# "Meet Polly," Tilly said. "Polly Prim, I call her.

"Just wait, Duncan. Don't say a word until you hear her sing."

He didn't trust the laughter in Tilly's face and thought it best to turn the new girl away.

While he paused, the young woman glanced to either side, as if to count the audience. Then she tossed back her hood, revealing a riotous wealth of rich brown hair.

Her voice stunned him. Pure notes rose through the rain and rush of the waterfront, carrying emotion that brought a tightness to his chest. It was as if her song discovered the most deeply buried hurts and longings and promised healing.

A fancy, but one who would have lonely miners tossing nuggets at her feet. He knew that as surely as he knew how deeply she touched him.

Duncan looked closely into the woman's earnest, upturned face. She wore paint on her cheeks and around her eyes, but such artifice looked wrong for her. "Who are you?" he asked. "What is your name, really?"

Dear Reader,

For your summer reading pleasure, we present our Harlequin Historicals titles for August, four adventuresome tales that bring the past to life.

In Mary Daheim's *Improbable Eden,* an unsophisticated young woman discovers love when she is swept up into the dangerous world of intrigue at the English court of William and Mary.

With *Golden Prospect,* her second Harlequin historical, Shirley Parenteau takes the reader to the Yukon and Alaska as she weaves a delightful story of fame and fortune during the Klondike gold rush.

Surrounded by madness and deceit, the lovers in Catherine Blair's *Devil Wind,* must put to rest the past before they can build their future, while the characters in award-winning author Elisabeth Macdonald's *Estero Bay,* are swept into the age-old fight between the old ways and the new, set against the backdrop of California's wild central coast.

We hope you will join us for some summer reading fun.

Yours,

Tracy Farrell
Senior Editor

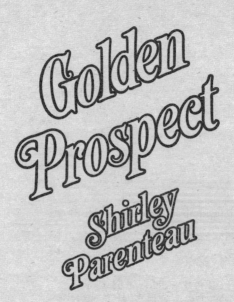

# Golden Prospect

## Shirley Parenteau

# Harlequin Books

TORONTO • NEW YORK • LONDON
AMSTERDAM • PARIS • SYDNEY • HAMBURG
STOCKHOLM • ATHENS • TOKYO • MILAN

Harlequin Historicals first edition August 1991

ISBN 0-373-28688-0

GOLDEN PROSPECT

**Books by Shirley Parenteau**

Harlequin Historicals

*Hemlock Feathers* #34
*Golden Prospect* #88

---

## *SHIRLEY PARENTEAU*

is a contemporary romance author who has now moved into the exciting field of historical romance. Shirley grew up in small logging towns along the Oregon coast and presently lives in an eighty-year-old farmhouse in northern California, which she and her husband restored themselves.

# Chapter One

*Seattle, March 1898*

Julia Ames added a box of candles to a display in the window of her uncle's outfitting store, then paused to gaze into the street. "Half the world must be heading to the Klondike." Her aunt murmured an absent reply from the back of the shop where she weighed evaporated apples from a barrel. Over her head, dangling gum boots added their pungent scent to the tang of apples and the musty smell of packing crates.

Julia remained at the window, watching rain bluster over a steady stream of drawn-down hats, hunched shoulders and glistening mackinaws. She knew that railroads daily discharged thousands from across the continent. Bankers were leaving their desks, lawyers their books and clerks their tie and ribbon counters. Men who had never in their lives so much as raised a blister on their palms were now pouring into the wilds of Alaska, certain they were about to wrest their fortunes from the earth.

Not all were men. Many of the women trekking toward the wharves appeared to be near Julia's own twenty-two years of age. Most accompanied husbands and brothers, but a few daring females traveled to the gold streams alone. There were others, women whose purpose in the Klondike was better not questioned. Uncle Aaron had commented dourly that the Canadian authorities should refuse entry to *that* kind of woman.

Still there was a grand adventure in the journey, whatever its end. Those who crowded the shop glowed with anticipation. Their steps were light, their faces eager. Julia felt a part of it all when she helped outfit them for the quest.

Her thoughts broke off as she glimpsed her uncle returning from the post office, shoulders hunched against the rain. Julia cast a quick critical glance toward her image in the rain-slick window. Her large gray eyes looked wary; her uncle often termed them "sassy." She tried to assume a serious expression as she assured herself that her often stubborn chestnut hair was tidied into a coil that even his sharp gaze could not fault. She'd spent the morning stocking shelves, but her white shirtwaist was immaculate. The plain gored panels of her blue woolen skirt discreetly covered the tips of her shoes.

She barely had time to criticize her image before damp wind swirled through the shop causing a flutter of price placards. After a curt nod, Aaron strode to the rear of the shop and slapped a packet of letters on the counter. Julia returned to the window display, but at a sharp cry from her aunt swung around. "Ruth? What is it?"

Her aunt's slender form looked as wire-strung as a marionette. One hand jerked up to cover her mouth; her eyes were enormous. Julia hurried forward, then stopped. On the counter between a bucket of hickory ax handles and a stack of gold pans glowed a heart-shaped nugget. A slender chain shimmered around it.

Julia raised her fingers to a carved cameo pinned to her collar. The stone had belonged to her mother, yet for once failed to yield comfort. Suddenly, she understood the force drawing thousands to the Klondike. She longed to possess that golden lump, to press it to her lips, to bury its red-gold warmth against her breasts where its pulse might echo the rapid beating of her heart.

Wild thoughts. Perhaps she bore her mother's heritage after all. As she rebuked herself, an envelope fell from Ruth's hand. Julia saw only a scrawled signature and the tantalizing words, *Dawson, Yukon* before her uncle crumpled it into the trash.

Her aunt had taken a step back. Face white, she cast a quick troubled glance toward her niece and a beseeching one to her husband. "We can't keep it, Aaron. It isn't right."

Julia's questions were momentarily silenced by her uncle's scowl. He was a slender man with an impressive moustache and a gleaming bald crown. His voice was the largest part of him and well used. "You're acting the fool again, Ruth. We did the man a turn. Now it seems he's made a strike and remembered the debt."

Julia looked from one to the other while irritation replaced her earlier enchantment. Her uncle would have his way as always and regard questions as an insult. Even so, she asked, "Who, Uncle Aaron? Who sent it?"

She could have mouthed his answer; it was worded exactly as she expected. "Do not be impertinent, Miss."

Ruth shook her head. The whites showed around her pale eyes while wisps of graying hair strayed across worried lines in her temple. Her distress seemed deeper than could be warranted by fear of unpleasantness between husband and niece. She should be well used to that.

The nugget had upset her and despite the silent plea, Julia felt compelled to know the reason. "Uncle, I should like an answer."

Aaron Ames's moustache bristled. He towered to his full height, which, although only slightly more than Julia's own unfashionable five foot eight inches, allowed him to glare down at her. "Will such knowledge gain you a husband? I hardly think so, Miss, given your mother's folly."

He slammed the flat of his hand into a pyramid of condensed milk cans, tumbling the tins to the floor in an angry clatter. "Stack the shelves. Curiosity is unseemly in a young woman."

Julia bent to gather the cans, but would not be silenced. "When have you done a favor worth such a nugget?" she muttered. "Let a gold coin fall into your hands and most of Seattle hears the eagles scream from the bruising."

Her aunt's soft protest made her add impulsively, "No doubt, Aunt Ruth did the favor. The chain makes it clear the gift is intended for a woman."

She thought he might strike her. His fists clenched until the knuckles turned white. Julia braced, but a muted thud broke the tension. With a rush of guilt, she saw that Ruth had swooned. "Tend to your aunt, you misbegotten daughter of lust," Aaron shouted. "Once again, you have made her ill."

It was not she who caused Ruth's weak nerves, Julia thought as she helped her aunt to her feet. Only the need for a barrier between Ruth's delicate health and Aaron's rampages kept her from distancing herself from Ames Alaskan Outfitters. Even work as a housemaid would be preferable to this daily battling of wills.

Still, Ruth was her only family, and Julia urged her gently through curtains into living quarters behind the store. "You will feel much better for a cup of rose hip tea."

While Julia busied herself at the stove, Ruth pressed her hands nervously together. "Your uncle is a good man, Julia."

"Yes, Aunt." Julia poured hot water into the china teapot, biting back her true thoughts. Charitably, she added, "I suppose the responsibility of outfitting argonauts has shortened his temper."

Ruth sounded distracted. "Argonauts, yes. We have never had such trade."

Yet Aaron raged that he was missing his full share. One hundred outfitters now operated from Seattle. They would drive each other to the poorhouse, he forecast. If only he were located on a more prominent street or could afford advertisement or was nearer the better-known Cooper and Levy and could draw from their trade, he would make a fortune from the gold seekers. Aaron's tirade was so often repeated that Julia heard it even in her sleep.

The day Cooper and Levy sent a wagon filled with provisions to tour Seattle streets in advertisement for their establishment, he nearly collapsed of apoplexy. Yet he would not pay to have fliers printed.

Carefully, Julia poured hot tea into cups and guided one into her aunt's trembling hand.

"Dear Julia," Ruth said anxiously, "My poor sister had so little. You were born when she was only sixteen."

That was another often-heard refrain: her mother's weakness for a gambler's whispered promises, followed by a young life lost in bearing a daughter who would never hear her father's name. While Julia felt grateful that her aunt and uncle had taken over her care, she wished they would not constantly remind her of their generosity.

"Enjoy your tea," she urged. "The rose hips will give you strength."

"But Julia." Ruth pushed the cup aside. "The nugget. You should know—"

The curtains brushed apart. Voices rose in the other room as Aaron looked from one to the other. "We have trade. Stay and recover your strength, my dear. Julia, attend me at once."

Ruth looked even more distressed. This was not the first time she had seemed on the verge of confiding some secret, but Julia saw that again Aaron had silenced her. Whatever the source of Ruth's worry might be, it would remain unstated until the next time she found courage, or perhaps a time after that.

Julia pressed her aunt's shoulder, then followed her uncle into the store. She noticed the gold nugget displayed now above a glass case of dollar watches. No doubt, Aaron felt it would further excite customers to purchase supplies for the Yukon.

To her astonishment women crowded the room, their wet skirts leaving puddles on the floor. Their brush bindings were worn, their colors vulgar and their manners unrestrained. They were certainly wild lilies of the field. Near the door, a tall, broad-shouldered man studied the list of provisions required by the Canadian government for passage into that country.

There was a taut, untamed air about him. Standing braced in dungarees and mackinaw, he looked as if he were taking possession of the shop. He wasn't wearing a hat; rainwater glittered in unruly dark hair that waved against the back of his neck. He rubbed one hand below his collar, as if to stop water from running lower. Julia looked at the women. He could not possibly be with them. Yet one of the lilies spoke to him familiarly, calling him Duncan.

When he turned to answer, Julia saw the gleam of the sea in dark blue eyes and beneath that a simmering anger that made her throat tighten not with fear but with some emotion she couldn't name. He regarded the women as if they were unruly pets that must be restrained.

Julia couldn't help looking at him. He was arrestingly handsome, but not easily approached, she thought. His face was deeply tanned and creased near his eyes as if from facing sun and wind. There was a startling sensitivity in those deep blue eyes that was at odds with the smoldering tension.

Beneath the mackinaw, he wore a blue flannel shirt, open at the collar. His throat was tanned as deeply as his face. She felt riveted by the implied intimacy in his lack of collar button and tie. His glance crossed hers, and she saw that to him she was invisible, merely a clerk to serve his needs. Nervously, she smoothed her skirt, both annoyed and relieved that his gaze did not linger.

The women lowered capes, their hair springing into disarray. All five flirted their taffeta skirts, revealing carmine or saffron petticoats and filling the store with an unseemly rustle and the scent of cloying perfume.

As Julia stared, a woman with hair as red as her skirts sauntered over to Aaron. "We're headed for Dawson City, love. We hear there's plenty of gold to be found." She paused to wink. "If a lady knows where to look."

It seemed Aaron would not turn even questionable trade aside. Julia hoped her aunt would remain in the kitchen. Yet she herself watched the women with open curiosity. They were going to the Klondike. Her heart envied them even as she marveled. What courage did they possess, that they dared to leave all they knew for the frozen wastes of the Yukon? There must be bravery beneath their painted faces and satin shirtwaists. She could not help but admire that.

However, they were not all of a mind, for a dark-haired woman pointed to the list of provisions and snapped, "Do I look like a packhorse?" She posed provocatively. "My talent is in riding, if you get my meaning."

While the others laughed, Julia wondered where the humor lay and why the man's tan had darkened. "Enough of that." His hard tone struck the smirk from the woman's painted face. She glared for a moment, then darted from the shop. He caught the door before it could close. "Tess! The *Gypsy Gull* boards at six tomorrow morning."

Her answer came through a gust of rain. "When I'll be snug in my bed."

He shoved one hand through his hair. Julia suspected that had he been alone, he would have cursed. The redhead chuckled. "She's no loss, Duncan, honey. Your brother wants entertainers for his music hall. Tess can't sing a note." The others hooted as she sang the scales in a raucous voice.

While Julia cringed at the sound, the man called Duncan took the nearest lily by her arms and planted her firmly on a chair beside a display of gum boots. "Select your sizes," he told them all. "Then be on your way while I settle the account."

The bright colors and chatter of the women fascinated Julia. While they teased and flirted, they seemed not quite sure of Duncan's temper. Clearly, he held himself under rigid control, disliking this business and eager to be done with it.

What could have brought such a group together? A music hall in faraway Dawson City hardly seemed the setting for the man. She pictured him at the wheel of a trawler fighting heavy seas. His hands were well-shaped with lean, tanned fingers that she admired as he selected a harmonica from Aaron's stock. "I'll be glad of diversion during the long Yukon night."

He had a low, mellow voice that she liked, but his comment brought further ribald laughter from the ladies until his cold gaze silenced them. Glowering, Aaron continued to fit the group for boots. Moments later, one of the women whipped up her skirts and tucked a silver-backed comb into her stocking. Pushed beyond limit, Aaron exploded. "Sir, control your women!"

When the younger man spoke, it was obvious his anger was tightly reined, but the disgust in his voice shook Julia more than a blow; she felt thankful it wasn't directed toward her. "Vida, if you need a comb, add it to the supplies we're buying."

With a careless shrug, the woman retrieved the comb and slapped it into his palm. In the same moment, Ruth shrieked from the kitchen. "Julia, stop her! That red-haired hussy has your father's nugget."

Julia could not move. She felt drenched with cold while she watched Duncan catch the woman at the street door. After a sharp exchange, he returned the nugget to Ruth. "I apologize, ma'am. We won't trouble you much longer."

As Aaron snatched the nugget from Ruth and locked it in the case of watches, the redhead protested. "I wasn't trying to steal the pretty thing. I only wanted to see it in a decent light."

"Get out of my store!" Aaron roared.

The woman flipped her skirts as high as her chin, giving him a scandalized look at lace-trimmed drawers. "La-di-da."

Aaron's purpling face boded ill for his health. Again, Duncan reddened beneath his tan. A vein throbbed in his throat. Grasping the woman by the waist with both hands, he thrust her into the street, then curtly ordered the others to follow. Expression grim, he returned alone to pay for their outfitting.

His problems no longer interested Julia. She waited until the door closed behind him, then advanced one slow step at a time to her aunt. Ruth watched with dread in her eyes.

"Don't faint," Julia warned. "Don't dare faint until you have explained your words. My *father's* nugget?"

Aaron intervened. "Your aunt is ill. Do not distress her."

Distress her? Julia wanted to scream with impatience while hope dazzled like sunlight.

Ruth quavered. "I wanted to tell you. I tried...."

Aaron broke in. "Your father is a gambler and a libertine. He ruined your mother. We raised his by-blow only on the promise that he should never attempt to contact you."

"You knew my father? You know where to locate him?" Truth struck Julia like a cold wash of surf. *"You have always known."*

"We raised you as our own," her uncle answered in a tone meant to silence her. "Not many men would take their sister-in-law into their household with her in the family way and no ring on her hand."

"A child needs a stable home," Ruth whispered. "We have done our best for you, Julia, dear. And how that man wanders around, with every letter from a different place. Even from out of the country. Now, of all places, the Yukon."

"*Every* letter?" Julia could hardly hear her own voice through the roaring in her head. "He has written before?"

"He sent funds when he could." Ruth's mouth trembled. "We must give him credit for that."

Julia's body shook. The floor felt fluid beneath her as if the planks rolled with her shock. Darting behind the counter, she grasped the trash container with both hands, scattering the contents, then scrambled on hands and knees through the litter.

"Mind yourself!" her uncle exclaimed. "You are behaving like a common trollop."

She ignored him. Her hand hovered above the envelope. For a lifetime, she had yearned for a parent's love. The crumpled yellow paper beckoned as no gold ever could. Anticipation and doubt warred. Then she snatched up the envelope and smoothed it over one knee.

A name scrawled in a bold hand became her entire focus: *Joseph Everett*. Beyond, an oval postmark with two words stamped inside: *Dawson, Yukon*. With a sob, Julia pressed it to her heart. "I must go to him."

"Go to him?" Ruth repeated. "Impossible."

"Do not distress yourself," Aaron assured his wife. "Steamers are booked ahead for months. By the time passage becomes available, the girl will have regained her senses."

Julia closed her eyes. Her mind filled with stories carried by prospectors heading for the Yukon, of the threat and challenge of the Chilkoot Trail where fifteen hundred steps were carved in ice over the side of a mountain. That was only the start of the long journey inland.

Did she have the courage she had so often admired in Klondike-bound travelers? There was no question. She must go quickly, before her father should move on. If Ruth told the truth, he did not stay long in one place. She would change that when she joined him. Or she would travel with him, wherever his wandering might take them.

She gulped for breath. Her heart beat so hard she could hear it. For as many of her twenty-two years as she could remember, she had dreamed of a father who would one day come for her, bringing his love into the cold emptiness of the life she shared with her aunt and uncle. In her mind he glowed like one of the knights in the storybooks Aaron scorned. As an adult she realized her dreams were spun of wishes. Even so, she never let her hopes die completely.

She forced spinning thoughts into order. Aaron spoke the truth. Every steamship was booked. With thousands of would-be miners pouring into Seattle each day, how could she hope to find a berth?

"Pull yourself together, Julia," her uncle said severely. "Clean the mess you have made."

She glared into his dour face. "There is a berth available aboard the *Gypsy Gull*. That woman Tess refuses to go, and her passage has been secured." Stunned, Julia sat on her heels. The words hurled to shock Aaron held the lure of possibility.

Ruth gasped. "You can't think to travel with those creatures."

"Can't I?" Julia's mind reeled. Could she? Dared she? Anticipation swelled through her. Her father was in Dawson City. *Her father*.

Aaron snorted. "You cannot think that fellow would take on the responsibility of escorting a gently bred woman through the wilderness. Why, he cannot even control his sluts."

Julia ignored the coarse term, so overwhelmed was she by her own daring. Her thoughts sobered when she remembered the strength of the man who thrust the redhead from the store as if she were weightless. By joining the troops, she might be exchanging domination by one man for that of another; yet the situation would be temporary.

Springing to her feet, she shuffled through some paperwork. Her glance flashed down the list of supplies for a group of six and stopped at a signature in a bold hand: Duncan Adair.

"He needs to replace Tess," she said with decision. "From the sample we heard today, I believe that I can sing well enough for a Dawson City music hall."

Ruth swayed against the counter. "Do you mean to sing in public? Julia, what has become of your good sense?"

"You will end just like your mother." Aaron's glower deepened. "Do not expect to use my name for common display."

She wanted to retort that she would use her father's name, but could not let them think they had driven her to desperate straits. "Of course, I will not sing in public. I need only to convince that man, Duncan Adair, that I am capable. When we reach Dawson, my father will repay the cost of my transport."

Ruth raised a lace-edged handkerchief to her lips. "That is less than ethical. Can you mean to mislead the man?"

"Ethical? An odd word for you, Aunt." Julia knew the harshness covered a twinge of conscience. Ruth had never been intentionally cruel, but she had no strength to face her husband. From now on, that problem would be hers alone.

"The troop will lack one entertainer, at any rate. Why should her passage be wasted? My father will make good the expense."

What beautiful words those were. *My father.* She savored them briefly while Ruth's and Aaron's warnings and imprecations went unheard. Abruptly, she rose. "I'll have the key to the watch case, Aaron. I mean to wear my father's nugget."

He drew back. His lips clamped tight. "Enough of this nonsense. You are wasting our time with missish behavior. Return to your tasks at once."

He held his hand over the pocket where he had concealed the key...just as he had kept her father's letters from her all these years.

Feeling raw anguish, Julia grabbed an ax handle from the bucket on the counter. She swung the rough length of it with both hands. Glass shattered, echoing Ruth's scream.

Dropping the handle into the shards, Julia recovered the nugget. She held it reverently before clasping the chain beneath her collar.

"Go to the devil then," her uncle shouted. "Leave this house at once and never think to return."

Ruth moaned. "Where will you stay the night?"

Sweeping her cloak from a peg, Julia pulled it around her shoulders. "If I can endure the trail to Dawson, I can certainly survive a night on the Seattle wharf."

## Chapter Two

For the first minutes after leaving Ames Alaskan Outfitters, Julia rode a wave of white-hot indignation. On the thronged Seattle streets, she soon became one of a jostling multitude. To her relief, the rain had blown past, at least momentarily. A zest for adventure electrified the air, charging her with fresh excitement.

Slowly, the enormity of her situation dawned. She had taken nothing but the gold nugget and the clothes she wore. Until she reached her father in Dawson City, she would be totally dependent on strangers. Her steps faltered briefly as she cast a glance in the direction of the only home she had ever known.

The smooth warmth of the heart-shaped nugget beneath her collar renewed her courage. Edging between a pair of carriages she continued down Yesler Street toward the wharves that lined this part of Elliott Bay. Every store window displayed goods for the use of miners, with all else crowded out. Nearly every sign referred to Alaska or the Yukon.

Eager crowds of prospectors, traders and adventurers were dressed for the trail in red and yellow plaid mackinaws, dungarees tucked into high boots, and caps to match any description she could imagine.

Men whom Aaron would term "the sure-thing gentry" roamed everywhere. Julia stepped around a crowd avidly watching one of their members attempt to discover which of three walnut shells covered a mysteriously elusive pea.

She had lived all her life in Seattle. Yet the city, taken over by fortune seekers seemed foreign. As night settled, the crowds never lessened. Music and men spilled from hotels and rooming houses. Women of dubious purpose lounged on the streets. The crowds appeared to represent every ethnic group; clearly, Seattle had become a melting pot with greed for a ladle.

Julia took care to avoid any stairs leading downward. She could still remember the horror nine years before when fire stormed through this end of town. Rebuilding began so soon afterward that the area had to be flooded to keep workmen from burning their feet, or so Aaron boasted. Seattle not only recovered but improved itself by raising the streets from ten to thirty-two feet above the original.

She didn't need her uncle's warnings to avoid dark entries into the twenty-two blocks of mostly vacant basement-like shops that remained at the old level. Their shadowy depths now harbored denizens more dangerous than the shell-game men and the women with come-hither eyes.

Julia wandered slowly along the wharves. Fresh air fought past pungent manure left by dozens of horses and other animals. She stepped aside for a dog team and bumped against canvas bags of provisions stacked higher than her head. Again she was reminded of her dependence on the man called Duncan.

Suppose he refused her passage? Suppose Tess changed her mind and there was no extra berth? Julia drew a deep breath. There was little sense in begging trouble, she told herself crisply. From now until she got to Dawson City, she would take each moment as it came.

She stood for a while watching oxen being driven aboard a sturdy vessel at Schwabacker's Wharf. The animals bellowed. Horses whinnied. Men shouted. Steam whistles blasted. A steamer pulled away while men on the dock waved their hats and cheered. At this very wharf just last July, the steamer *Portland* had arrived with miners from the Yukon and gold said to weigh a ton. The next day, the *Excelsior* reached San Francisco with a similar cargo, sparking the frantic rush north.

Now ships left every hour. What a parade they must be making along the inland passage to Skagway. Julia's heart quickened. The party atmosphere brought a surge of impatience. She began to walk again.

Even at this late hour, an occasional prospector was accompanied by his wife. Many of the women wore their skirts an immodest distance above their ankles. Was that the Klondike mode? As she shook the train of her skirt free of cigar butts and other debris, Julia longed for a pair of scissors.

A low voice spoke softly at her shoulder. "Ma'am, do you have passage? Will you sell?"

She faced a young woman with curly black hair, dressed in a corduroy velvet costume of the latest style. A saucy straw sailor's hat topped her dark curls, but it was the fire of her gaze that held Julia. Never had she seen such desperate purpose.

"I'm told passage is booked ahead for months," she answered. She did not intend to confide her hope for Tess's berth.

"I have money. I can pay."

Julia spread her hands in a shrug. "But I have no berth, even if I wished to sell. I fear we are both in the same situation."

"I must leave Seattle." With a hunted look in her eyes, the curly-haired woman glanced around. Appearing to see no one she recognized, she turned and studied activity at the edge of the wharf. "I mean to leave," she said as if to herself. "Even if I must stow away and take my chances."

Julia gasped. "Skagway is a seven-day journey."

"I cannot stay in Seattle." The woman glanced around again, then slipped past a dog team and was lost to Julia's sight.

The city was filled with desperate people, most driven by adventure or the lust for gold. There had been something more in that haunted face. Julia shivered, feeling fortunate for the first time since leaving her aunt and uncle. She was journeying toward her father with strong hope for a berth, not facing the bitter prospect of seven days' stolen passage with no guarantee of food and a constant fear of capture.

Wearied by hours of walking, she sank onto a bale of hay. Her cape fell back while she let the misting rain refresh her. Gradually, her heavy eyelids drifted down.

An amused voice roused her. "Say, if it ain't Polly Prim. What'd they do, throw you out? The old man ain't no honey, that's clear."

Julia jerked forward. She had fallen asleep despite the turmoil on every side. Her eyes focused on a boot raised to the hay bale near her hand and followed it upward past carmine ruffles and a straining satin bodice to a pair of laughing eyes and flyaway red hair misted with rain.

Recognition shocked her. "You're . . . one of the entertainers who came to the store."

"I sure am." The woman grinned. "Thought I might get in a little *entertainin'* before the ship leaves." She peered more closely. "You, though. Ain't you afraid some miner'll stick you in his poke and haul you off to the Yukon?"

Fervently, Julia answered, "I wish one would."

The woman tilted her head. "You runnin' a fever or somethin'?"

"Your friend, Tess," Julia probed. "Has she changed her mind? Is she going with you?"

"Tess?" The red hair tossed in a swirl of disgust. "She ain't much for a cold bed. Don't know why she followed along with the idea at the first." The redhead's eyes narrowed. "What interest you got in Tess, anyway? She owe you money?"

Julia began to tremble. She clenched her hands together in an effort to hide the shaking. This was her first test. She must convince the woman to accept her. "I mean to take her place on the *Gypsy Gull,* to travel with you to Dawson City. I can sing."

The woman slapped her knee, laughing so boisterously that passersby turned to frown or smile. Rubbing moist eyes with her knuckles, she exclaimed, "That's a good one! Worth comin' out in the weather to hear. You, a singer? Travelin' with us? To Dawson?" Laughter carried away her words and again she slapped her knee, making her taffeta skirts rustle.

"Will you help me?" Julia asked.

Sobering, the redhead studied her. "Honey, ain't you heard nothin' about the trip? Didn't you even take a good look at the bunch of us? This ain't no stroll through the damned park."

Kindness warmed the words, however coarsely spoken. Putting trust in that, Julia offered the truth. "You saw my uncle. I have left his house forever. My father is in Dawson City and I must get to him." She added urgently, "I *can* sing."

The redhead placed her fingertips beneath Julia's chin and tilted her face toward a gleam of light. "Proper mouse, ain't you. Voice to match, probably." Suddenly she hooted. "But what a joke on Duncan. Serve him right for actin' like he's got his hands full of week-old fish instead of gems like we happen to be." She grasped Julia's arm and tugged her upward. "If you're gonna be an entertainer, Polly Prim, you gotta look like an entertainer. Come along with Tilly. She'll fix you up."

Feeling as if she were dreaming, Julia allowed the red-haired woman to tow her along the waterfront and over the new cobblestones of Pioneer Square. Then she balked.

"Come along," Tilly exclaimed.

Julia clung to a curled iron railing. "Down there?" The horror that shuddered through her voice carried every story Aaron had ever told of debauchery and sin in Seattle.

"That's where I live, Miss Prim," Tilly said firmly. "But I ain't fightin' with you. I already got *my* passage north."

The sour smell of old burned wood drifted upward, muting the fresh air. Bile rose in Julia's throat. Her fingers clamped around the railing until the knuckles whitened.

"Nerves like that ain't gonna take you over the Klondike Trail. Go on back to your uncle." With a flounce of carmine skirts, Tilly darted down the stairs and out of sight.

"Wait!" Julia gasped for breath. Her heart seemed frozen between beats. Yet without Tilly, there was no hope for passage. A fleeting image of the young woman with desperate eyes and a vow to stow aboard ship loosened her fingers from the railing. "Tilly, wait. Please, wait for me."

Terror gave speed to Julia's steps. She dashed into a passage and nearly collided with the redhead. Tilly caught her by the shoulders until she regained her balance. "Nervy mouse, ain't you? Come along, then."

The journey over the Chilkoot Pass could not be more fearsome than this. Julia stayed close to Tilly, reassured by the perfume that had offended her hours before. They went through dark, rubble-choked passages. Julia held her skirts close, dreading to think what they might brush against in this smelly underground. As they passed doorways, she glimpsed burning fires inside cavernous spaces. At first, she thought the conflagration still smoldered, then realized that unseen people warmed themselves at bonfires of scavenged wood.

Shivering, she hurried on and nearly collided again when the redhead stopped. "Here we are, Miss Prim. Duck your head, now." Bending, she darted into blackness. Julia was suddenly alone. A low mutter of voices echoed through the passage. Skittering feet brought a vivid suggestion of rats. She jerked her skirts higher.

Light flickered in the blackness and became a single candle flame. Julia darted forward, banged her head on the low lintel, gasped, recovered her balance and scrambled into a cluttered space illuminated by golden candlelight.

"Told you to watch your head," Tilly said.

They were in a small area bounded by broken screens and packing crates. A pallet at one side boasted a handmade quilt of faded squares. Feeling as if her knees would no longer support her, Julia sank onto it.

Tilly bent over a chest. "It's all I have from the old days, but I can't take it to Dawson. Why bother?" Her eyes glinted. "We'll soon be rich enough to buy everything new." Fishing a key from a ribbon around her neck, she worked it in a lock with a mixture of dexterity and curses until the lock emitted an audible click.

With a theatrical gesture, Tilly threw open the lid. Julia glimpsed a dusky treasure of satins, taffeta and silk before the redhead pulled a gown from the tumbled collection and held it before her. Julia doubted that Tilly could fit within its slender confines even corseted, which she clearly was not.

"I was on the stage." The redhead flounced the skirt upward with a kick. "Had all the gents after me, too." She swirled around the room, lost for a time in memory.

"Worse luck, I listened. My fellow set me up in a little loft and brought love gifts each time he came by." She sighed, then tossed the gown on the chest. Her voice became harsh. "Nothin' lasts. Least of all love. Don't you let no man tell you otherwise."

Julia had pulled her legs beneath her. With her arms wrapped around her knees, she watched the other woman uneasily. It must have been a few years since Tilly graced any stage, and life had taken its toll. Julia cast a glance toward the bedspread beneath her, then rose with distaste.

"You'll need petticoats." Again, Tilly burrowed into the trunk. "Men like a girl's frillies to rustle."

"Who is Duncan?" Julia ventured. "Why is he going to the Yukon with . . . us?"

Laughter brightened Tilly's eyes when she emerged with taffeta flounces filling her arms. "That's right, Miss Prim, *us*. We'll pull it over once you're dressed and painted, see if we don't."

Painted? With an inner cringe, Julia forced aside the strict limits of her upbringing. Whatever must be borne to secure passage north, she would bear. With an unsteadying flash of memory, she pictured the man who was to lead the troupe. He had struck her as dangerous, yet she sensed competence in him and thought he would be a capable guide.

Aaron had warned her often enough of things that could happen to an unprotected woman. She shivered as her mind presented her with a clear image of Duncan: unruly hair glittering with rain, unbuttoned collar, sensitive mouth and intense, incredibly blue eyes. If Duncan wanted easy company, surely the others would satisfy him.

Determined to go ahead, whatever the risk, she concentrated on Tilly's answer. "Duncan Adair is the name he gave us. His stepbrother has a music hall in Dawson and arranged for our passage.''

In the candlelight, impatience glittered in Tilly's eyes. ''What are you dallyin' for, Miss Prim? Let's get a look at you in all that finery.''

Duncan Adair paced the rough planks of Schwabacker's Wharf, frowning into a crowd of mackinaws and rain slickers. The waterfront was thronged and noisy, but he saw no flash of taffeta and heard no feminine voices through the shouts of men.

He shoved one hand into a jacket pocket for his stepbrother's letter, but didn't pull it out. The words were emblazoned on his mind. ''If the girls can sing or dance, so much the better. The Yukon breaks up in May. Bring them in then. We'll earn enough with the Bonanza Playhouse to buy any boat on the Pacific coast.''

Glibly stated, Duncan thought, crumpling the letter he had barely resisted tossing into the fire on first reading. After months of alternately cursing and fearing for his stepbrother, he might have known Owen would land on his feet.

Far out on Elliott Bay, a fleet of fishing boats headed toward the sea. As he watched, Duncan felt a part of himself go with them. If not for Owen, he would be out there preparing to test his strength and skill against the honest sea. He could see the breakers in his mind and the deep green water beyond, could smell the clean salt wind and feel the salmon thrashing silver as he hauled in his net.

*If not for Owen.* How many times had those words crossed his mind in the eleven years since his mother remarried? He continued to pace, too keen-edged to remain still. His thoughts slipped back to his father's death at sea. If not for a vicious bout with influenza, Duncan would have been with him. He made up for that by taking his father's place in the family. At fifteen, he was a man putting in a full day on a neighbor's trawler, but there were always more expenses than income with several younger brothers and sisters to support.

Then, after five years of widowhood his mother married a ribbon clerk, a man who drew the drapes tighter at the first sound of thunder, who would never so much as wade into the surf for fear of denizens beneath the foam. The thought of his stepfather rankled as bitterly now as on the day his mother first introduced them. And with the ribbon clerk came twelve-year-old Owen, cocky, lazy and rebellious.

Again Duncan looked at the distant trawlers steaming through the bay. His stepfather had taken some of the financial weight from his shoulders; that had to be credited to him. In the years succeeding, Duncan had worked long hours and finally saved enough for a boat of his own. A few good fishing seasons made it possible to buy a second. At thirty-one, he had begun thinking it was time for a family of his own.

In one brief summer, because of Owen—now twenty-three, but no less cocky—everything changed. Both trawlers were gone, one foolishly driven onto rocks, the second filled with dock loungers and taken to Alaska without word of warning. According to the letter, his stepbrother had left the *Fortune* at the wharf in Skagway.

"Take the Chilkoot Trail, not the White Pass," Owen had advised, adding, "whichever route you take, you're sure to wish you had chosen the other."

The devil could have them both, Duncan told himself. His journey would end at Skagway, where he would recover the *Fortune* and return to fishing where he belonged. If he saw his stepbrother again, he was likely to do him some harm that would distress their mother. As for the troupe of entertainers, it shouldn't be difficult to find an escort to take them on to Dawson.

Where in blazes were they? Owen had banked on his older sibling's sense of responsibility—and his desire for retribution—when he wired home that Duncan was charged with escorting the ladies north. Owen had obviously never doubted that Duncan would waste no time in confronting him. But Owen was in for a rude awakening. Duncan meant to go as far north as Skagway, recover his trawler, find the women a capable guide, and wash his hands of the whole business.

Again, he searched the crowds. He should have gathered the women in one place for the night, but had chosen to spend the past few hours in the quieter company of his mother and sisters. With relief, he recognized Vida walking toward him, sheltered from the rain by a heavy green cape. As he watched, she bumped a portly businessman. Her eyes flashed as she smiled. Her hand flashed as well, while it moved from the gentleman's pocket to her own. Duncan frowned. She was not his responsibility until they were aboard the steamer, but he had better warn her that her light-fingered ways would not be tolerated.

Mae and Belle sauntered around a head-high stack of canvas bags, Bell pausing to wink at a sailor. When he slipped his hand inside her cloak, she laughed provocatively. Her cape fell back. Rain glinted in her wheat-colored hair.

Mae hurried toward Duncan, her round face flushed with anticipation. The miners would take her to their hearts, he thought. They would want to bed her and protect her at the same time. And they would return again and again to the Bonanza Playhouse to see her. Owen would do well, but then, he always had.

"They're boarding already," he said curtly, adding a nod for Vida as the dark-haired woman joined them. "We're in staterooms two and three." Belle sashayed over and he motioned toward a gangplank. "Go on inside. Choose your bunks."

Tess had apparently stuck to her decision. Where was Tilly? Had she, too, decided against trekking into the frozen north? She had seemed eager for Yukon gold.

As if the thought drew her, he spotted Tilly's red hair unhooded in defiance of the rain. Another woman walked beside her, taffeta skirts flirting with each step. For a moment, he thought Tess had changed her mind. Then wind lifted the woman's cloak and he knew otherwise. Not Tess. This woman's rose satin outlined a far more delicate frame.

Her height emphasized her slenderness. Except for that, her gray eyes were the largest thing about her. They were fixed on him with a fierce bright light. "Meet Polly," Tilly said, her eyes dancing. "Polly Prim, I call her. Just wait, Duncan. Don't say a word until you hear her sing."

He didn't trust the laughter in Tilly's face and thought it best to turn the new woman away. He anticipated problems enough without Tilly devising some mischief.

While he paused, the young woman glanced to either side as if to count the audience. Then she tossed back her hood, revealing a riotous wealth of rich brown hair. Wine-red lights flickered in vagrant rays of watery sunlight.

Her voice stunned him. Pure notes rose through the rain and rush of the waterfront, carrying emotion that brought a tightness to his chest. It was as if her song discovered the most deeply buried hurts and longings and promised healing.

A fancy, but one that would have lonely miners tossing nuggets at her feet. He knew that as surely as he knew how deeply she touched him. Longshoremen had stopped to listen. Even the brawling cries of horses and dogs momentarily halted.

Duncan looked closely into the woman's earnest upturned face. She wore paint on her cheeks and some dark coloring on her lashes and around her eyes, but such artifice looked wrong for her. And he couldn't shake the feeling that he'd seen her somewhere before. "Who are you?" he asked. "What is your name, really?"

She answered simply, "Julia."

He thought of the horror stories coming out of the Yukon. "You're determined to travel north, despite the rigors of the trail?"

Her eyes burned with her answer. Greed for Yukon gold had become a familiar expression on the Seattle docks. Julia might later regret her decision, but clearly she had no doubt of it now.

He nodded, thinking she would be safer in Skagway. That would be up to her. If she did go on, he hoped the trail wouldn't destroy her. "Stateroom two or three. We sail in ten minutes."

# Chapter Three

"Lord, there's not room left to swing a cat!" With a grin at Julia, Tilly pushed her way onto the crowded deck.

All along the wharf, ships were loading people and supplies. Thousands of eager prospectors and adventurers jostled forward, each hoping to convince a captain to cram in just one more passenger. Steamers, sailing vessels, even dories had been pressed into service for the journey to the goldfields. Feeling dazed, Julia wondered how many would end that journey on a bleak shore somewhere along the Inland Passage.

As she followed Tilly, she tried to still her doubts over the dirty, cramped vessel that was to be their home for a week. People sat or leaned on every surface, while the holds bulged with animals and freight. Additional freight mounded as high as the gunwales on deck. It seemed to Julia that water lapped dangerously up the laden vessel's sides.

It was obvious that carpenters had reshaped the *Gypsy Gull* to accommodate as many people as possible. Staterooms were mere cubbyholes, each containing three bunks. Tilly considered them critically. "We'll share with Vida. Mae complains up a storm, Belle's likely to invite in company—and I've a hunch that Duncan may snore."

The possibility of sharing sleeping quarters with Duncan Adair had never occurred to Julia. She had assumed he would have a room of his own, or at least bunk with other men. What arrangements had he made for the long trail?

Her mind flashed over the list of supplies ordered from Aaron's shop and stopped aghast at a tent. One tent. Large, yes, but one tent to house them all. Somehow, Duncan commanded even more space than his size suggested. There would not be an inch inside that tent where his presence wasn't felt. Shivering, she leaned against the door frame.

"You don't get seasick, do you?" Tilly demanded. "If you do, you'd best take the bottom bunk."

"Thank you." Julia forced faintness from her voice. It was not the threat of illness that made her unsteady, but she was glad to accept Tilly's offer. She had no interest in clambering up a tier of bunks like a performing monkey. The prospect did not trouble her companion. A flutter of carmine skirts revealed plump, stocking-clad limbs as Tilly scrambled to the top.

Stoutly Julia told herself, I am free of Aaron and I am going to my father. Nothing else matters. The words began to sound like a litany. She wondered uncomfortably how often she would find herself repeating them throughout the voyage.

The burdened ship sailed evenly through Juan de Fuca Strait and into the shelter of Vancouver Island. Once beyond that shelter, rough seas made travel miserable. Julia thought waves must be blowing onto the deck, so cold was the wind coming in from the passageway. She welcomed the chill air. Deep breaths helped still an uprising in her stomach. For two days, the thought of food revolted her. On the third afternoon, Vida shared an orange, refusing to reveal where she had obtained it. Julia didn't care to know. She bit into a fragrant segment and let the sweet juice burst over her tongue.

Her spirits plunged moments later at a bellow from the saloon down the passageway. Tilly had reported happily that poker, blackjack and drinking went on day and night. Now her shrill voice competed with shouts from the captain.

As Julia cringed at the language, Vida gave her an amused tap on the shoulder. "You must be feeling righter, love. You never noticed rough talk or much else till just now.''

That was true, but Julia was fairly certain there had never before been such an uproar. Lavender taffeta fluttered over mended stockings as Mae scurried in from the hall and crowded into the bunk beside Julia. ''A fine ship Duncan's brother chose for us,'' she said plaintively. ''That Captain James despises us all. He only honors the bottle. I wish I had never come aboard.''

Watching Mae pick nervously at a mend in her skirt, Julia became conscious of her own garish costume. Her mutinous stomach and the unsavory condition of the ship had made her appearance unimportant—even the fact that she had discarded her corset. Now she pushed her fingers through the curling tendrils that framed her face and longed to brush her hair into a proper coil.

Down the passageway, the captain and Tilly continued to rant at each other. Julia peered through the doorway, but a wall of men's shoulders blocked any view. The captain's complaint came over them. ''If I must have women on my ship, I will not have them at the poker table. All the world knows they cheat.''

''My grandmother's backside!'' Tilly screeched. ''You're only sore because you've lost. Pay up!''

As other men joined in, Julia was torn between staying as far as possible from the unpleasant scene and a feeling that she should aid her companion. Vida's eyes sparkled. ''I'll wager the rest of my orange against your pretty silver comb she tames the nasty brute.''

''If she has won fairly,'' Julia said, ''Captain James must pay his debt. We should tell him so.''

While Mae squealed, Vida exclaimed, ''Not me. He's a mean one, that captain. I saw him near knock a sailor overboard just because the lad took time to flirt with Belle.''

Mae pressed a fold of her skirt to trembling lips. ''Don't go in there, Julia.''

''We must do something,'' Julia said, thinking that if Aaron were a gambling man, this was the sort he would be: he would refuse to pay his debt simply because he had lost to a woman. Dealing with Aaron had prepared her for confronting that sort of man.

When the others refused to join her, she squeezed between the men in the passageway. She knew she needed to help not just because Tilly had befriended her. This was a chance to prove she was a decent woman despite her tight satins and loosened hair.

Unfortunately, the men blocking the door would not move aside. Someone yelled, "If she ain't allowed to play, how are we going to win back our money?" A chair crashed to the floor. People crowded closer. The intimacy was uncomfortable, but Julia felt as eager as the rest for a glimpse into the saloon.

She stood on her toes, trying to see over burly shoulders. The man in front of her backed away so unexpectedly that she clutched him to keep from falling. As the others flattened to either side, Captain James steamed through. Julia was too late to duck, and he stopped directly in front of her. Whiskey fumes on his breath made her choke.

"Another infernal woman!" he raged. "Is my whole blamed ship infested?"

As she sought a breath of less-tainted air, Julia found herself wishing for Tilly's colorful vocabulary and the courage to use it.

Warned that one of his charges was embroiled in argument with the captain, Duncan dashed for the saloon. It was nearly impossible to push through the crowded passage. Screams and shouts rose, but he couldn't make out the words.

Halfway down the passage, Julia's bright chestnut head popped into view. Shouldering his way into the crowd, Duncan began to force open a path. One of the men behind Julia patted her familiarly. She didn't seem to notice. Likely she was so accustomed to such pats she failed to take offense.

Duncan told himself it was not his mission to defend fallen women. Still, he marked the man's features with an eye to later inviting him into the makeshift boxing ring some of the fellows had set up in the stern.

The crowd parted abruptly. Men pressed to either side as the captain charged from the saloon. With an inward groan, Duncan saw Julia plant herself squarely in the man's path. Obviously, she lacked good sense.

And she was getting no better than she deserved from the irate captain. Duncan forced his way to her side. "Captain," he said quickly, "The women's passage has been paid, as you know."

"Then keep the vixens out of my way!" James brushed past, knocking against Julia. Duncan steadied her. For such a spirited woman, her shoulders felt fragile beneath his hands. She shrank from him, looking more distressed by his touch than by the familiar pat to her behind from a stranger.

Annoyed, Duncan exclaimed, "It seemed a simple matter to convey a theatrical troupe to Dawson City. Must you all be as scrappy as gulls?"

She stiffened. "I only wished to see that Tilly was treated fairly."

That made as much sense as anything else involving this group. Duncan crowded Julia against the wall of the passage. Her eyes became so large they seemed to fill her face. He saw again the delicacy of her features. If this woman was an entertainer, she must have only recently joined those rough ranks. She stood out from the others like a sea rose among rocks.

To deny a reluctant sense of protectiveness, he spoke harshly. "I don't believe there's a grain of sense in any one of you, with Belle slipping into more beds than she can count and Vida slipping into pockets. Now Tilly has taken the captain at cards." He frowned at Julia's strained expression. "Shall I guess or will you tell me just how *you* have occupied your time?"

"Please don't lump me with the others!" As the words left her lips, Julia knew it was a mistake to suggest she might be different. With dread, she recognized suspicion in Duncan's face. His hands clamped harder on her shoulders. She didn't dare complain.

"No?" he asked softly. "Why not?"

Panic fluttered inside her. She *must* maintain the subterfuge that would take her to her father. The ship sailed both ways, after all, and Duncan felt himself burdened already. If he learned the truth, he might send her back to Seattle.

Calling on mannerisms she had observed among the entertainers, Julia pouted her lips and fluttered her lashes. "I'm not at all like those street angels, love. I'm the girl that's got talent."

For an agonizing moment, he continued to study her. When at last his suspicion apparently faded, she felt limp with relief. He turned her toward her cabin. "Be a good girl, then. Stay inside and practice your scales."

As he regained the deck, Duncan silently applauded the songbird. For a time, her manner and voice had reminded him of his mother. Then the minx's true self returned. She mimicked gentlewomen she must have observed in the shops. She was a pretty thing, a little too tall, perhaps, but with fire behind her gray eyes.

She might well make Owen's fortune. As familiar anger against his stepbrother began to rise, Duncan forced his thoughts to the difficult trail the women would face if they went on.

Owen had arranged for packers to haul their goods from Dyea, a community smaller than Skagway, but closer to Chilkoot Pass. The showgirls would have to make only one crossing of the icy mountain range. They could take their leisure at Lake Bennett, waiting for the ice on the Yukon River to break up.

The only problem might be in finding someone to guide them on from Skagway. God knew he'd be glad to be free of them. Responsibility chafed, but he shook it off. They had entrusted themselves to his care without knowing anything about him. Why should they be any more particular in Skagway?

Once he reached that harbor and recovered the trawler Owen had so cavalierly commandeered, Duncan meant to locate a guide for the women. After all, he reminded his uneasy conscience, the lot of them were tough enough to have survived Seattle's darkest side. Compared to their usual lives, the trail to Lake Bennett should be a Sunday stroll.

They might even decide to stay in Skagway. Surely, they would find plenty of employment there. He turned toward the stern and the boxing arena. A man needed a strenuous workout after days aboard a cramped steamer, and a good match might drive away any uncomfortable sense of duty toward the showgirls.

Even so, Julia lingered in his mind. He paused against the rail, seeing not the passing scenery but Julia's luminous eyes. What unhappy fate could have brought her to this station in life? She made a man want to offer shelter, yet her eyes burned like twin suns through fog when she got her spirits up. And when she sang, her voice went right to the heart. He straightened. Julia could get under a man's skin. It was probably a good thing he wouldn't be traveling with her over the long trail to Dawson City. Still, he felt almost tempted to abandon his plans.

On the following day, the water became quieter. The ship slid between islands covered with low spruce trees. Mae crowded into the small cabin and curled her feet beneath her at one end of Julia's bunk. "Belle sent me out so she could entertain. I hope Duncan catches her at it."

Vida shrieked with laughter, nearly falling off her own bunk. "Stay here if you like," Julia said. "I feel the need for fresh air."

There was little warmth in the thin sunlight. She wrapped her cloak tightly around her while she picked her way along the crowded deck. Soon her enthusiasm returned. At every side excitement soared in the voices of men who compared the merits of evaporated fruits and vegetables, of packing horses and dog teams, of the White Pass or the Chilkoot Trail. A few had brought along collapsible boats and were engaged in heated discussions on whether the craft could survive the Yukon River.

The Yukon. The very words sent anticipation swirling through Julia. She was certain she had only to complete this journey to find happiness; when she located her father, her real life would begin.

She lifted her eyes to the waterway ahead. Smoke puffed from three distant ships, while sunlight glinted from a set of sails. As many vessels were probably visible from the stern. Could there really be gold enough for all the thousands of eager prospectors? No doubt, it was a good thing she sought her father and not her fortune.

On a nearby island, snow dusted low-growing trees. Julia's heart caught as her glance fell on a burned-out hulk lying half on the beach and half in the canal. Only days ago, its decks might have been crowded with cheering prospectors. Remembering her doubts on the wharf in Seattle, Julia murmured a quiet hope that all aboard had survived.

What of this overloaded vessel? Sobered, she continued her walk along the crowded deck. Eager shouts drew her to the stern. With a start, she recognized Duncan as one of two combatants in a makeshift boxing arena. Her breath caught. Despite the cold, both men had stripped to the waist. She knew it was unseemly to stare, but could not help herself. The closest she had ever come to seeing a man even partially unclothed was when Aaron hurried her past Greek statues in a Seattle museum. She saw at once that living flesh had little in common with cold marble.

Corded muscles shifted smoothly in Duncan's arms and back. She recognized a leashed sense of danger as he circled, daring his opponent. The other man swung. Evading the blow, Duncan lashed out. Julia gasped at the thud of his clenched fist against unprotected flesh.

Onlookers cheered. Others shouted encouragement to the second man, who crouched then darted forward. Bare knuckles cracked. Julia pressed her hand against her cheek, feeling a sympathetic flash of pain. After shaking his head as if to clear it, Duncan circled again.

A barbaric excitement raced through the crowd; Julia felt susceptible to it. She thought Duncan was magnificent. His opponent's chest and arms looked nearly as white as those marble statues of her memory, but his skin was sun-warmed gold. Dark hair curled over his chest, arrowing toward his flat stomach. She wondered how deep the tan continued, then pictured him aboard a trawler, his skin glowing while fish flashed silver in his net.

She turned away as abruptly as if Aaron had said she was no better than her mother. No decent woman would stand here admiring a half-naked man. Julia forced her way through the shouting crowd to the port side of the vessel. Again, the sound of a scuffle caught her attention, but this was different. Furtive. A woman's shriek was cut off. Julia hesitated, then hurried around a stack of hay bales.

Beyond the bales, the pretty dark-haired woman from the wharf struggled with a hulking bearded man. Her hat, which had looked stylishly saucy in Seattle, lay trampled beneath his boots. Her curly hair was in wild disarray. Her collar was torn open, her skin an angry red.

His hand covered her mouth. Above it, her eyes were desperate. Julia lurched forward. "Stop that! Release her at once."

Instead, the man slobbered kisses over the woman's throat. His victim clawed at him, but with a shrug of his massive shoulders he brushed her hands aside.

The rails were lined with men. Julia bit back the impulse to cry for help. Her thoughts raced. The curly-haired woman had threatened to stow aboard, and must have done so. Rescuers would certainly take her to the captain. Julia shuddered to think of the treatment she might receive from him.

The young woman's manner of speaking and her rich clothing suggested a respectable background. Julia cast her cloak aside. Grasping the sleeve of her borrowed dress in one hand, she pulled downward. The aged fabric separated. A ragged tear bared the length of her arm.

Satisfied, she dashed toward the men at the rail. "Please help! That brute tried to ravish me. Now he has attacked my friend!"

Men turned at once. As she pointed frantically, Julia almost convinced herself. "The monster! See how he ripped my sleeve!"

The bearded man was wrestled to the deck. Julia continued to scream accusations to hold the crowd's attention while the other woman slipped away.

A hard hand clamped over her shoulder. As she wheeled around she recognized Duncan Adair. He had pulled on his shirt and black woolen vest, but left his collar open. Hastily, she averted her gaze from his throat and a glimpse of dark chest hair. She saw that his eyes were cold.

He spaced his words, using a tone suitable for a recalcitrant child. "Didn't I tell you to stay in your cabin?"

She had practically saved a life. She should be applauded, not treated like a truant. "How was I to know some fiend would accost me?"

Duncan shoved one hand through his shock of dark hair. "Seven hundred men aboard and no more than a dozen women—yet you feel it safe to sashay alone around the deck."

"You must have lost your childish fisticuffs," Julia retorted, "that you are now so mean-tempered."

As his eyes narrowed, her mind filled with an image of muscles glistening under the thin winter sun and of dark chest hair directing her fascinated gaze toward a flat stomach. She saw Duncan register the fact that she had seen him in a state next to nudity.

Her face flamed. As the silence became awkward, he caught her shoulders and shook her slightly. "And you have lost your wits, or perhaps you had none to begin!"

A murmur of disapproval rose from the men nearby. They had rescued one woman, only to somehow lose her in the crowd. Now they looked eager to rescue another. "Gentlemen," Duncan said. "This woman is traveling with me. I thank you for coming to her aid."

Woman—as if she were no more than the showgirls. Common sense stopped her from denying it. She felt a rush of cold when he made the very threat she dreaded. "Songbird, I'm tempted to send you straight back to Seattle."

She had drawn on the artifices of the entertainers to delude him before. Now she drew on apology. "Please forgive me. I spoke without thinking."

Lines deepened in his forehead. Taking her elbow in an unforgiving grasp, he hauled her along the deck toward her cabin.

"You could be gentler," she protested.

He stopped, holding her beside the rail, which Julia clutched with both hands, for a moment fearing he meant to toss her over the side.

The fear must have shown in her face. He shook his head with disgust. "Don't worry, Songbird. You won't have to put up with me for any longer than it takes to reach Skagway."

"Skagway?" she repeated blankly. "What are you talking about? We're going to Dawson City."

Wind lifted his hair as he leaned against the rail. Beyond, gulls dove for scraps tossed from the galley. She heard shots, and hoped that men were not aiming at the birds.

"*You* are going to Dawson City," he said. Julia closed her eyes in relief. Her stomach had tightened until she felt sick. What kind of man would toy with her this way?

Duncan watched a gamut of emotions cross Julia's face. "Don't worry," he assured her, wondering at the intensity of her reaction. "I'll find someone to guide the troupe the rest of the way." His voice tightened with a scorn he knew was unfair. "You'll reach the goldfields as soon as the others."

"But you promised . . . you said . . . why would you turn back at Skagway?" Julia's thoughts spun. Did it matter who led her to Dawson City as long as she got there? She realized that in a short time she had begun to rely on Duncan's strength and competence. She reached out toward him, then drew her hand back. "I don't understand."

"My stepbrother owns the opera house where you'll be singing. There are hard feelings between us, most recently because he stole my trawler to make this trip the day he learned of Klondike gold."

Her eyes were so wide, he imagined he could see her thoughts racing in their depths. Their color had become as luminous as opal. He told himself that her talent lay in causing men to want to protect her, yet he found it hard to believe that she shook her fist at fortune as eagerly as did Vida and Tilly.

"I'll find a reliable guide for you," he promised. "But my trip north will end at Skagway, where Owen left my trawler, the *Fortune.*'' Again, rage surged. Damn Owen for getting him into this, when all he wanted was the honest work of a seaman. "I mean to take my ship back to Seattle and fish along the way.''

She understood the need to recover his vessel, but she felt betrayed. She had counted on him and he was proving to be no more trustworthy than Aaron. Straightening her spine, she put an edge into her voice. "I wouldn't think of further imposing on your time, Mr. Adair. Never mind searching for a guide—who would likely prove to be as dishonorable as you. I will find my own way to Dawson City.''

She turned swiftly and hurried toward her cabin. Duncan caught up to her and stopped her outside her door. Deliberately, he skimmed his fingertips over the length of her exposed arm from shoulder to wrist. "Don't put on airs, Songbird. We both know what you are.''

Julia jerked backward, then stared at the tanned fingers forming a dark contrast to her fair skin. His insult was meant to put her in her place, and yet beneath a shiver of outrage, she felt other sensations less easily defined.

Complex emotions darkened his eyes; his expressive mouth tightened. She realized with dismay that she was unchaperoned. Aaron's warnings swam in her mind. If Duncan chose to take advantage of her pretense of being a showgirl, how could she protest that she was virtuous? He would certainly send her back to Seattle. A part of her that must have echoed her mother's reckless spirit allowed a rush of anticipation. After an electrifying silence, he turned abruptly and made his way toward the deck.

Duncan's words blazed in her heart: *We both know what you are.* Outrageous. But it was exactly what she wanted him to believe, what he must believe.

Shivering, she forced her thoughts to needle and thread. Instead of looking for either, however, she stood inside the cabin door and held the torn taffeta over her arm while she relived the stroke of Duncan's hand against her skin. That he meant the touch to be an insult had no effect on the lingering sensations. It was as if sleeping senses had been startled awake and would never again be lulled.

Was this what her mother once felt? Rousing herself from her musings, Julia marched into the stateroom to search through her few possessions for a needle. She had saved a fellow creature. That was a safer direction for her thoughts. A sense of satisfaction replaced her confusion. Reflectively, she stitched the fragile taffeta. Could the stowaway have eaten in all this time? There would be bread and cheese in the saloon and perhaps a pot of tea.

Julia bit off the thread. With the sleeve mended—and after a cautious look for Duncan—she hurried into the saloon to steal dinner for her new friend.

# Chapter Four

Julia approached the hay bales feeling as if her heart was in her throat, but it couldn't have been, because it was thudding painfully against her ribs. Suppose that bearded hulk was still around? He would certainly wish to even the score.

It had taken far longer than she expected to gather a mug of tea and a saucer to cover it. Then she was forced to watch the tea cool while she waited for an opportunity to locate the stowaway. Most of the passengers were at supper. As she crept along, the shadows lengthened, creating threats in every stack of cargo.

"Miss," she whispered while Duncan's warning rang in her head. *Seven hundred men... less than a dozen women...* Even that was not as frightening as his threat to send her back to Seattle.

She was beginning to doubt she could trust herself alone with Duncan, and felt again his lean fingers in a slow caress down the length of her arm. Shivering, she placed her hand over the mended sleeve. He could not touch her so boldly again. That a flash of regret followed the thought made her strengthen her voice and call more loudly, "Miss? Are you there?"

Beyond the hay bales, shadows deepened but only the woman's crumpled hat remained. Setting the mug on a bale, Julia picked up the hat and wistfully tried to reshape it. Silk tulips drooped from a tattered band. Each had had a pearl-tipped stamen. She remembered their glow in the dawn light of Schwabacker's Wharf. Now half the pearls were missing. Julia turned the hat in her hands. Why would a woman who could afford such a hat have stolen aboard the ship?

She remembered the low plea. *I have money. I can pay.* Money could not buy passage when every square foot of deck space was already booked.

Footsteps sounded on the deck. Julia edged behind the bales as men's voices cut through the dusk. "I've brought an entire bag of wool socks. I only hope they'll be enough."

His companion's answer was earnest. "You'll want moccasins, as well. And buy a fur robe in Skagway. Arctic hare is best, but fox or wolf will do. Or lynx, if it's available."

Julia crouched behind the bales until the men strolled on. When their voices faded, she let out a long-held breath.

From nearby, a low voice asked, "Ma'am? Can you find me a crust of bread?"

Julia swung around. The woman from the Seattle wharf hovered in a shadow. She looked desperate, her hollow cheeks forming deep shadows. Wrenched with pity, Julia thrust forward the mug. "I've brought tea. It's grown cold, I'm afraid."

The woman drank gratefully, then sighed with pleasure when Julia produced a hard roll and a slab of cheese from her pocket.

"Where have you slept?" Julia whispered after the woman had devoured her meager meal.

Dark eyes glittered. "I've found a hole between a trunk and a wall." Her voice grew harsh. "The captain is a devil, drunk half the time. I believe if he finds me, he will have me thrown into the sea."

"Surely not," Julia exclaimed. She glanced swiftly around half fearing that such a horror would take place before her eyes.

"That hulking brute captured me when I crept from my hiding space hoping to find a bit of bread."

Julia reached out impulsively. "Come with me. I share a cabin with two others. We can make room for you, crowded as we are." Tilly spent most of her time in the saloon, she thought. Why shouldn't this poor creature make use of the bunk?

As for Duncan and his warning to stay out of trouble . . . There was no need to tell him they harbored a stowaway. The woman avoided her grasp. "I'll go on as I have, miss. Thank you for your kindness, but I'll be pleased if you will forget that we've met."

As she edged into shadows, Julia called softly, "Won't you tell me your name?"

"Hannah." The answer came from a distance. Julia raised her eyes at once but failed to locate the woman. After peering for long minutes into growing darkness, she realized she was alone.

Julia's sleep was troubled with worry for the woman she now considered her responsibility. By morning, she was determined that Hannah should be hidden in the cabin, where food and drink could be brought to her. Cautiously, she spoke to the others. "I have discovered a stowaway, a woman."

Quick interest brightened Vida's eyes. Tilly leaned from the upper tier, her red hair making an unlikely halo around her head. "A woman? Where could she hide? Why, every inch is taken."

"She found a hole," Julia answered, "but I'm afraid for her. Suppose she should be discovered and taken to the captain?"

"She's lost the gamble in that case," Vida said.

"And I'm late for mine." Tilly swung from her bunk, her stocking-clad foot just missing Julia's face. "There's cash on the table callin' my name."

"But we must help her," Julia protested. "She would be safe here with us."

"Here!" Vida sat up so abruptly that her head bumped the upper bunk. "Did you pay for your passage?" she demanded. "Neither did we. By rights, this cabin belongs to Prince Duncan. Ask him to take in your stowaway."

"Impossible." Julia realized with annoyance that she was wringing her hands in a perfect imitation of her aunt. "Tilly is rarely here in any event. Hannah may as well take advantage of the empty bunk. When Tilly does wish to sleep, Hannah may crowd into mine.''

Tilly shrugged. ''Why not? We're nearly there, anyway. I've heard the fellows say we'll be outside Juneau tomorrow night and Skagway the day after.''

Furiously, Vida objected. ''Risk getting our necks into trouble with that foul-tempered captain? No, thank you!''

''If you would just agree to meet Hannah,'' Julia pleaded, ''I know you would wish to help her. As for Duncan, he is probably engaged in another round of fisticuffs.'' She had a sudden unsettling image of him stripped to the waist, his sun-bronzed skin gleaming in the thin cold light.

Julia slipped one of Vida's purloined oranges into a pocket of her cloak and strode to the deck. A cautious search of the area near the hay bales failed to provide any sign of the stowaway. Even the hat was gone, for Hannah had plunked it onto her dark curls before slipping into the shadows.

Julia became aware of an almost visible excitement among the passengers. With each passing day, the crowd had become noisier. At the stern this morning, several were practicing their aim with rifles and revolvers. She pulled the hood of her cape more tightly around her ears as men blasted at floating chunks of ice, showing little concern for the cost of bullets.

Despite the noise, she was afraid to call out Hannah's name. Instead she peered as discreetly as possible behind every stack of supplies. Her mind filled with impressions of the stowaway lurking in fear behind ice-rimmed trunks or pungent bales of hay. The crumpled hat would be perched bravely on her curls, but bravado could not keep Hannah warm or safe from the captain's wrath.

The sun rose halfway up the winter sky before Julia completed her fruitless search. Either Hannah was safe, she conceded at last—or she had been discovered.

A shout went up from the rail. ''Whale! Look there!''

Julia pushed to a spot at the rail. Yards away, an immense barnacle-crusted back surged above the surface.

"Magnificent." Julia heard a familiar low voice, and spun to see Hannah staring raptly at the whale. "Have you ever seen anything grander?"

Irritation sheared Julia's nerves. All morning long, she had imagined herself nobly assisting the stowaway while the most fearful visions rose through her mind. Yet here was Hannah standing in plain sight as if she belonged among the passengers. Julia glared at her. "Where the devil have you been?"

She shocked herself. Such words had never before passed her lips. She imagined Aaron's snort.

Hannah's slow smile began with an upturn of her full lips and spread to lift the corners of her eyes, the depths of which held a mischievous sparkle. "Why, miss, have you been looking for me?"

Despite her boldness, Hannah was leery of leaving the familiar stern, where she felt safe. "Those who've asked believe I'm traveling with my brother and that the poor fellow's seasick in our cabin this whole time. But I make myself invisible when the captain's around, and I've no wish to encounter him far from my hole."

The days had become markedly colder. Even while they talked, a light snow began to fall. "Suppose we reach Skagway only to find you frozen in that hiding hole?" Julia demanded. "How do you think I will feel then?"

"Worse than I." Hannah said with a grin. "For in that case, I'll not be feeling at all." Her spirited words failed to mask her fears, however, and Julia was relieved that she soon gave way to reason.

As they hurried along the port side of the ship, they drew no more than an occasional appreciative glance. Most of the men directed every passion to planning their pursuit of gold. In the passageway outside the stateroom, Julia said thankfully, "There. Ours is number three."

Hannah started forward, but a bellow from the stateroom stopped them both. "Thieving Jezebel!"

Hannah jerked into Julia. For a moment, they clung together, certain the captain's outrage was directed toward the stowaway.

Julia whispered, "He can't have seen us. Quickly, hide in here." She ducked her head into stateroom two for a quick glance. Fortunately, Belle was not entertaining, and Mae was not present. Neither was Duncan. Fiercely, Julia pushed Hannah inside. "If anyone comes in, tell them you're waiting for Julia. I'm going to see what's upset Captain James."

"No, don't," protested Hannah. Her eyes were so wide the irises looked black. "What can you do? Wait until he has gone."

Julia was not eager to turn the miserable captain's attention toward herself, but she felt she had no choice. "Vida and Tilly have been kind," she said with reluctance. "If one of them is in trouble, I must try to help."

Hannah shrugged. "My advice is to stay clear."

Vida's shrieks rose about the captain's curses as Julia crept closer. The meanness of drink filled the man's voice. Something crashed to the floor. Julia's heart leaped and she reached out to steady herself against the passage wall. Whatever Vida had done, the captain had no right to mistreat her.

Trying to conceal her quaking nerves, Julia pushed open the door to her stateroom. Her eyes widened with horror. The captain had Vida by the shoulders and was shaking her as if emptying a bag of grain. "Trollop! How dare you enter my cabin! How dare you steal my oranges!"

Julia gasped. The orange she had earlier slipped into a pocket now felt as large as a melon. Even so, she stepped into the room. "Captain James. Please. Control yourself."

Tilly burst in from the passage, using far more colorful language. As James glared at them, Vida wrenched free.

"It's not enough the steering gear acts up," the captain growled. "Now I've trouble with a thieving woman, as well."

Looking as if he believed Vida responsible for all his problems, he reached for her again. She darted aside and he caught only her cloak. As it pulled loose in his hands, a silver object dropped to the floor between them.

He grabbed it before Vida could snatch it up. His face grew even redder. "My watch!"

Swiftly, Julia said, "You must be more careful where you leave it."

"Lucky Vida found it," Tilly put in. "Sure as the tide, someone else would have pinched it."

The captain looked as if he was about to explode. Then he sucked in a long breath. The redness faded from his face and was replaced by a cold intent that frightened Julia more. "Want to see the goldfields, do you? Then you'll walk, for I'm setting the pack of you thieving lightskirts ashore at Juneau."

He shoved past them and went out of the cabin. The women looked from one to another, for once all of them silent. Finally, Tilly shrugged. "The devil take the old mud puppy. There must be music halls in Juneau."

"Sure," Vida agreed as blithely as if she had not been the cause of their disaster. "Why tramp over a frozen pass? Besides, I hear them Canadian Mounted Police are dull as pancakes."

"That's it, then," Tilly said and with a careless shrug headed toward the saloon.

Julia felt as if the floating ice she had watched earlier now coursed through her blood. To be set ashore in Juneau...impossible. Wasn't it enough that Duncan meant to abandon them? Her eyes misted. She was nearly a thousand miles from home. How would she support herself? Perhaps she could clerk in some shop. Or she might sing in a music hall, after all. She shuddered.

From her bunk, Vida said, "I'd like to spit in his face." She leaned toward Julia, her eyes brightening. "Say, where's that stowaway you found? It'll serve the old party right if we help her steal a free passage."

The ice inside Julia gave way to anger. Yet to chide Vida for stealing would be as useless as to scold the tide for rising. There was little for it, she told herself with resignation, but to face one problem at a time. The most immediate problem lay with Hannah.

Minutes later, squeezed into one end of Julia's bunk, Hannah entertained them all with stories of her experiences. "It was when Julia sang on the dock that I slipped aboard," she said at last. "I sauntered right past a sailor who was supposed to be checking for tickets." She grinned at Julia. "You had them all bewitched."

Feeling more responsible for Hannah's safety than before, Julia asked the question that had burned in her since they met. "Why were you so desperate to leave Seattle?"

Hannah poked ruefully at the tulips on her hat. "I had a problem."

"Now, there's news," Tilly said.

With a spark of defiance, the curly-haired woman glanced at them. "I am a model, and well paid for it most of the time. Why, I even posed once for Mr. Dana Gibson. You must know his work."

*A model.* Julia almost exclaimed, *But you have such nice manners.* She kept the words back. A woman headed for a public music hall had no right to question another's morals.

Vida looked impressed. "Mr. Gibson. He's a swell. What kinda trouble did he give you?"

"Mr. Gibson is every inch a gentleman," Hannah said quickly. "It was another artist, one who refused to pay unless I would . . . be nice to him. And that was the least of it. He made a series of classical poses. Aphrodite was the last." Anger and despair flushed her face, then left it pale. "In each, I posed in heavy veils. He kept the pictures from me until he finished the last and then I saw . . ." Her voice trembled and she paused to steady it. "He painted me nude."

Julia sucked in her breath while Tilly made a coarse reference to the unknown artist's private parts. Vida leaned closer. "What did you do?"

"There was no one to protect me," Hannah said. "He tried to kiss me. We struggled. I fell against a column he used as a prop. An urn fell from the top, striking his head. I will never forget that sound." Moaning, she covered her face.

"He was dead?" Vida whispered.

Hannah's head shot up. "No! But I took his pocket-book to collect my fee. I knew it was in his waistband. He had taunted me with it. The money was owed." Again, she looked defiantly at them.

"We'd have all done the same," Tilly assured her.

Hannah picked nervously at the silk tulips on her hat. "While I was fumbling after my money, he groaned and tried to get up."

Tilly gasped.

"I ran," Hannah said in a whisper. "I forgot I had his pocketbook in my hand. When I remembered it, I knew he would send the police after me. I couldn't face the shame."

"But you must have told the police what happened," Julia exclaimed. "Why, you weren't at all to blame."

"I didn't tell them anything. I headed straight for the wharf." Hannah shivered. "Soon after, I met you."

They all fell silent for a moment.

"What will you do now?" Julia asked.

"Why, make my fortune in the goldfields like everyone else."

"You're brave enough to do it," Vida said with approval.

Julia was reluctant to cast another problem at the young woman after all she had been through, but she would have to know the truth. "The police refuse entry into Canada unless you bring provisions enough for a year."

"So much!" Hannah exclaimed. "Why?"

"There was trouble last winter," Julia answered. "Many in Seattle were horrified by the reports." Not all, for Aaron had been pleased. The plight of starving miners meant the chance to sell more supplies to those to follow. "Rumors were that thousands would starve," she added slowly, "though I believe most of the prospectors managed to survive."

"So I must procure supplies to last a year," Hannah said. "There must be shops in Skagway."

"Or in Juneau," Julia said. When Hannah looked at her, she added, "You must show us how to hide aboard, I'm afraid, for the captain has declared he will put us all ashore."

The door burst open. Duncan filled the narrow space, his head brushing the lintel as he glared at them. "What in blazes have you done to set the captain off?"

Julia moved to shield Hannah, but only succeeded in drawing Duncan's attention. Through a maze of sensations, she realized he was staring at the model with the look of a man whose last hope for sanity had faded. "Who the devil is she?"

Julia had spent a lifetime facing Aaron's wrath, and would not back down now. She placed one hand protectively on Hannah's shoulder. Duncan's narrowed gaze made her quail, but she kept her voice steady. "This is Hannah. She is traveling with us to Skagway."

"Skagway?" he repeated bitterly. "Hasn't the captain informed you of his plans?"

"No doubt you will remind him that our full passage has been paid." She warmed her tone to convey confidence in Duncan's ability to reason with the temperamental man.

He studied her with fresh distaste. "All I have done during this damnable voyage is remind him of that fact, while all of you have done your level best to harry the man."

Duncan was the one looking harried, and Julia felt a quaver of guilt before she reminded herself that he could certainly not hold her responsible for Vida and Tilly. She lifted her head as grandly as Aaron whenever his prices were challenged. That was a mistake. The speculation she had been dreading returned to Duncan's face, a look that said she didn't belong where she was, dressed as she was, pretending to be what she decidedly was not. "Pretty Songbird," he said softly. "You and I are overdue for a long talk."

Panic whirled through Julia. She was not good at lying. He would see through her in a minute. He already suspected the truth. If only Vida had behaved herself—if only all of them had.

"Where have you sung before?" Duncan demanded. "How did you meet Tilly?"

Julia stared at him. It seemed easier to look at the smooth tan of his throat than into his angry eyes. Yet it wasn't easier, after all. She felt entranced by the shadows cast by his open collar and by a hint of dark chest hair that she knew reached to his flat stomach. Disturbing images mingled with the memory of lean fingers coursing the sensitive length of her bare arm.

He gave her a light shake. "Are you daft? Answer me. What is your full name?"

Tilly interrupted crossly. "Leave off."

Julia braced herself. She had always believed that lies brought more trouble than the most unpleasant truth. "My name is Julia Ames," she began, but stopped herself. "That is, Julia Everett."

An enormous grinding sounded, as if the ship were protesting. She barely had time to wonder at the noise before a jolt threw her to the floor. "What is it?" she gasped, while the other women screamed. "What has happened?"

Duncan lifted her to her feet, holding her briefly in a protective embrace. "That damned captain is a fool. Faulty steering gear has pulled us to starboard all day, but he swore we could make Juneau."

Julia felt a dread far worse than any fear of being stranded in the wrong city. She remembered the burned hulk on the beach and wanted to cling to Duncan. Scarcely able to force words between stiff lips, she whispered, "Have we foundered?"

"We've drifted onto the bank." His voice was gentle though grim. "Stay here while I see what's to be done."

Shouting men were pounding past the open doorway. Duncan started to follow, then turned with a warning that pinned Julia in place. "Did you hear me? All of you stay here."

# Chapter Five

As he raced to the deck, Duncan hoped the women had sense enough to follow his orders. God knew what sort of panic was likely to develop among the passengers.

Once again, Julia had seemed to be more than a showgirl; he was sure of it. She was gentle beneath her fire. When he had stroked her bare arm, her skin had felt achingly soft. He had longed to carry her into the cabin and kiss every inch of that soft skin.

It wouldn't be smart to give any of the showgirls that kind of attention, even though he would leave them soon. He had torn himself away, but the restlessness stayed with him. When he held her in his arms, he felt almost overwhelmed by a need to protect her.

Ames or Everett? Why was she using two names? The law might be after her. That would explain why she insinuated herself into his care. She could be running from a husband. The idea disturbed him. Now there was another, Hannah. Where in blazes had *she* come from?

It was almost a relief to see the ship held fast by the muddy east bank. Here was a problem he could tackle. Grateful for the challenge, he pushed his way through a crowd of men standing twenty deep below the bridge.

Above them, Captain James shouted, ''Nothin' to worry about, lads! The tide's headin' out. It will carry us straight off. My crew will fix the steerin' gear while we wait.''

The man was a fool. With a mental image of the ship foundering, of Julia swept into the sea, Duncan raised his voice to reach them all. "Do you call yourself a seafarer? The tide will pull the *Gypsy Gull* over when it drops."

His warning was picked up and repeated. The captain bellowed above the rising voices, a slur in his words proving recent familiarity with the bottle. "Tha's a lie, sir. An' I'll thank you not to fright'n my pass'ngers."

A thin man in a plaid mackinaw shouted from the rail. "Look there on the bank. The tide is already below the high-water line. And the current is racing!"

"Nothin' to worry about," the captain said again.

Several turned to Duncan. "How far does the tide drop, do you know?"

Duncan had already learned this was the first voyage for most of the passengers. He cast a quick glance around, judging courage and agility. He didn't want to cause a panic, but if they were to save the ship, they would have to understand the danger.

"I studied charts before we left Seattle. This channel sees a fall of ten to fifteen feet. Unless we tie her to the trees, gentlemen, in a few more hours the *Gull* will lie on her side."

His nerves tightened as he thought of Julia. There was little sense in it, but the threat of losing her before he had learned who she was made his stomach knot.

White-faced men stared over the rail, but most soon gathered around themselves the comfort of the captain's assurance. Pulling off his knit cap, a burly fellow said stoutly, "Captain James knows his craft. The tide will pull the ship into the channel."

"And what then, if we're tied to trees?" another demanded.

"Why beg trouble?" the first man asked. "The tide is our salvation."

Duncan glanced again at the shore. The lap of waves sounded cold. A rank smell of rotting weeds pervaded the air. The smell would grow stronger as more of the mud bank was exposed. Gulls swooped overheard, their shrill cries sounding alarmed.

"Whatever the case," he said, "the horses must be secured tightly in their stalls. When the *Gull* lists, the animals may fall and break their legs." Grimly, he added to his mental tally against the captain. When this was over, any horses with broken legs would have to be shot.

"I'm going below to look for sturdy rope. If the rest of you want to lean on the rails and watch the tide drag the *Gypsy Gull* to her death, that's your choice."

He strode to the hatch, gratified that several men followed him. Heavy pounding and curses came from the area near the steering gear, where a crew worked on the faulty part. Horses snorted and banged in their stalls. A cow lowed, echoed by howling dogs and the bray of donkeys.

The pressure of time drove him as he quickly separated the men into three groups. "You men secure the animals, and you others gather all the ropes you can find. Haul them on deck. We'll tie the ship to the trees. And it will be up to you fellows in the third group to make sure supplies are lashed tight on deck. A sliding crate could shove a man into the sea."

The briskness in his voice set the men to work at once. "There are ships behind us," ventured a young man with freckles and bright red hair. "Maybe they can take us on."

An older man shook his head. "There's not a ship in this channel that isn't already packed from gunwale to gunwale."

The younger man blinked. Duncan guessed his age as sixteen or seventeen, no more than that. Freckles were sharply defined against skin that would blister under the Yukon sun should he ever reach that territory. He fought visibly to steady a quaver in his voice. "We can't be far from Juneau."

"It ain't walkin' distance." A bearded man in buckskin spat into a stall. Chambers, he was called, a trapper returning to the Yukon territory. He spent every evening regaling an eager audience with tales of his exploits. Now Duncan was glad to see him take action. He broke into passengers' supplies without hesitation and handed out coils of rope.

Duncan placed an arm around the shoulders of the worried young man. "We'll reach Juneau, and on the *Gypsy Gull*. Our job is to keep her from listing. You're an agile fellow. We'll need you to haul lines ashore and tie them to trees." He paused. "What are you called?"

"Ben, sir." Blinking rapidly, the younger man hoisted a heavy coil of rope over one shoulder. "I'm ready to start whenever you say."

He would do all right, Duncan decided. And the trapper Chambers had already taken charge of securing the animals. Duncan climbed over the stacked provisions and began hauling out more rope.

By the time he returned to the deck, the slope of the ship had become noticeable. As he expected, the hull clung to the mud while the ship leaned toward the sea in the outgoing tide. The air had grown colder. Snow swirled among knots of people with frightened eyes and pinched mouths. Even in the open air, Duncan smelled sweat, fright and gin.

Several men worked to lower lifeboats. It was clear there was not space enough for all. In minutes, an argument exploded. "You slimy wharf rat!" A lean man grabbed another and spun him around. "You only lowered the boat to stake your own claim aboard."

"I don't see you earning a place," the first shot back.

Duncan shouted at them. "Listen to me. Get lines into the trees and we can forget the boats. We need your help over here."

At his direction, men began tying ropes to the eastfacing, starboard side of the *Gull*. Others skidded down the sloping hull into the water. They splashed toward shore, letting out their lines. Within an hour, the entire length of the ship looked as if a mammoth spider had webbed the vessel to the trees.

Crossing the deck was like walking up a pitched roof. A loose hay bale slid a few feet, but stopped against an upright pipe. Men scrambled to lash it into place. Snow swirled faster. Faces were reddened with cold. Rubbing his numbed hands together, Duncan edged down the deck to the seaward rail. The men in lifeboats lay off a short way, their voices deadened by falling snow. Even so, he heard a furious argument from some who wished to row the small boats all the way to Juneau, never mind floating ice and growing darkness.

From the rail, a woman shrieked, "Let me off. Let me go, I say!"

As her scream cut through other shouts, Duncan saw Mae halfway over the far rail. Julia and the newer woman, Hannah, were struggling with her. If Mae wrenched free, she would slide down the hull into mud and water. With all those skirts, she would be lost.

Duncan started up the deck. In the same moment, Mae shoved away her would-be rescuers. While Hannah clung to the rail, Julia flailed for balance. Her leather shoes skidded on the steeply angled planks, and she came tumbling down the deck. Duncan lunged to intercept her. She collided into him with a jolt that knocked out his breath.

Holding her around the waist with one arm, he braced them both against the rail. There was no stiff corset beneath her taffeta gown. As her cape enfolded them both, he wanted to hold her even closer.

Snow crystals drifted onto her glistening hair. More of them melted on the curves of her face. She gazed at him as if mesmerized, and he raised one hand to brush icy flakes from her cheek. Her lips were soft and slightly parted. He thought of melting the snowflakes with kisses, but this was not the time.

With a start, she regained her senses. "Mae! She's climbing overboard. We must stop her!"

"It's all right." He settled her protectively. "Tilly and Hannah have her."

He indicated the women, who were successfully tugging a hysterical Mae into the saloon. Their struggle dislodged a trunk. It skidded drunkenly down the deck into a cluster of men. Their shouts and curses seemed far distant while Duncan looked into Julia's crystal-lashed eyes.

Snow drifted around them, blanketing the sour smell of low tide. When Julia peered over the rail, lantern light from inside the ship revealed mud barely sheened with water. Knees and elbows of driftwood protruded. Sucking sounds came from the raw bank as the last of the tide drew away. Only the network of lines in groaning trees kept the *Gypsy Gull* from settling more.

She turned to Duncan, trusting him to keep panic away. "What must we do?"

He wondered if Julia's calm masked shock, and he longed to tell her not to worry, that he would keep her safe. Her clear eyes demanded honesty. He said simply, "We've done what we can. It's slack tide now. If they can repair the steering, we should get back into the channel when the tide returns."

From the hold below came a sound of sliding cargo. The ship vibrated as something heavy slammed into the side. Horses screamed. With a tremor in her voice, Julia said, "People are clinging to the outside of the ship, clutching every knot and nail. They say those on deck may be thrown into the channel."

"The *Gull* won't lean any lower." That was scant comfort, considering their harrowing forty-five-degree tilt. He didn't want to picture what might be taking place in the hold, yet Julia looked confident of his promise to deliver her safely to Skagway. Again, he felt a stab of conscience. Yet he could not leave the *Fortune* in Skagway harbor through another winter.

The need to see his trawler swept him with almost physical force as he visualized every line of the vessel he loved more than he had ever loved a woman. Before heading home, he would check with the authorities, to locate a reliable guide for Julia and the others. He settled her more securely against his shoulder, aware that she stiffened as if she wanted to pull free. She was an odd contradiction of uncorseted satin and shrinking virtue. Again he wondered at the deceptive costume and whether she was running from the law or from a husband.

Tentatively, she said, "I must see to Mae."

"You would never make it up the deck with those shoes."

She looked at her feet as if the soft soles had betrayed her. Clearly, she wanted to hold herself away from him. That was impossible with the deck slanting like a steep-pitched roof.

Duncan felt as if he could easily spend the night holding her like this, so close that the heat of their bodies mingled. Her cape concealed them from curious eyes, and as time passed, she seemed less inclined to pull away. He curled his fingers around her slender waist, tempted to raise his hand to the sweet shape of her breasts, but unwilling to risk losing her trust. It would be an hour or more before the tide made an appreciable difference to the slant of the deck.

Despite their peril, Julia felt secure. Then she felt the steady beat of Duncan's heart beneath her palm and nearly forgot to breathe.

The fear of the passengers grew more obvious as the sky darkened. Sobs and prayers soon came from every side. Julia began to long for her cabin, yet felt safe in the open air with Duncan. Trembling, she spread her hand against his chest and wondered if she dared wrap her arm around his waist.

Duncan sensed the growing panic of the passengers. He'd seen hysteria before. Minds snapped, men became animals. He couldn't let that happen. Quietly, he said, "Julia, on the wharf in Seattle, your singing transfixed everyone who heard. Choose something soothing to sing to us now."

"Sing?" She sounded as if he had suggested something distasteful. "I—I'm not accustomed to singing in public."

He tried to study her face, but the night had become too dark to see her clearly. "Where do you think you will be singing in Dawson City? Do you plan to entertain one man at a time?"

She knew he meant to have an answer. If only fear didn't make it so difficult to think. A shiver ran through her at the thought of being discovered.

Singing would keep questions at bay; yet she simply could not do it. The wharf had been a different matter. Determined to convince him to take her to Dawson City, she had scarcely been aware of others listening. They were going about their business, or so she had assumed. Now he wanted her to call attention to herself, to her voice. She could not bring herself to try.

"Listen to them," Duncan urged. "Half the men aboard are barely old enough to shave. I warrant most of them are wishing now for their mothers."

Julia raised her head, trying to hear above the hammering of her heart. Someone was crying close by. The aching sobs wrenched her. To calm the fear of that one terrified young man, she began a familiar hymn. The clear notes carried reassurance through the swirl of falling snow.

To her surprise, Duncan added a rich baritone. A man's clear tenor rose from the starboard rail. Others joined in. Their combined voices formed a blanket of comfort.

Duncan's strong voice embraced Julia's notes as surely as his arms held her. She felt close to him in spirit as well as body while he protected her from the sloping deck and chilled rail. Her voice lifted, briefly alone until his baritone joined in.

Julia faltered, her feelings for Duncan chasing the familiar words from her mind. Embarrassed, she concentrated fiercely on her singing. When the hymn ended, silence drifted over the ship. Then she heard the creak and groan of straining lines.

Water slapped against the hull. How cold it sounded. With a shock, she realized the tide was returning. Before, there had been only mud. Eagerly, she said, "Listen? Do you hear? How long will it take to right the ship?"

"Not long," he said. "An hour, perhaps."

An hour! Would her nerves hold so long? Would theirs? "Miss," a man called through the dark. "Do you know any ballads?"

"'Sweet Marie,'" urged another.

From the opposite rail someone asked, "Will you sing, 'After the Ball'?" From one of the lifeboats, a man begged for "Little Annie Rooney."

Julia's doubts faded before the urgency in the lonely, frightened voices. Placing her confidence in Duncan as he supported her against the frightening pitch of the deck, she began again to sing.

She chose first the lilting "Little Annie Rooney," then followed with "Sweet Marie." Lanterns were carried from cabins and fastened above the deck. Their glow seemed to add warmth. Even better, they illuminated the gradual straightening of the ship. Soon the lifeboats drew alongside. Their passengers clambered up rope ladders.

The lines fell slack between ship and trees. Duncan directed men into the small boats to go ashore and recover the ropes, which would be needed in the Yukon. At the same time, those who had climbed over the upraised hull returned shivering to the ship. They stamped their feet and blew on numbed hands.

The ship shuddered as the engine came to life. Julia had remained at the rail. She held her breath while mud and water churned. The sour smell of mud flats was scarcely noticeable. Her entire being waited for the ship to move. And then with a lurch the ship shuddered, righted and was buoyant.

From the bridge, the captain shouted, "Gentlemen, we are free!"

Every throat burst into rousing cheers. Impulsively, Julia flung her arms around Duncan. "It's over!"

Lantern light cast changing shadows from the angles of his face as he caught her to him. Before she could draw back, his mouth covered hers.

No man had ever kissed her. She thought she must make him stop, and yet she nestled closer, more aware of the warmth of his body than before. Her muscles somehow lost their strength as unexpected sensations rushed through her. She clung to him, her arms beneath his coat, her hands straining against the strong muscles of his back.

The caress of his mouth was sweeter than she could have dreamed. The aching fear of the past hours fell away. She was no longer aware of snow settling over her face and hair. For an endless moment, she gave herself to breathless pleasure. She felt his hands at her waist and back. Slowly, he moved one hand, the caress making her think of hot snowflakes swirling over her skin. His warm fingers made her ache with longing as they stroked forward to cradle her breast.

For one liquid moment, she felt as if she was drowning in sensation. Aaron's training and her own better nature brought her to her senses. She jerked backward, nearly falling. "What are you doing? Let me go!"

He steadied her but did not set her free. She wanted to see him more clearly, then was thankful he could not see the confusion that must be in her face. At the same time, she realized with surprise that the kiss had shaken him, as well. His voice sounded distracted. "Who the devil are you? What are you doing with the likes of Tilly?"

She wanted to tell him everything, to trust him with her secrets and her life. She was saved from such foolhardiness by men who crowded around them, many pressing her shoulder or simply touching her cape. Moisture glittered in grateful eyes.

"You were like an angel come down to us," one said.

Another interrupted in a voice that trembled. "More like my sweet wife at our little daughter's cradle."

A young man said wistfully, "My mother used to sing like that. Miss, you gave us her favorite songs."

Julia felt her throat ache with gratitude for their praise. It was a far safer emotion than those she had been feeling moments earlier. In months past, she had raised her voice only in her own parlor or as part of a church choir. Never had she thought that her voice might touch painful chords in others. She was ashamed of her reluctance to sing.

The deck still sloped. She heard a worried undercurrent in the voices around Duncan. "I want to check the hold," he said quietly to Julia. "Please go into the saloon. I'll join you there."

With reluctance, she watched him go, remembering that cargo had shifted. The scream of horses had burned into her memory. As some of the men walked toward the hatch with Duncan, she was glad for the tide of admirers who escorted her into the comfort of the saloon.

The cook had water heating. A cup of tea was brought at once. Julia sipped gratefully, but was conscious of waiting for Duncan, scarcely hearing the praise of the men. At last, he pulled a chair to the table next to her. Her eager greeting clashed with questions in his eyes. She could not put off answering him much longer and felt newly grateful to the men who competed for her attention with stories of home and sister, wife or mother.

Hannah slipped through the crowd, her eyes bright as she approached Duncan. "I quieted your friend Mae by making her a promise."

Leaning back in his chair, he studied her warily. "Go on."

Hoisting her skirt a scandalous distance above her ankles, Hannah executed an artful buck and wing. Breathless, she said, "Mae is terrified of going on. She'll only give you trouble. I will gladly pay her passage home if I may take her place."

Duncan took a long draft from a mug of ale. It occurred to Julia that Hannah was making herself dangerously noticeable, but the dark-haired woman seemed unconcerned. Perhaps she still relied on the fabrication of a seasick brother in some cabin where passage had been paid. That would not convince the captain.

"Why do you want Mae's place?"

"Why else?" Hannah laughed. "To get to the goldfields, of course, but I'll dance in your saloon for as long as you need me."

Captain James plunged into the crowd. Men were pushing and circling around him. All of them wanted to relive the danger now that it was past. As the captain accepted their praise, it became clear that he saw himself as a hero. Julia looked worriedly toward Hannah, wishing the stowaway would slip from sight.

"I've arranged for five showgirls to be taken to Dawson City," Duncan said at last. "It's nothing to me which five they are."

Julia tried to return Hannah's beam of pleasure, but her smile felt frozen. The dreamy pleasure of those long hours in Duncan's arms shattered like a pricked bubble. She would not sing in Dawson City. Her father would see to that. Duncan planned to turn back at Skagway. She tried to feel anger at his betrayal, but felt only a sense of loss.

"You won't be sorry," Hannah told him and with a blown kiss, slipped into the crowd.

That she posed for commercial portraits suggested a less than savory reputation, and yet there was about Hannah the sense of a proper upbringing. Who was she? Julia wondered, and felt a twinge of discomfort as she remembered that Duncan asked the same question of her. Uneasily, she turned her teacup in her hands.

The captain shouted to Duncan. "I believe that I owe you my thanks, sir. Not that we were ever in danger. Yet I am a fair man. I have decided to carry your rowdy party on to Skagway."

In the tension of the past hours, Julia had nearly forgotten the threat of being put ashore in Juneau. Her body had not. She felt almost faint with relief. It was a distinct shock to hear Duncan answer, "You are mistaken, captain. The women are to go up the Lynn Canal to Dyea."

"Dyea!" Thunderheads formed in the captain's face. "Yours is the mistake, sir."

Duncan lowered his chair to the plank floor. Slowly, he rose to his full six feet. "Some mistakes are more dangerous than others."

The captain's thoughts became transparent. If word of this incident reached Seattle, even the most desperate of gold seekers might think twice before risking a voyage with him. The sooner he sent his passengers on to the goldfields, the better.

"I owe you, I've said so," he admitted grudgingly. "Another day won't change things much. All right, then. It's on to Dyea."

Julia noticed the captain's gratitude did not extend to her. Only loose women exhibited their talents in public. Aaron had always said so, and the captain's distaste brought her uncle's spirit uncomfortably near.

She was grateful for the distraction of a young man with red hair and freckles who spoke with warm admiration. "You were a wonder, miss. As brave as could be, despite the ship being half tipped over. And with the lines groaning like banshees in the dark." He grinned self-consciously. "I was scared the ones I tied might let go."

"You must have done your work well," she said and watched his face redden with pleasure.

Another fellow took up the story. "People crying and praying. Did you see how many clung to the upper hull? If they had dropped, they would have sunk to their waists in soft mud. In that current, they'd likely have been dragged under the ship."

"There's no reasoning with terror," the young man said as if he had been calm through the entire experience.

Julia enjoyed the retelling as much as the men did, especially when praise came her way. Yet she was intensely conscious of Duncan and of the hours she had been held against the warmth and strength of his body.

She caught herself watching his mouth, reliving the kiss she should never have allowed. Dismayed by the prospect of repeating her mother's mistakes, she forced her mind to a more practical concern. Duncan's questions had been avoided, but she couldn't hope to keep the truth from him much longer.

He meant to abandon her. That he promised to locate a substitute guide was no consolation. She was as much on her own as she had been when she left her uncle's care. Raising her head, she studied the men crowding the tables and standing at the bar. During the disaster, she had gained their respect. Why not select a guide from among them, rather than depend on a stranger?

All were headed for Dawson City, some by way of Skagway and the White Pass, others by way of the Chilkoot Trail from Dyea Inlet. Ben would certainly do his best for her, but he was inexperienced. If the trail was as rigorous as it was described as being, she would require a strong, competent guide.

Someone like Duncan.

Trying to ignore a tight feeling in her throat, she turned her gaze to a tall man wearing buckskin. He leaned negligently against the bar, looking bored by the excited telling and retelling of the night's events. His name was Chambers, she remembered. He was a returning trapper and a hardened man from the look of him. He would know the trail.

Would he agree to escort her? It was time she took charge of her own destiny. Never mind Duncan Adair and his plans. Chambers looked like a reasonable man. She would approach him in the morning. Surely, he would help her locate her father.

# Chapter Six

Duncan was accustomed to sleeping soundly, no matter what might go on around him. This night, however, he lay awake in his upper bunk staring into the dark.

Mae's terror had subsided into steady sobs. The prospect of returning to Seattle did nothing to comfort her, for she would be returning on the same ship with the same irresponsible captain. Duncan considered inviting her aboard the *Fortune,* but put the thought aside. Mae was given to hysterics, and there would be no crew to handle the wheel should she panic. She was safer aboard the *Gypsy Gull.*

It was Julia who kept him awake long after the others slept. An image of her bright, lively face rose in his mind. He thought of her soft lips and the artless sweetness of her kiss. He knew her garish costume was a mask. She was not a tart aping the manners of a gentlewoman. It was the other way around, and he wanted to know why.

There was no pretense in her determination to reach Dawson City, but he couldn't quite reconcile a greed for gold with the woman he was beginning to know. It suddenly occurred to him that she was not running from a husband or lover but toward one. Of course. The fellow had gone to the goldfields, leaving her behind. She might even be expecting his child.

Duncan twisted to pummel his flat pillow. The answer was obvious and unsettling. Thinking of Julia was doing him no good, he told himself. He would leave her company tomorrow and be glad of it.

That was only part of his restlessness. However long it might take, he knew he could not take the *Fortune* home before he located a reliable guide for Julia. He stared into the darkness, unable to sleep.

Julia shared her bunk with Hannah. She felt as if she was about to fall off the edge. Hannah's steady breathing accompanied soft snores from Vida and Tilly. How could they sleep so easily with the ship listing from the unbalanced cargo?

One grows used to danger, she told herself. For these women, an unbalanced ship was likely a minor threat compared to others they had faced. She envied their ability to sleep, but not their circumstances. She turned her thoughts to the trapper, Chambers. Tomorrow she would ask him to guide her to Dawson City. Perhaps promise of payment from her father would help, but how much should she offer? Did the nugget mean her father had found a wealth of gold? She had already committed him without his knowledge to repaying the cost of her passage.

Her thoughts drifted to the stories told in the saloon that night. Duncan's quick thinking had kept the ship from going over. Shivering, she realized how close she had come to death before even reaching the Chilkoot Trail.

Her circling thoughts returned to the need for a guide and her bitter disappointment in Duncan Adair. Chambers was the more trustworthy man. With Chambers, she told herself fervently, she would not have to guard against her own unsettling reactions. Restlessly, she turned onto her stomach and soon fell into a fitful slumber.

It seemed as if she had barely closed her eyes before the other women stirred awake. Hannah proved to be the sort who greeted the morning with vibrant enthusiasm. Julia pulled a pillow over her head to close out her new friend's eager chatter.

The two of them walked to the saloon together for breakfast, Hannah spilling over with plans for the trail. Julia knew she should tell the women that Duncan meant to abandon them, but had little heart for it. Let him tell them. Why should she make it easier for him?

After collecting tea and toast, the two of them found seats. Hannah's eyes danced. "I will admit this is far better than having to hide."

Julia nodded absently. Chambers had just ambled into the saloon. The young red-haired man, Ben, was with him. When they sat nearby with their breakfast plates, she couldn't help hearing their conversation.

Ben was as eager as Hannah to start on the trail. "White Pass is the easiest, I've heard."

Chambers answered with a cynical grunt. "Son, there ain't a way into the Klondike that's easy."

"Relatively, I meant." Ben hesitated. "Which way are you going?"

"Chilkoot."

"I guess you'd know best, having been there before. I wonder...that is, I'm a good hand at building fires and pitching tents. Seems like a man hadn't ought to travel completely on his own, so maybe we could team up. Just over the trail."

His words rushed after each other as if he thought a pause would give the older man a chance to refuse. At last his breath ran out and he stopped, watching Chambers with an intensity that echoed through Julia. If the trapper was willing to accommodate Ben, then surely he would agree to guiding one more. She could offer to do the cooking and washing up. After years spent under Aaron's tyranny, she felt confident of adequately performing such chores.

Chambers cut into a stack of hotcakes and chewed thoughtfully, in no apparent rush to make up his mind. Ben looked as if he was torn between repeating his plea and retracting it. Julia heard Hannah's voice but could not listen to the words. At last, the trapper set down his fork. Julia set down hers as well.

"Done." The trapper stretched out his hand. Ben shook it with obvious relief, while Julia nearly exclaimed aloud, "Oh, good."

Now was the time. Drawing on her courage, she pictured herself turning her chair toward the neighboring ta-

ble. She would apologize for listening . . . no, apology was
wrong. She would simply explain that she had overheard,
then emphasize the useful skills she could add to their party.
*Now,* she told herself. *Nothing is gained by timidity.*

"Good morning, ladies." Duncan's voice startled her.

Though her plans crumbled, Julia felt a pleasant leap of
her senses as she turned to look at him. His thick brown
hair was tousled, and he had nicked his chin while shaving; perhaps he had spent a restless night, as well.

As he hauled a chair to their table, Hannah greeted him
with so many eager questions that Julia could not get in a
word. She began to wish she had left the stowaway at the
rail. Not that words were necessary. When she looked into
the incredible blue of his eyes, she felt as if she were
drowning. Her hand trembled while she tried to butter a
slice of toast. She couldn't decide if she was more distressed by the prospect of his questions or the memory of
his kiss.

At last Hannah faltered to a stop when she seemed to realize that Duncan's attention was on Julia. Quietly, he said,
"I've been down in the hold. We're listing pretty badly, but
we'll make it through all right."

"I've almost become accustomed to the tilt of the deck,"
Julia said, thankful that her voice didn't betray her scattered emotions. "How are the animals?"

Duncan's face darkened. "Two mules were crushed by
falling cargo. And three of the horses had to be shot."

"Shot!" Hannah said with a gasp of terror. "Why?"

"Broken legs." He drank deeply of his coffee, his forehead creased.

Julia saw that he was bitter over the loss and knew he
blamed the captain. Toying with her fork, she said, "We
didn't expect an easy trip." That reminded her of his in-
tention to leave them. "I expected problems to begin when
we set out on the trail, not aboard ship and not in Skagway."

She rose abruptly. "I feel a need for fresh air."

A light snow that coated the decks had already turned to
muddy slush under passing feet. The air cooled Julia's hot
cheeks, and she pulled her cape more tightly together as she

took pleasure in the freshness of the morning. A still, icy world enclosed the ship. To either side, white-frosted trees covered the shores. Beyond the east bank, soaring mountains dwarfed the parade of vessels up the inland channel. Sunlight dazzled the rugged peaks. The magnificence of the scene held her at the rail.

A group of men stopped beside her, oblivious to the surrounding grandeur as they talked of the trip ahead. She interrupted the nearest to ask, "How much longer, do you think, until we reach Skagway?"

Anticipation glittered in the man's eyes and voice. "We passed Juneau before daybreak, miss. Should make Skagway late today, unless we have more problems."

Last night, her songs reminded many of women they loved. Perhaps Chambers, too, had been reminded of sister or mother. If that was the case, he would surely help her. She had so convinced herself he would help that when he strolled toward her along the deck, she stopped him without hesitation. "Excuse me, sir. May I have a word with you?"

Chambers looked her over in a way that would have offended her in Seattle. She told herself his lonely life had clouded his manners. Still, her heart pounded as she explained, "I couldn't help overhearing Ben talk with you this morning. It is good of you to permit him to join you on the trail."

"He'll earn his keep."

"I'm sure that he will, as I will—would—if I may join your party...."

His brows raised. Fearing he was about to refuse and uncomfortably aware of the men listening, Julia rushed on much as Ben had done earlier. "I can cook and tend a fire and, well, there must be many other ways I can aid you on the trail."

He threw back his head and laughed. Even her inexperienced ear could not fail to hear the insult. When he looked at her again, there was no question that he stripped her naked with his eyes. "Likely so, honey. I just ain't sure it's worth the trouble to haul along a bed warmer."

She had built a lore about this man. All of it crumbled with his words. "You misunderstood me," Julia said with shocked disappointment. "If that was what I had in mind, I would have chosen someone more manly."

As the other men laughed, Chambers's face clouded. Aaron had often said her tongue would be her undoing. Julia shrank back, but not quickly enough. The trapper caught her by both shoulders and dragged her to him. "You don't look too choosy to me, honey, with your trollop's flash."

To Julia's astonishment, it was the captain who intervened. He came storming along the deck. "What the hell is going on here? Didn't I tell you women to keep out of sight?"

He wrenched her free of Chambers's grasp, spun her around and slapped her behind to start her toward her cabin. "I don't care if you sing like the angels. Don't go making trouble on my ship!"

Relieved and furious, Julia marched down the deck. She passed the entrance to the cabins and continued forward, where she went to the bow rail and glared at the magnificent scenery.

Was her only hope in trusting Duncan to find a reliable guide? She no longer felt confidence in any man. Maybe she didn't need a guide. Maybe she could take herself over the trail. *Along with more than a thousand pounds of supplies.*

How had Duncan planned for those goods to be transported? Until now, the question had not occurred to her. Vividly, she remembered the dark-haired woman in Aaron's shop who protested that she was not a packhorse. How could anyone pack a thousand pounds?

A little at a time. Her memory brought up bits of information she had heard in the store. The Chilkoot Trail was twenty-six miles long. To cross with the required supplies, a miner made at least twelve round trips, each time packing a hundred pounds of goods up the trail. That meant a total trek of six hundred and twenty-four miles. And after that there were six hundred miles or more of river travel.

Her heart felt as solid and cold as the chunks of ice floating alongside the ship. The journey was doomed from the start. How could she have been such a fool?

She knew Duncan was beside her even before she turned. He stood so close that she felt warmth from his body, but when she faced him anger blazed from his eyes. "I've been looking all over for you. What the hell is this about propositioning Chambers?"

Julia felt as if she'd been punched. For a moment, she couldn't draw breath enough to answer.

Duncan watched the color leave her face and felt immediate regret. Impatiently, he pushed one hand through his hair. "I can't figure you out. Which are you, lady or tramp?"

"What I am is betrayed," she answered sharply. "By you and your promise to see us all safely to the Klondike."

"I've explained... Damn it, don't try to turn this around! What did you say to Chambers?"

His eyes were the intense cold blue of the glaciers. How could she ever have felt safe in his arms, Julia wondered.

"Captain James warned me to stay inside the cabin. For once, I feel inclined to take that advice." Turning her back, she hurried from him. He didn't follow. She told herself she was glad.

The closed space of the cabin nearly drove her to distraction. As the day passed with agonizing slowness, the other women wandered in and out. All were as restless as Julia and as eager to leave the ship for the next part of their journey. Again she thought of warning them that they might be stranded in Skagway, but in the end said nothing.

By late afternoon, even the thought of running into Chambers could not keep her from a walk along the deck. She paused to watch the crew haul a miniature iceberg aboard to stock the steamer's ice room for the return voyage.

Gold fever raced from passenger to passenger. From every hand, she heard wagers on the exact moment when they would reach the Skagway dock. It was impossible not to be caught up in the enthusiasm, however uncertain she was of her own prospects.

She made her way to the bow. Small craft of every description crowded the channel, all laden with miners' supplies. As far as she could tell, she was the sole person aboard to notice the dazzling scenery. The talk was all of packhorses and mining laws.

The snow had stopped. Pushing back her hood, she peered toward a thin line of white across the mouth of a deep valley. As she frowned, trying to make sense of it, a man nearby whooped. "There it is! That's the tents of Skagway!"

Others took up the shout until the entire ship seemed to vibrate. One fellow grabbed Julia and whirled her once around in an impulsive dance. The white line began to take shape; a narrow valley lay behind it, held between cloud-topped mountains that towered upward like hands peaked in prayer. Could there truly be a way out of that glacier-bound haven?

"That's the White Pass," said a man nearby. He pointed, and his voice shook with eagerness. "See there? Follow the line of trees up the valley. See where they fade into the blue distance? That's it. That's the golden trail."

She felt frightened by his intensity. Days ago, she had wondered if there could possibly be gold enough for all. Now, as she looked from one eager face to another, she felt a dreadful apprehension. What would become of these dreams of wealth? What sort of men would journey to Seattle when the rush was over?

Slowly, the *Gypsy Gull* steamed up Skagway Bay, crowding among stern-wheelers, yachts, barges and scows. Duncan joined her at the rail, and she tensed before she saw that his expression was troubled.

"Julia," he said quietly. "I admit to reacting without thinking. When I pictured you with Chambers—" He broke off, then said simply, "Let's not part in anger."

The apology in his voice touched her, and she offered her own. "I only approached him in hope of a guide and meant nothing more than to help with camp chores."

He nodded, watching the harbor as they approached. "You'll have a reliable guide. I would never leave you here without making sure of that."

He was the companion she wanted on the trail. The promise of a guide, however carefully chosen, was no comfort. Around them, the crowd seethed with excitement. On the flat ahead, hundreds of cooking fires wreathed the tents with bluish smoke. A few frame buildings rose above the canvas peaks. Mountains of goods were stacked around. Canoes and small boats moved around the steamer until it seemed as if the ship plowed through a floe of water craft. Their operators shouted offers to ferry passengers ashore for twenty-five cents.

Long docks stretched into deep water. Feeling an uneasy truce with Duncan, Julia pointed out the crowd of small boats that lined each wharf. "They look like ants at a spill of syrup."

Several large steamers lay at the docks. One was burning fiercely. With pity, Julia realized that some prospectors had had all their supplies destroyed.

Duncan hadn't answered. In his face, she saw the same hunger as in the face of the gold seekers. As others pointed out the White Pass, his avid gaze searched the wharves for his trawler. Feeling ignored, Julia said tartly, "I believe your passion for fishing equals other men's lust for gold."

He answered as he watched the harbor. "You would understand if you ever rode a trawler through the breakers at dawn. Sunrise is a glory over the eastern mountains. Your wake cuts a ribbon of light through the dark green of the sea. Crystals flash in the foam. Life is never better."

The rapture in his face and voice entranced her. She had never expected such a revelation into his heart. "The sea cradles you," he added. "It's as if you're embraced by the great heart of nature." He stopped as if he remembered where he was and was embarrassed to have spoken so candidly.

"You make a strong case for the life," she said.

He answered more casually. "The best part of it is in heading home with a hold full of salmon."

Feeling closer to him than she had during the hours in his arms, she said softly, "Thank you for talking with me, Duncan. If we must part here, I'm pleased that we do so as friends."

He stiffened suddenly, and his face grew tight. She watched with apprehension as he hailed a rowboat. "What vessel is that, the blackened one there?"

Julia glanced quickly from his face to a burned-out hulk half sunk on the mud flat. Apprehension turned to dread. The man in the rowboat glanced at the hulk. "She's a trawler out of Seattle. Been here since last fall. I believe she was called the *Fortune.*"

Duncan had known from his first glimpse of the burned vessel. Julia thought of the longing in his voice when he talked of the ship and the passion in his face when he searched for a sight of it. As she watched, his lips became a tight, hard line. The skin stretched taut over his cheeks. He blinked several times, then stared at the ruined trawler, his body rigid with grief.

She placed one gloved hand over his, longing to offer comfort. "Duncan, I'm so sorry."

# Chapter Seven

Duncan clenched his fists over the rail until the knuckles whitened. "This time, Owen is going to pay." Tearing his gaze from the *Fortune,* he said in a hard voice, "You have your guide, Songbird. We're *all* going to Dawson City."

She lowered her gaze to hide her relief.

Coolly, he began to plan. "I'll need an outfit for the trail. I brought only what I expected to need aboard the *Fortune.*" He broke off, and her heart felt his anguish. Then he turned back, and she flinched beneath his sharp regard. "We're going ashore. I mean to have a photograph of you girls made for my brother Owen. The sooner he starts drumming up trade, the sooner I can get out of this hell-hole."

If any place was less forsaken than this magnificence of dazzling white mountains, Julia didn't expect to see it. She kept her thoughts to herself, however, and sympathized with his loss.

"Get the others together," Duncan added. "I don't trust Captain James. He'd strand us if he could."

Julia swallowed. "Perhaps one of us should remain here to remind him of his word."

Duncan had started down the deck. He turned impatiently when she failed to follow. "There's time enough, Julia. James will be a few hours getting the ship unloaded. Come along."

The moment of tenderness between them might never have happened. Regretfully, Julia made her way among shouting, shoving men. Some intended to go on to Dyea; others pushed their goods onto barges to have them ferried to the beach.

Julia skipped hastily aside as a hay bale was thrust into her path. She spotted Hannah at the rail, her face alight with excitement, and sent her to roust Tilly from the ongoing game in the saloon.

As she wedged herself between mackinaw-clad men, Julia glimpsed Vida. The woman's deft fingers flashed into a pocket then into deep folds of her cape. "We're going ashore. Meet us on the dock," Julia told her curtly.

If Tilly was still at the poker table, Belle might still be... Just as she decided to discontinue her search, Julia turned a corner and ran into Belle. Both gasped in surprise. "We're all to meet on the dock," Julia explained, catching her breath. "Duncan wants a photograph to send to his stepbrother."

Belle fluffed her hair, a pleased smile warming her face. "Do you think he'll stand the cost of an extra picture? I've never had my likeness done..."

Skagway was a combination of dog kennel, lumber camp and Bedlam. As the group stood on the dock, feeling as if their bodies were still in motion with the ship, the cries of yelping sled dogs so filled the stretch of beach ahead that Julia wondered if the entire town had been taken over by the animals. Over the yaps and howls came a racket of lumbering. Skagway was rising from its beginnings as a tent city, but it was a noisy confusing process.

The long walk down the wharf became a parade through a gauntlet of catcalls and whistles. Julia had grown accustomed to satin and ruffles and unbound hair. Now she became intensely conscious of her wanton appearance, but she seemed to be the only one who felt uncomfortable.

Below the wharf, the beach held a litter of crates, sleds, boxes and canvas bags. Men in rubber boots clambered in the mud, arguing and occasionally breaking into fights as they struggled to haul provisions beyond the reach of the incoming tide.

At the base of the dazzling mountains, the tent city filled a triangular plain no more than a quarter of a mile wide at the beach and narrowing into the trees at the far end. The smoke Julia had noticed rose from fires where men cooked at large sheet-iron stoves. The smell of sizzling bacon reminded her that the captain hadn't bothered to provide an evening meal.

A dog team slushed by, spraying mud. Yards away, a commotion started up. Shouts rang above the barking dogs. "Look out!" Duncan pulled Julia aside as the others flattened against a rough frame wall. A frightened horse bolted toward them, a half-filled cart bumping and jouncing behind, tent ropes snapping loose in its wake. Canvas collapsed in billowing waves. People scattered, but once the animal had passed, they returned to their work as if a runaway horse were a common occurrence.

Duncan released Julia as abruptly as he had sheltered her and continued down the wharf. Annoyed that she felt a sense of loss, she lifted her skirts and followed. Several intrepid photographers had set up studios in tents and frame buildings. Unlike Belle, Julia dreaded the idea of a photograph and wondered how Duncan's stepbrother would display their likeness.

Duncan chose a studio from examples of work placed outside a large tent. As the entertainers preened and fluffed out their skirts, Julia tried to become invisible. "What are you doing back there?" Duncan asked impatiently. "Come out from behind Tilly. I want you in the center." With reluctance, she moved into place before a painted backdrop of snow-covered mountains.

"Wait here while the photographs are developed and printed," he told them. "I'll return as soon as I can buy outfitting."

The moment the tent closed behind him, Julia felt as if she had been abandoned. Suppose he didn't return? It might be possible for a woman to journey alone to Dawson City, but she could no longer imagine herself doing such a thing.

The photographer shut himself into his darkroom with the exposed plates for a length of time that stretched until Julia's nerves felt raw. The others made free with props, flirting behind fans and feathers like a band of rowdy children. At last, the photographer emerged. At the same time, Duncan pushed open the canvas tent flaps. Relief washed over Julia.

"Mae isn't the only one who's decided to turn back," Duncan said grimly. "The White Pass is clogged with men trying to go forward. According to some reports, hundreds of horses have fallen to their death."

Julia pressed her hand to her mouth at the vivid image. "Plenty of men have come to their senses," Duncan added. "They've put their outfits up for sale to earn passage home."

His expression told Julia he would welcome the chance to be among those heading south. He accompanied her only because he had no other choice.

Bracing a notepad on his knee, Duncan began to compose a letter. Julia peered over his shoulder and saw that he was writing to Owen. "You have wrongly spelled 'treacherous,'" she observed.

He gave her a sharp glance, then crumpled the page and tossed it aside. He began again on a fresh sheet, shifting his position so it was impossible for Julia to see what he wrote.

She drew back instantly, embarrassed and surprised at her own rudeness. Perhaps she was shedding her manners along with her modesty, Julia thought ruefully. She strengthened her resolve to leave the troupe the moment they reached Dawson City, though she dreaded having to confess as much to Duncan.

For two days, she had censured him for planning to abandon the group, never once admitting that she was no better. Still, she was determined to reach her father, and she couldn't let anything—or any one—stand in her way.

Julia turned to join the women at the tent flap. Tilly pointed out a hotel sign while Belle indicated a restaurant. When Duncan joined them, they begged for a treat, and at last he agreed to buy them a meal.

He paused along the way to post the picture and letter by courier, then led the troupe into a rough frame structure housing a restaurant. Julia had little appetite. Duncan's remote manner hurt her more than she wanted to admit. Apprehension followed. Once he learned that she wouldn't sing in Dawson, there would be no hope of regaining the friendship she had begun to cherish. She picked unhappily at a slab of halibut fresh from the canal.

Miners muddy from the trail tramped through the candlelit restaurant, a few of them with their wives, who had cut their skirts so short that their leather leggings were exposed. Some wore men's trousers.

Belle giggled as one trudged past. "And they call us shameless."

Quietly, Duncan asked, "Having second thoughts, any of you? No doubt, you can find employment here, if you choose to avoid the trail."

He spoke to them all but looked at Julia. His eyes were dark. The candlelight emphasized the hollows in his cheeks. The man who sang with her through the dangerous night aboard a sloping ship had been lost with the *Fortune*.

She answered with a shake of her head while the others stoutly vowed they were ready to go on. By the time they returned to the muddy streets, darkness lay over the town. Every tent glowed with candlelight, which made the entire city look softer; however, shots, shouts and curses rang from several directions. In her breathless voice, Belle said, "I'd rather risk the trail."

Moments later, a fight broke out almost beside them. Cursing men struggled together. Julia ducked, then hurried toward the hand Duncan held out to her.

Cold made bitter by a steady wind made them hurry their steps. The *Gypsy Gull* was still at the dock; with ironic relief, Julia hurried to the ship and captain she heartily disliked. The other women rushed for the warmth of their staterooms while Duncan checked over the goods he had had delivered. Julia remained with him, watching from beside the rail. "The ship has been home for so long, I almost believe I will miss it."

"You'll miss it, all right," he warned her. "Out there on the trail, you'll wish with all your heart for the dubious comfort of the *Gypsy Gull*." He rose and placed his hands on her shoulders. "You can still change your mind."

"No."

The world seemed to swirl with the cold wind. She was aware of waves splashing the hull and lapping the dock. Duncan drew her into his arms, and she nestled in the warm protection of his embrace. Voice husky, he said, "God forgive me for not ordering you home to Seattle."

She closed her eyes, drawing comfort from the steady beat of his heart. As long as he was with her, she could go anywhere. "Tell me about the trail. How are we to transport all our thousands of pounds of supplies?" The question had been in her mind for days. She asked it now only to prolong the embrace.

His breath stirred her hair. "Owen has hired packers for all but our personal needs. We'll only have to cross the Chilkoot once." His voice deepened. "That once may be more than your worst nightmare."

"You'll be there."

He agreed. "May God help us all."

The warning stayed with Julia through a second sleepless night. When she pictured the trail ahead, her mind filled with dazzling peaks. She comforted herself by thinking of her father. The need to be with him blazed as high as when she smashed the watch case in her uncle's store.

At dawn, the steamer pulled away from Skagway. Julia dressed quickly and hurried to the bow to watch the journey up the Lynn Canal, a deep trench of glacier water as icy as the mountains on either side. Sunlight glittered as she stood at the rail. For the first time since leaving her aunt and uncle, she felt at peace. At least two-thirds of the passengers had left the steamer. This morning she had the bow almost to herself.

So she thought, until a harsh voice cut into her thoughts. "The captain told you sluts to stay out of sight."

Julia swung around to face the trapper named Chambers. A chill that had nothing to do with the icy morning burned a trail down her spine. She became aware of a wind whistling past them and of surf washing heavily onto the shore.

Stiffly, she said, "I'm afraid we've begun badly, Mr. Chambers. Surely there is no need to continue this way."

His grin was only a little less threatening than his scowl. Julia edged along the rail, now wishing for the throng that had crowded there hours before.

"For a simpering little tart, you got grit, I'll give you that." With one long step, Chambers trapped her against the rail. He smelled of animal skins and sweat. The smell made her throat close in protest. "I been givin' your offer some thought. Might take you along, after all."

"There is no need. Mr. Adair had expected to return to Seattle, but has decided to go on."

"Yeah? Adair must be just the sort of stud you was lookin' for."

"I apologize. I spoke in haste." Julia knew she must be white with fear. She glanced nervously to either side, hoping to spot Duncan or even the irascible captain. Instead she spotted Ben's red hair down the deck. He leaned his arms on the rail, dreamily looking at the frozen horizon.

Would he help her when his journey was bound with the trapper's? "I—I believe we are nearly to Dyea." Desperately, she raised her voice. "Ben? Isn't that true? Isn't the town just ahead?"

He looked up, pleasure lighting his face. If the boy was aware the air snapped with tension, he didn't show it. "Yes, miss," he said, pointing. "It's just ahead there."

Julia spun around and felt her knees weaken with relief. A white line of tents stretched in the distance. Already, others were hurrying to the bow, exclaiming eagerly that Dyea was much like Skagway. Here, too, a tent and frame town had risen almost overnight on a narrow flat between forbidding peaks. A long wharf reached past mud flats to deep water. And, as at Skagway, the beach was stacked with supplies.

"Reckon we'll meet on the trail," Chambers said. With a curt word to Ben to start moving their goods, he strode away. Julia made a silent vow never again to be caught alone, then put the trapper from her mind.

Duncan escorted the troupe to a frame hotel. "You'll have one last night in a bed," he told them, and Julia heard again the warning that they should consider the possibility of ending their journey.

When he left to check on their supplies, most of the dancers bounced on the mattresses or hung out the windows, as excited as children at a carnival. "The mister paid for baths for each of you," said the woman proprietor, then added a warning. "'Twill be the last, you know, until you reach Dawson City."

With shrieks of pleasure, the women began peeling off their clothing. Julia let the others go before her. When at last it was her turn to slip into the copper tub, she eased slowly into fresh hot water and leaned back with pleasure. Never again would she take such exquisite comfort for granted.

The others had dressed and left to explore the town. It was a treat to have the room to herself. Julia felt her eyelids grow heavy after nights of restless sleep. The water embraced her and she slipped lower, her scrubbed hair pinned into a thick coil at the top of her head.

A continuous knocking at the door startled her awake. The water had grown cold, and for a moment she was disoriented. "Julia?" Duncan called. She straightened, frantically looking for a towel as she saw the glass doorknob turn.

"No, wait!" Her warning came too late. He was already inside. With a gasp, she crossed her arms over her breasts, her shocked gaze on his. She twisted around, presenting her back, uncomfortably aware of the chilly water. "Go away."

"I thought you might have drowned. Mrs. Kelly said she brought your bath two hours ago."

"You see that I have not."

"Then you must be chilled." To her dismay, she heard him approach. She leaned forward, her face in her folded arms, making herself as small as possible. Gooseflesh rose on her arms and legs.

In a stern voice, Duncan said, "Stand up, Julia. Let me wrap you in this blanket before you catch cold. I don't want to be delayed on the trail."

She saw that he was holding out a flannel blanket. Modesty conflicted with her longing for warmth. She hesitated, and with a wearied expression he raised the blanket higher to shield his eyes.

Julia stood so quickly that water splashed onto the floor. She reached blindly for the blanket, and he wrapped it around her like a cocoon.

As she savored the concealing warmth, Duncan stroked one fingertip along her jaw. The rough sensation against her skin caused a rush of heat to flood her face.

He pulled a chair close and sat, pulling her onto his lap. The impropriety made her entire body flame. "Lean over." Pushing her forward, he released her wet hair, then toweled it roughly. She had never before realized that her scalp could feel as ecstatically aware of a touch as her lips were aware of kisses.

Feeling confused and acutely aware of her nudity, she tensed every muscle, trying to lift herself above the hard muscles of his thighs. Currents of feeling raced through her.

"Relax," he said, sounding amused. "You're an entertainer. You should be used to this."

"I sing," she said in a voice that sounded strangled. "I don't . . . do other things."

Again, she sensed his amusement. Then he nuzzled her bare throat, his lips creating shivers across her skin. "Things like this, you mean?"

"Yes!" She flinched. "You do understand, don't you?"

Duncan believed he did. After puzzling over her behavior for days, he had convinced himself she was carrying her lover's child. Probably the father was the only man she had lain with. She seemed ready to take flight from his lap.

Still her clean fragrance and the blush that suffused her healthy, glowing skin made him enjoy teasing her. "I don't suppose you do this, either," he said, and tilting her chin toward him, he kissed her soft parted lips.

The usual racket rose from the muddy streets outside; hammering, sawing, shouting and the constant yapping of dogs. Duncan heard it all absently. The kiss began as innocent teasing but became far more when she responded by raising one bare arm from the blanket and sliding it around his neck. The silken caress of her lips made him feel as if he had driven his trawler into a storm.

Now that storm encompassed him. The blanket had slipped lower. Unable to resist her creamy skin, he kissed her throat and bare shoulder and felt her sigh. He was going out of his mind with wanting her. Never had he wanted anything as much as he wanted to carry her to the nearest bed.

Heat from Duncan's body made Julia cling even closer. Yet she wasn't cold—in fact, she was uncomfortably warm. The air felt delicious on her bare shoulders. She was tempted to lower the rough blanket. Startled by the thought, she was about to tug it higher when he kissed her shoulder, then licked the heated skin.

The damp heat of his tongue seemed to spread through her, creating whirlpools of sensation and an odd longing that she couldn't define. She wanted to stay in his arms, wanted to lower the blanket and feel his lips and tongue on more of her skin.

Shocked, she wrenched away. Aaron's grim visage swam before her stunned eyes. "This is wrong!" A rosy flush spread over her delicate cheeks and throat and the exposed rise of her breasts.

"It feels right," Duncan said. His desire mounted. Yet she pulled away, so startled that he knew he must force himself to take control.

Looking at her was as exciting as kissing her. The blanket clung to taut nipples, and he imagined taking one into his mouth. Her frightened eyes forbade him. She meant to preserve herself for her lover.

If Julia was expecting a child, there was no outward evidence. Yet her appetite was uncertain, and from time to time she rushed into the fresh air as if her stomach threatened to betray her. Now she looked terrified of his intentions.

The need to protect her helped him overcome his passion, and he nestled her into a more gentle embrace. "Julia, I want you to stay in Dyea. It won't be easy, but it will be easier than the pass. I'll come back for you when I've settled with my stepbrother and see that you get safely home."

He wasn't prepared for a blaze of denial that set her upright on his lap. She looked as if she was about to claw his face. "Again, you want out of a promise!"

"For God's sake!" he said. "Be reasonable. Dawson City is nearly six hundred miles from the coast, a journey beginning with a climb over mountains more forbidding than you can begin to imagine."

"Try to leave me behind now," Julia answered fiercely, "and I'll follow at your heels like a shadow. I am going to Dawson City, whatever the cost."

"To sing in a saloon."

His tone said he believed otherwise. Julia reached for the arch tone of a showgirl. "To make my fortune. I've as much right as the next."

Her defiant gaze challenged him to believe her. Instead, Duncan felt pity. Poor, fierce songstress. Her family must have thrown her out. More certain than ever that she was expecting her lover's child, he made a silent promise to keep her safe from other men as well as from himself.

There must be no more teasing . . . and no more kissing. Lifting her from his lap, he got to his feet. "Think about it. Will you do that much? If you decide not to go on, you can tell me over breakfast."

"I'm telling you now. There is nothing to go back to. I must go on."

With reluctant admiration, Duncan conceded that her fiery spirit might well carry her across the golden stairway of the Chilkoot Pass. Camping at the lakes while they waited for the ice to break up would be primitive but not particularly strenuous, and the remainder of trip was by boat.

"All right, Songbird, you win." Tilting her face upward, he broke his newly made vow by kissing the stubborn line of her lips. Their sweetness made him want to continue, especially when her lips softened as if she welcomed his caress. He reminded himself of his promise. Her heart was already claimed. He pulled away.

For a long moment, he gazed into her luminous eyes. "I just hope he's worth the effort you're making to get to him." Her mouth fell open, giving proof to his suspicion. Turning abruptly, Duncan strode from the room.

Julia stared after him, her thoughts wheeling. How could Duncan know she was traveling to her father? No one knew

that except Aaron and Ruth. Confused, she scrubbed her
fingertips across her lips, trying to rub away the unsettling
memory of his kiss.

# Chapter Eight

"Sheep Camp is our next home!" Hannah cried gaily. Dogs raced, barking, between the legs of horses with provisions strapped to their backs and among wagons piled high with goods. Other dogs were harnessed to sleds stacked with crates and bags and were tugging eagerly at their lines.

The day had dawned fair and cold. As Julia watched the early sun turn the mountain peaks a glorious rose, she glowed with anticipation. Her true life would begin when she reached her father. All else was preparation, including this trip across the Chilkoot Pass.

Chambers strolled around a corner of the building; Julia looked away at once. If she were such a poor judge of human nature, she told herself with disgust, she had better think hard before trusting anyone again.

Then Duncan Adair strode from the hotel and her resolution vanished. Her lips felt softer as she remembered the pressure of his mouth on hers. A few kisses meant nothing to a man of Duncan's probable experience, she reminded her traitorous senses.

He had watched her over breakfast with brooding intensity while she picked at her sourdough pancakes. Perhaps she would grow used to the flavor, but so far even syrup failed to sweeten them to her taste. It hadn't helped that their landlady spiced the meal with dire tales of the trail ahead until Julia pushed her breakfast away, most of it untasted.

They were each to wear a frame packed with the goods they would need along the way. As Duncan helped settle the canvas straps over Julia's shoulders, he murmured an apology. "When it gets too heavy, let me know."

The tent and tools he hoisted to his own shoulders weighed twice as much as what she carried. Vowing not to complain even if the pack pushed her onto her face, Julia took a careful step forward.

From Dyea, they followed the canyon along the rushing greenish-white waters of the river. Almost at once, the path climbed through a rain forest of lush ferns, shrubbery and leafy trees. Hardened by their lives in Seattle, the show-girls trooped along cheerfully despite their packs. The spicy forest scent made the muddy trail more bearable, though their skirts were soon heavy and slapping at their feet with every step.

Duncan called a halt at a toll bridge and, after dropping his pack, turned to Julia. "Let me help with that."

Suspecting that he was once again regretting the responsibility of shepherding a group of women, she protested, "We're all doing well. Don't you agree?"

"So far," he said with a smile that didn't erase the concern in his eyes.

While he helped the others, Julia picked up a rock and scraped mud from her skirt. At the bridge, a steady stream of travelers waited to pay their way across. For men like the toll operators, fortunes were made along the trail rather than at its end.

Duncan paid for their goods to be carried on horses. Those thousands of pounds had to be hauled over the Chilkoot Pass. Julia decided that whatever price they demanded, the packers were well worth their cost.

Throughout the morning, she had caught herself watching Duncan. Despite the heavy weight on his back and shoulders, he walked with an easy grace; clearly, he was at home in the outdoors.

Whenever his glance caught hers, she looked quickly away, remembering all too vividly his waking her from her bath and the shameless kisses that followed, the more shameless because she had longed for them to continue even when he broke away. This morning, he seemed overly solicitous, occasionally holding a branch from her path, then removing her pack before he helped the others. She caught speculative glances from the women and felt uneasy over receiving special treatment.

Finnegan's Point was a surprise. They were miles from Dyea, but a good two dozen tents, a blacksmith shop, a saloon and a restaurant had been set up along a wide place in the trail.

Julia was shocked when she saw the price of a hot meal. "Three dollars! Why, that's twelve times the cost of a meal in Seattle."

"You're not in Seattle, honey," the proprietor said with a grin.

As Duncan counted out the money, Julia felt a pang of conscience. He expected her to sing in public so that he might recover his expenses.

Despite her uneasiness, she dug hungrily into a plate of hot beans and bacon. Duncan glanced at her with approval. At these prices, he was probably pleased to see the food wasn't wasted. When they picked up their packs, Hannah grumbled, "I believe someone added stones while we were inside."

Julia agreed. Her pack seemed to get heavier with every step. Silently, she vowed never to complain. They climbed at a steady pace through a long, narrow crevice. Shadows stretched over them, casting the group into a quiet mood. Even Hannah, who had alternated between singing and chattering during the hike to Finnegan's Point, grew silent, her glance flashing into every dark shadow.

Enormous rocks and boulders littered the trail. Duncan placed a hand under Julia's elbow to help her over a boulder. "If you're tiring, leave your pack and I'll hike back for it."

"I'll do no such thing." She thought he smiled as she marched forward, but would not give him the satisfaction of looking back to make sure.

They trudged into Sheep Camp late that afternoon, limping on bruised soles and blistered heels. On both sides of the river, tents were set up shoulder to shoulder beneath a spruce forest. Wood was burning in camp fires and cooking stoves. The area was so crowded the canvas walls all but joined, becoming one huge billow of white mazed with tent ropes.

A number of frame hotels rose among the tents, but a glance showed they were merely crowded one-room hovels. Julia's brief hope for a private room died as quickly as it was born. Duncan dropped his pack on a boulder, then removed hers.

She sank wearily onto it while he helped the others. "Wait here," he said. "I'll find room for our tent."

The women clustered together against the wind as the time stretched on and on. At last, Hannah spoke for them all. "There can't possibly be room to pitch another tent." The others shook their heads.

"Duncan will find something," Julia said.

They looked at her. "You're awful sure of him," Tilly said.

"What choice is there?" Julia demanded as the women exchanged knowing glances.

He returned minutes later and proved her trust well-founded. "I've located some fellows who are packing to move on to the Scales. They'll hold their tent space until we get over there." As Julia reached for her pack, he added, "I'll come back for that."

Belle sat straighter. "Then you'll come back for mine, as well."

"And mine," Tilly said while Vida and Hannah agreed. Duncan looked startled by the outburst.

"Leave them all," he said shortly. "Let's get over there before we lose the site."

The wind had grown stronger while they waited. Shivering, Julia rubbed her hands to warm them. It seemed a lifetime ago that she had worried about sharing a single tent. Now she longed for it to go up so she could get inside. By the time they reached the tent site, bulky clouds tumbled through the mountain pass, two miles distant.

As a rising wind scattered snowflakes, Duncan unrolled the tent over boughs left by the departing prospectors. Julia stiffened suddenly. Chambers and Ben were pitching a tent just yards away. The trapper's cold gaze met hers before he turned back to the stake he was pounding. Shaken, she turned away.

"Vida, Belle," Duncan said. "Help me put this thing up and we can all get warmer. Where in blazes is Hannah?" He glanced around, then scowled at Tilly. "Look around for firewood. Dry, if you can find it. If not, cut some green branches."

He pressed a saw into her reluctant grasp, adding, "If you see Hannah, tell her to help." He paused. "Julia, get some rest."

This time there was no question of his favoritism. Julia bristled. Couldn't he see he was causing problems? "I'll help Tilly," she countered, and limped after the dancer.

Firewood was not easy to find. The army of campers had ranged far for their supply. By the time Tilly and Julia had filled their arms, they faced a long walk back. They were both too tired to talk, but as they started for the forest of tents, Tilly gave Julia a slanting glance. "I guess you musta told Duncan who you are, the way he's pampering you."

"No!" A dry branch slipped from Julia's arms. Tears filled her eyes. If she bent once more, she might never get up. But dry wood was too rare to waste. Feeling every muscle protest, she knelt to restack her load. "I haven't told him anything," she added. "I want no favors."

With a grunt of disbelief, Tilly trudged toward the candlelit tents. Wind raked Julia mercilessly, and her sore muscles burned. But she struggled to her feet and plodded after Tilly.

The tent was up, with snow banked around the lower edges to keep out the wind. Despite her weariness, Julia looked around with interest while Duncan took the wood from her. Tilly dropped her load with a clatter that sounded like an accusation.

At last, the musty smell of canvas mingled with a fresher smell of burning spruce in their small stove. The women crowded close, straining to heat their chilled hands. The irritation that had marked their last hour of travel began to wane.

When Duncan left the tent, Hannah said, "There are shops in half the camps here."

"Shops?" Vida repeated, perking up for the first time in hours.

"People have lost heart," Hannah explained. "A shocking number have put their goods up for sale."

"Milk-livered," Tilly said. "Most of 'em never had it hard before."

"I'd be wanting to turn back, too," Belle said in a voice made rough by her cold, "if I'd made that hike a dozen times and still faced most of the trail." Clasping her waist, she moaned. "My back will never be the same."

Poking gingerly at a blistered heel, Vida said, "With any luck, it will storm tomorrow and we'll get a day to rest up."

When Duncan returned, the troupe shared a meal of beans and dried peaches. The rising wind drowned out conversation. Julia had expected to feel shy about sharing the tent with Duncan. Because of the cold, they all climbed into their blankets fully dressed. She welcomed the extra warmth. She welcomed his nearness, as well; with Duncan close by, she felt safe despite the howling storm and the uncertainty of the trail.

The canvas walls billowed and boomed like the sails of ships. For a moment, she pictured all the tents tumbling free on the wind. Music came softly, countering the wild sounds from outside, and she realized Duncan was playing the harmonica he'd bought from her uncle. The sound wrapped comfortingly around her and she smiled, snuggling into her blankets to sleep.

For a long while after the women bedded down, Duncan sat near the stove, playing the harmonica and listening to the storm. Wind made the stovepipe jump, causing a rattle of metal. The women were safe enough here, but he wondered how long they would be forced to wait in Sheep Camp. There was no danger of running out of food. The poor devils turning back were eager to sell their goods.

His gaze turned to Julia. She had hiked fourteen miles with little complaint. They all had. His fear of being saddled with crying women had proved false. Instead, they had done better than some of the men on the trail.

The other women were more full-bodied than Julia and could afford a loss of weight. If the trek took much from her, she was likely to fade away. As his gaze moved over the slight mound she made under her blankets, he pictured her slender naked body and the heated eagerness of her kiss. That brought an uncomfortable stirring, and he thought instead of her resistance to preferential treatment.

She could be as spirited as a live salmon on a boat deck. What kind of man would leave her behind? Admitting that he was jealous of her unknown lover, Duncan hoped he would have a chance to meet him. He would have plenty to say to the fellow.

Forcing his thoughts to more immediate problems, he listened to the storm. From the sound of it, there would be plenty of time for the women to recover their energy. For most of this troupe, that would likely mean time to get into fresh trouble. That would at least distract him from Julia.

## Chapter Nine

By morning, ice crusted the ground. When Julia looked toward the pass, massive clouds roiled around the mountains. People who had started out at dawn were hiking back. "Don't bother," one called. "Nobody's going over today."

Duncan rested a possessive hand on Julia's shoulder. Currents of sensation raced through her, heating her despite the icy morning. "I'm going to ask around for information on the pass," he said, seemingly unaware of the confusion his touch had caused.

As he walked away, his steps crunching through ice, Julia returned to the tent and rummaged through their supplies for flour, baking powder and evaporated milk. As long as she had the time, she would make hot biscuits. And if she hoped to impress Duncan Adair with her cooking, she refused to admit it even to herself.

The women had not returned from the woods where they shielded each other while taking care of personal needs. It was pleasant to have the tent to herself. Julia sang softly as she worked, feeling unexpectedly content here at what must be the top of the world. Even Dyea seemed to be part of another life.

As she set a pan of biscuits on the back of the stove, the tent flap lifted. "You're just in time," she said, turning, then with a start recognized Ben. "Why...good morning."

Blushing almost as red as his hair, he held out a package. "I don't have much, Miss Julia, but maybe you'd take a pound of coffee?"

"Why, thank you," she said, surprised. She remembered how he had admired her with his eyes that night in the steamer's saloon. Apparently, she had made a conquest.

Smiling to put him at ease, she accepted the gift. To her dismay, he grabbed her by the waist and pulled her into his arms. The coffee fell from her hands as she braced against him. "Ben!"

He stopped her protest with an eager, wet kiss. As she struggled to free herself, she wondered if he thought to court her with roughhousing. He was young and obviously inexperienced. She tore her mouth away. "Control yourself!"

With a foolish grin, he put one hand over her breast. She jerked back so abruptly that she tripped and dropped to the canvas floor. More astonished than angry, she stared at him. "What on earth are you doing?"

"Oh, Miss Julia, you are a beauty!" Falling onto his knees beside her, he pushed her skirts to her thighs.

With an indignant gasp, Julia scrambled backward. "Have you lost your mind? Get away from me!"

Instead, he shoved her onto the blankets and tried to kiss her again. She wrenched her head from side to side. He had the wiry strength of youth, and she began to feel fear edging through surprise and anger.

His hand crawled beneath her skirts, clutching her thighs with eager, bruising pinches. An unpleasant heat rose from him. She shoved at his chest, frantic to escape.

Suddenly, he flew upward and slammed into the far side of the tent. Julia scrambled to her feet, wrenching her clothing into order while Duncan hauled the younger man up and drew back his fist. The punishment given his boxing opponent flashed through her mind, and she cried, "He's just a boy!"

"With a man's game in mind." Instead of slugging him, Duncan shook Ben until his head wobbled. "What the devil are you doing in here?"

"He said she'd do it for pay," Ben stammered, his eyes so wide with terror that Julia felt sorry for him, despite a flush of anger. She knew who *he* must be. Chambers.

"I've never done it," Ben added miserably. "He said it was time. And Julia's so pretty. He said she'd probably take a pound of coffee."

She had thought the coffee to be a gift. Feeling soiled, Julia scathingly asked herself if she would ever learn common sense. Just yesterday in Dyea, she had resolved to think hard before trusting any man.

Duncan's eyes were dangerous, the planes of his face taut and drawn. "You damned fool. I should throw you into the nearest snowdrift. Maybe that would cool you off."

"I didn't mean any harm," Ben muttered. "She's the prettiest of them all. Not rough like the others."

Julia was beginning to shake and clasped her arms tightly across her chest. She caught a harried glance from Duncan. "Stay away from her, do you understand? She's expecting a baby."

For a stunned moment, she wondered who he was talking about. He could not have **said** what she thought . . . except that suddenly, his strange behavior toward her made sense.

Ben's clumsy attack was nothing compared to Duncan's low estimation. Even Aaron had never so hurt her. She spoke with ice in her voice. "I certainly am *not* expecting a child. I have never lain with a man."

She swung her angry glare from Duncan to Ben, who flushed as he straightened his collar. "Whatever you may have been told, I am not a whore!"

Ben winced. His throat worked visibly. "Sorry, Miss Julia, I'm awfully sorry. I don't know what to say. Except I hope you'll keep the coffee."

She snatched up the package, and as he scrambled through the tent flap, she hurled it after him. Miners to either side looked around. Her furious glance sent them back to their business.

Turning into the tent, she saw Duncan lift the lid on the biscuits. Mildly, he said, "Smells like they're starting to burn." A slow smile crossed his face. "I'd say they're not all that's burning."

His grin failed to charm her. "How could you believe such a thing? I thought we were friends." She clenched her hands together to keep from pounding his chest.

Duncan set the biscuits on a folded towel, deliberately taking time to answer. While feeling flooded with relief, he knew the volatile moment could either end things between them or offer a new beginning. God knew, she had good reason to be angry. Questions swarmed around him. She was following someone. If not a lover, then who? He risked a glance and saw she was calmer, but far from appeased.

Closing the short distance between them, he gently pried her fingers from the tight clasp on her arms. "Julia, believe me, I didn't mean to insult you."

Storm clouds moved through her gray eyes. Before, he had judged her spirit would carry her over the trail. Now he welcomed her anger. Many women would have dissolved into tears or faints. "Trust me with the truth," he said quietly. "Why are you so hard set on Dawson City?"

"My father is there. You seemed to know that yesterday. When all the time, you thought..." Her words faded as a flush rose again into her cheeks.

"Your father?" He led her to one of the blanket rolls and drew her down beside him. "You and I are long overdue for a talk."

Julia smoothed her skirts over her knees. She had avoided the truth for over a week and only succeeded in lowering herself in Duncan's eyes. Now that they were on the trail, she could risk an explanation. She needed to share the truth, and words blocked for days poured out in a rush. "You have to understand...I never knew my father. I thought he had abandoned my mother when all the time it was my uncle who refused to let him near her and then she died when I was born and Aaron—that's my uncle—"

Duncan interrupted. "Julia. Take a deep breath. Try to give me one thought at a time."

She sighed heavily, then opened her collar to retrieve the gold nugget, warmed by her skin. After releasing the clasp, she held it out to him, and as calmly as she could manage, began at the beginning, though her voice picked up speed as she neared the end.

Duncan listened in silence, absently stroking the nugget with one thumb. He felt as if he were stroking the warm pulse at her throat. He held the chain, swinging the nugget, conscious of the impropriety of caressing an object that had lain intimately against her breasts.

The outfitter in Seattle was her uncle. Now he recognized her from that shop. He had scarcely afforded her a glance. The uncle might be an ogre, but Julia had been gently bred. Responsibility for her lay as heavily as if his mother stood at his shoulder warning him about proper conduct.

Those rules were worlds apart from the rough conditions of camping with showgirls. "How is your father going to react when he learns you reached him by wearing the clothing of a showgirl…and sharing sleeping quarters with a man?"

"Why, I…" She faltered, then said simply, "I didn't expect to tell him."

"Just as you didn't expect to sing."

She frowned at her hands. She could hardly blame him if he yelled at her or shook her, as he had Ben.

Raising her chin, Duncan carefully clasped the chain around her neck. He seemed troubled. She felt intensely aware of the brush of his fingertips against her throat as he fastened the chain.

"I lost my father sixteen years ago," he said quietly. "His trawler went down in a storm. I was fifteen then. It was a chance of fate that I wasn't aboard."

"I'm sorry," Julia murmured. The pain in his eyes said he felt partly to blame. Surely, he didn't feel he should have died, too, or that his help might have somehow saved the trawler. "I'm sure you were a comfort to your mother."

Duncan leaned his arms on his knees. "For five years, I did all I could to make her life easier. I admit I was jealous when she married again." He raised his head, his eyes sparking. "To a ribbon clerk! A man who never faced danger and never will. You won't see him in this trek—" He broke off. "What are you grinning at?"

She pressed her hands to her lips but couldn't hide the smile that he had already seen in her eyes. "I'm sorry. You looked so righteous, as if a ribbon clerk had no business falling in love."

"Not with my mother," Duncan muttered.

Julia put her hand over his. "How long have they been married?"

He turned his hand to capture her fingers and absently stroked her wrist with his thumb. "Too long." His grin admitted that his attitude was ungenerous. "Eleven years." The smile faded. "Owen was twelve at the time. A husky kid who should have helped with fishing. Instead he was given his leisure. A lot of good that did his character."

Duncan straightened his shoulders, looking slightly embarrassed. "I'm afraid you've brought out feelings I usually keep to myself. I don't begrudge my mother's need for a safe future. Truthfully, Julia. It's Owen who pulls at me like a bad tide."

"I understand how you feel about the *Fortune,*" she said.

"And the *Patience* before that." He rose and began pacing restlessly. "I named my first trawler after my mother. I was twenty-five when I saved enough for my own ship."

"What happened?" Julia asked warily.

"Owen happened." Duncan slammed one fist into the other. "The blazing idiot ran her on the rocks last year while showing off for his worthless friends." He brushed one hand through his hair, leaving it tumbled. "I'd earned enough with the *Patience* to buy a second boat, the *Fortune.* Yet the very day that I talked a wealthy banker into a loan to restore the first, Owen heard of gold in the Klondike."

"You had no warning that he would go to Alaska?"

"Warning! I'm told he sold spaces aboard to men on the dock and set off within minutes of the *Portland*'s arrival with gold."

"I'm sorry."

He was staring through the tent doorway. At her words, he came to take her hands and pull her to her feet. "Three times you've said that. It must be true."

He held her hands for a long moment. She thought he might kiss her and hoped that he would. Then he startled her by using her formal name, though the huskiness in his voice betrayed emotion. "Miss Everett, I apologize for having insulted you in Dyea. My excuse is that you were convincing in your disguise."

"I'm glad you have used my father's name and not my uncle's, but I see no reason for either," she exclaimed.

Lightly, he skimmed her lips with one thumb. His eyes darkened. A muscle flicked in his jaw. Abruptly, he straightened. "Keep that nugget out of sight—Miss Everett—or you may have to shake out Vida's pockets."

"Duncan," she protested. "Why address me so formally?"

"As a reminder."

She knew what he meant. With a sense of loss, she slipped the nugget beneath her collar.

Duncan stared out at the camp. "Of all the people who have decided to turn back, there must be a married couple who can accompany you to Seattle."

Julia's disappointment blazed into outrage. "Are you suggesting I go back to Aaron? I've told you. I no longer have a home there."

He let the flap fall, closing them again into dimness. If it was true that her relatives wouldn't take her back—and he suspected as much—then he would be sending her to a cold welcome on the Seattle streets. But if he took her on to Dawson City, compromising her reputation in the process, he was likely to receive her father's gratitude at the wrong end of a rifle.

*Be honest, Adair,* he told himself. *It's the prospect of spending the next months in close quarters with her yet never touching her—that has you feeling like a bear eyeing a steel trap.*

Even in the dim tent, her gray eyes were luminous. She wore showgirl satins with a poise that had always struck him as contradictory—and that heightened her appeal. "It's been hell keeping my hands off you when I thought you of easy virtue," he explained, his voice again sounding husky. "When I thought you belonged to another man, it was easier."

That was a lie. When he thought she had a lover, he had wanted to kill the fellow. Now he was tormented with the memory of her soft, eager kisses and the sweet fresh scent of her skin.

She was a decent woman, and she depended on him. He shoved open the tent. "I have to think this through. There must be a solution, but I'll be damned if I know what it is." Hesitating, he turned back. "I apologize for the profanity, Miss Everett. I didn't mean to offend you."

She raised her hands in helpless protest before the tent flap fell between them. He waded through ankle-deep slush, feeling more at a loss than he had when he saw the burned trawler. Controlling his language was a minor problem. With months of the trail ahead, how was he going to resist a constant hunger for Miss Julia Everett?

## Chapter Ten

Duncan strode through the camp, his attention on the few women present. Most were dressed severely, in dark clothes. Many wore skirts cut short enough to raise eyebrows in Seattle; some wore trousers. Most of them were traveling with their husbands. They looked cold and bone-weary, and courage glowed from faces reddened by exposure to the weather. They must have come from sturdy stock. How could he put Julia through the rigors of the trail?

The shock of coming into the tent and seeing Ben on top of her, with her skirts hiked halfway up her legs, had so infuriated him that he'd wanted to slam into them both before he realized she was putting up a desperate fight.

Ben was lucky to get away with a shaking, but the matter was not entirely his fault. Duncan felt his fist clench. It was a long way to Dawson City. Before then, he was likely to be drawn into a fight with Chambers. He almost welcomed the thought.

He walked to the boulder-strewn river and studied the mountain. Clouds hurtled through the slash between the peaks. He thought the glaciers looked unsteady. The sooner they all crossed, the safer they would be. But there would be no crossing today. Nor tomorrow, whatever the weather.

With the decision made, he returned to the tent and was glad to find all the women inside. "I'm going to Dyea," he said briskly. "Stay together and out of trouble. I'll be back tomorrow."

"What's in Dyea that you can't get here?" Belle asked with a provocative pout.

Duncan turned to Julia. "Write to your father. I'll send your letter on."

"I'll be glad to," she said, aware of the women's curious glances. "But why Dyea? Hannah has learned that couriers collect the mail even here in Sheep Camp."

Duncan swung an empty pack frame over his shoulders. "You'll go no farther up the trail dressed like that."

"What's wrong with it?" Tilly demanded.

Julia glanced down at the tight bodice of her borrowed dress and the satin skirt with its worn hem bindings. It had served her well enough that she had grown used to the costume. "Are you saying you will hike all that extra distance to buy clothing for me? That isn't necessary."

Duncan's tone rejected compromise. "Unless you relish another roll with the likes of young Ben, you had better be decently dressed."

Ben's attack was still raw in Julia's mind. In silence, she accepted a pencil stub and a sheet of paper from the pad he had purchased in Skagway. After collecting her thoughts, she wrote simply, "Dearest Father, I am approaching the Chilkoot Pass and will join you soon. With great love and anticipation, your daughter, Julia." In the same clear script, she addressed the envelope: Joseph Everett, Dawson, Yukon.

The words seemed to take on life. Nothing else mattered—not the trail nor the unsuitable clothing or even Duncan's stubborn attitude. Her father was in Dawson. Nothing could stop her from going to him.

When Duncan's long steps carried him swiftly from camp, Tilly squeezed into the doorway beside Julia. "You told him."

"I had no choice." Letting the tent flap fall into place, she went inside to explain to them all.

"It seems to me," Vida said when she finished, "your first problem is that trapper. Best not be caught alone with him."

"I don't intend to be." Julia felt a sense of family from the women. Not only had they heard her through with sympathy, they were ready to help. "Tell me, what should I do?"

"Hit him with something solid," Hannah said promptly. The others nodded, remembering the disastrous experience that caused Hannah to hide aboard the ship.

Practically, Vida added, "Keep a skillet close at hand."

"But don't swing it at his head," Tilly advised. "Slam it up between his legs."

While Hannah winced and the others laughed, Julia felt a gulf open once again. Perhaps Duncan was right. The showgirls were kind, but she was not one of them.

The gulf opened even wider when Vida revealed a pair of scissors she had appropriated from one of the tent sales. At once, the women slashed their skirts short in the practical Klondike mode. Julia looked ruefully at her worn binding. Duncan clearly meant for her to struggle through mud and snow with modesty and long skirts intact.

In Dyea, men and supplies all but blocked the muddy streets. Duncan took a room in the hotel they had stayed in before, but regretted it when he found himself vividly remembering Julia in her tub. Her skin glowed, while tendrils of chestnut hair trailed beguilingly over her shoulders. When he held her, it was all he could do not to pull the blanket from around her as if pulling leaves from around a flower. It was fortunate he had thought she was with child. Otherwise, he would surely have seduced her.

As he had longed to do nearly every minute since. He thrust himself from the bed and located the nearest saloon. As he sipped whiskey he didn't really want, he watched painted women who were exactly what they appeared to be. He had no taste for them, either.

His stepbrother was the lady's man in the family. Women were always sighing and crying in the parlor while his mother tsked over them and Owen made himself scarce. Courting was clearly a complicated game that took too much of a man's time. Owen didn't appear to gain much besides temporary pleasure followed by a lot of grief. Work had always drawn Duncan more than a pouting smile.

When he did feel the need for a woman's body, he chose to satisfy it where there would be no complications. He meant to marry when he could afford a family, but pictured a woman like his mother—quiet, modest and capable. Why was it different now? Why did he keep remembering the fiery softness of one stubborn set of lips?

A strong swallow of whiskey burned through his body but did nothing to ease his restlessness. He intended to turn Julia over to her father with her reputation unsullied. There was purpose in the plan, something he could put his mind to when distracted by the music in her laughter or, God help him, by the touch he felt on his heart whenever he made the mistake of looking directly into her shining gray eyes.

When he returned to Sheep Camp, he heard Julia singing. The pure, clear notes floated like crystal through the still air. He followed them to the bank of the river where she knelt on a boulder, her hands red with cold as she filled the enameled steel coffeepot from the glacier-fed torrent. He was glad to see the other women nearby. The day was clear, and most people from the camp were out on the trail.

For the past several miles, urgency had gnawed worse than the wind. Now that he saw she was safe, his steps felt light as he walked to the tent to unload the pack frame.

When Julia carried the filled coffeepot to the tent, she saw the empty frame with a rush of pleasure. Shoving past the tent flap, she cried happily, "You're back!" She stopped. "What on earth are you doing?"

He didn't look around until he finished fastening a blanket across one corner of the tent. "Privacy, Miss Everett. You'll sleep in there."

"'Miss Everett,'" she repeated. "'Privacy.' You *will* set me apart. The showgirls are sturdy companions, Duncan. Their present stations are not entirely their fault. You're mistaken in thinking I will set myself above them."

He held out a parcel. "Go in there and change. I don't ever again want to see you decked out like a fancy woman."

"Duncan Adair, I am the same woman who traveled with you from Seattle. Must you suddenly act as if I'm made of glass and have a mind as fragile?"

"You're not the same woman to me, Miss Everett."

She slapped the coffeepot onto the stove so hard that water splashed through the spout and sizzled on the hot metal. "This journey has been an education. I was not aware before that men have double natures, one rather dull for proper use, the more interesting side presented only to *improper* company."

"Julia," he said. "Help me, won't you?"

The appeal in his face made her feel petty. Picking open the parcel, she shook out a dark green walking suit. When she held it up, she knew the hem would gather every bit of debris between Sheep Camp and Dawson. Lifting the blanket, she stepped into the private corner he had prepared, pausing first to slip the scissors from Vida's bag.

When she returned with the frayed walking skirt swinging free at her calves, she was disappointed to find herself alone in the tent. Never mind; the deed was done. Humming softly, she turned to the stove and began to measure coffee into the pot.

The women wandered in, one at a time, each admiring Julia's new outfit and applauding her decision to shorten it to a practical length. "You'll be warmer in this," Belle said wistfully as she fingered the heavy fabric.

"I suppose I will." It was difficult to concentrate while waiting for Duncan. Needing to keep herself busy, she mixed a batch of baking powder bread. As she bent to push the pan into the oven compartment of the small Klondike stove, the tent opened with an inward rush of snow and cold air.

"What in blazes have you done now?" Duncan exclaimed.

She whirled, the skirt flapping against her stocking-clad legs. Belatedly, she thought that she should have worn boots to lessen his shock. She answered with a defiant set of her chin. "Why, I've made bread."

To either side, the women watched with dancing eyes. Duncan gave them a brief glance. "This is not a game one of us must win."

"I agree." Julia kept her gaze steady. "But I'll thank you to take down that blanket. While I appreciate your kindness, it prevents the heat from reaching my bed."

Belle's grin suggested other ways that Julia might warm her bed but, fortunately, she said nothing. After a glance that told him all the women were siding with Julia, Duncan gave up on curing her stubborn nature. He ripped the blanket from the pins holding it to the tent, tossed it aside and walked alone to the river.

How had he ever let things get so out of hand? Maybe he should have talked with her before changing the arrangement. For a well-bred woman, she was as stubborn as one of the mules. That was the uncle's fault, Duncan thought with a curse for Aaron Ames.

It occurred to him that after hiking twenty-eight miles in two days, not to mention the fourteen the day before, he was a fool to let her drive him out to walk still more. No doubt, he was the subject of merriment among the women.

Feeling as annoyed with himself as with Julia, he returned to the tent. The rich aroma of fresh coffee and baking bread reached out more provocatively than perfumed arms. His stomach reminded him that it had been hours since he'd stopped for a cold lunch along the trail. Inside, the women were laughing. He paused.

Hannah's voice came clearly through the canvas. "Julia, you put in too much. Wherever was your mind?"

"We know where her mind was," Belle said tartly, and all of them laughed again.

Thinking he would rather step into a den of bear cubs, Duncan pushed open the flap and sealed it behind him. The women were crowded around the stove. Julia was on her knees, working with fierce concentration at the oven.

"Now what?" Duncan demanded, then as they stepped aside and he saw what had happened, he threw back his head in a healing release of laughter. Julia's dough had risen in every direction, wedging against the sides and walls of the narrow oven. The aroma of fresh-baked bread was rapidly becoming a burning stench.

"Move away," he said when she looked up. "You'll scorch yourself. Tilly, hand me a knife."

Julia was glad enough to let Duncan take over. As she watched him hack away at her treasured loaf, she realized with relief that the tension between them had vanished.

The bread came from the oven looking mutilated and overcooked, but when they hacked off chunks to spread with jelly, nobody complained about the taste. Julia's gaze met Duncan's and both smiled. She felt herself relax and thought gratefully that it was going to be all right.

For two days more, they were kept from the pass by storms in the mountains. The snow and mud in Sheep Camp were tramped solid by hundreds of feet as people hauled goods in from Dyea or hiked out to check conditions on the pass.

With deepening concern, Duncan talked to people who had carried part of their goods ahead. None of the news that reached Seattle had prepared the Klondikers for the terrible rigors of the Chilkoot Pass.

If he had known of the deathly illness and heartbreak, of the thousands who would turn back rather than continue the ordeal, of cherished possessions abandoned along the trail and of the deaths of men and animals that turned generous hearts to stone, he would never have agreed to escort the women.

The weather broke at last. He stood frowning in the tent doorway, a tin cup filled with coffee steaming in his hand. The pass gleamed rosily in the early sunlight. He sipped his coffee in silence while behind him the women chattered like an eager flock of birds while they loaded their packs. They were tired of Sheep Camp. He couldn't blame them.

Neither could he risk their lives. Turning, he said quietly, "Unpack. You're not going on."

They all stared at him, Julia's eyes taking on the indignant glow he knew only too well. With an impatient gesture, he silenced her. "The trail is too hard for women to carry heavy packs. Set out the minimum you'll need for the next two days. The minimum, do you understand? I'll haul the rest to the top.''

None were happy with that, but he refused to hear argument. ''If there was a choice, we would all turn back to Dyea. But I mean to reach Owen and I can't leave you on your own.''

He had been ready enough to leave them before, Julia thought. The women could work as well in Dyea as in Dawson. It was she whom he would not leave. In silence, she began to take essential items from her pack.

Duncan returned late that night, too weary to do more than eat supper and slump onto his blankets. Julia could see he was more worried than before. Belle had come down with sniffles, while Vida had nearly frozen her fingertips in the icy river while picking out nuggets that proved to be only fool's gold.

Julia watched him sip his coffee. Candlelight emphasized the weariness in his face. He had made this extra trip to lighten their packs; not just her pack, but all of them. ''Thank you,'' she said quietly.

He glanced at her briefly. ''Don't thank me yet.'' He rested the cup on one knee, silent again, his eyelids half closing. ''When I see Owen, I mean to...mean to...''

Julia rescued the cup moments before he slid sideways onto the blankets, asleep. Tenderly, she drew a blanket over him. How different he looked in sleep. His lashes were dark over skin even more deeply tanned than it had been the day before. His jaw was rough with stubble, but his mouth relaxed and the lines in his forehead eased, giving him a youthful look that touched her more deeply than she wanted to admit.

Very gently, with her shoulders blocking the view of the other women, she leaned over him and kissed his temple.

The next morning, they all set out on the two-mile climb to the Scales. Thousands hiked ahead and behind, pans and tools rattling and banging against their packs. Tents lined either side until the gorge climbed between high stone walls. Soon even trees were left behind.

A series of nearly impassable steep inclines led between the icy walls. Julia felt guilty for complaining even silently when she remembered that Duncan carried the heavy tent and the stove.

At times, he bent almost double, using his hands to pull himself forward. At last, they reached a flat stretch beneath the sheer mountain wall. At several stations, men weighed the goods of prospectors. A steady wind blasted wet snow over their faces and shoulders. Gasping for breath, Julia leaned one hand against a boulder beside Hannah, who tried to smile, though her face was red with effort. "The best thing we did was to cut off our skirts."

Julia nodded, too breathless for conversation. Ben's voice startled her. "You look prettier than ever, Miss Julia."

With dismay, she saw they had set themselves in line behind Chambers and his young companion. She had thought them to be still hauling from Dyea. "Is there anything I can do for you," Ben added hopefully, "something I can carry, maybe?"

Duncan interrupted, "You'll call her Miss Everett and keep a respectful distance."

Flushing a deeper crimson, Ben stumbled over his own feet as he stepped back to his store of supplies. Julia relented. Ben and Chambers were packing their entire outfits over the pass. They had a difficult road ahead.

In a forgiving tone, she said, "Take care of yourself, Ben. I expect you'll have the muscles of a young Hercules when we see you again at the lakes."

He grinned while Duncan narrowed his eyes in disgust. Chambers looked pointedly at Julia's booted ankles. "Seems you said it before, miss. We started off bad. No point goin' on that way."

She nodded, putting as much chill into her manner as possible. There were few women here whose ankles weren't exposed, and the man was a brute for suggesting an apology while his eyes continued to call her wanton.

The dancers giggled or groaned with distaste while they rubbed oil and charcoal over their faces. "Looks like we're ready for vaudeville," Tilly said grinning.

Julia put her hand reluctantly into the mixture. It was better than blistering from the wind and sun. She felt foolish until she remembered a neighbor at Sheep Camp putting slices of raw potatoes over swollen eyelids.

The trail rose through a valley where boulders larger than tents were strewn around in haphazard testimony to the power of nature. They continued to climb, higher and higher, then the valley ended and a frozen wall rose forever into the sky. At the base, tents billowed in the wind, their guy ropes held down by boulders. At the top, gray clouds lashed through a jagged gap.

The air vibrated with a low animal moan. Julia had been feeling and hearing that hum for some time. She thought it was wind howling through the rocks. With horror, she realized it was the combined groan of thousands of people, all of them laden too heavily and forcing themselves upward one agonized step at a time.

The mountain was alive with movement. She stared in disbelief at a long, dark line snaking to the gap at the top, a line of human forms, each leaning forward under the weight of pack, box, barrel or pieces of furniture. To the right, others flew downhill on sleds or simply rode their pants bottoms as they returned to goods piled at the base.

Duncan stopped beside her as the sun turned the snow an eye-dazzling white. "The Golden Stairs, Miss Everett." His voice became harsh. "Shall I ask around for someone to guide you back to Dyea?"

She shook her head, but couldn't find her voice to answer.

## Chapter Eleven

The familiar stubborn set of Julia's mouth said argument was useless. With reluctant admiration, Duncan guided her into the line of people waiting to begin the Chilkoot Lock Step, a devil's dance done to the lure of gold. Fifteen hundred stairs had to be climbed. At two and a half steps a minute, the top could be gained in six hours. If Julia should collapse, he knew he would have trouble living with himself.

With a sturdy alpenstock in one hand and clutching the guide rope with the other, each member of the troupe began the ascent. Clouds gathered high above, gray and forbidding. To either side of the dark-clad prospectors, the snow stretched dull and white.

Duncan carried a good hundred pounds strapped to his back, but for awhile, as he watched Julia's shortened skirt swing against her trim hips and slender legs, his struggle seemed easier. If she turned to see him admiring her so frankly, she would likely shove him backward, and the entire row of climbers would topple. She wouldn't turn; no one wasted even that much effort.

They skipped the first opportunity to rest, but at the second the entire troupe staggered into a space stamped out in the snow and leaned their packs against a ledge of ice. Breathing hard, they waited for their hearts to stop pounding. It would be difficult to get back into line, but they needed a rest. Duncan eased the weight on his back and turned to look at Julia.

To his surprise, her eyes were shining. "What a magnificent sight. It must be truly wonderful from the summit."

She turned to look upward. Her breath had begun to steady. Now it caught as clouds at the summit parted, revealing a massive glacier hanging over the trail. Sunlight glimmered within the ice. Shifting shades of turquoise and sapphire suggested a portal into eternity. "What holds it there?" she whispered.

Duncan studied the glacier, as uneasy as Julia to see a three-hundred-foot wall of ice overhead. He had noticed the glaciers shifting. Now he gauged the feel and taste of the wind. "It's likely to be storming by the time we reach the top. Come on," he called to them all. "We have a long way to go."

Belle's cough worried him as the group trudged along, but tonight they would be at the lake and they would have more forgiving weather. One at a time, the women slipped between climbers reluctant to let them in. Many of the climbers were coughing and sniffling. Eyes were runny and faces flushed beneath sunburned skin.

Snow blew around the group when they paused again. The snow had become wetter and heavier by their third rest stop. By then, they were all too weary to do more than plod ahead, lifting one foot and then the other. Duncan wanted to spare them, but now there could be no turning back. Their moans and gasps blended with the vibrating animal sound heard from the Scales while their breath formed a vapor of ice crystals around their mouths.

Slowly, Julia became aware of a different sound, a mewling, surely the cry of a cat. Gradually, she realized the sound came from a basket strapped to the shoulders of a woman ahead. Why on earth carry a cat over the pass? Speculation took her mind from her agonized muscles as she continued automatically to lift one foot, then the other.

She was startled when her raised foot smacked down hard on solid ice. The summit, at last, when she had become sure the goal was impossible. Her knees and hips ached desperately; if she stopped moving, they would surely lock.

Mountains of supplies loomed through blowing, swirling snow. With another surge of thanks for their hired packers, Julia realized that one of those snow-buried mounds belonged to them. The other women trudged ahead, shoulders bowed against the storm. When Julia joined them, tents took shape—the border encampment of the North West Mounted Police. An officer came forward wearing a buffalo-hide jacket with embossed buttons over pants striped in yellow. "I'm Officer Gray, miss," he said to Hannah, who was nearest. "Take care to mark your goods with a pole so you can find them under the snow."

He then gave a wrenching sneeze and mumbled an apology while he hauled a crumpled handkerchief from a pocket. Julia thought with sympathy that the officer looked even less healthy than the people climbing the pass.

"Is it possible to get a drink of water?" Hannah asked.

"Yes, miss," he said. "Water is five cents the glass."

"Five cents! For water?" Hannah's weariness gave way to indignation. "I've never heard of such a thing."

"It all has to be packed in." He sounded apologetic but firm, as if this was an argument he heard several times a day.

Duncan left his pack beside a long pole, then joined them. "We'll have a fire, too, Officer. Five dollars' worth." The women looked at each other. In Dyea, they had overheard a cynical comment that in this country a man charged a dollar to say hello. Apparently it was true.

While the women huddled around the fire, Duncan located the goods that had been brought up the day before. The storm cleared while he worked, and sunlight soon dazzled the snow. To the west across American territory, spruce made a soft green blanket over the hills. When Julia turned toward the Canadian side, she looked over a barren prospect of rock massed as far as she could see.

Shivering, she held her gloved hands toward the fire. A pitiful mewling caught her ear. She saw the heavyset woman who had climbed just ahead of her. She had the basket in her hands and was peering beneath the woven lid.

"Is it a cat?" Julia asked.

The woman looked up with a wide smile. "It's more than one cat, miss. Amanda will give us a fine litter of kittens while we're camped along the lake."

"Kittens!" Julia's voice rose in surprise.

The woman chuckled. "That's right, miss. There's a few things a lonely man yearns for, and a loyal pet is one. Look at these prospectors. A goodly number are just a step this side of their mother's aprons. There'll be more like them in Dawson, men ready to pay in gold for a loving pet."

Astonished, Julia wondered if it wasn't cruel to benefit from another's loneliness. Yet the kittens could bring comfort. Even those unable to buy would find pleasure in watching them.

The young officer returned, looking so ill that Julia's heart went out to him. Hannah, however, spoke tartly. "If you mean to share our fuel, Officer Gray, you must either add to it or return a portion of the cost."

"Hannah!" Julia chastised.

The officer looked startled. "I only meant to ask if there was anything more I can do for you, miss."

"You should be in bed," Hannah said.

A deep dimple appeared in his cheek when he smiled. For a moment, his eyes sparkled despite his illness. Then he coughed again, half turning from them.

"Where is your superior?" Hannah demanded. "Someone should speak to him."

"It wouldn't do any good, miss, though I appreciate your concern. None of the men are in good health. Everything we own is wet most of the time, and it's impossible to keep our quarters warm."

"The Queen must not care much for her men," Hannah said darkly.

He looked offended. "We're paid an extra fifty cents a day for the difficult duty, miss. I hope you don't think I meant to complain. It's just that the last blizzard forced us to Crater Lake for the night."

They all turned at his gesture and saw, far below, a frozen surface. "The lake rose under the ice and came into our tents. We had to pull the sleds inside and sleep on top of them." A wracking cough shook him before he could add,

"I'm afraid bronchitis is a familiar friend to most of our force."

In a knowing voice, Tilly said, "It's not that the Queen doesn't care for her men, it's that she's greedy for the duty charged us just for passing through. That's what keeps you up here in the blizzards, isn't it, Officer Gray?"

Hotly, Hannah said, "The duty! The larceny, you mean."

The officer's attempt to look offended was ruined by another sneeze. When he emerged once more from the crumpled handkerchief, he tried at length to convince Hannah of the need to tax goods brought into Canada.

Julia looked from one to the other, surprised to recognize mutual attraction in the sparks flying between the two. Belle dug her elbow into Julia's ribs, her sly nod proving that she, too, had noticed.

"Officer Gray," Hannah said firmly. "While I may be merely a woman with merely a woman's outlook on the world, it does seem to me your government should be pleased that a rush of people is helping to open up this forbidding countryside."

Gray kicked a burning brand into the fire. "The duty must be collected. That is all there is to say."

Julia thought there was a great deal more he might say. How did these young men feel when they heard of gold being taken from their country by the thousands of pounds? How did they feel when Americans settled into Dawson City in droves?

Duncan joined the group, prepared to bolster flagging spirits, and was startled to see that in the presence of the uniformed officer, the women blossomed like spring flowers. Hannah, in particular, looked as pert as if she had partaken of a brisk morning walk and was ready for fresh challenge.

The Mountie didn't look well. No doubt, that brought out the maternal streak in the women. Annoyed to recognize a brush of jealousy, he spoke to Julia. "Enjoy the last of the fire while I reload our packs. We'll soon start for the lakes."

* * *

Late that day, sagging under their loads, the troupe followed the stream of prospectors across fields of boulders and pools of ice dotted with stunted spruce. Rough-peaked mountains scraped the gray sky. Julia felt as if she was crossing the center of a giant bowl with jagged, broken edges.

To her relief, the trail soon fell rapidly to Lake Lindemann. There again, tents crowded every level spot. The din of lumbering rang through the woods. Boats of nearly every type and in all stages of construction crowded the water's edge. Julia glanced at Duncan. "It looks as if all the men who thronged the Seattle wharf are now at the lake, still shoulder to shoulder."

"We'll camp here tonight," he said. "Tomorrow, we'll move on to Lake Bennett and set up a permanent camp. With luck, we won't have long to wait before the packers bring in our goods."

As weary as they were, the women helped raise the tent and gather wood. "At least it's free," Hannah said as she tossed a small branch onto the flames.

Wind soughed through trees with the rolling sound of breakers. In the lake, waves lapped beneath the ice. They were far warmer than it had been on the pass. Julia saw Hannah gaze toward the clouds on the peak and knew she worried over Officer Gray as he endured another freezing night.


Duncan was eager to hike to Lake Bennett at dawn. While complaining of aching muscles, the women dutifully hoisted their packs and followed. Hannah paused, looking toward the pass where sunlight cut through massed clouds. Gently, Julia said, "I believe you will meet again."

"I hope not." As Julia looked at her in surprise, Hannah said fervently, "Don't you understand? He's the law and I . . . Why, I'm not only a showgirl, I'm a felon."

"Nonsense!" Despite the bulky packs, Julia managed to hug her. "If you hadn't become frightened and run away, that monster would have been arrested for attacking you."

Hannah looked scarcely comforted. Together, they hiked past men working on boats. Stacks of lumber were piled between tents, canvas lean-tos and huge marquees.

Duncan located a site about to be abandoned by a group preparing to drive a heavily loaded dog team down the frozen lake. They left behind a log frame three feet high. Once the tent was raised within, Vida pranced inside. "Now this looks like home."

"Beats the Seattle underground," Tilly agreed. Grin widening, she added, "All this fresh air may be the death of me."

Julia hauled her pack into the tent and dropped it on the canvas floor while Duncan went in search of their packers. "Let's get the stove set up," she urged the women. "Who will go after water? Belle, we had better make a mustard patch for your chest."

"Who died and made her Mama?" Vida demanded, but grabbed a bucket and went out to look for a fresh-running stream.


In the morning, a terrible silence fell over the busy camp as news of disaster traveled from one man to another. "Do you recall a glacier overhanging the trail?" their nearest neighbor called. "Blue as the devil? Gave way yesterday. Buried at least fifty men."

Hannah gasped and clutched Julia's arm. "What of the officers at the top?"

Their neighbor scratched a stubbly chin. "I imagine they're looking for survivors, miss. They say dozens were buried under the snow."

"It might have been us," Julia whispered. "We might as easily have been caught." A vivid picture rose to her mind of Ben and his surly companion fighting for their lives beneath tons of churning ice and snow.

Through her horror, she realized that Hannah was whitefaced and turned to clasp her hand. "I'm sure he's safe and helping to locate people still buried."

"He's probably already dead of bronchitis," Hannah said fiercely. "If he isn't, he soon will be. There's no sense in wasting worry on a dead man."

"You don't mean that!" Julia exclaimed.

Tears threatened to spill from Hannah's eyes. Turning suddenly, she hurried away. Several tents distant, she dropped to her knees beside a basket, despair fading from her face. Puzzled, Julia followed and saw Hannah stroking a purring, cinnamon-colored cat with several brand-new kittens.

"Aren't they lovely?" Hannah murmured. "Look, Julia. Eight of them."

As Julia bent over the basket, the woman she had talked with at the summit came from her tent. "Like them, do you? They'll cost. You'd best attract a Klondike king, my ladies if you want one of Amanda's pretties."

Julia was annoyed by the woman's attitude. Still, she was thankful to see Hannah's distress soothed by the cat and her kittens.

They would be at the lake for nearly two months until spring breakup. Anticipation glowed through Julia as she imagined long hours spent with Duncan. It seemed a lifetime ago when she dreaded sharing a tent with him. Now with the hiking ended and her energy returning, her imagination offered vivid possibilities.

Her imagination proved to be mistaken. From the first day, Duncan's waking hours were spent in the spruce forest felling trees to be carved into lumber for boats. It had not before occurred to Julia that transportation would not be waiting and that they must build their own.

"The trunks are small and branch low," he told them over dinner. "We'll only be able to cut planks nine or ten inches wide, and they'll be full of knots."

"If it's all there is, it will have to do," Julia suggested.

His smile was grim. "I'm glad you haven't lost your optimistic nature."

If she hadn't lost it then, it faded as the long days passed with her dream of tender hours spent with Duncan proving as hopeless as his of cutting clear planks. Since the trail over the White Pass ended at Lake Bennett, a steady flow of people arrived from that trail as well as from the Chilkoot. Many of the newcomers set up business, opening cafés and bakeries, offering barbers, hot baths, mining information and other services. Horror entered men's voices when they talked of the trails, but most looked forward, not back, and were bright with anticipation.

As the days passed, it seemed to Julia that the only time Duncan spoke to her was when she annoyed him in some way. He was rarely at their camp, but somehow always appeared when she acted on an impulse that could get her into trouble, such as practicing the cancan with the dancers.

The late-April afternoon was sunny and crisp. The women's energy caught Julia's imagination. They shouted and tossed their skirts, wheeling and kicking with a vibrant precision that enchanted her. On impulse, she ran into the line and linked her arm with Belle. The heavy wool skirt impeded her, but it was cut to midcalf, and she kicked almost as high as the others.

Duncan chose that moment to walk into camp. His roar might have carried all the way to Dawson. Hastily, Julia straightened her dress. Even the dancers looked wary as Duncan strode toward them. "What in blazes are you doing?"

Julia glared. "As you can see, we're dancing."

"*Were* dancing," he said darkly. "If you make any more trouble Songbird, I swear I'll tie you to my belt."

The idea almost appealed to her. She suppressed a quick smile, but not before he saw it. "The other end of the belt," he warned, "will be linked to the tent pole."

Julia's heart sank. The women moved protectively around her while Hannah protested, "We won't let her dance, Duncan. Leave her alone."

"Julia?" he asked with a glitter of ice in his eyes.

She told herself that he worried about her. More important, through Duncan she would reach her father. "I'm sorry," she said. The words tasted like sawdust. "I wasn't thinking."

With a curt nod, he turned toward the forest.

"It's the mills," Belle explained as Julia glowered after him. "They've made all the men cross."

"You should know!" Hannah exclaimed. "You must have visited nearly all of them."

"Not quite," Belle said with a satisfied smile, "but it's the goal I have in mind."

To head off an argument, Julia caught Hannah's arm. "Let's follow and watch the work. I can't think how a tree can be made into planks."

"We'll go tomorrow," Hannah promised. "If I'm to dance in Dawson, I must learn the steps." While Julia sat on a boulder, the women wheeled in formation, kicking and shrieking with contagious energy.

That night, Duncan came to camp only long enough to eat. He left again before Julia could find a way to get through the fresh barriers that had risen between them.

The morning was clear and cold as she and Hannah hiked to the forest edge where men's shouts rang over the rasp of saws. Duncan and another man were rolling a log onto a head-high platform. "The frame looks awfully flimsy," Julia said doubtfully. The platform trembled beneath the weight of the log and men as they marked chalk lines to indicate the planks.

The other man stood on top and Duncan stood in the pit beneath as they worked the long whipsaw through the log. The saw cut only on the downstroke. With each cut, Duncan received a rain of sawdust in his face and hair.

Hannah laughed, and with a burst of colorful language he ordered them back to camp. "All we wanted was to watch," Julia complained.

The tension that had lain over Hannah since the avalanche could be heard in her voice. "Men don't care to be watched while they're not at their best."

"Still," Julia objected. "He's become a jailer. Just days ago, he insisted I return those novels—"

"Racy books," Hannah corrected.

"But interesting," Julia said. "And he forced me to return them as if I were a child."

"With a few hard words for the owners, I believe." As Hannah's voice lightened, Julia decided her struggles against Duncan's authority had some value if they brought amusement to her troubled friend. Deliberately, she in-

creased her complaints. "You heard him rage just because
I repeated a song I heard at the lakeshore."

"Julia!" Hannah exclaimed. "You cannot have understood the meaning in the words you were singing."

Tilly joined them, and Julia turned to her with an exaggerated sigh. "This could be a lovely place if we hadn't
Duncan Adair to worry us."

"Do you suppose she means that?" Hannah asked.

"I certainly do," Julia said. "He treats me as if I were
not particularly bright. Just think of the way he shouted
when he found me practicing the cancan."

Tilly grinned. "There'd be no problem if you were Belle
or someone with an easy taste for men. But you're a lady.
That's got him tied up in knots, so he paces the beach at
night and snaps at you during the day."

"I'm not likely to remain a lady under such treatment,"
Julia said darkly. Inside, she felt a rise of wonder. At night
he walked the beach? Troubled over her? She believed he
spent his evenings comparing information about the trail
with other campers.

Thoughtfully, she returned to camp with Hannah and
Tilly. As the day wore on, she considered and discarded
plans to follow and intercept him the next time he paced the
shore, if it was true that he did so.

There seemed no way to approach him without risking
the embarrassment of sounding like a lovestruck school-
girl. Late in the afternoon, she discovered Tilly absorbed
in a game of poker with three of the gamblers who each
evening matched wits with prospectors. The game didn't
appear to be especially complicated. In fact, it looked interesting.

One of the gamblers glanced at her. "Like to sit in,
miss?"

"Oh, no," she said and saw their amusement. The invitation had been meant as a joke. Tired of being set apart,
she said, "It's just that I have no..." What was the word?
"No stakes."

His eyes twinkled. "Of course you do. A pan of your
baking powder bread would match any stake on the table.
Boys, am I right?"

As they all agreed, Julia suspected she might still be the butt of a joke. But she was bored and willing to lose a pan of bread. Besides, if she walked away now, it would be to the sound of their laughter. She rolled a log closer to the makeshift table and settled upon it.

Poker proved to be more fun than she expected, especially when she won the first hand. The others chuckled at her open delight in collecting her winnings, but she didn't care. With Tilly advising, she pushed out a coin for the next ante.

The cards were dealt again. Julia picked them up one at a time, trying to keep her face blank when she discovered that three were aces. "Care to raise?" the dealer asked.

From behind her, Duncan said, "Deal her out."

"What?" She wheeled around. He took the cards and slapped them onto the table, face up. With a gasp, she reached out to turn them over.

Duncan caught her around the waist and lifted her over one shoulder. Shrieking, she pounded her fists against his back, but she might as well have pounded a tree. In fact, sawdust rained from his shirt with every smack of her hands.

Choking, she braced herself against his back, raising her head as high as possible. "I was winning!" she said furiously. "You saw my cards. I only put up a pan of bread. You have no right to haul me away like this."

Outside their tent, Duncan lowered her to her feet. "I don't care what you put up or that they let you win at first or what they would have taken from you later. A lady does not gamble."

Stung by his suggestion that the gamblers had let her win, Julia snapped, "My aunt plays hearts."

For Duncan, the words conjured a proper drawing room with polished game table, the setting where Julia belonged. Roughly, he demanded, "Does she play for money?"

"She gets so excited over points, I don't see the difference."

"Which only proves your lack of good sense."

"That is one more foolish thing you have said to me."

He caught her by the shoulders, unsure whether he meant to kiss her or shake her. The flash of her eyes defied him to do either. They glared at each other, the air simmering between them. He recognized a flare of sensual excitement. Her eyes revealed the same yearning he had tried for weeks to suppress in himself. His hands grew gentle as he became aware of the delicate curve of her shoulders beneath his palms.

Her lips softened from their earlier angry line as the fire in her eyes became a sensual glow. "Why are we fighting?"

A slight pull would bring her into his arms. Only inches separated their lips. But he couldn't kiss her here, before curious onlookers. And he didn't trust himself to take her into the tent. Possibilities held them apart for long breathless moments, broken by an eager shout. "Miss Julia!"

Her eyes widened. "Ben! It's Ben! He's alive."

Duncan's hands slipped from her as she swung toward the young man approaching from the beach. Her voice carried a lilt of relief. "We've been desperately worried since we heard of the avalanche."

"We weren't caught," Ben called. "But plenty were. All of us worked like dogs to get to the survivors." His expression suggested a great deal of maturing since their last meeting. "We buried sixty-one at Dyea."

"But you are safe," Julia said, and the darkness eased in his eyes.

Duncan watched her treat the kid who had once attacked her as if he were a long-lost brother. Pushing one hand through his hair, he decided he would never understand the woman. More newcomers caught his eye. At the end of the trail to Chilkoot Pass, a number of the Queen's finest marched onto the shore.

From behind Duncan, Hannah cried, "Officer Gray!" Nearly bowling Duncan over, she dashed to the shore, then made an obvious attempt to look interested in the construction of a large sailboat while making sure the Mountie couldn't miss seeing her.

Duncan picked up a stone and hurled it onto the frozen lake. It skittered across the lake and stopped. The Yukon ice couldn't break up fast enough to suit him.

## Chapter Twelve

While Ben and Chambers set up their tent, Julia perched on a rock nearby, insisting that Ben tell her everything about his experience. She knew that Duncan must think she had lost what little sense he attributed to her. The truth was that Ben's unexpected arrival had stopped her from making a shameless mistake.

She still felt stunned by the intensity of her feelings while she argued with Duncan. How could she have been so angry and yet longed to kiss him? She had all but forced herself into his arms. He must have seen passion in her face. She could only hope he had mistaken it for anger.

It was perfectly well for men to show desire, but for a decent woman to feel so strongly must be a sin. What if she had tried to kiss him? She felt herself cringe. All the neighbors would have witnessed her shame, whether he accepted her kiss or refused it.

Would he have accepted? She broke off the thought, determined to put the incident behind her—but not to return to the tent until Duncan had time to do the same.

She still felt a strong dislike for Chambers, but Ben had matured during his experiences on Chilkoot Pass. His earlier eagerness for adventure was subdued by death and injury. She forgave him completely for the misunderstanding at Sheep Camp and tried to lighten his spirits by describing the lakeshore community.

"You must see the kittens. And there is a man hauling mosquito lotion who expects to make a killing. Another is bringing in a carton of cough syrups. Two sisters down the lake are packing in sewing machines. They believe there will be great demand for their services.''

"I expect they're right," Ben said with a rueful glance at a tear in his sleeve.

From across the tent, Chambers shouted. "Damn it, boy. Quit making sheep's eyes at the woman and set that tent post."

Ben and Julia shared a wry smile before he returned to work. At the edge of the lake, Hannah stood talking with Officer Gray. Her body angled toward him while she laughed and teased. If she was worried about the long reach of American law, Hannah was not letting it stand in the way of her interest in the Mountie.

Julia waited for Hannah to return to the tent before she went inside, then was chagrined that Duncan was not there. He returned late, after all the women were snug under their blankets. He lowered himself to his blankets, which were near the stove, then played softly on his harmonica until Julia's lashes drifted lower and she lost herself in sleep.

Punts, rafts, scows, barges, double-enders and other boats were under construction along the lakeshore. Mounted police roamed among the boat builders, giving instructions to men who had never in their lives built anything more complicated than a birdhouse. More caulking was ordered so often that Hannah began to tease Officer Gray about having a sadly limited vocabulary. He answered in French, delighting her and provoking her to greater teasing.

"Aren't you afraid you'll discourage his attention?" Julia asked curiously as they prepared dinner one evening after a particularly animated exchange between Hannah and Edmund Gray.

"If he can be discouraged, he isn't worth having," Hannah said tartly, then with a sly smile added, "I don't see you making things easier for Duncan."

"There is nothing between the two of us!" Julia exclaimed and felt her face heat. Duncan had avoided her since the afternoon when she all but threw herself into his arms. Embarrassed by the memory and unwilling to admit that his absence hurt, she said fiercely, "He can hardly wait to be rid of me. And I will be thankful to see the last of him."

Hannah's knowing smile denied it.

They fell silent as they heard him stamping his feet clear of sawdust outside. He came into the tent, looking short of temper, a state of mind common after work in the saw pit.

Near the primitive sawmills, Julia had seen men burst into tears of frustration. Some grabbed their share of provisions and split up their partnership on the spot. One mill had collapsed, injuring the man beneath, who accused his partner of deliberately sabotaging the frame. After that, Duncan ordered the women to stay away from the mills. Julia was willing to take the advice.

As she opened the oven to put a pan of bread inside, sarcasm edged his greeting. "Do you think this time you might serve it without the stove?"

"That only happened once." She turned an indignant look on Hannah that said her case had just been proved. Hannah simply smiled.

Dropping onto his blanket, Duncan accepted a cup of coffee. After a long swallow, he said, "Your friend Ben is about worthless. He breaks out in a weeping rash from the sawdust."

"I'm sorry for Ben," Julia said, flaring. "I don't know why you sound as if that had something to do with me."

"I've agreed to give Chambers a hand," Duncan continued. "In turn, he'll help build our boat."

*Chambers.* Julia stiffened, then silently pushed the bread pan into the oven. The trapper was one of the few men at the lake whose every glance was an insult. "Do you trust him?" she asked after a strained silence.

"He's a good worker. I saw that aboard the *Gypsy Gull.*"

I saw just the opposite, Julia thought, but said nothing.

Setting the cup aside, Duncan stretched out on his back, his arms pillowing his head. She decided this was no time to argue, despite her apprehension over the new partnership.

That night, she lay awake watching shadows on the tent walls from the fire in the Klondike stove. A whistling wind pushed the canvas in and out. The tent grew colder and she tugged her blanket close. To either side, Tilly and Hannah slept soundly. Across the tent, Vida and Belle were also asleep, but as her thoughts moved to Duncan, she heard him stir.

He no longer slept in his clothes, since his shirt and trousers were thick with sawdust. As she pretended to sleep, Julia saw him climb from his blankets clad in long drawers and undershirt of cotton mesh. He walked to the stove and pushed in another piece of firewood. Beneath the fabric, his muscles moved fluidly. Firelight danced over the strong planes of his face and tangled in his hair. A wave of longing made her tremble so that she was afraid he might see she was awake.

Never had she felt such an odd and urgent hunger. Surely, Ruth had no such feelings for Aaron. If her mother had been drawn this way to Joseph Everett, the desire had caused pain and finally her death. When Duncan turned and looked directly at her, Julia lowered her lashes to hide her eyes.

Only taking time for a biscuit and a cup of coffee in the morning, Duncan left the tent to the women and headed at once to the tree line and the makeshift sawmill. Julia wondered how two men as different as Duncan and the trapper could work well together.

On the third morning, she restlessly set her toast aside and, taking the water bucket, walked to a spring in a ravine. Jays scolded from the trees. Red squirrels chattered loudly, as if even the animals sensed her troubled feelings. She knelt by the spring, glad of the cold water that splashed over her hands when she filled the bucket.

A shadow blocked the sunlight. With a start, she looked up at Chambers. His smile did not warm his eyes. "You're looking right perky this morning, Miss Julia. It comes to me that we ain't been civil to each other. No need to keep on that way. Why don't I just take that heavy bucket for you?''

Uneasily, Julia said, ''Thank you, Mr. Chambers. I can manage.''

''Now, Miss Julia, it wouldn't be neighborly to let you haul that heavy bucket.''

What was behind this? He had never offered aid before. ''I won't keep you from your morning tasks,'' she said firmly. ''I'm sure you are eager to get to the saw pit.''

He spat onto the rocks. ''The devil's pit, whether a man works top or bottom.''

Julia swallowed an uncomfortable lump. Why wasn't Chambers with Duncan? How in this busy camp could she have found herself alone with the trapper? ''I was sorry to hear of Ben's difficulty with the dust.'' Clenching the pail, she started toward the camp.

The trapper walked uncomfortably close beside her. ''That fool pup. Lazy as a summer hound.'' Chambers spat again, oblivious to her wince. ''Your fellow tell you that me and him joined up?''

She stiffened at the implication. ''Mr. Adair said he thought you a good worker.'' Hoping the compliment would satisfy him, Julia moved aside as she continued downhill. The camp had never seemed so distant.

''I reckon you and him's pretty close,'' Chambers suggested. ''Sleepin' in the same tent and all.''

As she swung to confront him, water washed over the edge of the bucket and soaked into her skirt. ''Mr. Chambers, I expect an apology.''

He grabbed her wrist. For a moment, they competed for the pail, then he won and set it on the rocks. ''Seems you're particular about your kisses, savin' 'em for that young pup and Adair. The way I figure it, you just ain't yet kissed a real man.''

He reached for her, but Julia moved faster. Snatching the bucket, she swung it in an arc that struck his knee with a satisfying crunch. Water sprayed over them both. Cursing, Chambers grabbed at his knee. A part of Julia's mind repeated the women's advice to aim for his crotch. Instead, she fled downhill, still carrying the bucket.

"That's not much water," Hannah observed when Julia set the bucket on the table.

"It will do." A word to Hannah could set the police after Chambers. They kept a strict peace here, as they did in Dawson. Julia was unwilling to cause trouble. The trapper would say that her smiles and glances were to blame. She told herself again that her best choice was to stay away from the man.

At the saw pit, Duncan waited impatiently. He hadn't believed Chambers was a man who would lay abed in the morning. He should have been here by now. At last he saw the trapper clumping up the hill. He walked with a limp and looked to be in a black mood. Duncan greeted him without enthusiasm. "I see you've injured your leg. You had better work in the pit today."

Chambers's flood of profanity seemed more than was called for. By midday, neither man was speaking to the other. Duncan walked to camp feeling an unholy pleasure that Chambers faced a cold lunch of his own making, for Ben was no more adept at the stove than in the pit.

As he approached the tent, Duncan savored the astonishing aroma of roasting grouse. Hannah explained with a proud gleam in her eyes, "Edmund brought the bird. He and his men have time for hunting with the light lasting so late."

Despite his difficult morning, Duncan grinned. "Edmund, is it?"

He glanced at Julia, and beneath her answering smile he saw relief. This was the first time they had shared amusement since the gambling incident. He regretted her unhappiness yet he knew there was danger in becoming close to her.

Stoutly, Hannah answered. "Edmund also said there are trout in the lake. If our guide had packed a net, we might have fresh fish for our meals."

"Good idea," Duncan said, pleased to return her jibe. "You've all complained of having too little to do. Weaving a fish net should keep you occupied."

"I would have no idea how to begin," Hannah said, looking as if she wished she could bite back her words.

The other women looked equally annoyed. "I have plenty to do," Tilly announced. "Why, I've learned three new games already. They'll be handy diversions in your brother's saloon."

Vida said that she, too, was busy but didn't explain. Hannah gave her a sharp look. "I hope you're not forgetting the police look unkindly on thieves."

"Are you calling me a thief?" Vida demanded.

Despite herself, Julia broke in. "Vida, really. Is there anyone here who wouldn't?"

"Enough!" Duncan roared. While they glowered at each other, he told them all where to sit. "Hannah, bring me a ball of string." They were unwilling and resentful pupils, but they learned how to weave a net before Duncan left for the sawmill.

Chambers lounged on an uncut log, tapping a fresh cut of chewing tobacco under his lip. "I began to think you was too occupied with the ladies to bother comin' back," he drawled. "That Julia's a right tasty dish."

Anger flared in Duncan, but he blocked his initial response. He needed Chambers's help if they were to have boats ready when the ice broke up. Aware that Chambers hoped for an argument, Duncan sprang onto the mill frame. As he climbed to the top, a plank shifted. He caught his balance briefly, but then the frame collapsed. He had only time to think, *Chambers did this,* before something struck his temple. He knew a moment of blinding light, then absolute blackness.

When he opened his eyes, Duncan lay on the grass with his aching head cradled in a woman's soft lap. A damp towel eased the pain. "You're awake," Julia said in a voice that trembled.

He tried to look at her, but the effort caused a lance of pain. "Shh," she said unnecessarily. "Lie still. We've sent for a doctor."

He tried to ignore the pain by concentrating on the softness of her lap. As she bent over him, her natural fragrance rivaled the smell of the meadow flowers. The gentle stroke of her fingertips helped ease the shattering pain. With his head cradled by Julia's warm thighs, he felt almost at peace.

"At last!" she exclaimed. "Here is the doctor."

Reluctantly, Duncan opened his eyes and looked into the serious gaze of a rather pretty woman with lively eyes. When she smiled, a diamond glinted in one front tooth. "So the logs fought back, did they? I'm Dr. Luella Day, Mr. Adair. Let me take a look at that head wound."

He wanted to object when she knelt beside him. What kind of doctor was this? Not only a woman, but sporting a gemstone in her tooth. Flashing pain in his head warned against sudden movement. With his mouth tight, he endured her probing.

"It's encouraging that he regained consciousness so quickly," the doctor said to Julia as if Duncan hadn't the wits to hear. "Let's not fly in the face of nature. We'll keep him off his feet for a few days."

Duncan tried to sit up. Through a blaze of raw pain, he felt the women press him back. His voice grated. "I have a boat to build."

"The boat will wait," Julia said. He felt her shift as she directed her attention outward. "Ben will help Mr. Chambers with both boats while you recover. He's discovered that his rash is easier as long as he works on top of the frame and not in the pit."

She had gained an iron spine from somewhere, Duncan mused, then remembered that Chambers might have caused the collapse. If so, he'd done himself no favor. The pit was a worse hell than the top, and Chambers was stuck with that job.

Julia stroked his hair and he relaxed again. Dr. Day chuckled. "I can see he's going to be fine. Let us locate some men to carry him to his tent."

When he was lifted, Duncan nearly blacked out from pain. He clenched his teeth to keep from cursing aloud. Two men carried him. Every step jolted straight into his head. By the time they lowered him to his blankets, he doubted that Dr. Day knew anything of medicine if she believed he was going to live.

Julia slept little that night. She checked on Duncan whenever he stirred. In the morning, the discolored swelling beneath his bandage looked worse, but he insisted on getting to his feet. As she expected, he wasn't an easy patient. She gave up arguing when he leaned on Ben to walk into the trees for personal needs. He returned white-faced and sank onto his blanket. The women hovered and were snapped at for their attention.

When he rubbed the stubble on his jaw in annoyance, the women all responded. Tilly poured hot water. Hannah located soap. Belle and Vida argued over who should strop the razor. When Julia offered to shave him, he answered with such a growl that she backed away.

Hannah considered him with a thoughtful tilt of her head. "While we have him at our tender mercy, Julia, I believe we should also trim his hair."

"Ben!" Duncan roared. "Get me out of here." Then, groaning in pain, he lowered his face to his hands and pressed his fingers to his temples.

"You've brought that on yourself," Hannah said severely. "Since you choose to be difficult, Mr. Adair, I see no reason to remain in your company. Come, ladies, let us leave him to Julia."

He looked up morosely as the giggling women left the tent. "They mean well," Julia said, offering a cup of spruce tea. "Dr. Day says that spruce needles contain healing elements."

As he considered the steaming liquid with distaste, Julia reached toward the dressing, which had slipped lower on his forehead. Irritably, he pushed her hand away. "How in blazes am I supposed to recover with you picking at me?"

She drew back with the look of a kicked puppy, then rose gracefully. "Since you have no need of me, I'm off to find a poker game."

He lurched upright. "Julia!" His head throbbed violently. Nausea rose and he choked it down.

Alarmed, she pressed her hands to his chest, urging him to lie back. "Are you daft? You should have known I said that to repay your surliness."

Through a haze of red, he saw that she held a roll of string. She intended only to work on her fish net. "Julia, I'm sorry," he managed, while the roar in his head receded. "It's just that I feel as useless as a...a ribbon clerk."

"That again!" she exclaimed. "You are unfair to your mother. After all, she chose her husband."

"She chose safety." Duncan sipped the tea, which wasn't as bitter as he'd expected. More gently, he said, "I have nothing against my stepfather except that he spawned Owen."

"Perhaps, the rigors of the trail will have made him into a man."

Her attempt to pacify him made Duncan more conscious of his bad humor. When she reached toward the bandage, then hesitated, he captured her wrist and kissed the velvet inner skin. She looked so startled that he offered a lopsided smile. "In my own clumsy way, I'm trying to apologize."

Her eyes grew gentle and her lips softened. He decided the pain in his head was a good thing. Without it, he might have pulled her onto the blanket and kissed her until the rest of the world disappeared.

That was no way to begin another enforced month on this blasted lake. With both his trawlers wrecked, he was in no financial position to make a commitment. And Julia could accept nothing less. He released her hand, aware that she drew back with reluctance.

As Julia watched different emotions cross Duncan's face, she felt as unsteady as if she were the one with the head injury. Hannah had provided them with an opportunity to be alone, but again Duncan raised barriers.

She felt a flicker of irritation. "If you have no more need of me, I will work on my net."

"At least one of us is useful."

A flash of her earlier spirit lit her eyes. "Oh, you are useful, Mr. Adair. I can imagine a no more determined chaperon." His soft curse made her smile as she stepped from the tent with the ball of twine.

# Chapter Thirteen

That evening, Belle borrowed one of the kittens for Duncan's amusement. Bold enough for two animals twice its size, the fluffy gray kitten climbed to his shoulder at once and batted at the bandage. Julia was glad to see Duncan's taut expression gave way to amusement. Lifting the kitten in one hand, he said soberly, "You remind me of a feisty young lady from Seattle."

Promptly, Belle said, "That's all of us."

He looked from one to another with unexpected gravity. "So it is, pretty Belle. Every one of you has proved herself well."

As the women warmed to his praise, Julia marveled that they had become a family despite their differences. She would miss them all dearly when the time came for parting. Suddenly awash in sadness at that thought, Julia rose briskly and pushed a piece of wood into the fire.

After locating Vida's scissors, she sat beside Duncan. He looked at her warily. "What do you have in mind, now?"

"Many things, the first being to trim the hair above your collar before the kitten is lost in it and we're forced to pay her greedy mistress the last of our cash."

He didn't object. Julia worked as crisply as a barber, yet every time she brushed his skin, she felt a leap of her senses. When the blades sliced through soft curling tendrils, a shiver raced up her arms. She guessed from his stillness that he felt an echoing intimacy. Perhaps it was just as well the tent was crowded with showgirls.

In the following days, snow melted from the mountains along the lake sending rivulets of water through the camp. A tapestry of meadow flowers made up for the discomfort. In the week after Duncan's injury, one or another of the women brought in armloads of blooms until most of the cooking pots were filled with forget-me-nots, bleeding hearts and harebells.

He complained mildly. "The place looks and smells like a funeral home. Are you planning to bury me?"

With a grin, Hannah said, "He's feeling better."

Julia agreed, adding, "More people are coming down from the passes. I can't think where they'll find space for their tents."

"Leave them to Edmund the Incomparable," Duncan said with a teasing glance for Hannah, who flounced from the tent with a look of mock indignation.

Julia laughed. "You've driven her away just when we had almost finished our net." Ruefully, she pushed the strings from her lap. "I'm tired of it, anyway. Will you teach me to pan for gold?"

"So our Songbird has plans besides finding her father."

She walked over to him as he stirred the embers in the stove. "I noticed there are pans among the supplies you bought in Dyea."

Feeling it wise to leave the deceptive privacy of the tent, Duncan said, "We'll try up by the spring."

As they walked toward the timber, happiness raced through Julia. The day was glorious with flowers and the sky was laced with white clouds. Duncan unwound the bandage and shoved it into a pocket. With relief, Julia said, "The wound is healing cleanly. In truth, the scar along your hairline has a decidedly devilish look."

"Consider yourself warned," he said with a grin that made her pulse quicken. When they reached the spring, Duncan scooped the gold pan half full of earth, shook it to settle the material then tilted and rocked it in the water. Little by little, gravel and earth swept over the side of the pan.

Bracing one hand on his shoulder, Julia leaned closer. Her breast brushed his arm. The contact was electric. He gave no indication of having noticed. Cautiously, she leaned close again.

Only fine sand and light gravel remained in the pan. Julia watched his lean fingers, feeling mesmerized by the rhythmic movements. When only fine black sand remained, he searched it with his fingertip. "Nothing."

"May I try?"

Their hands brushed as she took the pan. Roughly, he said, "Scoop gravel from close to the bedrock."

Kneeling, Julia dug into the rocky streambed. As Duncan had done, she shook the pan from side to side, then swished it beneath the water to clear away dirt and gravel.

"Easy," he warned. "Angle the pan. The angle won't lose your gold, but water will."

She tilted her head, laughing. "Is there lots?"

"There could be." His gaze caressed her face and throat. He swallowed and forced himself to concentrate on the work. "Don't jerk the pan. Watch your angle."

For once, she didn't object to taking orders. When only the finer gravel remained, she turned and caught him watching her. "Am I doing it right?"

He shook himself and looked quickly at the gold pan. "Shake it again. Now wash out the gravel. Easy. Watch your angle."

When she tried again, all the gravel shifted. Duncan put his hands over hers. In the circle of his arms, with his breath stirring tendrils of hair, she felt his pulse quicken.

For a moment they were both still. Then, determined to ignore the sensations he knew were shaking them both, he carefully washed the pan through the water. "Like this." He sat back. "Try it again."

Missing his embrace, Julia tried to copy the rocking, washing motion. Gradually, finer gravel slipped from the sides.

"That's enough. Let's see what you have." Carefully, he smoothed a fingertip through the remaining sand. "Julia," he said softly. "Look."

She drew her gaze from the scar at his temple. She had been longing to kiss it to speed the healing. At the tip of his finger, a reddish lump a little larger than a pinhead glowed against the dark. "Gold," she whispered. "Is it really?"

"Your first color." He grinned. "You're a natural. You may leave this country as a wealthy woman."

Exultant, she rocked the pan. Water rushed in. "Oh, no, my gold!"

Duncan rescued it, but they toppled together onto the grass. Setting the pan aside, he gazed into her startled eyes.

She reached for him, hardly knowing what she was doing. Slowly, he lowered his head, his expression becoming tender. When his mouth covered hers, she wound her arms tightly around him, feeling as if the single gold flake ran molten through her veins. High above, sparrows sang in branches rustled by the wind, but Julia felt as if the entire world centered on Duncan's warm lips.

Her fingers trembled in the thick, soft hair at the back of his neck. They lay so closely together that her breasts were crushed against him, yet she wanted to pull him even closer. She wanted . . . She didn't know what she wanted except to go on kissing him.

Julia's lips were even sweeter than Duncan remembered. Her soft body curved into his. He drew her breath into his mouth, then traced the trembling outline of her lips with the tip of his tongue. Feeling as if he could never in a lifetime get enough of kissing her, he explored the soft curve of her throat.

His hand moved from her waist to curve around her breast. He felt her quick intake of breath, but she clung to him as he reclaimed her lips and deepened the kiss. With unsteady fingers, he unbuttoned the waistcoat he had bought her to keep men from staring at her. When he slipped his hand beneath her dress, the vibrant heat of her breast through her thin chemise drove him wild. He traced kisses over her throat and breast, stroking her breast, then brushing his fingertips over the taut nipple.

Julia felt lost in sensation. She clutched him to her, loving the way her body felt against him, wanting him to keep kissing her. Her entire body felt as if an electric storm thundered and flashed within.

For Duncan, reason came slowly through pleasure. Having resisted her for weeks, the first kiss drove him out of control. Now, he fought the need to go farther. It would be sweet to keep kissing her, to urge her to explore his body as he wanted to discover hers.

With Julia, lovemaking would be incredible. He longed for it, but forced temptation away. Raising his head, he kissed the tip of her nose, then each eyelid. The sun had given her a tantalizing sprinkle of freckles. He began to kiss each one, but again passion began to overwhelm his resolve and he forced himself to sit up. "Pretty Songbird, if I'm strong enough for this, I'm strong enough to work on the boats."

She opened her eyes with a glazed look of denial. Gently, he said, "Think of your father, if you won't think of yourself." He pulled her shirtwaist together and buttoned it carefully. Catching her hands, he pulled her upright, then wrapped one arm around her waist for a last embrace. "Sweetheart, you should go into medicine. You have wonderfully healing ways."

She shook out her skirt with the violence of a cleaning woman on wash day. "I'll have my gold nugget, please."

He was grateful for the release of laughter. "Nugget! This?" Retrieving the pan, he pressed one fingertip to the flake, then offered it to her. "Milady, your riches."

Moistening her fingertip with her tongue, she claimed the flake. The innocent gesture electrified him. As he watched her shield the gold flake with her cupped palm, Duncan warned himself fiercely, *She's entrusted to me for safekeeping, and by all that's holy, I will keep her safe.* Clasping her elbow, he directed her downhill toward camp.

May was a happy month along the lakes. Most men had finished at the saw pits and sang at their boat building, joyful that the last lap of the journey grew near. Duncan played such sprightly tunes on his harmonica in the evening that Julia wanted to dance, and she envied the showgirls, who did.

Whenever her gaze held his, the thought of dancing fled and greater temptation stirred deep inside. She knew that he took care they were never alone and wondered which of them he least trusted.

When the net was completed, Edmund helped Julia and Hannah anchor the far end to a block of ice and the near end to a rock. All along the lake, murky water showed near the shore. People still sent their sleds skidding over the ice as they traveled down from Lake Lindemann to Lake Bennett, but at increasing risk. Just this morning, an entire load had gone through the ice. Duncan was among those who left work to rescue the driver and his horses, but the supplies were lost.

As Hannah flirted with Edmund, Julia began to feel like an uneasy third. Leaving them to each other, she picked her way along the muddy beach to the boat Duncan was building with Chambers and Ben. She rested her bare hand on Duncan's sun-warmed shoulder and felt his muscles flex. He leaned back to look at her, but did not shrug away her touch.

It was difficult not to stroke the scar at his temple. That injury had brought fresh argument between them when she learned he meant to continue working with Chambers. "I believe he feels responsible for the mill's collapse," Duncan explained.

"*Feels* responsible!" Julia retorted.

"Is responsible, for all I know. He regrets the accident. He's a capable man in the outdoors, if not with women. Give him credit for wanting to make amends."

"You give him more credit than you do me," Julia muttered, furious that he would again risk working with the trapper, yet unable to discourage him. From then on, she shadowed him. If Chambers should make another attempt against Duncan, Julia meant to be close enough to intervene.

Now as Duncan looked at her in question, she searched for a reason to explain her interruption. "How are we to carry all of our provisions?"

"We're building a third boat. Chambers will take one, Ben another. You'll travel with me. The girls can draw straws to decide which boat they'll ride."

She wanted to travel with him, yet reacted instinctively. "If they are to draw straws, so will I. When will you learn that by favoring me, you set the others on edge?"

That wasn't really true anymore. The women saw the way she felt about him and sympathized, whether he held her at arm's length or gave her special favors.

"As you wish," he said shortly and turned to the cross planks he was nailing over the ribs. Feeling dismissed, Julia reluctantly walked on along the shore.

Inspector Samuel B. Steele had arrived to take charge of the police but rarely had time to leave the log cabin built for him between the two lakes. Edmund confided that the inspector rose by four or five every morning and worked sometimes until midnight, settling disputes and overseeing the registration of the vessels the prospectors were building.

"He may be the Lion of the Yukon," Hannah said unhappily, "but he works his men far too hard."

Julia smiled at her friend's complaint, which really was that Edmund had less time for her. Still, she felt as restless. Weeks had passed since Duncan's lovemaking at the spring. He acted as if it had never taken place, or rather as if he intended to see that it was never repeated. Turning restlessly, she walked past him again, pausing to give Chambers a sharp glance.

She was almost back to camp when Hannah shrieked from the lakeshore. Grasping her skirts, Julia raced toward her. Hannah was on shore, jumping up and down and screaming. "It's the net! Look! Look! See how it thrashes. Something is caught. What shall we do?"

"I've never heard such a commotion over a fish!" Julia exclaimed, while her heart pounded.

Hannah looked helplessly around. "Where is Edmund?"

"Never mind him." Wading into the mud, Julia grasped the net. "Help me."

Hannah's screams had drawn a crowd. Men gathered, calling amused encouragement. After a searching glance told her that the Mountie was not among them, Hannah gave them all a haughty look and waded in to help Julia wrestle with the fish.

Icy water sprayed their faces and clothes. A silver body leaped in the strings. "Hold on!" Hannah cried.

"I am," Julia shouted. "Watch your end."

Hannah shrieked. "It's getting away."

"It will, if you don't hold on," Julia countered. "Pull!"

They were amusing a good many people from the camp but were too busy to care. Thinking of fresh trout sizzling in her skillet, Julia stepped deeper to catch a loosening section of net. Her foot slipped into a hole. Icy water poured into her boot. Gasping, she staggered backward with the net.

Her heel hit a rock and she fell, landing on her behind in a splash of water and mud. The net whipped into the air. The trout landed squarely in her lap. It slapped its tail, spattering icy water into her face. With an arc of its back, it nearly leaped free. She clutched her arms around the net, fiercely trapping the fish. It flipped its tail, slapping her across the mouth.

Around her, men roared. *Never mind,* she told herself. *After all of this, I'm not going to lose my fish!*

Hannah rushed to help. As Julia struggled to her feet with the net and thrashing fish, she saw Duncan among the men. He had one hand braced on the shoulder of the next man and was bent nearly double, laughing.

As she glowered, he wiped his eyes and came to take the trout. Slipping his fingers into its gills, he hefted it thoughtfully. "Four pounds, at least. Congratulations, ladies."

"Perhaps it was worth all the trouble," Julia said, "if it has brought you out of your surly mood."

His eyes danced. "Surly, Miss Everett? Why, it was I who taught you to weave the net." She held her tongue, certain that any answer she might give him would only add fuel to his humor.

That evening, she followed when he took his plate outside and leaned against a boulder to eat. The aroma of fried fish overwhelmed the smell of the inevitable beans. For the few past weeks, Duncan had made a habit of taking a solitary dinner. Now with her plate in her hand and her heart rising uncomfortably into her throat, she asked, "May I join you? It's far more pleasant here than inside that musty canvas."

When he made room for her, she perched on the boulder and cut into the trout, then sighed with pleasure. "I have never tasted anything more wonderful."

"It's always a pleasure to taste the fruits of your own honest effort."

She looked at him sharply to see if he was teasing her, but his expression was unusually open. "Tell me about fishing," she said. "Has your family always gone to sea?"

Setting his empty plate aside, Duncan gazed out at the frozen lake. "In one way or another. My great-grandfather was a French voyageur who went through the North West Territories. His son settled in Seattle. I worked with my father from the time I could put any weight on a rope."

He circled one arm around her shoulders, and in shared silence they listened to the cold slap of water on the shore and the unceasing sound of hammers and saws as men took advantage of the late sun to work on their boats. Inside the tent, the women talked softly.

"I had grand visions of an entire fleet of my own," Duncan said at last. "Maybe, my reach was too high. Fate rewarded me by sending the *Patience* onto rocks and the *Fortune* to burn in Skagway."

"You must despise him," she said.

"Owen?" Cupping one hand beneath her chin, Duncan tilted her face toward his. "Owen was the force that brought you to me."

She felt her heart stop, then beat more rapidly. Her body seemed to blend into his as his arm tightened. Her lashes closed, and she lifted her face to him. Out on the lake, gulls called raucously. A chill breeze riffled Julia's hair, cooling her heated face. The expected kiss did not come. Dismayed, she opened her eyes.

Duncan spoke as calmly as if a kiss had never been suggested. "I have the promise of a loan to repair the *Patience*. And I've sworn to get the cost of the *Fortune* out of Owen. One day, I will have my fleet."

With stiff embarrassment, Julia said, "All is not lost, then. I'm glad for you. And now, good night."

With regret, Duncan watched her march into the tent. It was increasingly difficult to resist her. Julia was as vulnerable as a kitten who tackled the world with innocent claws, totally unaware of how easily she could be crushed.

Straightening, he walked along the muddy lakeshore. They both had matters to settle before thinking about a future. What would Julia find in Dawson City? He wanted to protect her, as he thought of the uncertainties ahead. Had the letter reached her father? What sort of man was he? Would he welcome his daughter or put her aboard the first steamer headed out?

Again Duncan felt a rush of protectiveness. He meant to make damned sure that Everett welcomed his daughter. But after that? He shoved one hand through his hair, keenly aware that he wasn't in a financial position to offer for her. Once he saw Julia safely to her father, he meant to change that.

A Dawson saloon should be reaping a rich profit. If his stepbrother didn't have the cost of the trawler set by, then he could damned well sell the place to get the money.

There was nothing to be done about it now. Lake Bennett felt like a trap while his future held as many uncertainties as Julia's. He continued down the shoreline. It might have been summer in Seattle, not icy spring in the Yukon, as the restless heat inside him sent him pacing away from the tent where Julia would soon be preparing for sleep.

# *Chapter Fourteen*

On the twenty-fourth of May, Hannah's shrieks rang out again, this time for Edmund. "You're winning. Pull!"

"Traitor," Vida exclaimed. "Let's throw her things out of the tent."

Julia laughed. "We all know Edmund has caught her heart. Surely you don't expect her to lead cheers for the opposing team, even if Duncan is a part of it."

The entire camp had stopped work to celebrate Queen Victoria's birthday. For the first time since she had arrived, Julia heard no ringing saws or pounding hammers. All along the shores, men took time to play.

"Edmund!" Hannah shrieked. "Pull!"

Julia clasped her hands, willing victory for the other team. The Mounties in their colorful scarlet jackets stood out against the sweeping grandeur of lake and mountains. They were trained to work together, and inch by inch they were tugging Duncan, Chambers and a number of hefty prospectors toward a line scratched in the ground.

The popular sport had divided the camp in a festive manner. Teams of British pulled against Australians. New Zealanders fought the weight of Nova Scotians, while a blare of bagpipes encouraged a team of Scots. Julia hadn't realized how much of the world's population had joined the quest for gold.

Slush furred the shoreline of the lake. Water shimmered over the surface of creaking, groaning ice. "It won't be much longer," Ben said, joining her.

Anticipation lanced through Julia. Now that breakup was near, she could hardly endure the waiting. For two months, her father's nearness had burned within her like a low fever. Now she felt on fire with the need to reach him.

"Chambers says we'll miss the real show," Ben added. "He says that in the river, floes as big as houses leap around like that fish you caught, crashing and plunging together. Water rushes right up the banks and floods everything. He says you see caribou floating along, trapped on the ice."

"I'm happy to miss that unfortunate sight," Julia said with a shiver.

Cheers rang out and she saw the Mounties had won. Hannah ran to congratulate Edmund, who turned as scarlet as his jacket at her kiss. As the losing team dusted themselves off and called good-natured challenges, Duncan walked toward Julia. She ran to him, reaching out. "You nearly had them."

He caught her hands before she could wrap her arms around him, but his smile sent a wave of longing through her. Putting one of her hands firmly over his arm, he said, "Let's see how the Scots are doing."

She felt as dizzied by Duncan's nearness as by the prospect of traveling on at last. The celebration revolved around them like a carnival. Excitement laced her voice. "Soon, we will have only a boat ride to Dawson!"

He answered with an indulgent note of caution. "A five-hundred-mile boat ride. In Dyea, I bought a book by an old-timer who describes the route. He mentions rapids."

"Pooh." She refused to allow any clouds into this bright, perfect day. "After surviving the trail and the horror of the saw pits, rapids will be nothing to you."

Impulsively, Duncan caught her by her trim waist and whirled her around, her feet and skirts flying. He lowered her, laughing and breathless, still clasped in his hands. "You do wonders for a man's pride, Songbird. I should keep you with me always."

The shine in her eyes softened into an expectant glow, one he had no right to encourage. Duncan tried to change the direction of her thoughts. "Since you have decided on drawing straws, I'll have to trust to luck for your company on the river.''

"I think you are often lucky," she said.

He answered with a warning. ''It was not luck that left me all but penniless.''

Understanding dawned slowly within Julia. Duncan would not court her unless he could provide for their future together. He had kept them safe with such ease that she had never thought of him as having uncertain prospects.

''I believe in you,'' she said with a fierce emphasis that caused his hands to tighten at her waist. Recklessly, she added, ''Most of these men may be headed for disappointment, but you will gain your fortune in the Klondike. I know it.''

For a moment she thought—hoped—he would kiss her. But he simply tucked her arm beneath his once more and led her toward another tug-of-war. ''The future can't be foretold.'' After a momentary silence, he added a quiet promise that left her as breathless as he had when he whirled her. ''I swear to you, Julia, I mean to do everything under my power to prove you right.''

That night, voices buzzed around every camp fire, sounding louder than before. Julia heard snatches of conversation as men talked of the Klondike, where they would discover nuggets like Easter eggs hidden in the grass. Laughter rang through the camp while bets were placed. Who would be first down the Yukon? Who would be first to find gold? Who would be the first millionaire?

The days were so long now that sparrows sang nearly all the clock around. Duncan and Chambers worked exhausting hours to finish their three boats. Ben helped, but was inclined to linger in conversation or simply stand and dream.

''You won't find gold that way,'' Julia told him, snapping the young redhead out of still another reverie.

Four days after the Queen's birthday celebration, Julia watched the men seal seams with hemp heavily soaked in tar. As she wrinkled her nose at the smell, Hannah arrived with Officer Gray. "We're inspecting the boats," she said cheerfully.

"One of us is," the officer reproached her in his gentle Canadian accent. He walked around the newly finished boat, hazel eyes alert. "Gentlemen, I'm afraid you have shorted yourselves on oakum." He indicated a seam near Chambers. "As Inspector Steel has warned, 'Build strong, not a floating coffin.'"

Apparently smarting from his mild correction, Hannah said, "You are a paragon, Officer Gray. Do you never accept less than perfection?"

"Not where men's lives are concerned," he answered.

"I believe you are altogether too rigid," Hannah exclaimed and with a flourish turned and started away.

"More oakum there," the Mountie ordered crisply and strode after her.

Several yards down the lake, they stopped. Julia wasn't quite sure how it happened but thought Hannah engineered it, for Edmund's touch on her shoulder somehow swung her around and into his arms. He held her, looking startled, then slowly lowered his head for a shockingly public kiss.

"Score one for the Queen's man," Duncan said with a grin.

Julia shook her head. "I rather think the score belongs to Hannah."

For a moment, their gazes held, shutting others out. She wished Chambers were a good mile away. Slush lapped against her boot. She moved her foot absently, then glanced down and saw the lake water far above its bank. "What's happened?"

"Breakup," the trapper said with heavy satisfaction. "That's why we didn't put our boats in the water."

Up and down the shore, shouting men fought to pull out craft they had launched too soon into a narrow channel of open water. Enormous blocks of ice ground against the fragile wood. The entire four-mile-wide block of lake ice creaked and groaned, looking as if it had come to life.

Even the implacable trapper showed a glimmer of anticipation. "Folks will be settin' out on the heels of the ice and
most likely run into a jam at the outlet."

"We'll be right behind them," Duncan said as he prepared to add a sealing layer of pitch to the oakum-soaked
hemp.

By morning the trapper's prophecy proved true. Hundreds of boats followed the grinding ice as it worked its way
through the lakes that fed into the Yukon River. Julia
paused in loading provisions to watch the first travelers pass
their camp. One boasted a blanket sail while another had
stretched a set of men's long underwear from the mast.
Musical instruments sprang from hundreds of packs. Ecstatic voices rang from shore to shore.

She felt as if she could dance across the water. It looked
as if one could leap from boat to boat. Warming the nugget at her throat, she assured herself that her father had
found his claim and would show Duncan how to find gold
enough for a fleet of trawlers—and for a family.

As if her thoughts drew him, Duncan circled one arm
around her waist. She smiled at him. "We'll never see such
a sight again."

He agreed. "Most of them seem to think they're sourdoughs already."

"And what is that?" she asked, laughing as she thought
of the pancakes she had disliked in Dyea.

Chambers offered a crude answer. "Sourdough? Hell,
that's an easy one. A fellow ain't a sourdough until he's
shot a bear and slept with a squaw." He spat carelessly.
"Maybe it's the other way around."

As Julia stiffened, Duncan set her behind him. Her
throat tightened when she saw anger blaze in his face.
"You'll apologize to Miss Everett."

An unpleasant challenge lit the trapper's face. He
straightened, his hands in wary readiness. "Maybe you
haven't noticed, Adair. I ain't the apologizing type."

"Please don't," Julia said, aware that a fight had been
building between the two for months.

"Go back to camp, Julia," Duncan said, his voice hard.

Chambers's expression became malicious. "Better listen, if you don't wanta watch him get whipped."

She took one step backward. A lump in her throat made breathing difficult. Part of her longed to see Duncan smash the smug look from the trapper's face, but most of her dreaded violence.

Gently, Belle took her hand. "Julia, you had better come with me."

Julia shook her head.

Chambers threw a punch while Duncan was stripping off his shirt. Reeling, Duncan went down on one knee. The next blow grazed him as he slung away the shirt, then with whiplike grace he charged the trapper. His punch landed squarely.

Chambers shook his head, then circled more warily. His next blows grazed Duncan's head and, with horror, Julia knew that he aimed for the healed scar at the temple. Avoiding the blows, Duncan traded solid body punches. Julia winced at the thud of fists against flesh. With increasing despair, she realized they were evenly matched. Chambers was heavier, but Duncan more skilled. That only meant the fight would take longer to settle.

Nearby men watched, but no one stepped in to stop the fight. She looked at them, wanting to appeal for help, and realized they were making wagers.

This was not at all like the shipboard bouts. They had been a game. This was deadly and frightening. The two men fought in silence except for grunts and the sickening smack of their fists.

Julia gasped as another of Chambers's blows connected. Duncan blinked and shook his head, momentarily clutching the trapper. They broke apart and faced each other warily. Blood trickled from Chambers's lip. Duncan's right cheek was already bruising from the first unexpected blow.

A strong voice interrupted. "Hold on, there!" Swinging around, Julia recognized the Lion of the Yukon, feet braced, expression stern. Inspector Steele was a man with a formidable physique. According to Edmund, he was as quick and as fair as he was strong. With relief, she heard iron in his voice as he ordered the fighters to stop.

Both looked as if they meant to defy him, then with obvious reluctance shook hands. Belle hugged Julia. "It's all right now. It's over." Her eyes shone as she watched the inspector stride away. "I have never seen a grander looking man."

Duncan picked up his shirt and walked over to them. Ignoring Belle's interested study of his gleaming chest, he said shortly, "I told you to go back to camp."

"Did you think I could?"

A muscle twitched in his jaw. Tentatively, she raised one hand to touch his bruised cheek. He captured her hand and after an electric moment, kissed her palm. Shivers shot through her.

Beside them, Belle gave a lustful sigh. Duncan lowered Julia's hand, acknowledging the showgirl at last. "Let's get the supplies loaded. We'll soon be starting out."

# Chapter Fifteen

Cowpunchers from New Mexico herded sheep onto barges from a corral of packed snow. Their high-pitched cries rang over the bleating of the sheep and a medley of other sounds as the camp prepared to launch.

The sisters with the sewing machines set out with a petticoat for a sail. Their voices raised in a chorus of "Onward Christian Soldiers," a triumphant tune soon taken up by others. Feeling as if she would expire of impatience if they didn't launch at once, Julia tucked a packet of wild onions into one of the heavily loaded double-enders.

They had all worn themselves out loading the tons of supplies. Now at last, they were about to start. As the showgirls gathered, Julia pinched five stiff grass stems into uneven lengths. "The one who draws the shortest will ride with Mr. Chambers." She paused for a silent prayer that she would not draw the short straw. Since the fight interrupted by Inspector Steele, Chambers and Duncan had held an uneasy peace, but Julia wanted more than ever to have nothing to do with the trapper.

"The next two lengths drawn will travel with Duncan," she said and resisted closing her eyes for another quick prayer. The girls would be sure to notice and make her the point of their fun. "Those who draw the longest two straws are to ride in the third boat with Ben at the tiller."

"Chambers is more able than Ben," Tilly objected. "He ought to take two."

It had not occurred to Julia to send more than one unfortunate passenger with the trapper. To Tilly, she said simply, "Draw your straw."

With a shrug, Tilly pulled a grass stem from Julia's tightly closed fist. She held it, waiting with interest while the others chose. Hannah would ride with Chambers, Vida and Belle with Duncan, Tilly and Julia with Ben.

Lightly, Duncan rested his palm against the back of Julia's neck. "Once again, shunned by Lady Luck."

She looked up at him, longing to beg Belle or Vida to trade places. "It only means fortune is poised to turn."

His hand rested for a moment longer against her skin, flooding her with tenderness, then he returned to the mast where he was tacking into place the taffeta skirt he had forbidden her to wear. Her ruffled petticoats already fluttered from the other two masts. Troubled by her longing for Duncan, and feeling that her innermost secrets were tacked into public view on the masts, Julia stepped into the boat with Ben.

Tilly leaned over to ruffle the young man's hair. "You're a nice-lookin' lad and it's not that I'd bruise your pride, but it's my way to put money on a sure thing."

With that, she climbed into Chambers's boat beside Hannah. Rather than looking insulted, Ben beamed with pleasure. As Julia returned his smile, she hoped he would not again test the limits of their friendship.

At last, they set out, scudding down the lake in a flotilla. Voices carried across the water. People sang a dozen songs in a dozen voices. Others shouted wagers.

Ben stood in the stern working the tiller while ice splinters chimed musically against the sides of the boats. It would be days yet before they stepped ashore at Dawson City, but the last of the journey had begun and Julia's soul filled with song.

The mountains had never looked grander. Snow iced their jagged peaks, while the sides swept up from the shore in a haze of blue. The majestic reflection was sprinkled with hundreds upon hundreds of boats only yards apart. From Chambers's double-ender, Hannah pointed out the blue reflection of mountains sprinkled with vessels, calling, "We're like polka dots on a blue curtain."

The day was clear and cold. A strong wind stirred the water so they seemed to fly down the chain of lakes and connecting streams. Julia's mood sobered whenever they spotted wreckage where a boat had been crushed by ice in the first frantic rush to get underway.

A custom house stood on the shore at the foot of Tagish Lake. Edmund had numbered their vessels, explaining that the mounted police would keep track of their passage and know which boats failed to make the next stretch. "You will notice redcoats at several sites," he told them soberly.

Hannah answered that she wanted to see only one and received a rare dimpled smile from Edmund, who expected to be sent on to Dawson City within weeks.

They camped near the custom house for a cooked meal and a few hours' sleep, but with daylight almost continuous and gold fever sizzling from boat to boat, no one wanted to stop for long. The current rushed past as if mocking the need for food or sleep. At eleven at night, the sun still slanted across the mountains.

They were off again when the sun reappeared after its brief journey behind the hills. Late the second afternoon, they entered Six-Mile River where many boat-shaped islands loomed from the water, splitting the current. Showing weariness, Ben fought to keep the boat from the suction of brush-choked side channels. Several hapless voyagers were already grounded in shallow water or fighting their way out of false channels.

As Julia looked back to see how the rest of their party was faring, Ben yelped. She swung around to see an island coming up fast. Grabbing an oar, she leaned over the side and thrust furiously against the pull of the current. Water sprayed up, soaking her face and hair.

With a grinding crunch, the bow came to a stop in sand. The stern swung forward with the current and ground against the island. Apologetically, Ben said, "I'll have to shove it off."

She clung to the gunwale while he stepped into knee-deep water. Though he shoved with all his strength, the current held the boat fast. In the main channel, Vida and Belle shouted and waved while Duncan's double-ender swept by.

Julia felt a wash of abandonment. They were going on and she was trapped. Pulling her skirt between her legs, she anchored it under her belt and stepped into the water. The icy temperature made her gasp. "You'll do better without my weight," she told Ben.

He nodded and again thrust his shoulder against the bow. Julia hesitated on the bank, then waded to his side and shoved with him. The boat swayed, grated against sand, then settled back. Her feet were numb with cold. Trying not to think of the cold, she thrust her full weight in unison with his. The boat lurched into the current with Ben clinging to the side. Julia's hands slid free and she splashed face down into the water.

Wide-eyed, she stared into crystal blurs. An eternity of seconds passed while she struggled against current and water-logged skirts. Then strong hands grasped her waist, plucked her out and swung her onto the shore. She burrowed into Duncan's arms, seeking warmth without wondering or caring how he had so miraculously appeared. From shouts downriver, she knew that Chambers was helping Ben with the wayward boat. "C-cold," she gasped.

Keeping one arm tightly around her, Duncan led her along the bank. "We'll set up camp here. You have to get dry at once." Her feet were so cold she could hardly move them, and she kept tripping over roots and driftwood. Duncan lifted her into his arms and carried her to a clearing, where he swiftly built a driftwood fire. Setting Julia beside it, he ordered her out of her clothes. The women gathered around, shielding her with a blanket. Her fingers were so numb she couldn't manage the buttons. Clicking her tongue in distress, Tilly moved in to help.

"What about Ben?" Julia gasped.

"Don't worry," Tilly assured her. "Chambers is getting him into dry clothes."

Even after she had been dried and wrapped in a blanket, Julia couldn't stop shivering. Duncan lifted her onto his lap. As she clung to the warmth of his body, he said quietly, "The next time we run into trouble, stay inside the boat. One of us will be along to help."

"But you went on by," she said in a forlorn voice. "I thought you wouldn't stop until you reached Dawson City and that I would never get there." The last words came out in an anguished rush. She raised her head in apology and saw such tenderness that her breath caught.

"Julia," he said seriously. "I will always come back for you."

She became conscious of his heartbeat and of the life-giving warmth produced by his blood. The women were preparing dinner; they seemed to fade into the distance. Even the cold slap and rush of the river became muted. She raised her arms around Duncan's shoulders as he kissed her. His breath sent heat coursing through her body, warming her at last.

Somewhere down the island, a rifle blasted. Julia jerked upright. "It's Chambers and Ben," Duncan explained. "Hunting for ducks. If Chambers is the sure shot I think, we'll have fresh game for dinner."

She hadn't thought of the others, only of the yearning that overwhelmed her while Duncan warmed her with his body. She should feel embarrassed by so public a kiss, but the women's smiles didn't bother her any more than the knowledge that her wool dress and more intimate garments were spread to dry near the fire.

"We'll face Miles Canyon tomorrow," Duncan said. "Try to rest tonight."

Clutching the blanket more tightly, she nestled into his embrace, thinking she could sleep happily if only he would hold her like this. Then with a new stirring deep within her body, she knew that if he held her all night, she would not sleep at all.

Hours later, after feasting on two plucked and roasted ducks shared eight ways, Julia lay awake in the half-light inside the tent. Near her, the showgirls slept soundly. So did Duncan. Julia realized she had learned to know his breathing and loved to listen to it. Nights would not be the same away from that familiar comforting sound. Turning restlessly, she longed for sleep.

* * *

Long before they reached Miles Canyon, they heard the roar as the river funneled to a third of its width and thundered between rock walls fifty to a hundred feet high. Fighting the current, Ben swung the boat to shore. "Duncan means to take a look before we risk the canyon."

They pulled into an eddy along a low beach where hundreds of others were doing the same. People shouted above the roar of the water. Their faces were white, their expressions strained. Many had raised tents. They milled around, afraid to go on and unable to go back.

In a scow nearby, a woman wrung her hands in anguish, pleading with her husband, who stood on shore. "Don't try to run it, George. You promised you wouldn't."

Grim-faced, he jammed his hands in his pockets. "The professional pilots are asking twenty-five dollars to put a boat through. That's a sizable fee, Annie."

"But you heard—more than a hundred boats have broken on the rocks. At least ten men have drowned." The woman began to cry while her husband stared stony-faced toward the black opening in the canyon walls.

With a quaver of fear, Julia looked away from the terrible invitation of the canyon and saw that Duncan and Chambers had started up a trail to the top. Scrambling over the canvas-covered provisions in the bow, she ran after them.

Hundreds of people were portaging their goods around the canyon as they had hauled them over the Chilkoot Pass. At the brink of the straight rock walls, Duncan and Chambers stood with a line of men peering down. Most had awed expressions. Trembling, Julia grasped Duncan's arm. The sheer drop made her feel weak with vertigo.

Below, the river boiled and heaved. Waves stood like fences across the frothing surface. Geysers erupted. The great force flung between unyielding stone walls threw the center into a ridge several feet high. "You want to stick to the ridge," Chambers said as a boat flashed into the canyon as if to prove his words by example. To Julia, it looked like a child's toy. The men on the bluff fell silent until cheers from downriver told them the craft had survived.

She began to realize that Chambers had run the canyon before. As he pointed out the safest route, anticipation glowed within Duncan. Protest lodged in Julia's throat while she followed the two men along the gorge. The sheer basalt walls looked like hexagonal columns melded together with the torrent of the river speeding between. At midpoint, the water had carved an immense circular court in the canyon walls. Chambers grunted. "A boat can be held in that pool for days. Get through and you dance to the tune of the Squaw Rapids and White Rapids farther on."

Duncan nodded while Julia looked at him with horror. When he started up the trail, she ran after him. "You're not thinking of going through that?"

She knew she sounded like the woman in the scow. Duncan looked as stubborn as the man. Still, she persisted. "You're a seaman, not a river runner."

She suspected he would not give in because Chambers might think less of him. She didn't care what that man thought, but her argument broke off at a change in the sound of men's shouts.

Nerves raw, she followed Duncan to the edge of the gorge. Far below, a raft with two men aboard had struck a rock and momentarily hung against it. Julia clutched Duncan's arm, watching helplessly as the raging current poured under the raft. The raft tilted. Men and supplies flew into the water. The emptied raft shot out of sight.

It had taken just seconds, but the scene was engraved in her mind. "There!" a man shouted. One of the victims struggled in the water, then disappeared. Duncan pulled Julia to him, pressing her face into his shoulder.

Grimly, he said, "They may swim free below." His tone belied his words. Julia's memory held a frozen image of the raft with the men still aboard, as if by thinking of it she could will time backward and give them a second chance. Passionately, she said, "You must not risk the canyon."

He didn't answer and she knew he was determined to try it. In a frantic plea, she gestured toward the crowds. "See all these who are portaging. Duncan, we can do that."

"You women will walk the trail along the top of the gorge," he said. "We'll pick you up below."

She ran after him as long strides carried him to the beach where the entertainers waited uneasily. "How will I ever reach Dawson City if you are drowned?"

His answer was to tilt her chin upward and kiss her in full view of hundreds of people. For Julia, there was no pleasure in that kiss. Wrenching free, she appealed to the showgirls. "Can't any of you talk to him?"

Ben licked his lips nervously, as if wondering if his manhood depended on running the canyon. Duncan clamped a hand over his shoulder. "I'll count on you to escort the women over the trail. They'll need a man to see them safely to the end."

Hannah reached blindly for Julia, then pointed toward a crowd. Inspector Steele's voice could be heard over the thunder of the river. "There are many of our countrymen who have said that the mounted police make the laws as they go along, and I am going to do so now, for your own good."

Men who had learned to trust Steele's competence at Chilkoot Summit and at the lakes waited eagerly for instruction. He gave it in concrete terms. "No women or children will be taken in the boats. If they are strong enough to come to the Klondike, they can walk the five miles of grassy bank to the foot of the White Horse."

Most of the prospectors carried neither woman nor child and muttered agreement, but Steele's next order shook them. No vessel would be allowed into the canyon until it was first pronounced seaworthy by his officers. From Hannah's suddenly recovered spirits, Julia knew that Edmund Gray was among them.

Steele's voice boomed over the people's objections. "Anybody who breaks any of these rules will be fined one hundred dollars."

As more men crowded around the inspector, Julia turned to Duncan. "Now, will you admit the danger in that maelstrom?"

Steele's words might have been meant for other men. After all, Duncan had already decided the women were to walk. Impatiently, he asked, "Would you have me pay another for something I can do myself?"

"Are we so low on funds?" The question made her pause. She had committed her father unknowingly to a share of mounting expenses. Even so, she pressed both hands to Duncan's chest, trying to force reason into him. "What is seventy-five dollars for a professional pilot? We have all the goldfields ahead."

"Julia," Duncan answered. "Show some faith in me. I've handled boats all my life."

Fear clutched her, but he tilted her chin upward and kissed her into silence. The knowledge that she loved him was like a door opening into her heart. *She loved him*. And she was about to lose him.

She grasped the front of his shirt, but he pried her hands free with fresh impatience. "We'll meet beyond the rapids," he said over the roar of the river, then stepped into the stern of his boat.

A dreadful sense of loss drove all other thoughts from her. She darted to the water's edge to plead with him. There were no more words. There had never been words he would hear. Desperately, she glanced toward the black gap of the canyon's mouth. Duncan swung the bow into the unforgiving current. Without second thought, Julia splashed into the river and flung herself aboard.

The boat seemed to poise for a breathtaking interval. Around them, the water looked slick and oily. As Julia scrambled to right herself, the craft slid down a pitch of water into the cauldron. She clung to slats on the bottom while the boat plunged and leaped ahead. Fearful speed shot them past rock walls.

Above, people fringed the brink, watching. She couldn't tear her gaze from the river. The roar of crashing water eclipsed all else. It seemed impossible the boat could hold together through the terrible pounding.

Duncan ran it onto the ridge as Chambers had advised, but the weight of their load sent them into the trough with disaster a hand's breadth away. Water flung over the sides in drenching waves. Loose cans and an oar floated at Julia's feet. She scarcely noticed.

Duncan's face glowed with an unholy pleasure. After one horrifying glance at him, Julia stared at the rock walls and crashing waves. The double-ender shot through a comber, drenching her again, then swept into the circular chamber.

The boat caught on a crosscurrent, swung around and for a moment ran sternwise down the canyon. Before Duncan could change his position, the boat again swung around, leaping and jumping through driving fury.

Still with that devilish passion in his face, he set the boat into a crosscurrent that flung it onto the ridge. They plunged forward and were suddenly in calmer water. He pulled the boat into an eddy where several boats were beached. Broken planks swirled against the shore.

The joy in Duncan's face told her that this was what he loved best, trying his skill against nature's power. He stood in the stern, legs braced, uncaring that icy water soaked his clothes. Wind lifted his thick hair, exposing the scar at his temple. He looked like a pirate, especially when he turned glittering eyes toward Julia. "That was the easy one. White Horse Rapids lie ahead. Do you plan to ride them, too?"

On the shore, men lashed steering oars in place, preparing to send their boat on without a crew and collect it in saner water. Could an unmanned boat survive? After rocketing through the canyon, the men clearly feared the rapids. Debris washed against the shore, the wreckage of boats built painstakingly at Lindemann or Bennett.

Julia's hair had come unpinned and fell wildly around her shoulders. Water dripped from the ends. Her wool dress clung. She lifted the wet skirt from her knees, then let it fall. Duncan waited for an answer.

Despite the men on the banks and the wreckage washing against the boat, she threw his challenge back at him. "Go on? Why not? I doubt I can get much wetter."

With a sweep of the tiller, he sent the boat rushing downriver. She had expected him to argue, had even, she realized with dismay, meant to give in this time and join those walking the trail. Now, they were caught again in the current, the chance past. She wondered whose pride was more at fault.

# Chapter Sixteen

The river widened and became smooth, but not for long. Julia scarcely had time to regret her decision before they swung around a bend and were in a froth of white water. Jagged rocks pierced the surface, visible only as they passed. Waves burst around them. The boat felt alive.

Duncan shouted a joyful challenge at the river. Julia dug her nails into the slats and felt one nail break. They sped through a gorge with low rock walls, lashed by a fury of rock, current and foam. The boat leaped up and down and from side to side until Julia thought the roiling current would reshape the planks. A sheet of water streamed over the bow and drenched her. A wave spun them around. Duncan fought until the bow was again straight. The roar grew louder. As Julia thought it must be a waterfall, the river dropped. They surged forward, poised briefly, then fell eight feet with the torrent.

Spray and foam filled the world. The roar was everywhere. They exploded into sunlight. As water streamed from her, Julia felt an incredible rush of joy. A cheer burst from her throat. Jubilant, she unlashed a bucket and began to bail water from the bottom of the boat.

Duncan watched her with amazement. When Julia had thrown herself aboard, it was too late to turn back, and he had felt his heart clench. It was one thing to risk his own life. He looked forward to the challenge. To risk Julia's safety was entirely different.

Yet any screams stayed locked in her throat. Her eyes widened until they seemed to fill her face, but she didn't make a sound. Not even when they fell off the ridge into the trough, racing past rock walls that could have crushed them. Instead of begging to be set ashore after Miles Canyon, she had dared him to take her through the rapids.

"You look like a drowned kitten," he told her. With a peal of laughter, she continued to bail water from the boat. Feeling drenched in her bright courage, he said, "We'll camp here tonight."

For at least a quarter of a mile, people lined the shore, stretching wet outfits to dry in the spring sun. Many worked to repair damaged vessels. At last a clear space appeared, and Duncan pulled the double-ender to the bank.

Gold fever rang through the voices of men preparing for the next stage of their journey. Those who had bested the obstacle of Miles Canyon and White Horse Rapids now saw wealth within reach. As Julia scrambled onto the beach, Chambers pulled the second boat alongside. She had completely forgotten that he, too, meant to run the canyon.

With honest enthusiasm, she called, "Congratulations, Mr. Chambers!"

To her surprise, he gave her a look of solid approval. "You have more courage than I ever reckoned you for, miss."

"Or less sense," she said ruefully, but was pleased with the compliment, the first pleasant words he had offered her.

Chambers helped set up the tent, but aimed a dour look toward the wet goods that must be spread on tarpaulins to dry. "I'll hike back for that last boat," he said, heading for the trail. "I'd a damned sight rather run the canyon then tend to housekeeping."

Julia's clothes felt as if they had come directly from her aunt's mahogany-framed ice chest. The exhilaration of beating the rapids slowed to admit common sense. She had to get dry. When the tent was up, she ducked inside with a canvas bag that held her few possessions.

The moment she eased the wool dress from her shoulders, the weight of absorbed water pulled it to the tent floor. Her cotton camisole and drawers clung to her skin.

Belatedly, she remembered that her only other outfit had been used for a sail.

"Julia," Duncan said from outside. "Here's a blanket."

With a startled shriek, she snatched up the wet dress.

He burst into the tent. "What's wrong?"

Clutching the dress as a shield, she stammered, "I thought you were coming in. I mean...you are in."

He had pulled off his shirt and undershirt. His wet trousers clung to his hips and legs. She stared at him, feeling as unsteady as she had when they were on the river.

In the dimness of the tent, his eyes darkened. He stepped toward her with the blanket, wrapped it around her and pulled her toward him. "Let me warm you."

The dress slipped from her nerveless fingers. The damp camisole was no barrier against his irresistible warmth. Her hands braced against his hair-roughened chest, her palms gingerly touching his bare skin. She felt sunlight still in his warm skin and slowly relaxed to absorb heat through her fingers and palms.

With one arm holding the blanket around her, he tipped her face up to look into her eyes. A mesmerizing tenderness in his expression dazed her. She wanted to be even closer, to forget restraint.

Duncan smoothed damp tendrils of hair from her temple. "Whatever possessed you to leap aboard? You were convinced I'd never make it through the canyon."

"That was why." She had slept in the same tent with him for weeks, but never felt such breathless intimacy. For the first time since Dyea, they were truly alone. Anticipation jittered through her, and she recognized the same poised suspense as when they hovered above the waterfall.

"What was why?" His gaze focused on her lips. His fingers stroked the soft skin of her throat and bare shoulder, leaving splintering sensations like sunlight on ripples.

She tried to order her thoughts. "Could I have spent hours hiking along the canyon rim, never knowing whether you had yet drowned?"

His smile began deep in his eyes, then slowly curved his lips. "Are you saying that you cared?"

From somewhere, a sense of caution kept her from revealing that she loved him. She felt as if she hardly knew him. The man who dared the canyon seemed new, exciting and dangerous. She said only, "I need you for safe escort to Dawson City."

"And nothing more?" Easing aside the strap of her camisole, he gently dried the skin beneath with his thumb. A shiver began at the spot and traveled all the way to her bare toes. "Julia?"

"I would not like to see you drowned," she admitted.

He slipped his arms around her, his roughened hands startling her skin. The freedom to touch him made her light-headed. Slowly, she let her hands creep to his back and discover the sleek shape of muscles she had admired for weeks. Her breasts brushed his chest, and she felt unable to breathe. The wet camisole made an erotic contrast to his heated skin. Then he lowered his mouth over hers, and she was able only to think of his kiss.

As he explored the sensitive shape of her lips, she clung to him, until she felt that her knees could no longer hold her. His hand slid down the blanket, curving over her bottom and holding her intimately.

She stiffened, shocked by hard pressure against her thigh, but his tongue pressed insistently between her lips. She was startled by the invasion, then lost to cascading emotions when he explored the sensitive inner surface. He withdrew and she moaned, "Please..."

"Julia," he said softly. "Kiss me."

In the moment that she looked into his darkened eyes, she became exquisitely aware of the pressure of his body, of his hand against the blanket covering her bottom, of her breasts all but bared against his naked chest and of a turbulent agitation that made her feel as if they were once again poised before the dangerous invitation of the canyon.

Slowly, she raised her arms to his shoulders. Sinking her fingers into the rich thickness of his hair, she drew his head toward her. Tentatively, she explored his lips with her mouth, then dared to press her tongue between them and caress the inner surface.

She felt the blanket slip to the floor. Her body shook as
if from cold, yet heat raced through her. Wherever his
hands stroked, she felt intensely aware of the touch, of heat
and of rising excitement.

He broke the kiss and pressed his lips to the curve of her
throat. She realized that he was shaking, too. "Julia...sweetheart," he said with difficulty. "I should not
have started this. We have to stop."

She didn't want to stop, and she was certain that he
didn't, either. If she continued to stroke him, to kiss him,
he would stay and then... Her imagination could not ven-
ture further. Against his cheek, she murmured, "I never
knew that kissing could feel like this."

"Neither did I." He straightened, looking distracted.

When she looked down, she saw that the damp camisole
was molded to her sensitized breasts, outlining the stiffened peaks. Very gently, he lifted the sheer muslin and drew
it outward, erasing the image. But then with a groan, as if
yielding to greater need, he bent forward and pressed his
lips to the damp fabric and with his tongue traced her nipple.

She gasped. When he drew the tip into his mouth, she
thought they must have drowned in the canyon, for no
earthly experience could so dazzle her entire body. He
raised his head, looking as entranced as she felt. "Julia."

Her name was musical when he said it. He moistened his
lips, then drew an unsteady breath and said her name again,
but with deeper purpose. "Julia. This has to stop."

She saw him steeling himself to leave her. Without pausing to think, she grasped the hem of the camisole and
peeled it off over her head. Wrapping her arms tightly
around him, she pressed her naked breasts boldly against
his chest, reveling in the soft roughness of his hair against
her skin.

She felt a change in him, the sense of a current caught
where there could be no turning back. When he kissed her
with an urgency that trembled through them both, she
knew he would not again try to leave her. Her knees weak-
ened and she sank with him onto the blanket.

He held her quiet for a moment, looking at her with an expression of wonder. Then he caressed her breast, brushing one thumb lightly over the nipple. She pressed her fingers into his hair, urging him closer. Against his lips, she murmured, "It's like the river, like a torrent that can't be stopped."

"It can be," he said with obvious effort. "Only say so."

She traced his lips with the tip of her tongue, urging deeper kisses. As Duncan thrust his tongue into the sweet warmth of her mouth, imitating the act that every nerve in his body cried out for, he drew on his will to slow his racing desire. All these weeks, he had longed for her, dreamed of her, and now she had become a seductress, so wildly tempting that he wanted to take her with quick, explosive thrusts. Shaking, he forced himself to wait.

The need to protect her was scarcely less than the yearning to possess her. Wild kisses drove out the last effort toward reason. Her fiery spirit masked a passion he had never suspected. He found it hard to believe she could be learning from him as they kissed.

The desire to bury himself in her hidden warmth nearly overwhelmed him. With trembling hands, he caressed her, fighting for a control that she instinctively resisted. His fingers brushed against the drawstrings of her cotton drawers, and she reached down to pull the ties loose.

Her eagerness astonished him while it sent his blood racing. He must have been mistaken to think her an innocent. He stroked lower with his fingers, discovering the delicate hidden part of her that every sense urged him to know completely. When she wriggled out of the last garment, he pressed kisses down her body.

He felt her surprise and trembling pleasure. She murmured his name in a husky moan. He reclaimed her lips, feeling he could never get enough of kissing her. Straightening long enough to strip off his clothes, he saw a marveling expression widen her eyes. Once again, he fought to quiet his growing urgency. She was looking at him as if she had never before seen a naked man.

He hesitated, but with a soft moan, she reached for him, urging him closer, lifting her hips so that his momentary doubt dissolved. He kissed her again, sinking into the sweet warmth of her arms and lips. At last, forcing himself to go slowly while longing to plunge, he joined their bodies. In dazed confusion, he felt a silken barrier. As if sensing his doubt, she held him tighter, instinctively urging him deeper.

For Julia, the brief sharp pain was quickly forgotten. Tantalizing waves rippled through her. She wanted more and learned quickly how to move with him to heighten the bright currents.

Their bodies were sheened with perspiration. Julia saw a tenderness in Duncan's expression that filled her with love. Even that dissolved into rapture. Closing her eyes, she let him launch her into a current that hurled her directly into the sun.

Long afterward, Duncan drew the blanket over them. As Julia cuddled close, the intensity of his feelings for her both thrilled and troubled him. She had been a virgin despite her fierce instinctive passion. The need to plan for their future sobered the soaring pleasure he felt.

He stroked the incredible softness of her skin while he made silent plans. Gently, he spoke her name. When she lifted her lashes with a look of sleepy pleasure, he said, "As soon as we reach Dawson, we'll book passage on a steamer to Seattle."

"What!" She sat straight up. "Seattle?"

Her shock startled him, but as he admired her naked body and remembered how eagerly she had shared it, he said, "I'm a fisherman, sweetheart, not a miner."

Julia felt in such a muddle that she couldn't sort out her thoughts. What had happened between them had been a result of the canyons and the rapids; it had felt like a continuation of that turbulent ride. Now Duncan said she was returning to Seattle with him, as if she had become his property. He was acting just as Aaron might have.

It was ludicrous to think of her dignified uncle so intimately engaged, and it was probably not mischance that he and Ruth were childless. Feeling betrayed, she exclaimed,

"Does every man try to control women with his strength of will? You sound a great deal like Aaron Ames."

Stung by the comparison, Duncan sat up to put his arm around her, reminding himself that her miserable uncle had caused her to distrust every man. "I can't say I enjoy the comparison, love, but yes, I believe most men wish to have the women they care for under their protection."

"Their protection? Is that the word you use?" She didn't want to argue, but the matter could not be set aside. She thought of Ruth quaking while her husband raged over some small mistake. He provided a roof and food, Aaron always reminded Ruth loudly. That was the "protection" Julia had escaped.

Confused and troubled, she thought of the single goal that carried her from Seattle, over the Chilkoot Trail and down the chain of rivers and lakes. "I must locate my father. I won't feel complete until I know him."

Duncan felt as if she had struck him. Julia had given herself with a joyful passion that raised him to heights he had never before experienced. He wanted to protect and hold her always. Yet here she was in his arms, looking even more appealing than before with the flush of their love-making still in her face—saying that he was not enough to make her feel complete.

Trying to mask a sense of injury, he sat up, lifting her with him. "You don't know Joseph Everett," he said, feeling lessened by the need to argue at such a time. "But you had better know this, Julia. The men who came here before the rush treasured solitude. That kind of man may not welcome a daughter thrust suddenly into his life."

Despite the warning, Julia's eyes shone. "If he gave my mother the joy that you have given me, then he must be wonderful." There was no way to answer that but to kiss her, and she responded as eagerly but more knowledgeably than before. Desire returned with an urgency that astonished him. No woman had ever made him feel so desperate for her kisses. As they discovered new ways to lift each other to unimagined heights, he knew he would never get enough of loving her. He knew, too, that lovemaking might put off argument, but never solve it.

Much later, as Julia nestled in his arms glowing with satisfied passion, Duncan tried again to plan. He thought that for most of an unhappy life, Julia had spun dreams around a peerless father while she was treated as a servant by her uncle. The dreams had strengthened her will and made her into the woman he loved. But she couldn't put them aside. This was not the time to argue.

He kissed her gently. "The others will be arriving soon, sweetheart. We must get dressed."

She sat up with a dreamy expression that made him want to take her into his arms again. Instead, as he got to his feet and pulled on his trousers, he made a silent promise. Whatever Julia might find in Dawson City, whatever goals she might have, her future was forever bound to his.

When Duncan left the tent, Julia looked at her soggy wool dress with distaste. She couldn't wear that. She felt time passing. How long would it take the troupe to hike the distance covered so swiftly by boat?

Gingerly lifting the tent flap, she poked her head through and located Duncan. He was still bare from the waist up. He was hauling wet gear to the tarpaulin. For a moment, she admired him. She had known at Miles Canyon that she loved him and yet the need for caution clutched her. After escaping the domination of her uncle, she was not ready to place herself under the rule of another strong man, however ecstatic he made her feel.

When he looked her way, she said quickly, "I have nothing to wear. Perhaps . . . the sail?"

He glanced at the taffeta dress, which hung limp from the mast, then pulled a canvas bag from the boat and hauled out a pair of pants and a shirt. "They're miles too big, but they're dry."

"But I can't . . ." Her voice faded. She was far past arguing about propriety. And she would not be the only woman wearing trousers. Accepting the clothing, she ducked into the tent.

As the flap closed behind her, Duncan slung a bag of flour onto one shoulder. There was satisfaction in hard work when that stubborn streak gleamed in Julia's eyes. Whatever impossible goal she might be set upon attaining, she belonged with him, and he meant to convince her of that.

An inner voice mocked him. Convince her how? By offering to share a bedroom with her in a home that belonged to his mother and stepfather? Julia would be a favorite with his younger brothers and sisters, he told himself cynically. They would keep her company while he was at sea, and she could watch over them while the older couple were out.

He slammed the flour onto the tarp. If that was the best he could offer, he had better keep his great love to himself. He couldn't imagine life without Julia. Reaching for another soggy bag, this one holding sugar, he vowed again to get the cost of a trawler from his stepbrother.

Julia came from the tent looking swamped by his clothes, and he broke into welcome laughter. His blue flannel shirt was knotted around her waist, the sleeves rolled above her wrists. The cuffs of his denim overalls were also rolled, but slipping precariously over her shoes while her hands were occupied in holding them up at her middle.

She looked like the saddest waif from the Seattle wharf. Still chuckling despite her silent reproach, he rummaged through the supplies for a length of cord. After wrapping it around her waist and knotting it, he looked into her face. "Sweetheart, it may take awhile, but—"

She broke in before he could mention Seattle again. "I have apparently taken your only dry shirt."

Duncan sensed the natural warmth of her body heating the fibers of his clothing. When he reclaimed the shirt and trousers, her fragrance would linger. Such thoughts were not helping him think clearly. Reaching for a steady tone, he said, "You won't have to hike the trail again. With the Yukon open, steamers will come up the river to Dawson City. As soon as I settle matters with Owen, we'll book passage home."

Julia pictured a leisurely voyage with Duncan, then set temptation aside. "Home?" she repeated. "Where is that? I understood you were still living with your family."

He felt accused, as if he were the lazy son, rather than Owen. The unfairness sent a rush of blood into his face.

For five years, he had been the sole support of his mother. He remained at home after his mother's remarriage so he could save funds for a trawler of his own, and he'd worked damned hard to accomplish it.

"I've made a mistake," he said, his voice low. "I've told you too damned much. I see you think me worthless, as if I'll never possess more than the shirt on my back."

"Which you have generously shared," she said, alarmed to see the scar whiten at his temple.

She saw him keeping his temper with an effort. "It's true I have little now," he said. "I asked you once to have faith in me. Now I'm asking again. A good hand and a strong back can always find work aboard Seattle trawlers. If the fishing's good, I can earn enough in one season to settle us in a home of our own."

Julia saw his eyes narrow as if he winced at the thought of working for other men. "You mentioned a loan to repair the *Patience*," she said, still trying to undo the anger her hasty words had caused.

"Exactly." Duncan snapped the promise, not meaning to lash her with it, but able to keep hurt from his voice only by translating the hurt into anger. They had shared each other's bodies with greater pleasure than he had dreamed possible. Now, she apparently regretted it.

If her regret stemmed from modesty, it would be understandable. But it was his lack of a sound financial standing that troubled her. Grimly, he attempted to set her mind at ease. "I'll ask the banker to hold off on repayment until the *Patience* brings in her first catch. And Owen owes me for the *Fortune*. Are you forgetting that?"

Julia felt a cold wash of guilt. Because she had urged him to love her, Duncan felt responsible for her. She knew what fishing meant to him. He became lyrical when he spoke of it. If he set up a home, he might have to put off the purchase of a trawler for years, while their love grew edged and resentful.

She had seen his eyes darken when he talked about working for other men. He detested the idea. As for Owen, she had heard the doubts about his stepbrother and could not believe Duncan trusted him.

Before she could lose her courage, she refused him. "What happened between us was from the insanity of the canyon passage. Feelings I never imagined made me..." She paused, her nerve failing. "Made me urge you to continue...when you would have stopped." She finished with an effort. "I've been told I am as heedless as my mother— but that's no reason for you to feel responsible for me."

It was easier to watch the clouds scudding overhead than to look at Duncan. When she forced her gaze to his face, she glimpsed surprise, disbelief, possibly anger, surely sympathy, but then as her hopes rose his expression grew remote.

Duncan fought a hot rise of anger. What else, after such a speech? She sounded as if he had disappointed her. He knew that wasn't true and wanted to kiss her into confessing that she enjoyed his lovemaking. Instead, he faced a bitter truth. Tightly controlling his voice, he said, "Why rebuke yourself, sweetheart? Why not simply say you have no interest in sharing the life of a penniless fisherman?"

He expected an apology, but received a burst of fury. "Duncan Adair, if I believed it right, I would share a mud hovel, but I will not hold you back. Nor will you keep me from locating my father."

She spun away, tripping over one slipping pant cuff, and began to spread her wet clothes on the tarpaulin to dry. He watched in silence made more painful by the longing to hold her. She looked vulnerable in the oversize clothing. Tendrils of drying hair curled around her face. The loose, unruly locks reminded him of her eager response to lovemaking. The pins that held her hair in a proper coil were somewhere at the bottom of the rapids or washed ashore with the wreckage of hapless boats. He felt as if some of that wreckage was within himself.

Damning them both for a rift that seemed to grow wider with every word they spoke to each other, he returned to the work of hauling wet provisions onto the canvas to dry. Long minutes later, a hail rang from up the beach. Duncan heard relief in Julia's voice as she called a welcome to Ben and the showgirls.

# *Chapter Seventeen*

Hannah ran toward them showing little sign of having hiked five miles. Eyes alight, she demanded of Julia, "Whatever are you wearing?"

"The only dry clothing available," Julia said, afraid to look at Duncan for fear the others would see too much in her expression. The past few minutes seared her, the argument repeating in her mind until she wanted to clap her hands over her ears.

"Never mind," Ben said warmly. "You look just fine, Miss Julia." His admiration made her answer with caution. Images flashed of herself and Duncan rolling together, grabbing at each other, kissing.... She risked a glance and saw that his feet were braced, his shoulders stiff as if he were denying that anything had happened.

That didn't make it untrue. The experience gave her new eyes as she turned again to Ben. She knew now what he had in mind when he shoved her to the floor of the tent at Sheep Camp. She felt far less willing to forgive him.

"We made it through, as you see," she told him, teasing him for his perfectly reasonable fear of the canyon. "The ride was exhilarating."

Duncan turned, his brows raised as if to remind her that the river trip was only the start of the exhilaration. As if she needed to be reminded. She could hardly think of anything else. Except for the conflict, when he had become as stubborn as Aaron in thinking he might tell her what to do.

She had often noticed that her uncle became most obstinate when he was most in the wrong and hoped Duncan saw a warning in the glance she returned. Eyes dancing, Hannah said, "Officer Gray threatened to hold our third boat against the hundred-dollar fine for taking a woman through the canyon. I told him exactly what I thought of that."

Julia's moment of pride collapsed. She hadn't given a thought to Inspector Steele's warning. Now guilt wrenched her. It was awful enough that she had shamelessly urged Duncan to... She had also cost the group the enormous sum of a hundred dollars. If she looked at him now, the group would surely see their entire argument in their expressions.

"You should have heard her," Tilly added. "Hannah told the Mountie to his face that he didn't know the first thing about love. That set him back."

Duncan laughed, a harsh sound without humor. "I doubt the Mountie is the first man to be so accused."

Julia felt herself tighten. She would not get into an argument. The laughing pleasure in the dancer's face said she had enjoyed every second of her confrontation with the handsome Mountie. "Well, go on. How did Officer Gray reply?"

"He said he was simply following orders." Fondly, Hannah added, "Edmund does enjoy his orders."

Belle sank onto a corner of the tarpaulin beside Vida, a sparkle in her eyes despite her weariness. "That's what he said, all right, but that devilish dimple of his was showing all the while."

It seemed to Julia that Hannah enjoyed arguing with Edmund Gray even more than she enjoyed kissing him. After arguing with Duncan, Julia felt as if there were blades gathered inside her. She was ready to flash out at his next sharp word, but all she really wanted was to be held and kissed.

With an effort, she asked, "How did it end?"

Lightly, Hannah answered, "Why, I paid the fine. Mr. Chambers will be here with the boat at any minute."

Duncan stepped between Ben and Julia, as if warning the younger man to keep his distance. She felt annoyed that he spoke for her by the gesture, then annoyed with herself, since she had no wish for Ben to stand near. Clearly, Duncan was not thinking of those wanton moments inside the tent. His attention was on the stowaway as he asked softly, "You paid the fine? How?"

Looking pleased with herself, Hannah said, "It seemed the thing to do. A woman caused the problem. Why should a woman not resolve it?"

With a glance at Julia, Duncan said, "I've found that women are often the cause of problems."

"That's unfair," Julia exclaimed. One sleeve unrolled over her fingertips. She shoved it back, wanting to ball her hand into a fist.

"My apology," he said with sarcasm. "I wouldn't want to make any *unjust* accusations."

He implied that she had done so. Refusing to repeat their argument for the amusement of the others, she lifted her chin. "If you are trying to find blame in our rescuing Hannah and bringing her into the troupe, then you are as solid in the heart as I'm beginning to believe you are in the head."

His brows shot up. "I am solid in the head? At least I'm willing to see beyond the next turn of the river."

Conscious of curious glances cast in their direction, Julia held to the subject of Hannah. "She might have frozen in that hideaway on deck."

"As I once told Julia," Hannah broke in, "I am not without funds."

"When did you tell her that?" Duncan asked softly, while his accusing gaze again questioned Julia. Sensing a storm building inside him, she answered. "Hannah is not exactly an entertainer."

Duncan shoved his thumbs into his belt. His feet were braced, and the scar at his temple looked white against his tan. Julia felt a sense of danger. In spaced words, he demanded, "What *exactly* is she?"

Hannah sank onto the tarp. She looked as if she wished she had kept her triumph to herself. Duncan's expression grew even darker. When he stepped toward her, she blurted, "My father is Simon Clark."

Duncan looked as if he had been struck. Words seemed to choke him. "The banker?" Hannah quailed as she nodded, then watched in fear as Duncan digested her surprising news.

"The banker who does not know his daughter's whereabouts?" Duncan said as he stepped closer to Hannah, a look of growing anger on his face. "What you are telling me on this godforsaken beach where I can do nothing about it is that you are the daughter of the one man who agreed to finance repairs to the *Patience!*"

A painful silence followed. Julia felt cold with dismay. Owen had deprived his stepbrother of two trawlers that were to be the start of a fleet. Now Hannah had innocently cast doubt over salvaging even one. And it's my fault, Julia told herself. I was the one to discover and shelter a stowaway. Feeling grieved, Julia clasped one of Hannah's hands.

Duncan ran his fingers through his hair, turned from the women to walk to the water's edge, then returned to ask in a deceptively gentle tone, "Miss Clark, forgive my curiosity, but what in blazes are you doing here?"

She looked up the trail as if hoping her Mountie would appear to rescue her, but there was no glint of a red jacket among the prospectors. She rose to her feet still clutching Julia's hand and said hopefully, "Father must believe in you, Duncan. He never risks money on less than a sterling investment."

For a moment, Julia thought he would shake her. Hannah gulped, looking as if she regretted the effort she had made to soothe him. Ben moved forward as if to intervene. A glance from Duncan made him step back.

"It's not her fault," Julia objected.

He glared from her to Hannah with such a dark look that neither dared speak. "Have the two of you conspired to drive me crazy? One with innocence and the other with secrets? The truth, Miss Clark. Now."

With a frightened rush of words, Hannah exclaimed, "Father is a hard man. You're right in that. It was without his knowledge that I worked as an artist's model!" She clasped her hands tightly together. "But the artist proved dishonorable. I had to escape Seattle."

In a reasoning tone, Tilly said, "Hannah's picture may beat us to Dawson."

Blanching, Hannah protested. "You're mistaken. He promised the works would go only into museums."

Vida's laugh caused a flush to come over Hannah's white cheeks. "His idea of a museum may not please handsome Officer Gray."

Hannah clasped Vida's hands. "You must never tell him. Never. Promise me. All of you."

"Better keep him out of the saloons," Tilly warned.

Hannah sank into horror. "My picture could not be all the way up here."

"Surely not," Julia agreed. She wrapped her arms around Hannah's trembling shoulders. Yet she couldn't help remembering that many remarkable items were on their way to the goldfields, some by way of ships steaming the long way around to the mouth of the Yukon River.

Duncan wheeled away from the women and strode down the beach, feeling as if his guts were in knots. Back in Seattle, Clark must be going through hell worrying about his daughter. Unless he had completely disowned her. In any case, word of her whereabouts must be sent as soon as possible.

Obviously, there would be no loan for the *Patience*. The only hope of getting another boat lay with Owen—who had never yet helped anyone but himself. A possibility Duncan had suppressed for weeks emerged. Julia's father had been in the Klondike when gold was first discovered. All these thousands of people streaming north were arriving after the fact and couldn't see it.

But Everett had been there at the right time, a time when threadbare miners dug shovels into the earth and came up rich beyond belief. Everett could easily be among them. If he was a rich man, he wasn't likely to give his daughter in marriage to a fisherman with nothing to his name but one trawler with its bow smashed in and another burned to embers at the Skagway wharf.

Clouds of mosquitoes eventually drove him back to camp and the tent where the women had taken refuge. Absently, he noted that in the future they had better set up camp on high ground where the wind would discourage the pests.

The tired women had fallen asleep. Julia lay on her stomach, her hair like a cloud over her shoulders. Suppose she decided to stay in the Yukon with her father? With nothing but hopes to offer, Duncan knew he could never ask her to share his life. Until his prospects changed, he had better keep his hands and his heart to himself. Aching with the thought, he tried to stop thinking of the future until he was in a position to change it.

Julia slept restlessly, waking from a dream of Duncan to a sense of his nearness. For months she had longed for his touch, then for his kiss. Now she knew greater wonder was possible, but he had closed her out of his heart so that even a touch was banned. During a quick breakfast pestered by mosquitoes, he spoke little.

Duncan's experience with boats served them well when they sailed onto Lake Laberge. White-capped waves blustered over the thirty-mile-long lake, turning it into a miniature sea.

Along the shore, green leaves fluttered above white birch trunks. Chambers commented during a stop for lunch that the birch made him think of cancan dancers with their long white limbs and frilly skirts. There was a twinkle in his eyes, and Hannah answered gaily, "Why, Mr. Chambers, your gruff exterior hides the soul of a poet!"

At least, that gulf had narrowed, Julia told herself. Since her reckless ride through Miles Canyon, the trapper had treated her not only with respect but with kindness. Regretfully, she looked at Duncan and wondered if the rift between them would ever close.

With every lake crossed and every connecting stream traveled, excitement grew. Julia heard it in shouts from the flotilla accompanying them and in excited conversations over camp fires whenever they stopped to rest.

Finally, they were in the tremendous flow of the Yukon River. Banks of sand and gravel soared upward at every curve. The inner bank stretched away in low, densely timbered flats where mosquitoes made sleep nearly impossible and camping briefer than ever.

"There's a tale about them skeeters," Chambers said while they hovered near a smoky camp fire applying eucalyptus oil to faces and arms to discourage the pests. Urged to continue, he settled back on his heels. "Started with an Indian princess. She gave birth to a monster child that grew faster than normal and hunted just to watch things die."

Julia shuddered and looked at Duncan. He sat a short distance away, studying a guide to the river, looking so unreachable that her heart ached. At the same time, her spine stiffened. Duncan needn't think she would obligingly return to Seattle simply because he said so. They might find joy in each other at first, but life would surely grow bitter as he tried to provide for her while longing for his own ship. Bitter men gave harsher orders and expected quicker obedience.

For the first time, she wondered what Ruth had been like at her wedding and whether Aaron had dreams that grew sour with the years. There had been a picture of them in the parlor. With a frown, she tried to remember whether there had been happiness in their stiff pose. If so, life had turned Aaron hard. That must not happen to Duncan. Without her, he would earn another trawler. With her, he might never be able to do so.

The trapper's story became gorier. Ben edged protectively toward Julia. With an inward sigh, she gave her attention to the story. "This child was a boy," Chambers was saying. "He had sharp teeth and hair all over his body."

Julia's mind flashed a swift image of dark, curling hair over finely chiseled muscles, and she stared into the fire to keep her longing for Duncan from her face. To compare him to a monster was not exactly flattering. She smiled despite her unhappiness when she pictured his reaction to that.

"Why didn't the people kill it?" Vida asked.

"The chief was his uncle," Chambers reminded her. "So nobody said much, but pretty soon people from the tribe started disappearing. They figured this monster thing was to blame. Finally, the chief himself decided to drive the thing off. Hour after hour, the two of them wrestled. Hour after hour. And then the chief cast the creature into the fire.''

''Good for him!'' Belle exclaimed.

Ben reached for Julia's hand. She moved it into her lap so sharply that he sank back. She glanced again toward Duncan. He looked remote as he gazed down the river. Avidly, Tilly demanded, ''Was the evil thing destroyed?''

Chambers studied the camp fire as if seeing the match played out in the coals. A howl from some dogs on the beach made the women glance uneasily around. ''The monster burned like dry wood, then his voice rose from the flames, 'I will drink your blood for a thousand years.' Ashes rose from the fire and circled around. A cloud of them hovered and swirled, and each one turned into a giant mosquito.'' Chambers grinned. ''To this day, the evil thing drinks the blood of every man or woman who comes here.''

Vida slapped at a mosquito on her arm with such disgust that the spell was shattered. Everyone laughed with relief.

Duncan turned to look at the group around the fire, envying their closeness. The trip had changed and shaped them all. He had never expected to see the women entertained by the dour trapper.

He strolled along the shore, selected a rock and skipped it across the water. He felt that time was running out, but that was wrong. The truth was that he could only mark time as he waited to reach Dawson and learn what was to be found there.

Julia hoped for a father in a golden carriage. Suppose her fantasy proved true? He bent to select another stone and sent it flying. Suppose they both reached their goal. Julia would be caught into the arms of a wealthy, loving father, while Owen would hand over gold enough for a fleet.

With a bitter laugh, Duncan realized they might end this journey to find less than they had when they began. Could they turn then to each other?

At the camp fire, Julia swatted a mosquito from her skirt. The size of the insects was startling. She couldn't help wondering if the legend might hold some truth. She certainly felt as if a curse had fallen over her. For the hundredth time, she raised her glance to Duncan and saw him sauntering along the shore.

She longed to regain the easy friendship they had shared at Lake Bennett, or to repeat the passion they discovered later. Ben touched her hand. "Don't look so troubled, Miss Julia. It's just a story. You'll be safe in Dawson. I'll see that nobody bothers you."

She looked at him with dismay. During their brief stops along the river, Ben had become as pesky as the mosquitoes. She knew he felt guilty for having once attacked her and for causing her to fall into the water the day he grounded the boat. Because of that, she suffered his constant attention. But she expected soon to be free of him.

As she jerked her hand away, Chambers spoke quietly, "Don't go making promises you can't keep, boy. You'll be needing a place to stay while you figure out the best prospecting. You might as well come along with me for awhile. But I ain't planning to hang around Dawson while you moon over Miss Julia."

Ben looked as if he felt torn, and Julia said swiftly, "What a wonderful plan. With thousands headed that way, there can't be space left in Dawson large enough to raise even a small tent. Ben, you are fortunate in having a friend in Mr. Chambers."

Gratefully, she smiled at the trapper. He was not a man who would freely offer shelter to a neophyte. His offer was an apology for his earlier behavior. She forgave him freely in return for taking Ben from her path.

Duncan returned to the camp. Their gazes met and held. Longing swept over her so strongly that she nearly went to him, but his expression closed. He turned away and tossed a length of wood on the fire. The moment was lost in a shower of sparks.

# Chapter Eighteen

Cheechakos flooded into Dawson City, which was situated on a low flat between a scarred mountain and the rushing white torrent of the Klondike River. Every inch of the waterfront was full of boats, and still they came, the people on them whooping and hollering. Julia shrieked with the others. The tents and frame buildings crouched over the flat were the most exciting sight she had ever seen.

Men scrambled ashore, most in a fever to find and stake their claims. Those who had traveled all this way to sell luxuries to novelty-starved miners set up stalls, creating a carnival atmosphere. Duncan found space for his boat, and the other two were tied alongside. Julia clambered ashore, certain that even in this throng her heart would know her father.

He would be looking for her. He must have received the letter sent from Dyea months ago. Aaron had often complained dourly that she resembled her mother, although she doubted that her mother had ever risked sun enough to produce a sprinkling of freckles or a peeling nose.

How odd to think that she was several years older now than her mother had been at her death. This was a time to think of beginnings. Her heart pounded so hard she felt light-headed. What would she say to her father? What would he say to her? It wasn't something that could be planned. Her heart would tell her what to say, just as it would know him.

She started forward, so intent on searching for the al-
ready-loved face that she nearly tripped over a dog sleeping in the street. Duncan caught her arm. "Steady."

She smiled at him, longing to share her excitement, but
his face was closed. Chambers approached with Ben in tow.
"Reckon we'll be moving on."

The bright day seemed to fade slightly. For months, the
trapper had been her enemy, then he became her friend.
Feeling as if a close company was breaking up, she gave the
trapper a quick, fierce handshake, then clasped Ben's hand,
as well. "Good luck to both of you."

The showgirls looked as if they were lit from within by
excitement. Ahead men blocked the way. They were
watching a parade. Julia rose onto her toes to look over a
massive shoulder and glimpsed a dozen uniformed men
walking in single file. The ones at the front and rear carried rifles and wore cartridge belts. Each of the others carried a heavy bag.

"What is it?" she asked.

An old-timer grinned, revealing broken teeth. "That's
gold from Alex McDonald's claim, miss. One of the richest
in the Klondike. Every one of them bags weighs a whop-
ping seventy-five pounds."

"Seventy-five pounds," she breathed. "And there
are..." she counted quickly. "Ten! Why that's..." Her
voice trailed in awe. Then her heart pounded more quickly.
If McDonald's claim was one of the richest, others could
be nearly as rich. Perhaps the one belonging to her father
was rich.

Remembering Vida's light fingers, Julia looked sharply
toward her, but even Vida would not risk those guards. The
men marched toward the steamship that would carry the
gold to safekeeping. The natural confusion of the waterfront resumed. As Tilly pointed out a performing bear,
Hannah applauded a team of acrobats.

Dogs were everywhere, getting underfoot or chained in
teams preparing to haul provisions to the mines. The long,
drawn-out howl of the native malamute added to a pande-
monium of voices, music and the whine of a dozen sawmills.

One newcomer had brought a cow over the White Pass, then carried it by scow down the lakes and was now selling fresh milk at a shocking price. A few yards farther on, men gathered around a crate of chickens, placing bets on when the first egg would be laid. The woman with kittens set a sign against their basket asking double their weight in gold.

Julia's searching gaze flashed past gamblers in black broadcloth and ruffled shirts to well-dressed women, some wearing satin and a few Indian women wearing deerskin. Many of the newcomers sweated in their mackinaw blanket coats. Julia's glance skimmed over all of these to focus on men dressed comfortably in coats of deerskin or parkas of navy blue twill, the fronts open and hoods thrown back in deference to the warm weather.

As she looked from one unfamiliar face to another, her ebullience began to fade. Admiring glances lingered over her more often than was comfortable, but in none was there a gleam of recognition. Drawing on courage she would never have possessed in Seattle, she spoke to the next miner whose eyes caught hers. "Forgive me, sir, but are you acquainted with a man named Joseph Everett?"

"Everett?" He considered at length, then shook his head. "Sorry I can't help you, miss."

Duncan watched the animation begin to fade from Julia's eyes. If Everett had received his daughter's letter, the man should be here. He might not be expected to recognize her, but there were only a few decently dressed young women to interview.

The trail had left her vibrant with health, making a mockery of his early misgivings. As always, he felt touched by the scattering of freckles over her cheeks. He wanted to pull her close and kiss each one until the lost look in her eyes changed to trust.

He cursed himself silently. The last of their travel together had been pure hell. He ached so with wanting her that he walked away from camp most nights until he felt sure she would be asleep. He sent his boat ahead of the other two rather than watch sunlight dance in her bright hair while she rode with Ben. Even so, his mind filled with her until it was a wonder he hadn't led them all down one of the dozens of false channels.

Now the need to take hold of the future and shape it to suit them both came over him so strongly that his fists clenched. He cast a sharp glance at sourdoughs arguing over novelties set out for sale. Most of the population must have turned out to watch the cheechakos arrive, but none showed any resemblance to Julia.

He turned to see her standing as if frozen, staring at a frame building. He walked closer and cursed beneath his breath. Someone had transferred Julia's likeness from the photograph to a life-size representation. The painting was slightly more voluptuous, with the skirt lifted to reveal a trim ankle. The glittering expression on the painted lips and eyes had never crossed Julia's delicate features.

She swung around, her wide eyes distraught. "Do you see this? Seattle Songstress To Appear at the Bonanza Playhouse."

"I sent Owen a message by postal courier from Lake Lindemann," Duncan said tightly. "It must not have reached him." *Or else he ignored it*—but Duncan kept that thought to himself. "Don't worry. We'll get it straightened out."

"But don't you understand? I've been told I resemble my mother. What must my father think of me?" Tears shimmered in her eyes. Her chin quivered, then she steadied herself. "He's ashamed of me. That's why he isn't here."

Through all the torment of the trail, she had never cried. Taking her hands in his while longing to take her into his arms, he said gently, "There could be any number of reasons for his absence. Give your father a chance to explain."

She looked up with tears glistening in her eyes. The trust in her face hurt him worse than the tears. Everett had better have a damned good reason for not showing up.

A few yards away from the colorful cluster of showgirls, a well-dressed young man toyed idly with a nugget on his watch fob. Duncan was looking fit, he mused. Count on his laudable stepbrother to look even hardier after a three-month trek in the quarrelsome company of bawdy women.

Owen turned his attention to the women. His gaze lingered over one with curly black hair and a lively expression. The sparkle in her eyes said she was eager for adventure and not yet jaded by the world.

Might be worth investigation, he told himself, then settled his attention on the fifth woman, who stood talking with his stepbrother. She was recognizably the one he had dubbed the Seattle songstress, but she was dressed in a limp brown wool outfit better suited to his mouse of a stepmother than to a singer.

Owen's brow creased as he studied Duncan. There was something unusually possessive in the way he spoke with the girl. Could he be smitten by that bit of Yukon flotsam?

What a joke if the peerless older brother so often scornful of affairs of the heart had gone softheaded for a showgirl. Not that she wasn't attractive with those big gray eyes and sun-brightened chestnut hair. She was a little tall and had a stubborn chin, Owen decided. He dismissed her. The black-haired girl was far more interesting.

His brother looked around then, caught Owen's eye and straightened, brows leveling, his mouth taking a familiar tight line. Owen set his shoulders at a jaunty angle and sauntered forward.

Through her distress, Julia saw a change come over Duncan. One moment, he was more tender and reassuring than he had been since Miles Canyon. In the next, he withdrew, becoming a stranger she didn't know, aloof, even arrogant. Tentatively, she asked, "What is it?"

His voice was as unforgiving as his expression. "You're about to meet my stepbrother."

The stylish young man sauntering toward them wore a blue serge suit and a rakishly tilted fedora. Julia had not expected Owen to be so handsome. She noted sensitive lips and merry brown eyes that held her own for a moment of mutual admiration.

As she automatically returned his smile, he offered Duncan an enthusiastic handshake. "Welcome to Dawson City! You're looking in fine feather. The trail must have suited you. I look forward to comparing adventures. But we don't need to stand out here, shouting over the racket. We'll go back to the Playhouse.'' He paused with a rakish grin. ''First, introduce me to our bevy of beautiful ladies.''

Julia glanced from one man to the other.

Duncan nodded coolly. ''Lead the way.''

With a vibrant smile, Hannah stepped forward. ''I'm Hannah. And here are Tilly, Vida and Belle.''

To each, Owen offered a gallant bow, then turned to Julia. ''And of course, this is our songstress.''

It was apparent to Duncan that his stepbrother hadn't changed one damned bit from the easy-living lounger he had known in Seattle. It was hard to believe he'd hiked over the White Pass. Maybe he got hold of a horse and rode in before the pass clogged with Klondikers. Before the Mounties guarded the borders, there was no need to haul in a ton of provisions. The entire experience had probably been a lark, and Owen had probably wasted no thought on the *Fortune*'s charred timbers at Skagway.

''Miss Everett is not going to sing, Owen. Where is your office? I don't mean to discuss private business on the street.''

As the brothers walked ahead, Tilly nudged Julia and nodded toward Owen. ''Nice-looking fellow. And a lot more pleasant than his brother. You could do worse.''

Julia studied the men. Duncan's rough dress contrasted with Owen's style the way a raven contrasted with a caged canary. Owen might be attractive, but she suspected that it would be difficult to sustain interest in him.

Just looking at Duncan made her breath catch and her lips long for his kisses. She would never grow bored with Duncan, but her heart ached with the fear of losing him. During the last days of their journey, he had scarcely spoken to her. She clung to the reminder that he had comforted her over the painted portrait, briefly becoming the tender, caring man she loved.

Now, while all the women whispered about Owen's charms, Julia watched Duncan. His sure strength was revealed in every lithe movement. It occurred to her that Duncan presented a breathtaking appearance out of his clothes, while Owen was perhaps more attractive wearing his.

What a direction for her thoughts to take. She pressed her palms against her cheeks, hoping no one noticed her blush. Fortunately, the girls were too enthralled with the town and Owen. The brothers were concerned with a conflict that had begun years before.

Clearly, there was little liking between them. Owen's gaiety seemed a bit desperate, and she felt sorry for him, even when she remembered the lost trawlers.

Tilly's awed tones rose above the clatter. "Just look at this place! Every other building is a saloon, dance hall, hotel or eatin' place."

Belle answered breathlessly, "That means plenty of openings for a working girl."

Julia felt newly conscious of the entertainers. She recognized class snobbery in the quick steps she took to put herself a few paces ahead of them. Her conscience twinged. On the long journey, they had befriended her without question.

Still, she was not one of them. And as she glanced at the men and occasional women on the streets of Dawson City, she saw that here, as everywhere, people were categorized by station. At one end were women whom society termed "decent" and at the other were those she had heard called "unfortunates." She wasn't sure where she felt most comfortable on that scale, except that it was not with Belle, Tilly and Vida.

Where she might feel comfortable was not important. Her father's position would determine her own. Where could he be? Was it possible that her letter had missed him? That could easily have happened, considering the dangers of the trail. Relief made her steps lighter. It wasn't that her father was avoiding her, but that he didn't yet know she was here.

Owen turned to take her arm, and she smiled with such radiance that his eyes widened. She saw Duncan frown but did not let it trouble her. She had reached her goal and soon she would meet her father. With anticipation, she looked at the colorful banners and signs painted on frame buildings. A general merchandiser across the street dealt also in drugs and medicine. A laundry offered mending free of charge. A small sign proclaimed that fortunes were told.

Outside the nearest saloon, two men worked at the rear of a horse-drawn cart. Painted letters on the side heralded its contents as Pure Arctic Water. A burly-looking fellow finished filling a barrel, then hoisted it onto his shoulder and trudged toward the laughter and tinny piano music coming from the saloon.

Owen smiled at Julia's fascinated gaze. "You might think it's bad for business, but it's traditional to keep pure water and a dipper at the end of the bar."

"I'm glad to hear that," she said with an answering smile that faded abruptly when Duncan grasped her elbow and jolted her toward him.

"You were about to step off the walk," he said when she looked up in protest.

With a grand flourish, Owen directed their attention across the street. "The Bonanza Playhouse. What do you think of it?" The two-story frame building sandwiched between a hotel and a drygoods merchant was notable for its ornate false front and the name in fading red paint above the door.

The dancers squealed appreciatively while Julia said, "It looks very welcoming, Mr. Powell."

"I believe it does, if I may be forgiven the pride of saying so." His smile rewarded her, but Duncan's dour glance did not. The women were already hurrying across the street, Hannah in the lead, no doubt to assure herself that her portrait was not above the bar.

Seeming untroubled by his brother's lack of enthusiasm, Owen led them grandly through a small anteroom and into the saloon. Barrel-shaped stoves were located at either side of the entrance. A few men played faro nearby. Tilly watched the game while the others moved into the room.

A double row of curtained boxes formed a gallery. Below, men lounged at tables or along a red-stained pine bar near the left wall. Behind the bar was a row of bottles and glasses.

"You don't draw much of a crowd," Duncan said.

Owen reacted so quickly his defense seemed rehearsed. "There's plenty of competition, but the girls will soon have them fighting for standing room."

Fear stabbed through Julia. She moved closer to Duncan. She had never before set foot inside a saloon and had never expected to. A small stage at the far end filled her with dread. Owen noticed her shiver. "Don't worry, Miss Everett. There is a third stove beneath the stage. You won't be cold."

Duncan corrected him, "As usual, you ignore what you don't want to hear. She won't be singing."

Grateful for the reassuring touch of Duncan's hand at the small of her back, Julia looked apologetically at Owen. A slight frown briefly creased his forehead. Then, squealing with delight, Belle ran past them and onto the stage. Owen grinned, his merry nature returning as he watched Belle stroke the ruby velvet curtains. That look of sensual pleasure in Belle's face was never there when she spoke frankly of her experiences with men.

Sadness came over Julia. During the journey, she had disapproved of Belle's easy way with men. Now, watching her, Julia knew that for all her experience, Belle had never shared the loving rapture she had discovered with Duncan. She looked into his drawn features and wondered if memories were all she was ever to cherish.

Vida had also run onto the stage. Her supple fingers caressed the gold outlines of flowers and vines that were embossed on the stage. Julia felt as if she had never been a part of their world. Their dance had seemed an exuberant exercise when she joined them at Lake Bennett. Now she knew Duncan had been right when he stopped her from dancing. She would rather beg on the street than appear on that stage.

"See our piano?" Owen asked proudly. "It came in over the Chilkoot last year on the back of the fellow who plays it." He tapped a small instrument at one end of the bar, adding, "Can you guess what this is?"

"We're not here for the grand tour," Duncan said shortly. "Where can we talk?"

Owen held up a hand for patience while a grizzled old-timer thumped a leather pouch onto the bar. ''Here's my poke. Bring me a whiskey, Gus.''

The bartender was a giant of a man with a forbidding expression. He poured out a drink, then picked up the pouch and spilled a glittering stream of gold dust into a small tray on the instrument Owen had been tapping.

The showgirls gathered around, drawing in such awed breaths that Julia thought they might inhale the dust right off the scale. When the bartender finished weighing the cost of the whiskey, he returned the poke.

Owen waved him over. ''Girls, I want you to meet August, the best bartender in town. He's only working long enough to earn a stake. If I had the nerve, I'd underpay him just to keep him on.''

When Owen's chuckle went unanswered, he added, ''Gus, here are our performers at last. Show them where they're to stay and fill them in on the routine. Tell Agnes to fit them in those new costumes.''

Turning his infectious smile on the troupe, he added, ''You might as well start getting rich, girls. When you finish the show, we'll push back the chairs and tables to give you room to dance with the customers. A dollar a dance. You'll get your cut, with a bonus for every drink you sell. Ask for champagne, it costs the most. And remember, the first show's at eight.''

Julia nearly moaned aloud. Never had she felt so trapped. Even the Seattle underground was more inviting than the Bonanza Playhouse. This was not her future. It couldn't be. Feeling as if she was already being squeezed in a prospector's sweaty embrace, she reached mindlessly for Duncan.

# Chapter Nineteen

The showgirls clustered around the bartender while Owen directed his stepbrother and Julia into a small cluttered office. After pulling two hard chairs before a rolltop desk, he lounged in an elegant leather-backed chair. In the depths of his eyes, Julia saw that he expected an ax to fall, but he appeared relaxed as he dug a bottle and three glasses from a drawer.

"Nothing for me," Julia said.

"You're protecting your voice," Owen approved. "I saw at once you were sensible as well as beautiful."

Duncan had remained standing. He leaned against the back of Julia's chair. His stepbrother's obstinacy rivaled Julia's. A memory of women crying in his mother's kitchen flooded him. He could even smell the cinnamon tea she offered as comfort. Owen, of course, was always far from the tearful scene, either at the pool hall or lounging on some street corner with his worthless friends. "For the last time, Owen. Julia will not be singing. Not in public."

Golden droplets spattered over the varnished desk as Owen jerked the bottle. "If this is your way of getting back at me, it's the wrong one. I'm sorry about the boat. You must know that. But if Julia sings as sweetly as you said in your letter, she'll earn back the cost of the boat in a fortnight."

"The damnable thing about all this," Duncan said angrily, "is that I actually hoped to find you'd grown up.

There seemed a chance the Klondike might have made a man of you. I see my hopes were misplaced.''

Owen gave an exaggerated wince. ''My sympathies, Miss Everett. You've endured months of his humorless company.''

She glanced uneasily from one to the other. While she wanted to urge Duncan to give his brother the courtesy of a hearing, she wasn't willing to risk their tenuous relationship.

''You haven't changed a hair,'' Duncan said. ''But if you think to manipulate Julia, you'll have me to deal with.''

She apologized to Owen. ''This is my fault. I joined the troupe under false colors.''

Duncan broke in. ''The only subject we need to discuss, Owen, is the funds I need to replace my trawler. I don't intend to wait around. If you have to sell this place, you'll sell. I want the money now.''

Julia heard him with astonishment. This cold man couldn't be the companion who had laughed with her while panning for gold and who shared that furious passage through Miles Canyon and the emotional fury that followed. He was treating Owen as if he were little better than a gambler with a folding tray and a set of walnut shells.

Clearly, Owen was trying to make the best of a difficult situation. She felt embarrassed for him when he reddened in response to Duncan's demand. He poured two drinks, pushed one toward Duncan, then drank deeply of the other. ''Miss Everett, I've been a poor host. Permit me to send for herb tea to soothe your lovely throat.''

To Julia's horror, Duncan moved like a sprung trap. He grasped his brother by his jacket and shoved him against a wall. Owen's glass flew across the room. His hands jerked up to tug at his collar.

For Duncan, the remembered scent of cinnamon tea hung around them. As always, Owen refused to hear what displeased him. ''*Tea to soothe her throat? Julia is not to sing. And you are to pay the cost of the Fortune.*''

Resisting an urge to tighten his grasp on Owen's fashionably high shirt points, Duncan saw a flash of images. In each, his stepbrother turned life to his advantage, no matter who he hurt. The first was the day of their parents' marriage, when Owen delayed the ceremony by feigning a sprained ankle and was rewarded with a double serving of cake.

He was not going to win this time, with neither father nor stepmother present to defend him. "Whatever you lose by selling this place will be less than you've cost me."

Owen's face reddened. White blotches showed on his face. "You don't understand."

Julia pressed her fist to her mouth, afraid to interfere. Owen finally managed to get out words that made his brother loosen his grasp. "It isn't mine. I'm only the manager."

While Owen gulped for air, Duncan repeated with scathing disbelief, "Manager? You're nothing but the manager?"

Owen regained his chair. He avoided looking at Julia, and again she felt embarrassed for him. With heavy reluctance, he said, "The owner couldn't take the cold weather. He offered me a percentage of the profits to manage the place while he recovers his health."

Duncan drained his whiskey, then slapped the glass onto the desk. "So you're worth no more here than you were at home. And the *Fortune* is a burned hulk."

Owen looked as bitter as his brother. "Nuggets were lying around like hen's eggs. That's what they told us when the *Portland* reached Seattle. What a joke that turned out to be."

Getting abruptly to his feet, he paced to a window. Through it, Julia glimpsed a storehouse set on legs to keep food from marauding dogs.

The rasp of Owen's voice drew her back. "That crowd swarming in by the thousands is going to be bitterly disappointed. It's backbreaking work getting at the gold. The pay is buried deep, and it's hard to follow. You have to be a gopher to stay with the vein...if you find one." He rubbed one hand through his hair in a gesture that startled Julia. It reminded her of Duncan's similar habit.

Disgusted, Duncan said, "A man who's not afraid of a little hard work would not be stopped by a few feet of soil."

"A little hard work?" Bracing his palms on the desk, Owen glared at his stepbrother. "You've just stepped ashore and you know all about mining. You're aware that the gold-bearing earth must be brought up during the winter so it can be sluiced in the spring runoff? You know that men burn fires on the frozen ground so they can dig? I suppose you know how damnably slow the ground is to thaw, despite a day's burning?"

He looked from Duncan to Julia, including her in his case against his brother. "Three inches will thaw in a day, if it's muck. Ten, if it's gravel. And a man may be forced to sink half a dozen holes to find gold. If he finds it."

"Mere inches in a day," Julia breathed.

"Even so, every gully is full of men working themselves into an early grave." Owen sank onto his chair. "It was already too late when I got here. The claims worth having were staked before the *Excelsior* and the *Portland* ever started down the coast. Still, people are thronging in to batter themselves against the Chilkoot Trail or the White Pass. Why the devil would anyone think there might be a square yard of pay dirt left unclaimed?"

"Every man has his dream," Duncan said. "Mine happens to involve fishing."

Owen leaned back, trying to appear nonchalant. "The truth is, a bunch of steady customers took up a subscription to send for the girls." He glanced at Julia. "They'll be eager to hear you sing."

As she drew a quick breath and Duncan started forward, Owen added quickly, "There's a saloon in every second building around here. We needed a draw to raise the kind of profit that can replace the *Fortune*. Now we have it. All I ask is your patience."

Patience. The word exploded through Duncan. "If I had a dollar for every time your father urged patience with you, I'd have a fleet of trawlers today." He leaned over the desk, his pose menacing.

"Understand this, Julia is not to sing here."

Frightened by Duncan's barely leashed anger, Julia interrupted. "I'm not a performer, Mr. Powell. I've come here to locate my father." Unclasping the chain from around her neck, she displayed the heart-shaped nugget. "He sent this to me in Seattle. I wonder if he has been a customer here? His name is Joseph Everett."

She thought Owen's hand stilled slightly in the act of straightening his collar, but the pause was so slight that she decided she was mistaken, especially when he shook his head with regret. "Everett? I'm sorry. The name is not familiar."

He leaned across the desk to pat one of the hands she had braced against the edge. "Believe me, I would rather be struck dumb than dash your hopes."

"I sent him a message from Dyea." Julia turned abruptly to Duncan. "He must be at the waterfront. I should be there. I must go back at once."

Her gray eyes glowed with such vivid hope that Owen revised his earlier assessment. Julia was quite beautiful. Her lovely lips would tempt any man. And he was beginning to sense a spirited nature that was rather appealing.

Rising smoothly, he offered his hand. "Please allow me to escort you to the post office instead, Miss Everett. We'll learn whether your letter has been claimed. I intend to make it my first order of business to help you locate your father."

As Julia gave him an uncertain smile, Owen was conscious of his brother's scowl. Obviously, Duncan felt a tenderness for the young woman. It would be an unkind cut—not to mention dangerous—to take her from him after costing him two trawlers. There was no question, however, that the moment he heard her name, Owen vowed to make Julia Everett his.

When they left the Playhouse, Owen saw Dawson City's Front Street through the freshness of Julia's eyes. He became aware, as he had not been for a long time, of the clutter that surrounded the rapidly growing city. A tide of men washed along the boardwalks, most of them newcomers in a frenzy for claims. It wouldn't be long before the truth broke them.

He noticed Julia clutching Duncan's arm as if her life depended on him. That was logical, considering their perilous journey. Now matters were different. For a time, at least, his peerless stepbrother was picking his way over a trail that Owen knew well. He meant to use his advantage to charm Julia Everett.

For most of his life, he had admired and envied Duncan, eight years older, stronger and more capable. When their parents married, he had felt embarrassed that his father was a clerk while Duncan's had been a rugged fisherman who drowned gallantly at sea.

Duncan named his first trawler after his mother. He must have resented losing her to a new husband, especially one with a twelve-year-old son. With a glance at Duncan's rigid profile, Owen wondered if there had been a moment when they might have become friends but chose to be rivals.

That's hardly the word, he corrected himself wryly. Duncan treated me as if I was invisible. So I put on a cocky act. What else could I do? A familiar ache rose through him, but he knew it didn't show. He had had a lot of experience in hiding his feelings beneath a careless smile. Owen caught Julia's glance and put a glow of welcome into his eyes. This time, he was going to win.

As usual, there was a line of men outside the post office. They were hoping for letters from home. "Word came out that a government boat brought in over thirty sacks of mail," Owen explained. "These fellows should realize it will be a month or more before the letters get sorted."

Julia's step faltered. "So many are ahead of us."

"Don't worry, Miss Everett. They'll open the back door for me." Pleased with her look of surprise, Owen gallantly placed her hand on his arm. The Mounties always welcomed women ahead of the waiting men, but Julia couldn't know that. As he led the way around the building, he prepared to impress her with his importance. Knocking sharply on a door frame, he called, "It's Owen Powell. Open up."

A young man peered through. When he saw Julia, he smiled widely. After introducing her, Owen explained her plight.

"It will take just a minute to check, miss," the clerk promised and disappeared into the building.

While they waited, Duncan watched Owen attempt to charm Julia and made a mental note to warn her of his stepbrother's faithlessness. He trusted her common sense, however, and was more concerned with the bitter truth of the Bonanza Playhouse. There was no cash to replace the *Fortune*. He had followed a lure as false as any on the long trail.

Men rushed along the streets, all looking as if they had somewhere to go and were late getting there. The same restless frustration tore at him, and he forced his mind to choices. He could take Julia back to Seattle and hire out on someone else's trawler. Maybe with years of effort, he could get enough ahead to buy another of his own.

A second possibility had been building since he learned the truth. He might take over the Playhouse and see that it made the profit that should be pouring into a Dawson City saloon. He would not feel easy warming a chair instead of fighting the elements, but he had had experience in managing two trawlers. He trusted himself far more than he trusted Owen, who was likely to cut corners.

It troubled him to see Julia laughing at a comment from Owen. He wished he could take her to Seattle at once.

To Julia's relief, the clerk was not much longer than his word. He soon stepped outside with an envelope in his hands. "Is this the one you were expecting, miss?"

Her writing on the envelope brought a vivid memory of her anticipation in Dyea when her father seemed only a short journey away. With an effort, she said aloud, "He never received my letter."

Duncan put one hand on the small of her back. "In a way, that's good news. It explains why he isn't here."

She wanted to bury her face against his shoulder, but she knew people watched them curiously. Blinking hard, she forced a wan smile. "I just hoped ... I just thought ..."

Her voice was too unsteady to finish, but her thoughts raced. Duncan had talked of leaving at once for Seattle. Whatever he decided to do, she had to stay. When word reached her father, he would come to her. The only question was how to make sure he heard where she was.

There was an answer, one that set her nerves on edge. She had taken her future into her own hands when she smashed the watch case in Aaron's shop. It was time she did so again.

Lifting her chin, she turned to Owen. "When I sing for your customers, Mr. Powell, you will introduce me as Julia Everett. Put that name on the poster, too. I want my name well known. Rumor carries messages more surely than the post."

The brothers looked startled. As Duncan's hand tightened on her waist, Owen clasped her hands. "Julia." He paused. "If I may call you that?" At her nod, he said firmly, "Now that I know you are not a performer, I cannot expose you to the stage. I mean to have that poster painted over at once."

"I appreciate your kindness," she said, pulling her hands free. "But I must sing."

She felt Duncan's disapproval. His hand felt possessive on her waist, reminding her that he expected to set the rules. "You thought Everett was avoiding you because of the poster. How do you think he would react to word that his daughter is performing on a public stage?"

She kept her voice steady. "He will know that I am doing whatever is necessary to bring us together." Clasping her hands beneath her heart, she added fiercely, "He'll come to me. I know he will."

Owen felt a twinge of compassion. Julia's gray eyes had widened until they seemed to fill her face. She had spunk. He liked that, but he couldn't have his future wife performing on stage. Duncan was arguing enough for the two of them, so Owen held back. When his stepbrother made her angry enough, she would turn to the man who offered sympathy.

By the time they returned to the Playhouse, Duncan and Julia were barely speaking to each other. Owen showed a compassionate attitude toward Julia.

After a sharp glance at the scattering of customers in the saloon, Duncan strode into the office and took Owen's chair at the desk. "Bring out the books. What's your agreement with the owner?"

Resentment stabbed through Owen. He hid it by making Duncan wait for an answer while he settled Julia into a comfortable chair. Then he reached into a drawer, produced a ledger and tossed it casually onto the desk. "I receive fifty percent of the profits and send the remainder to him."

Julia tried to hold onto her courage while she watched the two of them lean over the open ledger. She had watched Aaron at his accounts enough to know that Owen was trying to put a high gloss on matters, one which Duncan inevitably shattered by ferreting out the facts. For a man who prided himself on physical prowess, Duncan showed remarkable skills as a bookkeeper.

He closed the ledger with a snap and she started nervously. "Unless you and your bartender have been helping yourselves to the till, the profits have been far too low."

"I'd vouch for August any day," Owen answered hotly. "And if you are accusing me of theft, then I—"

Duncan cut him off. "We're going to send the owner a new contract. Our share is to rise to seventy-five percent depending on increased profits, with his income never to fall below the amount he has been receiving. Unless he means to return and run the place himself, he won't argue with that."

"How do we raise the profits?" Owen demanded. "Do you realize how many fancy women arrived with the cheechakos? Every bar in town will be boasting of showgirls this summer."

Drawing courage around herself, Julia broke in. "Aboard the grounded ship, men were reminded of wives and mothers. I believe those men will wish to hear me sing again."

"Dearest Julia," Owen protested. "You aren't to take our problems on your delicate shoulders."

"It seems that singing in public suits Julia's purpose as well as ours," Duncan said, surprising her. "Does the city have a newspaper?"

"The *Klondike Nugget.* It's just begun."

Duncan pulled a sheet of paper toward him, then dipped a pen into the inkwell. He wrote swiftly, then leaned back and read aloud. "Miss Julia Everett, heroine of the *Gypsy Gull,* is a recent arrival to our city. Many reports have reached this newspaper of a difficult voyage through the Inland Passage where the ship's captain allowed his vessel to go aground. Passengers daring enough to take matters into their own hands saw that lines were secured to trees before the outgoing tide could pull the vessel over.

"Even so, the deck tilted to a perilous degree. With composure to shame those who succumbed to panic, Miss Everett stood bravely on the listing deck and lifted her voice in comforting song. As the sweet, pure notes rose through the darkness, men halted their crying and cursing to listen.

"Dawson City can be proud to welcome Miss Everett, who is as brave as she is beautiful and whose voice can now be heard nightly at the Bonanza Playhouse."

He handed the paper to Owen. "Have that run at once. And see that the poster is repainted more in her likeness. The words beneath are to read, 'Miss Julia Everett, Heroine of the *Gypsy Gull*.'"

Owen looked from the paper to Julia. "Miss Everett—"

"Julia," she protested.

"Julia, dear brave Julia, may I be among the first to congratulate you on your courage. It will be an honor to have you appear on our stage."

His thoughts spun as he realized his brother had found the perfect solution. Julia would sing publicly and be praised rather than stained by it. When the story came out that she was searching for her lost father, every man in Dawson would want to help find him.

Would that present a problem to his plans? Probably not. Impulsively, he raised her hand and kissed the back of her fingers. As his wife, Julia was going to be an even greater asset than he had first believed. A man could raise himself in the eyes of the frontier town by marrying a heroine.

"How gallant you are," she murmured.

Dryly, Duncan said, "Tell me, Owen. How much shall we offer Miss Everett to keep her from accepting an offer from some other stage?"

"I'll not be greedy," she said sweetly. "Ten percent of the increased profits will do."

Duncan's brows rose while a smile flickered at the corners of his mouth. Owen gulped. "Ten percent?" Hastily, he added, "You're worth far more, of course."

"Far more," Duncan agreed. "Revise that offer to the owner. We'll assure him of receiving never less than in his best month. Anything above that will be divided between the three of us."

"Mr. Powell," Julia said gently. "You look rather pale. Shouldn't you sit down?"

With a swift mental kick, Owen pulled himself together. Why was he worried about his income suddenly dropping to a third of the profits? Once Julia became his wife, he would be receiving two-thirds of the Bonanza's pie. Warmly, he said, "You are as compassionate as you are courageous, dear Julia. It's a privilege to welcome you into partnership."

# Chapter Twenty

Julia didn't feel courageous the following night as she waited to step onto the Bonanza's stage. The day had been too filled with activities for her to have time to worry. Agnes, who managed both kitchen and stage, had taken her on a whirlwind tour of Dawson City stores, then fitted her for a costume.

Now she was dressed in a mauve theater gown that set off the color of her eyes. Heavy lace covered the sleeves and bodice. A band of black velvet circled her throat with a dazzling rhinestone sunburst at the center. The dress fit smoothly over her tightly corsetted waist and hips, then flared to the floor. Lace rosettes accented the graceful folds of the hem.

Agnes helped her put on elbow-length gloves, then fussily adjusted a matching wide-brimmed hat topped by an ostrich feather dyed purple. "You look lovely, dear."

"I hope I'm not too nervous to sing."

The older woman stepped back, her capable hands on her ample hips while she critically surveyed Julia. She nodded, satisfied with her creation. "No need for you to be nervous, dear. The boys'll be happy just to look at you. And after that story came out in the paper today, why, there will be plenty wanting to do that."

Whether the story of the *Gypsy Gull* brought people to hear her meant less to Julia than that they listened with courtesy. The dancers had entertained a raucous audience the night before. They were peering out around the curtains at the men gathering tonight.

Men who waited for her, Julia thought with a shiver that made her ostrich feather tremble. With a rustle of taffeta skirts, Tilly swirled into the dressing room. Hopefully, Julia asked, "Is the audience quite small?"

The dancer's eyes sparkled. She looked years younger. The long trail had removed surplus pounds while adding a healthy glow. Before she could answer Julia's question, the laconic bartender appeared briefly in the doorway. "The boss wants you cancan girls to open the show. Come out when you hear the piano."

Tilly's radiant smile surprised Julia, who had expected a snappy reply. "Don't you worry. We'll be there."

He regarded her with distaste. "See that you are. Some of the boys have threatened to burn us out if the entertainment doesn't please them."

"What an unpleasant man," Julia said as the door closed after him.

Tilly simply laughed. "Don't let Gus rattle you. He dislikes cheechakos, entertainers and women, in that order— but I'm pretty sure I can get women up to number one."

The piano sounded a loud chord. As the women ran whooping onstage, Julia felt as if the floor wavered beneath her. Never in her life had she expected to sing from a public stage. Clenching her hands on the back of a chair, she waited for her cue.

She thought she had her nerves controlled, but when Duncan stepped into the dressing room, courage deserted her. She ran into his arms and clutched him tightly around the waist. Her hat tilted at a painful angle, the pin pulling her hair. Gently, he eased her grasp. "Is this the daredevil who leaped aboard my boat for a journey through Miles Canyon?"

She had done more than risk the canyon and rapids, but she put the rest out of her mind. "Suppose I make a fool of myself? What if I start to sing and the customers leave?"

He reassured her gravely. "Sweetheart, you'll do fine. Remember, the men out there are no different from those on the *Gypsy Gull*."

She nodded, determined to pretend the same men were in the audience. This had been her idea, after all. She had to go through with it.

Very gently, Duncan tilted her face upward and kissed her. Longing flooded her as for a precious moment they shared the closeness they had known on the river. His heartbeat comforted and thrilled her. She raised her arms to his shoulders, clasping her fingers against his hair.

Then the dancers pounded down the hall, laughing with excitement. Feeling dazed, Julia drew back. "Owen is announcing you," Hannah called. "Hurry!"

Duncan held her still long enough to remove the pin from her hat and straighten the velvet brim so the ostrich feather swirled over her forehead. His mouth twisted in a wry smile. "I must be crazy to let you do this."

She pushed the tip of the feather away from her eyes. "Let me! I do as I choose, Mr. Adair."

His grin said he deliberately provoked her to give her courage. In her returning smile, she admitted that the plan worked. Still, she was glad to steady herself on his arm as they walked down the hall to the wings.

From the center of the stage, Owen said, "Here she is. Gentlemen, let us have a Dawson City welcome for a lady as talented as she is lovely, Miss Julia Everett."

Loud cheers and applause nearly undid her nerves. Feeling that her face must be white beneath the powder and blush Agnes had applied, Julia looked helplessly at Duncan.

He gave her a light push and she forced herself forward, one step after another. How could the stage have become so wide? Owen appeared to be miles away, but at last she reached the sanctuary of his outstretched hand. He drew her beside him, then squeezed her fingers and murmured, "Courage."

Suddenly, she was alone on the stage. People lined the bar. Bottles and glasses clattered over shouts for whiskey. In the gallery, the curtains to most of the boxes were drawn open, revealing empty interiors.

The men who sprawled at the tables on the main floor appeared to have little interest in her. Laughter mingled with curses, conversation and shouts. The spin of the faro wheel sounded loud. A gambler called, "Place your bets."

The piano player waited her nod, then banged on the keys. Julia felt as if her heart was in her throat. She would never be able to sing past it. She could almost see Aaron glowering in the wings. Not even her mother had done so daring a thing as to perform on stage.

Glancing into the wings, she saw that the cancan girls had joined Duncan and Owen. Tilly nodded encouragement while the brothers stood apart, waiting.

From the audience, a man shouted, "Don't just stand there, honey. Sing if you're goin' to."

She drew a shaky breath and began. "Oh, don't you remember Sweet Alice, Ben Bolt?" Her voice was no match for the crowd, or even for the tinny piano, and she faltered to a stop.

Somewhere in front, a man laughed. Stricken, she edged toward the wings. Duncan spoke sharply, "If your father is to hear that his daughter sings in public, at least let him hear that she sings well."

"Go easy," Owen reproved him. His troubled expression reminded Julia that the miners had threatened to burn them out if they were disappointed by the entertainment their donations had provided. He managed a reassuring smile. "We'll have the girls dance again while you regain your courage."

"No," Duncan said. "She'll finish."

Tilly ran on stage beside her. "Men are like donkeys, honey. First you've got to get their attention." Hands on satin-clad hips, she bellowed, "Quiet!"

When the clatter eased, she shouted, "Little wonder you gents have trouble findin' gold. You don't know value when you see it. Now Miss Everett's come a long, hard way. Shut your ugly mouths long enough and you'll hear the best singin' this side of the border."

"Melt their hearts," Duncan said from the wings. "You can do it."

For a moment, she felt as if she stood alone with him. Their eyes held as intimate an embrace as their bodies had moments before in the dressing room. From Duncan, there was no offer of cancan girls to take the stage while she cowered. He expected her to sing and to sing well.

Lifting her shoulders, she stepped to the center of the stage. Tilly swept a challenging glare around the silenced room, then said, "Go ahead, honey. Knock 'em off their chairs."

The piano began again. This time, Julia put the full force of her emotions into her voice. Haunting notes lifted from her throat, each as clear as glacier ice.

The men listened in a silence that astonished her. Feeling nervousness vanish, she moved nearer the gaslights at the front of the stage. Her gaze settled on one rapt face after another. With even deeper surprise, she realized that no one raised a glass to drink.

When she came to the end of her song, the hush continued, then broke as men flung back chairs and rushed toward the stage. Terrified, Julia backed away. Owen and Duncan appeared instantly at her side.

"No, boys!" Owen shouted. "Miss Everett is a decent lady who hiked the rigorous Chilkoot Trail. She has come here to locate her father. Until then, she promises to sing for us each night so long as you behave. What do you say?"

A chorus of approval rose, then the men returned to their chairs. With a nod to the pianist, Owen drew Julia forward to stand alone at center stage. She lifted her voice again, this time to the plaintive strains of, "The Picture That is Turned to the Wall."

A glimmer of tears appeared in more than one grizzled prospector's eyes, while a young man near the front sobbed and pressed his knuckles against his mouth. Emboldened, she followed with, "Two Little Girls in Blue." Men came in from the street and stood at the back to listen. The boxes in the gallery began to fill.

She realized she was enjoying herself. With a light step, she flirted her skirts above her ankles, dancing around the stage while her voice lilted through "My Sweetheart's the Man in the Moon."

When she finished, the men again crowded forward, cheering and shouting. A few nuggets rattled to her feet. A half-filled poke of gold dust thudded nearby. She raised her cupped hands, kissed her fingertips and blew a kiss into the audience.

Suddenly, velvet curtains swung from the sides of the stage, closing her off. From beyond, Owen shouted, "Miss Everett will sing again tomorrow night. Tell your friends to come to the Bonanza Playhouse."

The rest of the troupe darted onstage to hug Julia in delight. While they gathered the gold, Duncan drew Julia into the wings and held her in the circle of his arms. She saw smoldering approval in his eyes. "Word of mouth will soon pack this place to the walls. Your father is sure to hear."

"And then?" She needed his reassurance.

He didn't disappoint her. "Everett will fight through hell if necessary to reach you."

As the curtains swept open, the dancers ran shrieking onto the stage. Eyes sparkling, they whipped their skirts high to reveal layer upon layer of taffeta petticoats. Locking arms and facing in alternate directions, they wheeled and kicked and screamed with joyful energy.

Owen glowed when he returned to the wings. Catching both Julia's hands, he kissed one then the other. "You have stolen every heart, including mine!"

Laughing, she accepted the compliments and others that followed. Long after midnight, the troupe gathered in the kitchen for a light supper. Exhaustion began to seep through Julia, and she wondered when Hannah would be willing to return to the room they shared. All the dancers were crowded around Owen, watching him count the night's receipts.

Duncan touched her hair. "Come along, I'll take you to your room."

Street noises came clearly through the walls as they mounted the narrow stairs, then walked along a hall scarcely wide enough for one. Closed doors stood on either side, so many that she wondered if the rooms beyond could hold more than a single cot. Snores sounded audibly, joined at one side by a bawdy creaking of springs.

Uneasily, she said, "The walls must be very thin."

"They are." Duncan's step lengthened, as if he wished to get her quickly past the sound of bedsprings, now accompanied by grunts and giggles. "The city sprang up too fast for even a dozen sawmills to keep pace. These partitions are nothing but calico panels nailed to slats and papered over."

"It's no place for secrets, then. I'll have to remember that."

He opened the door of a room overlooking the street and glanced inside to make sure it was empty. "If you need me for anything, I'll be next door with Owen."

"I do need you." Impulsively, she raised her arms to his shoulders and sank her fingers into the thick waves of his hair. His eyes were shadowed as he gathered her into his arms and lowered his mouth to hers. She rose eagerly into the kiss, pressing her body against his. She felt a deep need for reassurance; she wanted Duncan to care for her not as a showgirl who might earn back his trawler, but for herself.

She found that reassurance in Duncan's arms and lips, then he raised his head. "Go to bed, sweetheart. Tomorrow we'll begin to search for your father."

Leaving him with reluctance, she stepped into the small plain room with a narrow bed on an iron frame at either side. A pine armoire filled one corner, a mirrored dressing table another. A fringed velvet curtain at the single window blocked the nearly constant daylight. Languidly, she unfastened the lovely mauve gown and let it slip to the floor. She was tempted to leave it, but Ruth's memory rebuked her and dutifully she retrieved the dress and hung it in the armoire.

She pulled the pins from her hair, then shook her head to free it. She released her corset and drew a deep breath that let her lungs expand fully for the first time in hours. Society's rules must be obeyed, but she far preferred the comfort of the trail.

The shopping trip with Agnes had resulted in a number of personal items, including a linen nightgown sprigged with rosebuds. Julia slipped it over her head, then sat at the table to brush her hair. Half asleep, she stroked the heavy tresses.

A thud sounded from the hall. She stared at the door, then lowered the brush to the table, stood and crossed the room. When she opened the door a crack, she discovered Duncan, still fully clothed, climbing into a blanket roll. "What in the world are you doing?"

He looked up, startled. "I thought you would be asleep by now."

"Well, I'm not. What are you doing outside my door?"

"Hannah shows no signs of tiring. I'll not leave you alone while the men you charmed with your songs linger over their drinks. All of them are doubtless reminding themselves how delectable you are."

"You don't expect anyone to come up here?" A quaver of alarm ran through her voice.

"Not while I'm here." He turned his back to her. "Good night, Julia."

She closed the door, but stood on the other side uncertainly. "I do wish you would go to your own bed," she said through the wall.

"After months on the trail, I wouldn't know how to sleep in one."

"Nor I," she said stoutly, though with a wistful glance toward the iron bedstead. She heard him pull his blankets more comfortably around him and knelt beside the wall nearby. Dreamily, she said, "What a strange day this has been. I confess I enjoyed the performance."

"Don't." Duncan's warning came so clearly through the calico, they might have been sitting together. "Take care, sweetheart. Remember how few women are here, compared to the numbers of men."

"Once Owen told them I was a lady, they behaved quite well."

"Owen has always been easy with words. Don't take him too seriously."

Could that be jealousy in his voice? Duncan was so much more than Owen could ever be, and yet she couldn't resist prodding. "Are you saying you don't consider me to be a lady?"

She heard him sit up and imagined him leaning toward her, one arm clasped loosely around his knee. She wanted to reach out to him, to stroke the fine scar at his temple, to trace the outline of his jaw. She pictured the shape of his sensitive mouth and longed to feel it once more on hers.

"Be on your guard every day, Julia," he said, breaking into her musing. "A man's natural desire for a woman's company can overwhelm his better judgment."

"You're rather hard on your own kind."

He answered shortly. "Trust me least of all."

She felt her breath catch. She had never fully come to terms with that incredible joining of their bodies, although she relived the rapture in dreams. That had been her doing, not his. She should feel shame but she remembered beauty. She answered him softly, "I do trust you, Duncan. You have always treated me with great care."

His voice sounded rough. "Julia, go to bed."

She thought for awhile. "I can't believe there is any danger. Everyone says the mounted police keep order."

"They can't be everywhere." Duncan's voice hardened. "I meant to warn you about flirting your skirts the way you did. That's too provocative."

She straightened so abruptly she lost her balance and sat hard on the floor. "My dance was nothing compared to the others!"

"Julia, you are not one of the others." The words sounded final. She heard him lie down and draw the blankets around him.

She made a face at his unforgiving tone, but the need for sleep grew, and she crept across the room and tumbled into her blankets.


Much later, a murmur of men's voices woke her. She glanced across the dim room and saw that Hannah slept in the opposite bed. The voices came from the hall. As her mind cleared, she heard Owen ask, "Do you have plans for that girl?"

Julia's heart leaped. The blood pounded so hard in her ears, she was afraid she would miss Duncan's answer. Were they talking about her? Coldly, he said, "My plans are no concern of yours."

*They are a concern of mine,* Julia told him silently. *Let me hear you say that you love me.* He had never said so; he had only stated that she was to go with him to Seattle. That was because he felt responsible for her. In her mind, she had traveled the Chilkoot Trail with him many times. While she dwelled on every tender moment they shared—especially the tumultuous rapture following White Horse Rapids—she always found her own behavior at fault.

From beyond the partition, Owen said, "You're wrong there, old man. How many marriageable women do you think come through here? A man gets bloody lonely in the long winter. I'm warning you now. I mean to offer for Julia."

She clamped one hand over her mouth to stifle a gasp. Then she lowered it, waiting for Duncan to answer. *Tell him we have an understanding. Tell him that you love me.* The springs complained as she leaned forward. She bit her lip, trying not to give herself away. Duncan sounded as if he were already half asleep. "I wish you luck, Owen. You'll need it."

Julia eased back onto her pillow as a door closed. She heard footsteps in the adjoining room, where Owen must be preparing for bed. "I'm asleep and dreaming," she whispered. "On such brief acquaintance, Owen would never consider marriage. And Duncan would not wish him luck."

Her mind chided her cruelly. Fishing was his life. If she should marry Owen, Duncan would be freed of an unwelcome responsibility.

# Chapter Twenty-One

Julia woke to the sound of Hannah's voice. Blinking away sleep, she sat up and looked toward the window. Her friend was there in her chemise, leaning halfway out and waving. "Edmund! Up here!"

"What are you doing?" Julia exclaimed.

Hannah turned with glowing eyes. "It's the Mounties. They've returned from the lake. Come and see, Julia. They're magnificent."

Barefooted, Julia padded to Hannah's side and peered around the protective cover of the curtain. Below, a troop of North West Mounted Police marched in the street. The back of a neck glowing almost as red as his dress uniform betrayed Officer Edmund Gray. Hannah called to him again. "Edmund. Look up!"

"You're embarrassing him. Hush!"

Laughing, Hannah ran to pull clothes from the armoire. "Hurry and dress, Julia. Come with me to the barracks. I must see him."

Julia dressed more slowly. "I suppose you had better talk to him. Before someone else confides that you are showing your limbs and petticoats onstage."

Hannah looked so dismayed that Julia felt a twinge of regret. Why chide Hannah when she had herself sung and danced for men?

She understood that the fortune seekers thronging the waterfront were those without claims. Of course her father was not among them. He was too busy to collect his mail.

Now that the rivers were running, her father was washing out the gold that would allow them to live comfortably together. Eagerness leaped in her, and she turned to Hannah. "Have you yet written home?"

The ebullience faded in Hannah's eyes as she dragged a brush through her springy curls. "Duncan insisted. I don't know what good it will do. I'm sure they have disowned me." Lowering the brush, she looked dolefully at Julia. "I am completely alone in the world."

Julia pinned her hair into a smooth coil, thinking that if Hannah was upset, she hid her emotions very well while hanging out the window in her chemise. "No doubt, Officer Gray will be captivated by your tragic story."

"That's just the trouble," Hannah said with a sigh. "I can't tell him. I believe he is just as rigid as my father. He may say that I incited the artist's attack, then stole the money."

Tartly, Julia answered Hannah, "If you believe that of Edmund, you cannot believe he loves you."

Hannah sighed. "Do you think that a man ever changes for love?"

Julia remembered last night's overheard conversation between Owen and Duncan. She had dreamed it. Surely, she had.

A man's angry shouts stopped her from answering Hannah. The voice sounded so near that she whirled, thinking a man in the room. At once, she realized the furious words came from next door.

"It's Owen," Hannah whispered, her eyes wide.

His voice came so clearly that Julia didn't need to press against the partition. "Brazen, thieving tramp. I've a mind to put you in the street."

When Vida answered, Hannah gasped, "It's like the steamer captain, all over again."

Julia rushed into the hall and through Owen's door. He held the dancer with one hand bunching the front of her dress. With the other, he angrily shook a quilled pouch.

"I didn't take nothin' from it," Vida protested. "Why are you so het up over an empty poke?"

He thrust her from him with a shove that hurled her against Julia in the doorway. They both nearly went down. As Julia steadied Vida, she was surprised to feel the dancer tremble.

Owen started, then visibly brought himself under control. "Forgive me, Miss Everett...Julia. If this woman is a friend of yours, please get her from my sight."

Julia urged Vida into the hall, where Hannah put one arm around her and led her toward the stairs. Turning, Julia said tentatively, "I'm sure she meant no harm. Vida has an unfortunate tendency..."

A lower drawer in Owen's armoire stood open. He hurled the pouch inside. For a moment, she expected him to kick the door shut, but visibly he controlled himself. "I won't have a thief on the premises."

"Of course not. I'll talk to her. We all will. It won't happen again." Julia hesitated, then added, "Her dancing made Vida very popular last night."

She knew it was true. The women had all danced energetically, swinging their skirts and offering scandalous views of their limbs. Vida was most enthusiastic of all. Her body proved to be as supple as her nimble fingers. When a miner threw a poke to the stage, she snatched it up and deposited it deep within her cleavage without missing a step, much to the delight of the audience.

Owen pushed one hand through his hair, lifting it from his forehead, then smiled with an enchantingly boyish appeal. "Forgive me, Julia. You must think I have the temper of a two-year-old."

Because she had been thinking very nearly such a thing, she returned a quick denial. "I suspect she is a bit smitten with you, Mr. Powell. Probably she wanted some small possession to dream upon."

He looked so alarmed that she suppressed a smile, but she was too worried to feel amused for long. "Vida was kind to me on the trail. You will give her another chance, won't you?"

He sighed heavily, clearly feeling put upon while doing his best to bear up. "She can stay as long as she behaves. Won't you call me Owen, please?" He leaned against the window frame, outlined by sunlight. "What a courageous girl you are. Not many would have the courage to pit their survival against such great odds as a trek through the frozen north—and in such company."

"The troupe befriended me many times," Julia said in their defense. "And Duncan kept us safe."

"Of course." As he studied the polish of his boots, Owen seemed to speak more to himself than to her. "I once hoped to impress Duncan through cleverness." With a self-deprecating shrug, he added, "It was bravado, I'm afraid, a twelve-year-old trying to impress a man of twenty. He saw through me at once."

A vivid image came to Julia of Duncan's agony in Skagway when he recognized the burned-out hulk of the *Fortune*. Even so, she sympathized with Owen, or at least with the boy he had been.

Gracefully, Owen lowered himself to sit on the sill. "Did he tell you I was showing off for friends and put the *Patience* on the rocks?"

Julia shook her head. "You don't have to tell me these things."

"There is no use sparing myself." With a disarming smile, he added, "In all fairness, dear Julia, permit me to offer my side of the story."

She felt uneasy, but his brown eyes were guileless. Encouraged by her silence, he said, "If Duncan had beaten me, I'd have felt better. His superior silence drove me wild. I suppose I reacted by becoming more cocksure, rather than less."

The blithe tone faltered, for the first time revealing an agony that sounded genuine. "When word came that gold nuggets could be picked from the beach like hen's eggs, I thought I could gather enough to repay the cost of the *Patience,* and that at last Duncan would look on me with approval."

Instead, the *Fortune* burned. Julia ached for both brothers. At the same time, she realized she must not linger. Suppose Duncan discovered her here? Aaron's censure burned in her heart. She kept her voice pleasant with an effort. "Thank you for your confidence... Owen. Now I must go. I promised Hannah that I would join her."

Springing to his feet, Owen walked with her to the door. "Please say you understand, Julia. I can't bear for you to think badly of me."

Although he had done his brother a terrible wrong, her heart felt touched. After all, they shared a common bond. She had struggled throughout her life to please an uncle whose every look condemned her existence. It seemed that Owen had suffered equally from his older stepbrother.

Her expression must have revealed her feelings. Owen's eyes grew gentle before he raised her hand and pressed his lips to her palm then to her inner wrist.

Alarmed, she pulled free. "I must find Hannah. Excuse me." It was a major effort to walk calmly down the hall, aware that he watched until she was out of sight on the stairs.

Hannah was just starting up from the bottom. "Julia, whatever is keeping you? I am dying to locate Edmund."

"If he wishes to see you, he certainly knows where to look," Julia said wryly.

"Do you think he may be upset?"

Laughing, Julia hugged her. "When has that stopped you from tormenting Officer Gray?"

"A pert tongue does not become you, Julia," Hannah warned.

Thankful that Hannah's troubles put Owen to the back of her mind, Julia turned her attention to a mirror framed with enameled rosebuds. "I've been afraid to show this necklace for fear of theft, but I've noticed even larger nuggets casually displayed in Dawson City."

"The Mounties keep strict order," Hannah said, as proudly as if she were responsible. She peered more closely. "What a lovely specimen. It has a very distinctive heart shape."

One her father would surely know at once. With fresh impatience, Julia turned toward the door. "Let's look for a milliner. Our hats are a ruin, except for those bought for the stage." She paused as Hannah balked. "If Edmund

Gray wishes to speak with you, your paths are likely to cross whichever way you go.''

"They will be more certain to cross if we go toward the barracks," Hannah grumbled.

When they stepped onto the crowded plank walk, the black-haired dancer looked eagerly down the street while Julia studied the prospectors. Newcomers were flooding in from upriver, all of them recognizable by their perplexed manner, as if they couldn't believe this trodden mud flat was the golden country they sought.

To Julia, Chilkoot Pass seemed almost a dream. The weather was so warm that many men were in shirtsleeves. She tried to picture her father. He would have a snug cabin beside his claim. If only she could join him and help wash out the gold.

A stout Indian woman stopped directly in front of her. Black eyes blazed in a round brown face. Julia gained an impression of a tanned deerskin dress decorated with intricate quill work while she tried to make sense of a stream of words in a strange language. "I'm sorry. I'm afraid I don't know what you are saying."

The woman closed the space between them, backing Julia against a wall of the Playhouse. Switching to broken English, she shouted, "Three too many. Three too many."

Hannah tried to intervene. "Ma'am, you have made a mistake."

The woman's hand flashed out. Julia felt the chain snap behind her neck. "No!" she screamed. "Stop her!"

Hannah flung both arms around the Indian. The street was filled with people who seemed willing to mind their own business, probably because she and Hannah had just stepped out of a saloon. Lunging forward, Julia grabbed the thief. "Give it to me."

She and Hannah had all they could do to hold the woman, who was like a small engine as she drove against their restraining arms. A shrill whistle made them all start. Instinctively, their holds slackened. The Indian woman slipped into the crowd. At the same time, a man asked, "Why are you two always in trouble?"

Joyfully, Hannah exclaimed, "Edmund!"

Julia was dismayed to see amusement in the officer's eyes as he said, "I'm afraid we must have order, Miss Clark."

"You will have to catch her first," Hannah said.

"He means us," Julia corrected sharply. "He means we are breaking the peace."

Officer Gray tilted his head. "What should I believe of women who shout from windows and brawl in the public streets?"

"You're teasing us," Hannah faltered, looking as if she feared he was about to put her under arrest.

When a dimple glinted in his cheek, Julia cried angrily, "While you entertain yourself at our expense, that woman has disappeared with my only link to my father."

Edmund grew sober at once. "What woman? Miss Everett please start at the beginning."

She ached to run after the thief, but there was no chance of finding her now. Blinking back the sting of tears, she told him of the nugget that had drawn her all the way to Dawson City in search of a father she had never known.

Edmund listened with a thoughtful frown. "Everett," he repeated. "Joseph Everett. I've heard that name."

Julia drew in a sharp breath. She felt Hannah's arm around her waist. Edmund snapped his fingers. "That's it. Sodie Joe. The miners call Everett Sodie Joe."

Heart racing, Julia whispered, "Then he . . . he is in the area?"

"Unless someone got after him for taking too much at cards." Edmund paused at her startled gasp. "Forgive me, Miss Everett. But you did know . . . I hope I am not the first to tell you he is a gambler."

Hannah tightened her arm around Julia, as if she feared Julia might faint. "You are far too insensitive, Officer Gray."

To Julia, Hannah's voice seemed to come from a great distance. The usual rush of Dawson City streets was unchanged. Dogs howled. Steamboat whistles blew. Yet it was not the same. With a few words, Edmund had toppled her world. Her father was not a Klondike king but a gambler. A sure-thing man. He was not working a mine. He was probably in hiding. The nugget she had worn so proudly may have been won at cards, perhaps unfairly.

The sunlight felt warm on her skin while the chill of the pass spread through her. She had directed her last few months toward finding a father who would make the world right. Now it seemed he could not make it right even for himself.

From deep within, she gathered new purpose. He was her father. That made a bond. It struck her that she might help him. Ruth had said that he moved around a great deal. He must be lonely. The company of a loving daughter would allow him to settle down.

Gently, Edmund asked, "Miss Everett, is he expecting you?"

"I wrote to him, but my letter was never claimed." Despite her efforts, tears welled into her eyes. The busy street blurred.

From the Playhouse doorway, Owen said, "Officer, I'm sure you won't mind checking the records to find whether Everett has left the Yukon."

"Of course." Edmund spoke earnestly to Julia, "Miss Everett, do you remember the customs posts you passed on your journey down the river? Records are kept on every man who enters or leaves the Yukon. We'll soon learn whether he is still here."

"I'll help you check them," Hannah told Edmund, then added guiltily, "you will take care of Julia, won't you, Mr. Powell?"

"Of course." Owen clasped Julia's hands. "Poor love, this has been an emotional time."

She would not dissolve into tears, Julia told herself fiercely. Tears solved nothing. Gulping hard, she said, "Did you see what happened? An Indian woman stole the necklace from my throat. It was..." Despite herself, her voice wavered. "It was my only connection with my father."

"Let us step off this crowded street." Linking her arm through his, Owen led her into the office at the back of the saloon, then held her tenderly. "Dearest Julia, I can't change what has happened, but I swear, if your father is in the Yukon, I will find him for you."

"Did you hear it all?" she asked. "That he is a gambler called Sodie Joe? He may have played cards in this very saloon."

Owen shook his head. "I don't know him, dearest, but I mean to ask for you."

They both started when the door slammed open. Duncan strode inside. "What the devil is going on?"

"Go easy," Owen warned. "Julia has had a shock."

She felt suddenly aware of Owen's arms around her. They had been comforting, but now felt possessive. She pulled free and reached in despair toward the man she loved. "My necklace—you remember, the nugget—the link to my father. An Indian woman popped up in front of me and I couldn't understand her, but then she screamed 'Three too many' and snatched the nugget."

As he drew her into the comfort of his arms, she looked up in anguish. "Duncan, she tore it right off my neck. Hannah grabbed her and so did I, but then Officer Gray threatened to arrest us for brawling in the street, which was Hannah's fault in the first place for shouting from her window, and that's not the worst of it—"

"Breathe," Duncan ordered gently.

Julia gulped for air. Duncan glanced at Owen. "A steamer came in this morning with a supply of whiskey. Check with August on how much we need." Owen hesitated and Duncan said with impatience, "Go now. Before the stock is sold."

When the door slammed behind him, Julia's problems receded briefly. Owen had tried to help her, and she hadn't even thanked him. She turned to Duncan. "You treat him abominably. He is your brother. And he's doing the best he can."

"When did you develop a tenderness for Owen?"

The accusation hurt. If he couldn't see which of them she preferred, he must not care for her. The overheard conversation rushed back. "That's what you want, isn't it?"

"What in blazes do you mean by that?"

"You wished him luck in courting me. I heard you."

Duncan's eyes darkened. "You should know by now what I want." Roughly, he pulled her closer. His mouth captured hers. Her attempt to free herself only made her more conscious of his hard body. Layers of clothing proved useless against a searing memory of bare skin.

"Let me go," she gasped. "There's nothing for us. I won't get in your way." His lips found a sensitive hollow behind her ear. Grasping his shoulders, she steadied herself against a flood of sensation.

She needed to be closer and pressed into him until her breasts felt crushed against his chest. Her thighs pressed against the lean, hard length of his. She felt his arousal with a sense of joy, but to her dismay, he drew back. "Sweet Songbird," he said with difficulty. "Your father may have his hands full in keeping you in your proper station."

The reminder sent a cold rush and chilled her desire. "He is nothing but a gambler known as Sodie Joe."

For days now, Duncan had prepared himself to accept that Everett was a wealthy Klondike king. A gambler? Nothing more? Against a wash of relief, he realized she would return to Seattle, after all. There was no wealthy father to forbid her from marrying a penniless fisherman.

The shock of seeing her in Owen's arms returned briefly, but she had left his stepbrother at once and had come to him. When she kissed him, pressing so close that clothing was no barrier to the secrets of their bodies, all he could think was of locked doors and soft beds. This was not the time. "Sweetheart," he began, forcing his mind to the practical problems of their immediate future.

Julia recognized the expression in Duncan's face. That look said she should forget the search for her father—a mere gambler. While resentment burned through the earlier haze of desire, she said tightly, "I intend to question every man in town, if need be, until I locate someone who knows where to find Joseph Everett."

"The devil you will!" Duncan caught her to him so abruptly that her breath puffed out in surprise. "Whatever your father may be, you were raised as a lady and I will not allow you to approach strange men."

She pushed hard against his chest. "You are fond of telling me what you will not allow."

The pain in her eyes sent an ache through Duncan. It was hell to want to give her what she needed so desperately and be unable to help. "If men are to be questioned," he said, his voice tight, "I'll be the one to do it. Can't you get it through your head that these fellows have been away from women for an uncomfortably long time?"

Before she could argue, he kissed her again, so deeply that her resistance eased and her body again molded to his. With an effort, he ended the kiss. "You've gone through enormous difficulties, sweetheart. Now you must have patience. Waiting will be difficult, but you'll know as soon as I learn anything."

Julia shook away a need to keep kissing him. "Wait?" she repeated, forcing her mind to clear. "Have patience? Do you think that a few kisses will encourage me to sit dutifully while my father decides to move on? I don't intend to wait, Duncan. I intend to find my own answers." Twisting free of his arms, she darted into the saloon.

# Chapter Twenty-Two

Nearly a dozen men lined the Playhouse bar or sprawled at the tables. Most of them were newcomers. Julia chose a man who looked as if he had been in the Klondike for months. His rumbling laugh gave her courage and before she could lose her nerve, she approached his table. "Sir?"

He looked up with suddenly avid eyes, then patted his knee. "Join me for a drink, pretty thing?"

Julia glanced toward the office, relieved to see Duncan watching. "I need information, not a drink, sir. Do you happen to know a man called Sodie Joe?"

The prospector whipped out one arm and pulled her close, squeezing her so hard that she gasped. "That'll take a bit of thinkin', honey." His eyes roved lewdly over her bodice. "Why don't you have a drink while I stretch my memory?"

His hand slipped lower to cup her bottom. Snatching a glass of whiskey from the table, she dashed it into his face. With an outraged yowl, he leaped to his feet.

While the other men laughed, Julia fled toward the bar. Several hands reached out for her as she rushed between the tables. "Sing somethin' romantic, honey," one shouted. Another caught her skirt, but she jerked it free. Someone patted her behind. She closed her mind to half a dozen coarse invitations, too stunned for the insults to register. How could these be the same men who listened raptly to her songs?

Tilly pulled her to safety behind the bar. "A lady like you hadn't oughta be in a place like this. You don't know how to handle these fellows."

"I certainly do not," Julia admitted. To her relief, the man she had doused with whiskey was settling into his chair, his laugh rumbling again as his friends ribbed him. She searched for Duncan, and with a rise of indignation she saw that he had returned to the office.

He was quick enough to pull her into his arms when they were alone. Why hadn't he come to her rescue? Did his sense of responsibility end with the revelation that her father was a traveling gambler?

Tilly dipped water from the barrel at the end of the bar. "Here, love, calm yourself."

The glacial water was pure and cold. As she sipped from the metal dipper, Julia's mind became clear. There was no sense in trying to guess Duncan's thoughts—or his feelings. She must depend on herself. What was her best course?

Her attempt to plan was interrupted by Tilly's flirtation with the brawny bartender. "Gus, you told me all the good claims were taken. Yet here you are, servin' drinks to earn a new grubstake so you can tramp out there with the rest of 'em. Why is that?"

Resting his elbows on the bar, Gus leaned closer. "Don't give me any sass, Red. There's honor in honest work. And there's still fractions to be had."

"Fractions? What kind of a claim is that, something you fellows work together?"

Julia listened absently, trying to gather courage to approach another sourdough. This time, she must make the man understand from the start that she was not a bar girl.

She jumped at a derisive snort from Gus. "I don't expect any woman to trouble her mind at understanding."

"Try me," Tilly posed provocatively.

"Thinking of stampeding, are you?" His laughter sounded grudging.

Tilly's eyes sparkled. Lightly, she batted his shoulder. "Listen to him, Julia. He's not as tough as he pretends. I believe I'm gettin' to him."

"You'd have better luck finding a rich claim than getting to me," Gus told her severely. "And you'd have better luck mining the dirt on the floor than tramping the hills."

"He loves me," Tilly said. "Else, he wouldn't give away tips like that."

Julia thought most of the conversation was incomprehensible. "It's true we know little about mining, Gus. What do you mean by fractions and stampedes?"

"Don't be worrying your pretty head," he said gruffly. "It ain't gonna matter to you showgirls."

Tilly winked as Julia stiffened in annoyance. "'Course it matters, Gus, honey. Anything that matters to you matters to me."

Turning his burly shoulders away, Gus pointedly spoke to Julia as if to emphasize that Tilly was beyond his interest. "You know how the first claim on a creek is called the Discovery Claim? The ones at either side are called One Above and One Below, then Two Above and Two Below and so on, as far up or down the creek as claims are made."

"And fractions?"

Merrily, Tilly said, "Them's the little slivers poor miners like Gus are lookin' for."

Producing a rag from beneath the bar, he polished busily as if trying to wipe Tilly from his life. She leaned over and grinned at her reflection, fluffing up her hair.

Her jibe must have reached him, for still pointedly speaking to Julia, Gus explained. "The men don't carry measuring devices when they prospect. They just step off their claims. Like as not when the survey comes around, the officers see the fellows marked off an extra yard or more. The law is five hundred feet to any one miner on any one creek. So the fractions are put up for claiming."

He looked belligerently at Tilly. "Small as they are, if the paydirt's rich, a man can do himself proud."

It was a long speech for August. An eager glint had come into his eyes, one that appeared to have little to do with Tilly. Julia knew the look. She had seen it all along the trail. Gold, not love, made a man's eyes take on that anticipating glow.

"So that's your plan," Tilly said. "Soon as you get a grubstake, you'll head out with the rest of these fools, hopin' to find yourself one of them fractions."

He shook his head. "Not me. Once it's known that fractions are open on some creek, half the town tramps out there, jostling to be first." He glared at her. "And that's a stampede."

Tilly shaped a kiss with her lips. "Could be fun, depending on who did the jostlin'."

Gus's long face darkened. "I aim to tramp off by myself. There's still pups out there that no man's claimed. Some of them'll yield up paydirt."

"Pups?" Julia repeated blankly.

Tilly answered, smug with knowledge. "Side creeks. Gus explained them to me yesterday."

It occurred to Julia that Tilly was as captivated by the dour bartender as Hannah was by her officer. Feeling romantically abandoned, she replaced the dipper on the edge of the barrel. Her time was better spent thinking about how to locate Sodie Joe than thinking about the elusive pleasures of romance.

Hannah swirled into the saloon, almost dancing between the tables as she rushed to Julia. She seemed casually unaware of calls from the men in the saloon. "There you are! Julia, we checked the records and there is none saying that Joseph Everett left the territory."

The lilt in her voice and bright shine in her eyes suggested that more flirting than studying had been done. Still, however coquettish Hannah might be, Julia trusted Officer Gray to make a careful search.

"So he is still in the Yukon," Julia said with relief. "We must only find out where. Did Edmund ask the other officers if they had heard of Sodie Joe?"

The glow in Hannah's face was momentarily subdued. "He hasn't been seen in Dawson City for over a month." Animation returned swiftly. "But that's good, because he must come in soon to buy supplies and claim his mail."

Should she leave another message at the post office? Julia decided against it. If Sodie Joe came into town, he would soon see the poster or hear word that his daughter was singing at the Bonanza Playhouse. Until she located him, she must go on stage every night.

After the insults she had received from the men in the saloon, it would be more difficult to perform. The day passed slowly. She gathered courage to speak to several more prospectors, but learned nothing of Sodie Joe except that one of the men had gambled with him.

That night, she dressed for the stage with reluctance. Even the peacock feather seemed wilted and kept falling into her eyes. When she watched the cancan dancers, she remembered every pinch and shouted suggestion during her dash among the rowdy miners. *Sing somethin' romantic, honey.* She was tempted to go out there and sing only hymns. Duncan joined her in the wings. "Remember, sweetheart, the more men become enchanted with you, the sooner word will spread that you are here."

And that was why she must please them. The tenderness in Duncan's expression made her thankful she hadn't accused him of losing interest in the daughter of a gambler. She admitted he had been right to warn her about lifting her skirts. Obviously, the men misunderstood her innocent dance. Smoothing the satin into proper folds, she waited for Owen to call her name.

It was even harder than before to walk on stage, but once again an enthusiastic reception eased her doubts. When her voice rose in pure, clear notes, the bawdy miners became fathers, friends and sons. She began with ballads, then switched to happier tunes and, despite Duncan's warning and her own earlier misgivings, whirled her skirts as her voice lilted through the songs.

When the curtains swung together, she looked in amazement at the nuggets scattered at her feet. Then she looked at Duncan. His eyes were angry. Dismayed, she straightened the skirts that she had promised not to lift. Bending swiftly, she gathered the nuggets, then ran into the wings, holding them in her open palm. "How much will you need to buy a trawler?"

He knocked her hand away. "Can you believe I would buy a boat with a woman's body?"

Vida scrambled to retrieve the nuggets while Duncan turned away. "You have seen far more than that of me!" Julia exclaimed. "If a look at my ankles will earn money to buy a fishing boat, I see no harm in it."

"I keep crediting you with sense when your head is empty," he answered coldly.

"You may be right," she said, stung with rejection. "I fear I lost my good sense in Miles Canyon."

He stiffened. She wanted to call back the words, but could not. She had thrown them less to annoy him than to hear him say he cared for her. But he walked away.

Hours later, she heard the muffled thud of blankets thrown down outside her door. Slipping from the bed, she padded barefoot to the wall, knelt and said through the calico, "There is no need for your continued discomfort out there."

Impatience sounded in his voice, "Is that an invitation to join you?"

"It is not." She had had time to reconsider her hasty words in the wings, time to admit she had perhaps overreacted and longed to end the quarrel. Instead, sitting on her heels, she told her traitorous senses that Duncan had a great deal to answer for. "You might have helped when that beast insulted me in the saloon."

"As I remember," he countered calmly, "you refused my help."

"I didn't expect the men to be so forward."

She heard him sigh. "Nothing I say sticks to your mind."

It would, if he would only say the words she longed to hear. "I remember all your warnings," she said crisply. "Unfortunately, there are men about whose egos prevent them from recognizing polite courtesy."

"I seem to remember warning you of that."

It was not enjoyable to lose an argument, especially through a wall. Although she was dressed only in her nightgown, Julia pushed open the door and went out to sit at the end of Duncan's blanket.

He sat up as if stung. "What in blazes are you thinking?"

"That I would rather watch your face when I'm talking with you." She traced a thread in the blanket, uneasily aware of her unbound hair curling over her shoulders to the round, low neckline of her gown.

Golden light flowed from an oil lamp down the hall. Music and laughter tumbled up the open stairs. The empty hall was an isolated haven. Her pulse began to hammer. "I have learned a great deal about mining," she said to hide her confusion. "Do you know that when word comes of a gold strike, much of the town runs out like stampeding cattle?"

"If word comes that you're sitting out here half-naked, there will be a stampede up the stairs."

She looked into his eyes and saw awakening desire that made her even more conscious of the pulse in her throat. Her hands trembled and she stopped trying to trace the blanket pattern and pressed her palms over her knees. They felt unnaturally hot through the linen. "Still," she murmured, "it does sound exciting."

"Julia, if you are thinking of joining a throng of gold-crazed fools, put it out of your head."

"How well you know me," she said with sudden spirit. "It's as if you read my mind. But I will thank you not to tell me where I may or may not go."

If he could read her thoughts he would know that her pulse was racing with the memory of his kisses. Even in this dim light, her skin felt as if it glowed through the fine material of her gown. She drew folds of cloth over her knees, then realized that her breasts were clearly defined through the rose-sprigged linen.

She looked into Duncan's smoldering eyes and felt light-headed with the memory of him kissing her nipples through her chemise. "If you don't go to bed at once," he said harshly, "I'll carry you there."

"Will you?" She put her hand over the blanket where it covered one of his feet and felt the impression of each separate toe.

With a muffled oath, he threw the blankets aside, rose swiftly, swept her into his arms and carried her into her room. "Which bed?"

She twisted her arms around his shoulders and slid one hand down the smooth muscles of his back. The beat of his heart thudded against her breasts, and she thought of their bare skin touching.

He moved quickly to drop her onto the nearest bed as if her body burned him. When she didn't let go, he fell onto the bed with her. She twined her legs between his. He gave a startled groan, then his control snapped. His lips captured hers, caressing and tasting, the kiss deepening as if it were an attempt to quench a lifetime of thirst for them both.

She pushed one hand inside his shirt to his heated skin, delirious with the freedom to touch him at last. Kissing, they rolled together until she was on top of him, her gown high up her thighs as she clung to him. She pressed closer, aching for sensations excitingly near but impeded by clothing.

Bunching the linen in rough hands, he pulled the gown higher. When she felt his hot palms press and cradle her bare bottom, she wriggled desperately against the hardness that tantalized her even while she urged herself against him. "Duncan... Oh, please."

Down the hall, someone laughed loudly. A woman giggled. A door slammed. Duncan rolled out from under Julia with a look of such self-reproach that she remained kneeling on the bed.

He turned his back. Every line of his body was taut. "Duncan," she whispered. "Why not?"

He shook his head. "Not here. Not like this. Not like them."

The anguish in his voice made her bite her lip in shame; he strode from the room, closing the door without looking back. Seconds later, she heard him drop heavily onto his blankets.

"Then when?" Julia whispered. "Where?" But she spoke the words too softly to be heard, or else he chose not to answer. Minutes later, Hannah came running up the stairs and into the room, full of gay chatter and an energy that never seemed to fade.

* * *

In the morning, her friend's cheerful greeting roused Julia from restless dreams. She rubbed gritty eyes, wondering how Hannah managed with so little sleep. Perhaps her days as a stowaway had hardened her to doing with little rest.

"I hope we are not off in quest of Officer Gray again," Julia said as she began to dress.

Hannah laughed gaily. "Why, no, for I have already arranged to meet him for lunch. He says there is a man down the street selling pies for a dollar. We are going to share one while we watch the foolish cheechakos come ashore."

"As if you were not one of them," Julia said, pleased for her friend's happiness, but with increased misgivings over her own. Duncan longed for Seattle, but he would not be happy there without a trawler, one he might earn if she were not with him. One she might eventually earn, if he would accept the nuggets her singing won. Her thoughts circled until she wanted to scream.

She splashed cold water onto her face from a bowl on the dressing table, but felt little refreshed. What must Duncan think of her behavior last night? Hannah might easily have embarrassed them both. With a sinking heart, Julia suspected that Duncan would avoid her.

As they entered the hall, a door opened farther down. A burly man stepped out, reddened when he saw them, then hurried toward the stairs. "Why, it's Gus!" Hannah exclaimed. She exchanged a glance with Julia, then darted forward. "Let's learn whose room he visited."

The mischief in Hannah's eyes encouraged Julia. She welcomed a new direction for her thoughts. The porcelain knob of Tilly's door felt cool to her touch and turned easily. "Open it," Hannah whispered. Cautiously, Julia cracked open the door.

Tilly sat up in bed, laughing at them. "What a lot of whisperin'. Thought you never would get the nerve to come in. Well, what's keepin' you, now?"

Julia stepped inside. "Was that August who left?"

"Gus? Here? Think I'm crazy?" Tilly paused, then leaned wistfully against her upraised knees. "Maybe I am. We make a pair, don't we?"

Teasing, Julia leaned over the iron bed frame. "What was it you warned me about in Seattle? Something about never trusting love?" As Tilly's sparkling eyes denied that words could direct the heart, Julia felt a rush of hope. If the cynical showgirl could learn to trust again, surely she and Duncan could find a way to be together.

Hannah had dropped onto the foot of the bed. "Tilly and August are no more unlikely a pair than Edmund and me. I live in fear that he will discover my past."

"It seems to me you would be happier dragging that monster out of your closet," Julia said, "rather than fearing the handsome Mountie will discover it there."

Mournfully, Hannah said, "You don't know a fig about love."

A few minutes earlier, Julia might have agreed, but Tilly's delight was contagious and she answered with only a smile.

"Well, I do," Tilly said gleefully. "I know who Julia's father loves."

"What?" Julia demanded, clutching the bed frame. "What are you talking about? Tell me!"

"Go easy," Tilly protested. "Give me time to get it straight." While Julia seethed with impatience, the redhaired dancer slipped from the bed and splashed her face and hands with water from a pottery bowl. Clearly, she was enjoying her secret.

"Don't be cruel," Hannah protested. "Julia is about to burst."

"I suppose August told you," Julia prompted. "He hardly looks the sort to know about affairs of the heart."

"That's what you think," Tilly said tartly. Lifting her walking suit from a peg in the wall, she slipped it over her head. Voice muffled, she added, "Gus said he married her."

Puzzled, Hannah asked, "Gus is married?"

"No!" Tilly's head popped into view. "I don't believe it. Gus, married? Who said so?"

"You just did," Hannah exclaimed, while Julia looked impatiently from one to the other.

"Dolt." Looking reprieved, Tilly attacked the buttons lining the front of her dress. "Not Gus. Julia's father. He married a woman with a claim at Forty Above Hunker. She was tryin' to mine it herself, Gus said. And that's hard work, no lie."

"Are you saying he married some woman for her claim?" Julia demanded.

Tilly shrugged. "All Gus knows is that Sodie Joe was huntin' a claim and this widow was needin' help, so they tied the knot."

Julia's thoughts raced. Forty Above Hunker. That meant forty five-hundred-foot claims upstream from the discovery site on Hunker Creek, wherever that might be. She felt as if she could fly over the tundra. "I'll go at once."

Catching Tilly's hands, she whirled her around. The room was so small they soon collided with the dressing table. However unlike their lives might be, in many ways they were sisters, and Julia felt an upwelling love for all the showgirls.

"How will you get to Hunker Creek?" Hannah asked.

"We have walked miles enough to get here," Julia said. "A few more will scarcely trouble me."

She repeated the vow at breakfast minutes later, sparkling with excitement as she shared Tilly's discovery with the others. "My father must be with her. I can't wait to get out there."

"Impossible. The country is far too rough," Duncan protested, while Owen nodded agreement.

Julia glared at them both. "If I could withstand the Chilkoot Pass, I find it difficult to believe a walk through the tundra will be any worse."

Duncan took a long swallow of coffee, then said, "On the trail, all men thought of was gold. Now most are disillusioned. They'll welcome a woman's soft body to ease the bitterness."

Was that what she meant to him? Julia was finding it impossible to keep thoughts of last night in the recesses of her mind. Her gaze kept returning to the open collar of his shirt and the bronze curve of his throat. She wanted to place her lips just there. And then . . .

She wrenched her attention to Owen. "Rough going," he was saying. "Brambles and brush. Better to send a messenger to invite the woman here."

Glaring, she asked, "Does it make sense to say the journey is safe for one woman, but not for another?"

Duncan watched Julia's lovely mouth set in the stubborn line that touched something inside him. He longed to make her happy. If only he could somehow present her with the man she had traveled all this way to find.

But Julia was impulsive. And there was something unsettling in the mystery surrounding Everett. The latest news of a gambler marrying a widow for her claim made him wary.

Julia's plan to march out to the creeks had better be stopped right now. "You can't even move safely between tables in the saloon," he reminded her. "How in blazes do you expect to navigate the goldfields?"

Her expression dared him to stop her. Slowly, he offered a possibility that had begun to bother him. "You don't even know that Everett wants to meet you."

"He does."

Pain flashed through her eyes. Julia lived in a dream of her own imagining. She needed to face the truth before it hurt her. Quietly, he said, "With the story in the newspaper and increasing numbers of men drawn to your singing, it's probable that he already knows you're here."

Julia said hotly, "If he didn't care for me, he would not have sent the nugget."

Owen interrupted, sounding uneasy. "He must be with the woman. Let us send a message, Julia."

"And don't expect too much," Duncan warned.

Julia tore a piece of bread from a thick bun and buttered it in silence. Then she looked straight at Duncan. "Don't worry," she said in a sweet tone meant to cover her aching heart. "I have become accustomed to disappointment."

Their gaze held for a volatile moment while both remembered their interrupted lovemaking. Duncan swung to his feet. "I'll talk to Gus. He may know more than he's told Tilly."

Julia darted after him. Whatever the bartender might know, she meant to hear without having to pry information from either man. Tilly followed, but stopped her as Duncan stepped into the saloon. "Just wait. You'll have an escort of hundreds."

Julia looked at her blankly. "What do you mean?"

"Watch." Raising her voice, Tilly said loudly, "That's what he told me. Fractions on Hunker Creek go up for claims at one o'clock today."

She winked as conversations halted at nearby tables. The words "fractions" and "Hunker Creek" swept from man to man. "Of course," Tilly continued merrily, "I haven't the foggiest idea what he meant." She turned to the nearest prospector. "What in the world is a fraction? Do you know, sir?"

"Yes, miss, I do." Gulping his drink, he dashed for the door. Several men ran after him. From the street, someone yelled. "Fractions opening on Hunker Creek. Hurry."

Triumph gleamed in Tilly's face. "Looks like a crowd's heading out to Hunker Creek. Shouldn't be much trouble to follow."

Julia cast a defiant glance at Duncan. In his face, she saw the same harried expression he had often worn at Lake Bennett. Beneath it she saw something more, a look of wary approval. "All right, Julia," he said, straightening from the bar. "Have it your way. But we'll go together."

She felt as if she had lit up inside despite the dark warning in his eyes. Eagerness welled in her, along with pleasure over the prospect of once again traveling with Duncan. Her delight made him add shortly, "Get enough food together for two days while I pack our supplies."

She resisted the flat order and the delay. "We're only going out to Hunker Creek."

"It won't be a picnic," he said, his voice hard. "Prepare for a rough journey, one that may end with far greater disappointment than any I've ever caused you."

# Chapter Twenty-Three

$\sim\!\!\sim\!\!\sim\!\!\sim$

Gold pans and shovels rattled in an eager chorus as many men and a few women hurried from Dawson City. They passed Julia and Duncan whenever possible. The Bonanza mated with the Klondike River a short way east of town, but claims on that stream—called Rabbit Creek before it spawned the gold rush—had all been staked more than a year before. The stampeders scarcely gave it a glance.

Walking became difficult after hundreds of feet churned the trail to mud. Rivulets of water ran from every gully and crevice and pooled in the footprints. Most of the stampeders appeared to be newcomers. Julia felt uneasy because the rush was caused by Tilly. Still, such wild chases were common to those burning with gold fever. They at least provided an outlet for people's hopes.

Duncan's long strides covered the rough trail as if he could hardly wait to be rid of her. Annoyed, she hurried after him. Her boots skidded in mud. He caught her before she could fall, but with a rigid grip that had nothing of tenderness in it.

Feeling bereft, she plodded on. She had looked forward to hiking with him, but he had become as remote as he had been on the last days of their journey down the Yukon. Why was he angry? She believed he cared for her. Maybe he didn't want her to meet her father. It wasn't just that Joe was a gambler. Duncan's disapproval started before he learned Joe's occupation.

Again, she found herself comparing him to her uncle. Duncan was a man who needed to be in control. He was angry because she risked her safety and her happiness by insisting on this quest when he felt helpless to protect her.

She loved him, but she resented his attempt to dominate. He was right about one thing, she decided as she hurried to catch up, the trail was far from the pleasant country walk she had imagined. By noon, every muscle ached from lifting her boots from mud, only to plow into more.

A burly fellow passed them, one who must have come in with the latest flood of cheechakos. His eyes were hidden behind a wooden frame mask with eye slits that prevented snowblindness. She wondered if they were any help beneath this summer sun.

A stocking cap was pulled low over his head and ears, topped by a natty beaver hat. His face looked flushed as he hurried past. He was obviously sweating in his heavy wool shirt. Fur-lined mittens were stuffed into his pack on top of a blanket coat. A cobweb of ropes held a bulging collection of blankets, Yukon stove, food tins, gold scales, spyglass and folding stool. Shovels dangling from the frame batted his generous posterior at every stride.

Julia covered a smile with her hand. Her glance flashed to Duncan, and as his eyes creased with shared amusement, laughter bubbled upward until she was helpless to stop it. Leaning weakly against him, she gasped for breath. Wryly, he said, "There is a man who knows the value of preparation."

"Do you suppose he means to mine?" Julia asked. "Or to sit on his stool and watch the labor of others?"

As Duncan smiled at her, she felt companionship returning, and it grew as they walked on. Relief gave new energy to her steps. Soon, Duncan pointed out the Hunker River.

Julia clasped her hands. "We're almost there."

"We still have a long walk," he warned. "We'll cross and have lunch."

Half a mile upstream, where the river narrowed, someone had thrown a rough bridge over the muddy water. On the far shore, they left the trail and climbed through underbrush to a patch of dry land beneath a birch tree. While they shared venison jerky and dried peaches, the silence became uncomfortable.

Laughter had bridged the tension momentarily. Perhaps it could do so again. Pointing to one of the men trudging up the trail, she said, "That fellow must be a dentist, the one with the pencil moustache and delicate hands. He smiled a moment ago, showing teeth as perfect as an advertisement."

From the corner of her eye, she saw Duncan's expression lighten. Encouraged, she pointed to another prospector. "There, that portly one, do you suppose he is a banker? I see him behind a great carved oak desk ruling over trembling souls who dare to ask him to lend them money... but at home he trembles beneath the iron rule of his wife."

Duncan leaned one arm across his knee, watching Julia instead of the men she indicated. She was as free-spirited as a child. He took pleasure in looking at her. Strands of hair had slipped free of the jaunty brim of her hat. They cast diverting shadows over her face. He enjoyed the interplay of light and shadow over the freckles scattered across the gentle curve of her cheeks. He ached that he couldn't hand her happiness in a golden box.

She looked at him, her head tilted. "Are you listening to me?"

Forcing aside the desire to kiss each freckle, he said, "Don't I always?"

Her look became incredulous, her eyes widening while she drew in a breath as if to list every instance when he might have given less attention than she wished. Before she could speak, he pointed out a brawny man with a reddened complexion. "There's a sailor. What's his story?"

Julia considered. "He has left his ship short one crew member, but I believe that's common. It occurs to me that fishers and miners are somewhat alike. Both seek hidden wealth."

"Only the skilled or lucky find it," he said. "When that fellow's sweetheart learned his ship was headed for Skagway, she warned him not to come home without gathering nuggets from the beach."

"How disappointed she will be, but if she is so greedy, she does not deserve him."

Duncan lay back on his elbows, again watching Julia. "She's thinking of the comfort of her children," he corrected softly. Then he added, "What sort of woman does a penniless fisherman deserve?"

She clasped her arms around her upraised knees, silent for a moment. "He looked like an honest man. If I were his mother, I would urge him to look for a woman who shares his values."

"His *mother?*" Duncan exclaimed.

Julia poked his ribs. "He must have one, you know."

"He looks about your age," Duncan mused. "Too old to heed advice, I'm afraid."

She returned the jibe. "His penniless state means nothing to his sweetheart, for she believes him to be a man of great prospect."

For a moment, they held each other with their eyes, conscious of nearby prospectors while longing to touch. Feeling the danger in the situation, Duncan lay back on the grass, his arms beneath his head. "She may grow to resent having to live on a sailor's share."

Fiercely, Julia answered. "She will do that and save, for she learned through a difficult upbringing to make a lot of a little."

When she leaned over him, her eyes sparking, he wanted to give her the world, but could only offer his heart. Roughly, he said, "He's a lucky man."

"Yes," she said. "As long as he realizes it."

He moved one hand to caress her cheek, but from the trail someone whistled. Julia sat straighter. "Why did you encourage Owen to court me?"

"It was a warning, sweetheart, that you were more than he could handle." Aware of traffic on the trail, he added more lightly, "It was also a warning that women who listen through walls can expect to hear nothing good of themselves."

She looked so indignant that he sprang to his feet, caught her hand and pulled her upward. "We're not here for a picnic. We still have miles to walk."

Neither moved toward the trail. For a long moment, they looked into each other's eyes. "Julia," Duncan said quietly. "You must know how difficult it was to leave your bed, but you will have to think of your reputation."

She needed love, not a lecture. She answered with a painful rise of temper. "A woman who sings in a saloon, the daughter of a gambler? That reputation?"

"Remember who you are," he said, "not who men may think you to be."

"Who am I to you, Duncan? The runaway niece of an unpleasant shopkeeper? Daughter of an unmarried mother? What reputation are you so determined to protect?"

He raised his hands to cradle her face. Her angry eyes sparked tenderness deep inside him. Aaron Ames should be horsewhipped for his treatment of her. And as for her father, the more he learned of the man, the more credit Duncan gave him for staying out of her life. He meant to do the same until he could support and protect her.

Quietly, he said, "From the first, I've seen a woman whose spirit outshines her sweetness. I've seen a dreamer who is far too harsh when thinking of herself and far too reckless for her safety."

The lovely eyes became troubled. He wanted to kiss her eyelids closed, then urge her to see herself as he knew her to be. There were too damned many curious glances cast toward them already. With reluctance, he lowered his hands. "We have a long walk ahead, sweetheart. We'd better get started." She was quiet. Despite the onlookers, he clasped her hand and continued to hold it as they walked.

Julia scarcely noticed the muddy river or the rough trail. Duncan had sounded as if he truly cared for her. The warm clasp of his hand made her feel safe. And yet he had made it clear he would not commit himself until he could provide a comfortable home for her.

He had spent long hours over the Bonanza Playhouse accounts. Was their future in those cramped figures? She knew he longed for the open sea, not a desk and ledger. How long would it take him to resent her for making that paperwork necessary?

She turned her gaze ahead, toward her father. He must have answers. She felt it in her heart as she had since she was old enough to know that she did not belong with Aaron and Ruth. Each thing she learned of Joseph Everett filled in a bit of her past and a bit more of herself.

At last, they approached the first of the mining claims. Julia felt her step grow lighter. Cabins built of raw lumber looked out of place against the earth and shrubbery. Men clustered along wooden chutes. As she came abreast of one, Julia watched two men shovel gravel into the high end. Others worked mysteriously along the length.

Great mounds of dirt and gravel forced the trail to veer. Frames built of logs protruded from the top of the mounds, crossed by bars supporting a pulley. "They each have their own well," she said. "I suppose the river is too muddy to drink."

Duncan burst into laughter. "Those are windlasses, sweetheart. All those heaps of gravel and muck were brought up through your wells during the winter, while the ground was frozen. As you see, the men are now occupied in sluicing their dumps, hoping to find gold among the rocks."

The dumps were hoards of buried treasure. Julia looked at them with new eyes, no longer grudging the extra steps it took to go around. How exciting it must be to work the sluice, watching for the glint of precious metal. She suddenly understood the force drawing so many thousands to the Klondike.

The prospect of meeting her father drew her more avidly. Pointing to a stake, she tugged at Duncan, who had paused to watch the miners. "Nineteen Below Discovery. We still have a long way to walk."

As they started on, a group of men came toward them. Blanket rolls dragged heavily against their pack straps. Awed, Julia turned to watch them descend the trail. Each of those blankets must be weighted by gold. How many millionaires had they already passed on this trail?

Cabins stood raggedly on the hillside on both banks of the creeks. Great mounds of gravel all but overlapped. Even the gulches—the pups, she corrected herself—were marked with

stakes. Wooden sluice boxes snaked over the brush, water
gushing from the lower ends.

A few of the mines were still being worked. The air carried acrid whiffs of burned wood. As they passed the discovery claim and continued uphill over earth as smooth-
packed as a city street, Julia saw miners haul up a steaming
bucket. The creak of their windlass added an eerie sound to
the clunk of gates in nearby sluice boxes and the swishing
from hundreds of rockers.

Many cabins appeared to be deserted. Apparently, their
owners had taken their gold into town. Julia felt her senses
lurch as she wondered where she and Duncan would spend
the night.

He indicated a marker. "We have only five more claims
to go."

Julia looked eagerly ahead. The streambed rambled so
that it was impossible to know which cabin or gravel dump
belonged to Sodie Joe Everett and his wife. She hoped the
marriage was happy. Excitement coursed through her as she
located each claim stake and read each number aloud.
"Forty above," she said at last and clutched Duncan's hand
like a lifeline.

A small log cabin stood above a gravel dump and an
abandoned windlass. A heavyset miner in boots, trousers
and a blue flannel shirt shoveled earth into the upper end of
a sluice. Julia's heart leaped. Could it be . . . ?

Then she realized the miner was a woman. Gray hair was
pinned haphazardly to the top of her head, with lank tendrils hanging down her neck and over her forehead. As Julia watched, the woman raised one sleeve to brush hair from
her face.

"Go ahead," Duncan said. "Speak to her."

Where was Sodie Joe? Taking courage from Duncan,
Julia picked her way to the sluice. "Pardon me, ma'am. Are
you Mrs. Everett?" *Are you my stepmother?* She held her
breath while the woman turned slowly and looked her up
and down, taking in unlined skin, new hat and store-bought
clothing.

"I'm Martha Everett. Who wants to know?" The voice
was low and cautious. Weathered skin aged her beyond her

years, but Julia guessed her to be in her late forties. There was a forbidding lack of welcome in the dark eyes, deeply creased at each side.

"I was told that you are married to Joseph Everett," Julia explained, trying to put warmth into her voice while the woman's frown threatened to freeze the words in her throat. "He . . . is my father. I came from Seattle to find him."

A flash of shock went through the woman's eyes before they darkened in pain. She turned to the sluices. "Haven't seen him in weeks. And I've no time for idle talk."

Julia's heart plummeted and she reached out to Duncan. Quietly, he said, "Ma'am, it looks as if you could use some extra hands. The only pay we ask is information when we're done."

She studied him, then made a sudden decision. "Get on the gate, then, mister. Let the water through when I say. You, girl. Take up a paddle."

Apprehension lay over Julia. Where was her father? What had he done to cause Martha to be so hostile? Realizing that answers would not be coming before the gravel was sluiced, she stepped onto a walk mounted beside the long chute. As she took up a wooden paddle, Duncan released a gate at the top. Water burst through, washing the lighter material with it. The heavier rock settled. Fancifully, Julia thought that the flow called forth the very soul of the gold.

She watched Martha. The woman's reddened hands pushed a paddle briskly against the muck in the chute, churning it so the water washed away the lighter earth and rock. Carefully, Julia copied the motions. The chill water shocked her, but as she worked, it began to feel almost warm.

In the dance of the paddle, she forgot about Martha, who was busy at the lower end of the boxes. The water felt silky as she stroked it with her paddle. It foamed like kisses over her hands, kisses sent from Duncan each time he opened the gate. Below, Martha swished the rocker. The sound blended with the rush of the water, taking on a primal music that echoed through Julia's body almost erotically.

Her hands reddened in the cold water, and yet she felt heated. Her breath whispered between parted lips. She felt her breasts swing forward with the motion of her paddle and knew that Duncan's gaze was on her and not the sluice.

Desire simmered between them. When he closed the gate and took a paddle to work the muck beside her, Julia felt as turbulent as the churning gravel. Her hand glanced off his. Sensation jolted her. Flooded with restless yearning, she remembered every moment of their lovemaking and longed to feel him lying naked against her.

"That's good," he said and she started nervously, sure that he read her thoughts. Fine gravel and black sand remained in the trough. Duncan pressed one fingertip to the dull glint of gold. Picking out a nugget the size of a hazelnut, he held it up for her inspection.

Martha cut in. "Enough. I'll finish the cleanup with the gold pan. You two can go on your way."

Julia's mood shattered. How could she have dreamed away the chance to talk with Martha? "You promised to tell us about my father."

Martha looked exhausted. No doubt she had labored long, hard hours with little rest. Remembering again that her father should be helping, Julia felt guilty for insisting on answers. Yet she had no choice.

"There's plenty of empty cabins," Martha said at last. "Pick one for yourselves. We'll talk at breakfast. Right now, I'm too tired to make sense, and I still have the panning to do."

Feeling she should offer to help, Julia saw that Martha would not welcome a stranger's hands on her gold. She would have to be patient a little longer. Even that thought fled when she thought of spending the night with Duncan. Euphoria held weariness at a distance. She placed her hand on his arm as he gathered their packs and felt his muscles flex beneath her palm. He nodded to a cabin door that swung open beside an abandoned sluice.

She felt as if she was moving in a dream. Light came through the open door before he closed it after them, then more dimly through a window covered with a flour sack. The floor was packed earth. A ledge at one side of the cabin held dried spruce boughs. Duncan spread his blanket over them, then unrolled Julia's over the top.

She wanted to hurl herself into his arms, but he turned away to build a fire in the stove. Empty crates offered seating at a rough plank table. Feeling a need to be useful, she searched through their pack for food to heat for dinner.

Tinned stew, crackers and dried fruit had never tasted more delicious. Each crisp snap of a cracker sounded distinct to her ears. The fruit lay roughly sweet on her tongue. She chewed slowly, savoring the taste and texture, while deep inside she savored the pleasure she hoped would follow.

Duncan gazed through cracks in the stove at the dance of flames. "What do you think of your stepmother?"

"She certainly doesn't seem to like people," Julia said slowly. "I wonder what attracted my father?" Before he could remind her that her father had apparently married for a claim he wasn't even working, Julia jumped to her feet and began to clear the table.

Duncan took his harmonica from a shirt pocket and pounded it absently against one palm. "The most unlikely people are sometimes drawn together."

"Like us?"

He let the harmonica answer for him. The tune wove through the cabin. She stood behind him, her hands resting against his shoulders. After a time, she began to sing the haunting strains of "After the Ball."

Julia's clear notes drifted like a veil around them. Duncan played the harmonica more softly, while her voice tightened a spell that had begun with their work at the sluice. She had looked enraptured by the flood of water and churning gravel. It wasn't the thrill of gold he saw in her smoky glance, but pure desire. He had wanted to carry her into the nearest empty cabin.

He knew he had to keep his head, but it was all he could do to keep his mouth on the harmonica instead of her lips. Julia began a love song, "Sweet Marie." As she breathed the words, he shoved the harmonica into his pocket and drew her onto his lap. All the day's yearning poured through his kiss.

Then he forced his emotions under control and stroked her hair with an unsteady hand. "Sweetheart, I think your uncle pounded doubts into you. You say you must know your father to know yourself. Can't you see you are the woman you have created, not a reflection of two people you never knew?''

He took her hand in his, turning it in the dusky light from the window and discovering perfection in each delicate plane. Instead of answering, she leaned against him. He felt as if he could spend hours learning the wonder of her bare shoulder and days in memorizing the change of light or shadow over her cheek or breast.

Whenever he talked of taking her to Seattle, she talked of searching for her father. He felt as if they were at cross-purposes, that they had little in common except a hunger for each other.

She curled as trustingly as a kitten in his arms, seeming half asleep as he stroked the heavy satin lengths of her hair. The pins lay in her lap, tortoiseshell symbols of propriety. He lifted a silky tendril and breathed its perfume, then touched it to his tongue.

That was a mistake. It made him yearn to taste the rest of her. He rose, lifting her, ignoring the tiny clatter of falling hairpins as he carried her to the bed.

''Sleep, now,'' he told her as he lay her on the blankets. Instead, a mesmerizing smile invited him to join her. He meant to return to the chair by the fire. She reached for him, holding him with one hand clenched in his shirt while the other traveled down the row of buttons, freeing them one by one.

He sat on the blanket beside her, pried her fingers from his shirt and raised them to kiss each knuckle. She slid her other hand beneath his undershirt. The sensation of her bare palm against his skin drove out all other thoughts. Slowly, he leaned down to kiss her.

Julia told herself that nothing could be more right than their lovemaking. The beat of the rockers pulsed through her blood. The rush of flooding water uncovering treasures became the pulse singing through her body as Duncan deepened their kiss.

The creak of windlasses sounded through the cabin walls. Rockers continued their work throughout the night. The sounds enclosed them more fully in their own private world of welling tenderness and need.

The sweetness of their lovemaking made her feel as if her heart expanded. She could not get enough of touching him. She stroked her hands through his hair and over his back as if she was implanting sensations in her mind to draw on for the remainder of her life.

She banished thoughts of the future and immersed herself in the searing pleasure of his kiss. Briefly, she felt cold air against her bare skin, then he drew a blanket over them both, and the warmth and wonder of his naked body heated her instantly.

This time, he entered her without pain. Eagerly, she lifted her hips, seeking the intense rapture she had known only once before.

Their motion repeated the rhythm of a distant rocker, and as pleasure turned to molten gold, Julia pictured the flood churning through an opened sluice gate. What could be more precious than the rosy metal? As she clung tightly to Duncan, feeling their rapid heartbeats slowing to shared fulfillment, there was no question.

He held her close, stroking her skin while the music of the mines filtered through the walls. There was a splendid isolation in this unknown miner's cabin. The world no longer intruded. All that mattered was the moment, and for Julia the moment was an eternity of pleasure and peace. With a misty sense of belonging, she cuddled close in Duncan's arms until at last sleep settled down, welcoming her home.

## Chapter Twenty-Four

Hours later, Julia woke with a start to find herself naked. When she realized that Duncan lay beside her with one arm circling her waist, she sat up. He stirred but didn't wake. His vulnerability touched her, and she looked down at him while their lovemaking flooded back.

The scar at his temple was usually covered by hair. Now it was revealed, and she nearly kissed it. His mouth looked gentle in sleep, while his cheeks and jaw were shadowed with a beard. Smiling, she remembered his annoyance when she offered to shave him at the lake. Love churned through her, along with an uneasy truth. Once again, she had urged him to love her. In his mind, she had surely tightened bonds.

Warnings flashed. He must return to fishing, and he must save for a trawler. She would wait for him forever, but she would not willingly hold him back for one day. Maybe she could slip out of bed without waking him, begin breakfast and pretend nothing had happened.

Lazily, he said, "You're not planning to do anything foolish, are you?"

She felt blood rush to her face. "Ever the mind reader, Mr. Adair."

"I think we've progressed to first names." He raised one hand to stroke the silken curve of her breast.

A tremor ran through her body, and her nipples betrayed her by hardening. She swung her feet to the floor. "We must reach Martha before she begins her day's work."

"Joe seems to have disappeared," Duncan said quietly. "She may not be willing to talk about him."

Keeping her back to him, Julia slipped hastily into her drawers. As she tied the bows, he stroked a fingertip down her spine. With a gasp, she jerked away, though every instinct urged her back to bed. "We must hurry."

"It's better when we take our time," he teased, but she stiffened, and with reluctance he swung from bed.

For a moment, Julia stared at his smoothly muscled body. She had never dreamed that a man could be so beautiful to look upon, even those parts of him she couldn't name.

He snapped his fingers, startling her. Amusement warmed his eyes. "As much as I enjoy your approval, love, you're right. We need to get out there."

She turned away to slip into her corset and petticoats. When she jerked her dress over her head and settled it in place, Duncan stepped behind her. With gentle fingers, he fastened the buttons at the back, buttons he had unfastened last night with trembling urgency.

With an effort, she held herself rigid, then he kissed the nape of her neck and she whispered, "There's no time!"

Wrenching free, she began to gather her scattered hairpins. Duncan pulled on his clothes, thinking that Julia was like a fawn. She trusted him. He believed she loved him, yet she remained wary and easily startled. As he watched her pin her hair, he wondered how long it would take to earn enough to provide a home for her.

Placing his arms around her waist, he drew her against him. "I wish I knew how to shelter you from being hurt."

She sighed. "You're so certain of hurt. Duncan, you had your father for fifteen years. I suspect you are much like him and find strength through the knowledge. I can't model myself after Ruth or Aaron."

He kissed the top of her head, touched by the careful part she had made in her hair. "Sweetheart, you've done a wonderful job of creating the woman you are, despite those two."

She turned in his arms and looked at him. "Suppose you were to learn that your father didn't drown but survived and was living on some distant island?"

"I'd move hell, if necessary, to get to him." That Julia's father deserved such fierce loyalty seemed less likely the more they learned of him. Duncan tightened his arms. "I'll help you find your father, love. Then we're going to talk about a future together."

Her eyes grew troubled. "I'll wait for you, however long."

"I don't think either of us feels much like waiting," he said wryly. "I want you with me, sweetheart, whether I'm working on some other man's boat or poring over account books like some damned clerk."

Her eyes widened, then she startled him by laughing. "Clerk? Is your stepfather on your mind?"

"He wasn't cut out for fishing, any more than I'm suited to an office," he admitted. "But he does what he must to earn a living for my mother."

Julia slipped her hands around his neck. "If he stands behind his counter wishing his life were different, it seems unfair to resent him for it."

"I don't resent him," he said. "For the first time in years, those feelings are gone." That love for Julia could have opened his heart to his stepfather seemed unbelievable. Yet it was true.

When they stepped into the yellow morning sunlight, the steady creaking of windlasses, the rush of water through sluices and the rhythmic swish of rockers surrounded them. The scent of burning wood as strong as smoke from fires rose lazily through the still air.

Martha was not in sight, but a plume of smoke rose from the chimney of a cabin behind her gravel dump. Bracing herself, Julia walked to the frame door and knocked. "Mrs. Everett?"

Martha's brusque voice answered. "Come on in."

The aroma of fresh coffee and sizzling flapjacks welcomed them into the cabin. Julia's quick glance took in provisions stacked against one wall and dishes on a low shelf. The single window held her for a moment, for it was cleverly filled with ginger ale bottles, placed alternately base to mouth.

"Might as well call me Martha," the woman remarked. "We don't stand on ceremony out here."

"Then please call me Julia. And this is Duncan Adair, who escorted me from Seattle."

Martha turned her attention to the skillet. "Long as you're here, you might as well have some coffee. Better eat some flapjacks, too. Go ahead and sit yourselves."

Impatience clawed at Julia as Duncan urged her onto a stool beside a rough deal table nailed to one wall. He took tin cups from the shelf and poured coffee for them both.

Martha looked at him curiously. "Never knew a man to take on a woman's tasks. Reckon you two ain't hitched yet."

Julia felt her face heat and saw amusement in Duncan's eyes. This was not the discussion she meant to have. Leaning toward Martha, she spoke earnestly, "My father sent me a gold nugget on a chain." The yearning that had swept her that day shook her. "It was the first I knew of where I might find him—or even that he was alive."

"He isn't here." Deftly, Martha flipped the pancakes onto a metal plate. She pulled the lid from a jar of marmalade, stuck a knife in and set it on the table. "Dig in, if you're not particular."

It was impossible for Julia to imagine her father married to this woman. She realized she was staring and looked away. An empty can in the center of the table held cutlery. Choosing a bone-handled fork, she lifted a flapjack onto her plate.

It was tender and delicious. Suddenly feeling starved, Julia slathered marmalade over another and ate hungrily. Duncan raised his coffee cup in a toast. "Martha, I wouldn't be surprised to learn that Sodie Joe married you for your cooking."

A pensive look came into Martha's face as she accepted the compliment. "So you're Joe's daughter," she said to Julia. "You kind of look like him around the eyes. He thought you were just a little thing, though, maybe ten or twelve years old."

"I'm afraid time slips by," Julia said, trying to keep her voice from shaking. "Has my father lived in the Klondike for long?"

"Long enough to learn that luck at cards don't hold over to luck in prospecting. Joe never did turn up more than a little color. It wasn't easy on him watching fellows like McDonald haul it out by the pound."

The image caused a lump in Julia's throat. It sounded as if her father had had little happiness in his life. If only she had known of him sooner. Duncan put his hand over the taut knuckles she clenched in her lap, as he asked Martha, "How long have you been in the Klondike?"

"Lord, who keeps track?" She considered at length, then shrugged. "My first husband, Abe, brought me in by steamer. That's been ten years or better."

She got up restlessly and filled their coffee cups. "We were in Circle City when news came of a strike in the Klondike. Soon as we could, we came up the river and staked this claim on the Hunker."

"What happened to Abe?" Julia asked softly.

She was afraid Martha would be offended, but the older woman tucked back a stray wisp of hair and offered a flat reply. "Abe couldn't take the cold. Never was well, all that time in Circle City. Finally died on me about the time we reached bedrock."

"I'm sorry," Julia breathed, adding after a moment, "you've worked the claim alone?"

Clattering the empty plates together, Martha dumped them into a pan of water heating on the back of the stove. "There wasn't much else I could do."

Julia felt as if she was probing a wound. She wanted to stop, but she couldn't. "I don't mean to distress you, but where should I look for my father?"

Martha dropped a cup into the pan, sending drops of water over the side. The droplets spattered on the hot stove. "Last I knew, he was all excited over a bench claim he'd staked. That's one of them old streambeds high on the hillsides. Joe got real excited and went into town looking for someone to grubstake him. That was maybe six weeks ago.

"Like I said, Joe was a gambler with a hunger to strike gold. Should've stuck to the cards, I told him. He was like to find pay there faster than in the ground."

Martha loved him. Julia heard it in her voice. Impulsively, she asked, "How did you meet?"

For the first time, Martha smiled. "Joe couldn't cook for sour apples. He was struggling along on the hill up there after he heard about gold in the benches."

A rough chuckle rocked her. "Soon after he got here, he made up a batch of bread and forgot to add soda. Came out of the oven brick hard, of course. Even the dogs wouldn't eat it. That's when the boys started calling him Sodie Joe."

Crisply, Martha dried her hands. "Here I was, working night and day to thaw the paydirt and hoist it to the top, hardly taking time to open a can of beans. And there was Joe with time on his hands, but the cooking skills of a moose. Seemed natural we'd team up, so we did. Like Joe said, when two people need each other, the law's got no right keeping them apart."

Her expression became challenging, and Julia hastened to reassure her. "He...never married my mother. And anyway, she died when I was born. So you have no need to worry about that."

"He talked about her some," Martha said. "There's a lot of time to talk when it's dark the clock around. Said he shouldn't have let her move in with him, but she was in his blood when he was young and eager, like."

Julia tried to imagine her parents, the sixteen-year-old girl in Ruth's old photograph and the man she loved. If there had been photographs of Joseph Everett, they had been destroyed long ago.

"He was living on his wits," Martha explained. "The girl couldn't take it after a while. When she went to her sister's place, the brother-in-law refused to let Joe near her. Wasn't until after she died that someone told him she'd had a daughter."

"And Aaron refused to let him contact me," Julia said, her eyes misting with tears.

Martha nodded. "The uncle agreed to raise you as long as Joe stayed away. What could he do? The way Joe was living, there wasn't any room for a kid, least of all a girl."

Julia's mind filled with an image of the Ames's parlor. Prisms glowed in the light of oil lamps, which cast a dusky beauty over worn carpets. Aaron towered in the center, a figure of righteousness, while Ruth huddled protectively over a baby. Joseph Everett, shoulders bent in defeat, walked through the open parlor door into the rainy street. Light formed a golden rectangle around him before he disappeared into the night. With an inner shake, she brought her attention to the rough Yukon cabin.

"Joe must have really loved your mother," Martha said thoughtfully. "He gets kind of soft looking when he talks about her. Makes it sound like it all happened yesterday."

Julia clasped the woman's roughened hands. "Thank you. That means a great deal to me."

Seeming embarrassed, Martha pulled free.

Julia felt as if she had been dismissed. She had learned a lot about her father, but she did not know where to look for him. Helplessly, she tried to think of a way to prolong the conversation.

Martha's look became accusing. "That heart-shaped nugget sure was a pretty thing. I'm surprised you're not wearing it." Without waiting for an answer, she tramped toward the sluice and gravel dump. Julia followed, wondering if she should admit that the nugget was stolen.

Martha grabbed a shovel then heaved a load of paydirt into the sluice. Her face was closed, the lines of her body angled into the work. She shoved the blade into the gravel and leaned briefly on the handle. "Joe won that heart-shaped nugget over at the Bonanza Playhouse. He said he might as well send it to his little girl. Otherwise, both of his wives'd be wanting it."

"Wives?" Julia repeated.

Stoically Martha said, "Most of the old-timers married squaws. No reason for Joe to be any different." She heaved another shovelful of gravel into the sluice. "Funny thing, though. I never figured he'd go back to her."

Julia felt as if the ground swayed. "Martha, are you saying he is living with—with Indians?"

Anguish roughened Martha's voice. "I've spent too much time gabbing already. Reckon I must be getting weak in the head. Get along with you both, before I take a shovel to you."

Julia understood the heartache beneath the brusque orders. Impulsively, she kissed the weathered cheek. "Thank you. For breakfast and for talking with us. I hope we'll meet again."

Martha didn't answer except to dig her shovel deeply into the gravel. When Julia joined Duncan on the trail downstream, she felt as if a lifetime of dreams churned through the sluice, leaving bitter truth in the riffles.

The princelike father of her imagination vanished with the waste, leaving a new image of a gambler, a bigamist and—what was the disparaging term she had heard a prospector use? Squaw man, that was it. Her stomach knotted so painfully that she stumbled and might have fallen if Duncan hadn't steadied her.

The trail was crowded, but Duncan ignored the curious prospectors and held Julia close. Her face was pale, her eyes the color of opal. Her distress was plain. "Sweetheart, don't think about him for awhile. Remember, we have each other."

Rockers and sluices played their cold music along the muddy stream. Julia called on the toughness she had gained in the difficult days when she swore never to quail before her uncle. "Martha decided I was strong enough to know the truth, and I am. It's just that I wasn't prepared."

She clasped Duncan's hand tightly as they walked. When they neared the river's mouth, he led her to a clearing beneath a birch and dug through his pack for the last of the jerky.

A spring ran from the rocks nearby. He watched her kneel and cup her hands to catch the water. Her face looked porcelain in the thin sunlight. Droplets slipped through her fingers as she sipped from her cupped palms. She pressed her cool, wet hands to her cheeks, and he felt his throat thicken with the need to protect her.

She sat back, gazing into the spring. "Remember that first day in Dawson City? It must have been my father's Indian wife who tore the nugget from my throat."

Duncan handed her a strip of jerky. "Don't think about it now. Eat something, sweetheart. It's a long walk to town."

"She shouted, 'Three too many.'" Absently, Julia bent the jerky between her fingers. "I suppose, like Martha, she believed Joe's daughter was a child. When she saw me wearing the nugget, she must have thought he married a third time."

Gently, Duncan massaged her taut shoulders. Sighing, Julia tried to relax the tight muscles. His hands were warm and felt wonderful, but she couldn't stop thinking of her father. What kind of man was he? Were Aaron and Ruth right to keep him from seeing her? Abruptly, she got to her feet. "I must meet him. Whatever he proves to be."

Duncan picked up the pack, then clasped one of her hands. "Whatever your father may be, sweetheart, you have taken the best from him." Her smile didn't reach her eyes. She pushed through the brambles to the trail.

They walked in silence for a time. At last, Julia said, "I must talk with the Indian wife. Someone will know where the village is located."

"There will be several," Duncan warned, wondering if he could spare her by locating the woman first. "Can you describe her?"

Julia tried to bring the Indian woman's face into her memory. "I was so shocked and upset that I only got a hazy impression."

A second image crowded into her mind, one of Owen shouting at Vida while Vida denied taking anything but an empty poke from his drawer. Julia saw the leather pouch clearly. It was decorated in quill work, much like the trim of the Indian woman's deerskin dress.

Owen had hurled the pouch into a drawer of the armoire and kicked the drawer shut. Joe had won the nugget playing cards at the Bonanza Playhouse, yet Owen insisted he had never met her father. Why would Owen lie?

The pouch must still be in the armoire. Impatience quickened her step. At the first opportunity, she meant to slip into Owen's room and examine what must surely be a clue.

# *Chapter Twenty-Five*

Duncan saw the light of a new idea in the sudden flash of Julia's eyes. She didn't offer to share the idea, so he knew the plan was one he wouldn't approve. "Sweetheart," he said warily. "Tell me you're not plotting trouble."

Julia shook her head, thankful for once he couldn't read her thoughts. The stepbrothers barely suffered each other. She had no proof that Owen lied about knowing her father. It would be a mistake to set Duncan even more strongly against him.

Hours later, when they stepped into the Bonanza Playhouse, Tilly and Hannah ran to her. "Julia! At last! Wait until you hear!" Hannah said.

Tilly whirled, her skirts flying as if the news were too much to contain. "What?" Julia demanded. "What is it?" Eyes sparkling, the women tugged Julia and Duncan into the office. "We promised to let Owen tell."

Owen sprang from behind his desk as they crowded through the door. "Dear Julia!" he exclaimed, catching her hands in an eager grip. "Darling, I have wonderful news. We've found your father."

She glanced around the room, expecting to see her father, but saw only the familiar furniture. It must be true they had found him. She saw it in the dancers' excited faces. She exclaimed, "You promised you would help me! Where is he?"

Pride in Edmund glowed in Hannah's explanation. "A message from the Indians arrived at the police barracks. It was Edmund who tied the clues together."

Tilly broke in. "Sodie Joe saw that nugget necklace. He guessed his daughter was in town and sent word he wanted to see her."

Hannah gave Tilly a light push, obviously eager to be the one to boast of Edmund. "None of the Mounties knew who his daughter might be, except for Edmund, who came straight here."

Julia felt she could not wait another second. Were they holding her father out of sight to surprise her? "Please tell me. Where is he?"

Owen held her hands and drew her farther from Duncan. "Your father is ill, dearest. The Indians have been caring for him."

"Ill?" For a moment, disappointment and fear left her weak. Then with impatience she faced Hannah. "Where is Officer Gray?"

She saw her friend's vibrant expression fade and braced for fresh disappointment. "He had to leave, Julia. He's on a mission to the Stewart River, but he promised to escort you to the Indian camp when he returns in a week."

"A week." Julia slumped onto a chair. When Duncan put his hands on her shoulders, she twisted to look at him. "I can't wait so long. Suppose something happens to keep us apart forever?"

He came around the chair and lifted her into his arms. "You need to rest. We'll make plans in the morning, after we've gathered all the facts." As he carried her up the stairs, she clung to him gratefully, letting her head rest against his strong shoulder. The weariness she had held off for hours dropped in a single dark wave.

He placed her on the bed. She wanted to urge him to stay, but sleep drew over her like a blanket, and her eyes closed. She wasn't aware of his leaving.

She woke some time later when a hand touched her shoulder. A woman whispered, "Julia? Are you awake? There's something I must tell you."

Julia managed to force her eyes open and turn her head. "Belle?"

With a quick glance toward the door, Belle spoke rapidly. "It's about Owen. When word came that your father was asking for you, he turned white as quartz, like he'd heard the dead was walking." She glanced again toward the door, then added, "I know men. Reading faces is what I do best. Look out for Owen."

Julia recognized a need for thought, but her need for sleep was stronger. When she woke again, the room was empty. Owen called from the hallway, and she knew that his voice had wakened her. "Julia? Dearest, are you awake?"

Feeling groggy, she looked for Belle. Perhaps the whispered warning was no more than a nightmare. Sitting up, she called, "What is it?"

He opened the door, looking apologetic. "Forgive me for disturbing your rest, dear, but it is growing late. The girls have finished the first show and the men are begging that you appear for the second."

She pushed her hair behind her ears, struggling to blink away the last tendrils of sleep. She had to sing, to help bring in money that would lead to a future with Duncan. She forced a smile. "It's all right. I'll dress and come downstairs at once."

To her dismay, he crossed swiftly to her and clasped her hands. "Darling Julia, you've set every heart on fire, mine most of all. Please say there is a chance for me."

"I'm sorry," she said hesitantly. "You've been kind, but..."

"You are still half asleep." Leaning forward, he kissed her temple. "Darling Julia, I don't mean to hurry you. I'll wait outside to accompany you downstairs. We'll talk of this later."

An image of the quilled pouch flared in her mind and burned away the last tendrils of sleep. "How kind you are, but please don't bother to wait."

Tenderly, he captured one of her hands and kissed the palm. "For you, my love, nothing is a bother." After a lingering look into her eyes he got to his feet. He smiled engagingly before stepping outside.

Feeling as if she had awakened in an upside-down world, Julia decided to take her time in dressing for the stage. The scent of a cigar told her that Owen waited in the hall. This must be his idea of courting her. Why couldn't he have chosen another time to prove his devotion?

When she emerged from the room wearing the mauve theater gown, his eyes glowed with approval. Placing her hand on his arm, he led her toward the stairs.

From the stage, she looked out at the cheering miners. She began to sing, and emotion filled her voice. The audience listened with rapt attention. She saw tears in some eyes and wistful smiles on the faces of many. When she finished, men shouted and cheered, and small nuggets rattled around her.

Duncan waited in the wings. As the dancers darted out to collect the nuggets, Julia went gratefully into his arms. Problems fell away as she felt the familiar comfort of his embrace. Quietly, he asked, "Have you eaten?"

When she shook her head, he took her into the kitchen and filled two bowls with thick, steaming soup from a pot on the back of the iron stove. Julia cut slabs of bread, feeling as if the homely tasks mirrored their future.

She was hungrier than she knew, and for several minutes she devoted herself to eating the restoring broth, then used the bread to wipe the last drop from the bowl. "Have you learned yet where the Indians make their camp?"

As he pushed his bowl aside, she saw that he was judging her courage. She prepared for bad news. "I'm afraid they move around," he said. "I'm told they follow fishing and hunting trails through the summer months."

Julia set her bowl down with a thud. "If my father is ill, surely they're not moving him around the countryside."

"Officer Gray can tell us that."

She tried to suppress her impatience. Lurching to her feet, she exclaimed, "How can I wait here while my father's health may be failing?"

The torment in her face brought Duncan to his feet. He held her until the tension eased from her body, then stroked tendrils of hair from her face. He ached with the need to make her happy. "Sweetheart, I've only been able to learn of roving bands. But they're a gentle people. Perhaps those caring for him have held their camp.''

Cheers from the saloon told them that the dancers had finished.

Julia reached for her hat.

"You don't need to perform," Duncan reminded her. "That was only to attract your father's notice."

She shook her head, thinking of the need to earn money for their future. "The men are expecting me."

By the time Julia finished singing, exhaustion weighted her steps. She had had only a short nap. She meant to search Owen's armoire before resting. She stood outside his room, listening. Footsteps sounded inside. Remembering that she hadn't seen Owen downstairs after the last show, she returned to her own room and stretched out on her bed to wait.

When she woke, bright sunlight patterned the carpet. She realized it was late morning. Hannah, an early riser, had apparently decided not to disturb her. Julia dressed swiftly, aware that the upstairs rooms were quiet.

Excitement made her hands tremble as she pinned her hair into a hasty coil. After checking her appearance in the small mirror above the dressing table, she cracked open the door.

As she had guessed, no one was around. Her slippers moved silently over the wood flooring. Holding her breath, she eased open the door of the adjoining room. Both beds were neatly made. Only a box of cigars and shaving brushes in mugs on the washstand gave evidence of the occupants.

She slipped noiselessly into the room and closed the door. The armoire loomed. She went toward it as if hypnotized. She knelt and grasped the wooden drawer knobs with both hands. The heavy drawer slid toward her with a squawk of protest. Biting her lip, she listened intently. There was no sound except the distant noise from the street.

Folded shirts lay on top of wool underwear. She slipped her fingers beneath the garments. She felt only soft wool.

Owen might have moved the pouch or even discarded it after that scene with Vida.

With her teeth pressed into her lower lip, Julia piled shirts and underwear on the floor beside her. The supple leather pouch lay at the back of the drawer. She pulled it out in triumph.

It was exactly as she remembered it, intricately decorated with colored porcupine quills. A drawstring closed the top. She could feel that it was empty.

How could she connect this pouch to the woman who had ripped the nugget from around her throat? She sat on her heels, thinking furiously. When Owen caught Vida in his room, the usually stoic dancer had trembled at his fury. Was he so angry because she prowled among his possessions? Or was there another reason?

The pouch lay in her hands, frustratingly silent in its mystery. There must be a clue, but where? She toyed with the drawstring, then pulled the pouch open and peered inside. Empty, as she'd thought.

She started to pull the strings tight, then stopped as faint markings caught her eye. She turned toward the dusky light from the curtained window and pulled back the upper edge of the bag. Initials had been burned into the soft leather inside.

"Julia!" Owen said from the doorway. "I came up to check on you and..."

His voice halted as she sprang to her feet. She thrust the pouch toward him. "Why have you lied to me?"

The color left his face. "Julia," he protested. "My love, I don't know what you mean."

"Don't you?" She shook the pouch. "You had never heard of my father?" She stepped closer. "That's what you told me, Owen. So whose initials are these? Does J.E. stand for someone other than Joseph Everett?"

She saw his Adam's apple move against his tie. He closed the door, then placed his hands on her shoulders. "Dearest," he said gently. "I wanted only to protect you."

"I'm not a child, nor a fool."

"No, you are a lady," he said earnestly. "From the first, I knew I had to protect you from learning Sodie Joe Everett was your father."

He was no better than Aaron, she thought, shocked. Owen hid his manipulations behind a merry smile, but he, too, had kept her from her father. She repeated, "Protect me?"

Quickly he said, "Sweet Julia, please hear me through. It's true that I knew the man. It was here he won the nugget you received. Out of sympathy for his tale of a lost daughter, I loaned him a grubstake. He left the empty poke as his word for the loan."

"So he came to you," she breathed.

Owen's expressive features softened with regret. "I'm sorry, darling. I never saw him again. I thought he must have been killed. The Yukon takes its toll, and Everett... forgive me, but he was a drinking man. I thought he must have passed out somewhere and been frozen to death."

"But he is alive." She remembered Belle's warning that Owen had looked stunned by that news, and hardened her heart against his gentle coaxing. She no longer trusted him.

"That's a relief to me," Owen said fervently. "I was afraid that by staking the man, I'd sent him to his death."

She tried to move away, but he slipped his hands to her waist and held her lightly in the circle of his arms. He seemed not to notice that she stiffened. "For your sake, Julia, it would be better if he had died."

Shocked, she wrenched backward, but he tightened his embrace. "Forgive me, darling, I don't want to grieve you, but you should know he is a gambler, a drunk, even a bigamist."

Over the past few days, she had faced the failings of her father. "You're telling me nothing new. All that matters is that he is my father."

"Darling Julia, we share the pain of an unhappy upbringing. Fate brought us together. We must give each other the love denied us as children. I need you, Julia, as you need me."

He was about to kiss her. She saw his gaze fasten on her lips. "Owen, please," she said, pushing her hands against his chest to hold him away. "A difficult childhood is all we share."

"You force me to speak sooner than I intended," he said passionately. "But darling, my feelings for you are no secret. From the first glance, my heart was yours."

"Mr. Powell, please," she said with alarm. "You must know that Duncan and I—"

He cut her off, pulling her so close that his starched linen collar rasped against her cheek. As she tried to twist free, he exclaimed, "I love you, Julia. I long to make you my wife. You are so lovely, so elegant. You deserve furs and velvets and jewels. Dawson will not always be the rough frontier you see now. Together, we will help it become the San Francisco of the north."

His hands felt hot through the fabric of her dress. She struggled to free herself.

"Can't you see it?" he urged. "It's beginning already. That's why you must not divulge that an accident of birth made Sodie Joe your father. You are nothing like him. Why tar yourself with the pitiful reputation of a scoundrel?"

She slapped him. The action startled her, but she was pleased to see the imprint of her hand on his face. "You're speaking of my father."

Owen's mouth twisted. For once, his voice revealed his true feelings. She cringed as he spoke. "You could wish differently if you saw him living in filth, feasting on moose stomach."

She cleared her mind of everything but the need to reach her father. "Where?" Owen hesitated so long she thought he wouldn't answer. "Where?" she asked again, her voice hard.

With regret in his voice, he said, "The camp is up Caribou Creek. You passed it when you floated down to Dawson. But you are not to go there, Julia. I won't allow it."

"You have no authority over me."

Anguish shook him. "But I love you. Can't you understand that?" He tried to pull her closer, but her rigid stance defeated him. "You're not thinking rationally, my darling."

"Owen, I am not your darling." Julia heard her voice rise with anger. "There is nothing between the two of us and there never will be."

Moving quickly, he caught her off balance and thrust her onto the nearest bed. His weight held her down as his mouth captured hers. One hand in her hair trapped her painfully. His lips were wet and hot. Feeling invaded, she managed to wrench her mouth away. "You've lost your senses. Let me go!"

He breathed heavily. His face was flushed. His coat had fallen open. When she shoved him, her hands caught in his satin suspenders. She fought to wrench free of the hand in her hair, despite the tearing pain it caused. "I despise you! Get off!"

Abruptly, he clambered to his feet. Anger blazed in his face, and she wondered how she could ever have thought his eyes merry. Warily, she tried to gauge his intentions as he stalked to the door.

A false smoothness in his voice failed to cover fury. "This is for your own sake, my darling. You could cause irreparable harm to the future I mean for us to share. I'm afraid I must insist you give the matter more careful thought."

Alerted by the flash of his eyes, she scrambled toward him, but he slammed the pine door in her face. She heard a key turn in the lock.

# Chapter Twenty-Six

Julia threw herself against the door. "Owen Powell, let me out!"

There was no answer. She pounded her fists on the wood, then wrenched at the knob. "Come back here. Let me out!"

The lock held. Julia listened, but heard nothing from the hall. Owen must have gone. She ran to the window. There was no way to open the single pane. Where winter lasted three times longer than summer, there was more need to seal a window than to open it.

Even if she broke the glass, who would pay attention to a woman screaming from a bedroom above a saloon? They wouldn't help when she was on the street fighting for her necklace. Knotting her hands into fists, she glared at the locked door. How long did Owen believe he could hold her prisoner? Duncan was certain to check on her before long. His steps would sound clearly through the calico walls, and she could . . .

With sharp annoyance for her own stupidity, Julia began to search the room. At once, her glance returned to the shaving mugs. Snatching open a drawer in the washstand, she found a folded razor and pried open the blade before stalking to the partition separating her from the hall. "Owen?"

If he waited there in silence, thinking to stop her, she would fight past him with the open razor. The thought shocked her, but with grim purpose, she slashed the wall-paper and calico from ceiling to floor.

A similar partition covered the other side of a raw lumber framework. She slashed through it easily and peered into the empty hall. She tossed the razor aside, pushed through the slashed fabric and rushed toward the stairs.

Duncan looked up from the account books as she stormed into the office. He sprang to his feet. "What is it?"

Her glance searched the room. "Where is your brother?" Dashing to the doorway, she shouted to Gus. "Have you seen Owen?"

As the bartender shook his head, Duncan grasped her shoulders and pulled her into the office. "What's happened? If Owen has insulted you, I'll stretch his hide to the wall like a bearskin."

She felt a rise of wild laughter and fought it back, afraid it would overwhelm her. "Insult me? He has offered a proposal of marriage."

Duncan's fingers tightened so abruptly that she winced. In apology, he massaged the spot. "You don't appear flattered by the offer."

With anger, she exclaimed, "Owen is afraid that Sodie Joe will embarrass our marriage."

A frown darkened Duncan's eyes. "You're not marrying Owen. You're marrying me. I think it's time we make that clear to him."

As he drew her close, she found comfort in the familiar warmth of his arms and body and even in his anger. Trying to suppress the indignity of Owen's unwanted kiss, she told Duncan about finding the pouch and about Owen's explanation.

She stopped short of mentioning the physical attack. Duncan's dark fury made her stop. But he would eventually see the slashed wall. "Owen locked me into the room. He said I should think it all over. I used a razor to cut through the wall."

Where was Owen? With alarm, she exclaimed, "He must have gone to the Indian camp on Caribou Creek. He means to keep my father from me. He may offer to stake Joe again and send him far from town.'' She trembled with certainty.

"I'll go after him," Duncan assured her. "Try to relax. Joe Everett knows you are here. Owen won't easily send him away."

"He may say that I want nothing to do with a gambler, a drunkard and a bigamist." Her voice faltered. She forced it to remain steady. "I'm going with you."

"I'll travel faster alone." Gently, he set her aside. "You've had enough travel for awhile, sweetheart. Stay here and rest. You know you can trust me."

He kissed her, then left quickly.

She ran into the saloon, feeling her nerves fray. She selected a man she judged to be a newcomer. Her heart raced, but she managed to smile and speak in a casual tone. "Did you see that old fellow with the pack and shovel? What tales men tell! He tried to convince me of rich bench claims on Caribou Creek. I'm sure he was simply trying to win my favor."

Before the last words were out, the man had leaped to his feet and turned to a friend. "Bench claims on Caribou. Come on!"

Julia followed them into the street, astonished at how quickly a crowd formed. Instead of rushing toward the bridge over the Klondike, however, the stampeders pounded toward the Yukon River. In dismay, she watched pairs and groups of prospectors leap into boats and shove off against the current.

Owen's directions mocked her. "You floated past on your way down to Dawson." What a fool she had been to think she could follow the stampede.

Duncan had propelled the double-ender several yards upriver before his conscience got the upper hand. An image of Julia's stricken face hovered before him. She had gone over the frozen hell of Chilkoot Pass to reach her father. She must be going through a worse hell now. He couldn't leave her behind.

When he forced the boat around, he was startled to see a number of vessels rushing toward him. Where in blazes were all those fellows heading? Was the town on fire? A quick glance reassured him, then he stared in astonishment as he recognized a figure standing forlornly at the water's edge.

Laughter burst from him. The blockheaded woman had launched another stampede. Obviously she had no idea that Caribou Creek opened into the Yukon miles upstream.

Still chuckling, he leaned into the oars to pull out of the current and toward the beach. Before he reached the shore, Julia lifted her skirts to her knees, waded into the shallows and climbed aboard. With a defiant glance, she pulled off her slippers and squeezed out water.

Duncan shot the boat upriver. "You're sure this camp is on Caribou Creek?"

"So your brother told me."

"And you expect to hike in those shoes, wet as they are?"

"If I must." She pulled the toes of her stockings forward and wrung water from the cotton.

"Take them off," he suggested, but she straightened her skirt around her damp legs. Other vessels swept ahead and behind. Men shouted above the rush of water. Mildly, Duncan said, "For your sake, I hope none of them learn who started this worthless stampede."

"It gives them something to do besides sit around the saloons," Julia answered, peering impatiently ahead. "Is it far?"

"It's slow going against the current. The return will be swift."

"We'll bring my father back with us," she said. "I can care for him far better than the Indians."

Duncan didn't answer. He concentrated instead on keeping the boat near the shore while speeding them on with each sweep of the oars. Julia turned to look at him. She realized he cared enough to come back for her.

Love welled through her as she turned to search for a break in the forested hillsides at the water's edge. At last, the leading boats turned in. She saw a change in the color of the Yukon that marked inrushing water from a muddy stream. "There!" she cried, pointing, but Duncan was already working the double-ender toward shore.

She shoved the wet slippers over her damp stockings and grasped his hand to clamber onto the bank.

Duncan climbed over a gravel dump to talk to some men working a sluice. He returned and said, "There's an Indian camp four miles away. They say there's a path along this bank of the Yukon."

After a brief search, they located a moss-cushioned path leading into the forest. It was so different from the muddy miner's trail that Julia felt as if she were entering another world. Black spruce formed narrow columns. Sunlight rayed through, brightening the light green leaves of ground plants. There was a mystical quality to the shapes and shadows as Julia and Duncan walked silently over spruce needles and moss.

Duncan strode ahead, sparing her the slap of an occasional overhanging branch. Far above, a raven called. It followed them, landing in tree after tree, its rough, primeval voice seeming to warn other forest creatures of their progress.

They knew they were near the village when the raven's warning was lost in the furious howls of dozens of dogs. The forest rang with the malevolent cries. Duncan snapped a branch from a fallen limb for a club, then warned, "Stay behind me."

The trail led into a meadow. Skin-covered domes nestled around the edges. Julia barely glanced at them. With pounding heart, she peered past Duncan at a dozen or more snarling dogs. They looked half-starved; their teeth were bared and their hackles raised.

A sharp command came from one of the huts. The dogs slunk back as a young man came into the clearing. He was dressed as a miner, though his features were those of a native. In broken English, he offered to trade for Duncan's hat and shirt.

Other Indians came from the huts, offering various objects. Julia stood as close as possible to Duncan while women tugged at her dress. "Everett? Joseph Everett? Sodie Joe?"

He received blank stares. The first man shook his head. "No Sodie Joe." He offered a hatchet. "How much?"

"This is the wrong camp," Duncan said angrily. "I might have known Owen would lie."

Heart sinking, Julia waved away grasping fingers. "Will they let us leave?"

Duncan reached into his pocket for coins and bartered for the hatchet. While the men argued, Julia tried to avoid pinches from the women and a throng of children who seemed suddenly to be everywhere.

One woman snatched at her hat, but it stayed pinned to her head. Another persistently tugged at her stockings while shoving her moccasins at Julia. Hoisting her skirt, Julia peeled off the wet hose and gave them and her slippers in exchange for the moccasins. They were snug but warm and dry, and she wriggled her toes appreciatively. Two women tugged at the stockings, voices shrill as they argued with the victorious trader.

Over his shoulder, Duncan said, "Start up the trail."

She backed away with uneasy glances. Duncan shoved the hatchet through his belt, then turned and strode after Julia. The Indians continued to wave items and shout, but they didn't follow.

Julia didn't breathe freely until two miles separated them from the camp with its hostile dogs and eager traders. The need to locate her father returned with a rush. "You said there are many villages. Where shall we go next?"

Duncan drew her into his arms. "We'll do as we should have done in the beginning; ask directions of the officers at the barracks."

Feeling frustrated, Julia tried to pull away, but he turned her and kissed her temple. "You heard Martha talk about Joe. Your mother meant a lot to him. And so do you. Maybe he's never seen you, but he's carried you in his heart all these years. He's not likely to believe anything that would keep you from him."

She sighed, wanting to believe him. Who was her father? A gambler, a luckless prospector, a man hungry for gold. Would the offer of a stake and a tip about a new discovery send him on?

No. When she looked into Duncan's eyes, she knew he spoke the truth. He understood Joe without knowing him because he loved her. If they were separated, no one's glib tongue would keep Duncan from coming to her. And wherever he might be, Sodie Joe would wait.

With a sigh, she raised one hand to his smoothly shaven cheek. She remembered stubble etching roughly erotic sensations against her skin as she woke naked in his arms.

Her fingers roved higher, to caress the scar at his temple. They had been through so much together; she felt as if she had always known him. He was companion, friend and lover.

He drew back to look into her eyes. His own were smoky with growing desire. Wordlessly, he pushed branches aside to open a passage into the surrounding forest. A red squirrel chattered suddenly from a spruce, then darted around the trunk and out of sight. Julia moved through shafts of sunlight between the trees and drew in the heady spicy fragrance of the forest. A spiderweb shimmered like spun gold. Carefully, she edged around it.

Voices rang from distant workings, but the buzz of insects and the lilting song of birds overcame human sound. Sunlight splashed over the ground cover and caused mysterious shadowed darkness beneath. Feeling as if they were the first people to step into this secluded haven, Julia turned to Duncan. His hand on her waist was a caress that made her aware of each finger and of the warm curve of his palm. She raised one hand to his mouth to trace a promise over his lips. He kissed her fingertip, and desire stormed through her.

They emerged through waist-high ferns to a shallow trough bedded with moss and fragile greenery. In the spring, melting snow must have rushed and tumbled over the slope, which was feathered by soft new growth. Dropping the hatchet, Duncan drew her into a kiss that deepened instantly. His hand shaped the soft curve of her hips, molding her intimately.

She raised her hands to his hair and pushed his hat back until it fell. The world seemed to spin until only by clinging to him could she keep her balance. He removed her hat, then the pins from her hair, so that the thick waves tumbled loosely over his hands. His kisses warmed her cheek and throat and caused tantalizing sensations when he parted her bodice and pressed his lips to the throbbing pulse at her throat.

Sun and shadow played among shifting leaves. She needed to touch his bare skin, and one by one opened the buttons of his wool shirt. As she discovered again the lithe strength of his muscles, she felt overcome with longing. Impulsively, she kissed his chest above the rapid beat of his heart.

He eased her away just enough to unfasten the remaining buttons of her bodice. Sunlight warmed the creamy curve of her breasts. She felt as natural a part of the forest as the sunlight, which seemed to ray from her as she felt herself glow.

When he drew her down with him onto the ferns and moss, she trembled with her need for him. He stroked beneath her open shirtwaist, easing the fabric from her shoulders, renewing every inch of her skin with his touch. With recklessness born of love, she straddled him. Leaning forward, she brushed her bare breasts against his chest. He cradled her face between his palms. ''My sweet Julia. How I love you.''

The words sang through her. He said them naturally, as if in his heart he had already said them a hundred or more times. Their kiss sealed the promise of the spoken words. Her skirt and petticoats had become raised to her thighs. When he moved his hands beneath to release the ties of her cotton drawers, she slid her hand over his flat stomach and daringly below. Desire deepened in his eyes.

She left him just long enough to slip out of the undergarments. As he opened his trousers to reveal his beautiful male body, she cradled him between her thighs and lowered herself with exquisite care.

Julia's sensual abandonment turned Duncan's blood to smoke. When she eased her sweet, enclosing warmth around him, he placed his hands on her waist to hold her while he fought to slow racing emotions. Sunlight tangled in her hair, creating fiery glows among the chestnut waves. He felt bewitched. Wherever he was, his thoughts turned to the memory of her laughter or the mystery of her lovely eyes.

Moving his hands to the delicate curve of her hips, he gave himself over to a tide of emotion. Sunlight haloed her body. He felt as if she were a wood nymph, but one who was wonderfully human. Her luminous eyes glowed. She moved intimately, causing erotic sensations to blaze within them both.

With shaking hands, he caressed the satin curve of her breasts, feeling overwhelming tenderness when he saw that their pebbled delicacy betrayed her desire. "I love you," she whispered and passion leaped through him. The passion was as intense as it had been their first time together. She would always thrill him, even if he spent a lifetime loving her.

She breathed his name with wonder, and thought vanished. Eternity existed in the high excitement of their shared bodies. Clasping her hips, he jolted upward to spill his love with an outpouring of blazing pleasure.

Gradually, the sounds of the forest returned. Red squirrels chattered. Overhead, a bird poured out a ripple of melody. Julia had never known greater happiness. As she lay nestled in Duncan's arms, an orange butterfly landed briefly on her bare shoulder, then lifted away. Feeling deeply at peace, she sat upright and smiled at him with wondering joy.

He stroked damp tendrils of hair from her temples, then drew her close enough to kiss. "For the first time in my life, I wonder how men can endure days and nights at sea while their wives keep their beds warm at home."

"Every homecoming is a new beginning," she suggested.

The future spread before him like a treasure chest thrown open. "We'll be married as soon as possible. During the long journey home, we may never leave our stateroom."

She scrambled to her feet, swiftly adjusting her clothing. Duncan restored his own before placing his hands on her shoulders. "Sweetheart, what is it?"

Trembling, she said, "Help me find him. Don't ask me to go empty into a new life."

He understood her longing and told himself it was foolish to feel hurt that his love was not enough to make her feel complete. He took her into his arms and held her tightly. He wanted to force her to acknowledge the wholeness they found in each other.

She raised her head. "This streambed . . . is it a pup of Caribou Creek?"

"So it seems."

She looked around slowly, as if to implant the woodland setting in her mind. Love and apology glowed in her eyes as she linked her arms around his neck. "This is a magical spot. I want to make it ours forever. What must we do to stake a claim?"

## Chapter Twenty-Seven

By claiming the site where they had shared their love, Duncan hoped, Julia would attain some of the sense of permanence she craved. At one side, the dark spruce gave way to slender white trunks of birch. Choosing one of these, he swung the hatchet. A few swings felled the tree. As he wiped the back of one hand across his damp forehead, he looked at Julia, who watched with sparkling eyes.

He longed to pull her into his arms and kiss her until she admitted that his love was all she needed. They would likely end in the mossy welcome of the dry streambed, exciting each other to new heights of lovemaking while the day grew old around them and nothing was solved. To end the temptation, he demanded, "Why aren't you pacing off your claim?"

As she jumped to her feet, he couldn't resist adding, "Make enough noise at it that any bears go the other way."

With a look of alarm, she pointed to a raw spot high up a birch trunk where sap oozed slowly from the edges. "Did a bear do this?"

He shook his head, already regretting that he had teased her. "A moose used the tree to scrape velvet from his rack. No doubt he thought lustfully of a sweet moose lady."

"That's a cow, isn't it?"

He chuckled. "Is there no romance in you, sweetheart?"

"Oh, yes."

The sudden huskiness in her voice nearly overcame his decision to leave further lovemaking to a proper bed. He put his emotions into a swing that severed the birch trunk. "Measure the claim, and don't forget to alert any bears."

The birch yielded four sturdy posts. Bracing his foot on the first, Duncan began to carve a point at one end. Yards away, Julia counted at the top of her voice while crashing through the brush. Soon she called out, "This makes two hundred and fifty feet. I'm rolling a rock into the middle to mark it."

By the time he finished the last post, she was making her way down the dry streambed. Duncan carried two of the posts up the bed until he reached her markers. This was a hell of a lot of work to satisfy a whim, but he would do anything to please her.

She shrieked his name. He nearly smashed his foot with the back of the hatchet. "Duncan!" she shrieked again.

God, maybe there really was a bear. Grasping the hatchet, he raced down the streambed. Blood pounded in his ears. His mouth went dry. When he saw her kneeling, he flashed a glance through the trees looking for bears, wild dogs or some other threat.

With dancing eyes, she held out her hand. "Look!"

Slowly, his heart quieted. "Why in blazes did you scream? I thought you were in trouble."

"Look!" She held a bean-shaped nugget toward him. "It's gold."

"I know." She looked up with glowing eyes. "I moved a rock from the hillside to mark the end of the claim and there it was!" Shoving the nugget into his hand, she began to dig into the earth and gravel with her fingers.

"Julia," Duncan said, "calm down."

"It's found in veins, isn't it? Where there is one nugget, there must be more." The fever that had leaped from man to man aboard the steamer from Seattle now sizzled behind her eyes. Her body angled eagerly.

He grasped her by the waist, pulling her back. "Listen to me. We're going to put that rock where you found it. Do you want to risk someone high-grading your discovery while you're in town recording the claim?"

She gasped, then scrambled to her feet. "Hurry. Mark the claim before somebody comes along."

He shook his head. "Now that you've found a nugget, you expect men to spring from the trees?"

"Don't talk," she said impatiently. "Do it."

"Good idea." Pulling her close, he kissed her until her arms went around him. Her lips softened as her fingers stole through his hair. With satisfaction, he looked into her eyes. "That's better. Now, push that rock back while I get the other stakes."

He had stuck a lead pencil in his pocket when he stopped working on the account books. Julia used it to write her name on the top of each stake. Struck with a new thought, she exclaimed, "The gold is on the edge of the claim. Shall we move the upper limit closer?"

"We'll both stake. I'll measure another five hundred feet downstream." He paused to grin suggestively. "Shall we first dedicate the ground?"

Her blush delighted him. He had to force himself to concentrate on the business of felling a second birch. Minutes later, he wrote his name and the date on a stake marking the limit of the second claim.

When they started downhill, they heard the ring of iron on wood. Pushing through the underbrush, they discovered a man and woman pounding a stake into the ground near the rocky creekbed. The woman looked at them with suspicion while the man gave his stake a proprietary whack with the flat end of a hatchet. "This here's claimed, folks."

"Good luck to you," Duncan answered. "Get any sign of a prospect?"

"Haven't had time to run a cut to bedrock." The fellow nodded downstream where the ring of iron on wood told of others marking territory. "Word came out of Dawson that gold turned up along Caribou Creek."

*Her false rumor.* Julia felt euphoria giving way. How likely was it that through their love for each other they had located a rich vein? It was possible that melting snow had carried her nugget from somewhere uphill. Hadn't Martha said Sodie Joe looked futilely for a gold claim for years?

The thought of her father reminded her that time was rushing past. As they followed the gulch downhill, every five-hundred-foot segment was marked by a prospector. Most of them appeared to be newcomers, though at least one had the grizzled look of an old-timer. Near the junction with Caribou Creek, three young Indian men were busy sinking a test hole.

Duncan held the double-ender while Julia climbed aboard. A flotilla of vessels crowded the shore. Duncan kept near the bank and out of the fierce Yukon current.

Julia crouched in the bow. Her urgency had returned. She wouldn't recall that rapturous time with Duncan, but she felt restlessly aware of the late afternoon sun. Duncan's steady effort sent the boat smoothly downriver. They must soon reach Dawson. Anguish gnawed her. She had expected to bring her father with her. "We shouldn't have taken time for . . . that," she said.

She felt the boat slow and turned to see Duncan rest on the oars. "Julia," he said, sounding strained. "See if you can't find a more expressive term for loving each other."

She knew she had hurt him. Regret cut through her swiftly, but her impatience was stronger. "If you love me, you'll understand my need to hurry."

"*If* I love you?" He looked more pained than before. "I see my word is not good enough, nor apparently is my lovemaking. What in blazes must I do to prove that I care for you?"

"*Row!*" she said with strangled impatience and reached for the oars.

He caught her hands in a tight grip. They stared into each other's eyes while the current sped them on. Resistance was brief. In the same instant, they leaned together for a kiss that deepened rapidly.

Minutes later, she slowly became aware of their surroundings. The loving haze disappeared. Upstream, tents were visible beyond the headland. "We missed Dawson City!"

He glanced from the rapidly receding waterfront to Julia. "Did we kiss for so long?" In silence, they both pictured the busy waterfront. They had drifted past while caught in an oblivious embrace.

An embarrassed flush colored Julia's cheeks, but then her gaze met his and a ripple of laughter bubbled through her. Leaning forward helplessly, she pressed her forehead into his hands. Wryly, Duncan said, "Your reputation is ruined. You'll have to marry me."

She raised her head, her eyes dancing, but insisted softly, "With my father's blessing."

He nodded, preparing to swing the boat around.

A break in the underbrush caught Julia's glance. "Look! An Indian camp. And nearer town."

Duncan held the boat steady while he studied the clearing. Skin-covered huts huddled beneath trees. His narrowed gaze took in the beach. Most of the Indians wore clothes bought in Dawson City, but their boats were distinctive. There, beached among the graceful birchbark canoe, was a sturdy skiff.

He shot the double-ender toward shore. Julia clutched the gunwales and yearned toward the clearing. "I always knew when I reached him, my heart would tell me. My father is there. I feel it."

"Remember," Duncan warned. "The man you've built in your mind can't exist this side of heaven."

Julia didn't answer, not because they had had this argument before, but because she feared he might be right. She resisted the thought. Whoever Joseph Everett might be...whatever he was...she loved and needed him.

Duncan beached the boat, and she scrambled ashore. She stopped suddenly, so overcome with emotion that she was unable to move. Duncan put one hand on her waist. "Let me go ahead."

Because her doubts shamed her, she resisted. Howling dogs had alerted the people of the village. Their owners shouted and the dogs fell back. Despite the dogs, Julia started up the trail.

One hut seemed to be the center of activity. Her heart hammered. Her mouth felt so dry that she doubted she could speak. As they reached the skin-covered doorway, the hide was swept aside. A man in blue serge rushed through, nearly crashing into them.

"Owen!" Julia exclaimed.

Startled, he glanced from Julia to Duncan. His voice was urgent. "Julia, thank God you're here. Joe's been asking for you."

He stopped her from lurching forward. "I'm afraid your father is not entirely lucid. Dearest Julia, I am sorry, but you must be prepared to overlook some of the things he may say."

For a moment, she believed him. Then she remembered the false trail to Caribou Creek and his lies. "Get out of my way."

Duncan moved him aside. "Let her pass. You and I have some matters to settle."

As she reached for the tanned hide covering the doorway, Duncan nearly went after her. He wanted to protect her. Yet it would be better if she faced her father—and herself—alone. He would be here for her when she needed him. In the meantime, there was Owen.

Grimly, he turned to his stepbrother. Owen blanched and backed away until he came up against a birch. "Start talking," Duncan said tightly. "How are you involved with Joe Everett?"

"I gave him a grubstake. Over a month ago." With a nervous laugh, Owen added, "I'd seen Joe excited before. This time, he was different. I thought maybe he really had something."

Clenching one hand on his stepbrother's shirt, Duncan said, "Go on."

"It was a two-day hike," Owen said quickly. "Joe took along some celebratin' likker. By the second day, he was more interested in the bottom of the bottle than in mining. He couldn't even remember where he'd made his claim."

With a glance toward the skin hut, he lowered his voice. "The damned Indians are all learning English. A man's not safe talking around them."

Biting back his disgust, Duncan let the younger man lead him to the Yukon. "Get on with it."

"I was about to give up when damned if the old bum didn't stumble over his own stake." Again, he laughed nervously, then an avid light came into his eyes. "The fool scrabbled in the weeds and pulled up a handful with nuggets tangled in the roots. I've never seen anything like it."

"So you tried to kill him."

"No!" His shock sounded genuine. "I swear on my mother's grave," Owen exclaimed, "I thought he was dead or I'd never have left him." He turned restlessly and placed one foot on the bow of his skiff as he watched a birch canoe sliding down the Yukon. "The fellow was drunk. He started singing and dancing like a fool. The next thing I knew, he tripped over his own boots and toppled down the bank."

"You left him."

Owen jerked. "His neck was twisted. He didn't move. I swear I thought he was dead."

"Did you make the effort to find out?"

Instead of answering, Owen said eagerly, "I thought if I could marry Julia I'd inherit with her, but now it doesn't matter. An unfiled claim is only good for sixty days. Don't you understand? Joe never filed, and the sixty days are up. All we have to do is restake."

Duncan's right hook caught him by surprise. He crashed into the boat. Scrambling upright, he said, "Listen to me. Joe doesn't even remember. We can—"

His words were cut off when Duncan wrenched him forward by his suspenders. A second punch hurled him into the muddy shallows. He came up spitting. Mud and water ran down his face. "Have you lost your mind?"

Duncan waded into the river. Owen backed away, floundered for balance and landed in waist-deep water. Duncan's lunge forward sent a muddy wave into his face.

Struggling to his feet, Owen swung the end of a canoe between them. "Listen to me. There's a fortune waiting. You can buy any trawler you want ... a dozen!"

"You no-good, lying skunk." Shoving the canoe aside, Duncan waded closer. "I'll see you behind bars before I'll let you steal Joe's claim."

"Look out!"

A birch canoe missed them by inches and glided to the beach a yard away. Three young Indians leaped to the bank. Duncan recognized them as the men he and Julia had seen testing the claim. One of them let out a high-pitched whoop. "Gold! Off Caribou!"

Another chimed in, "Whole pup looks rich!"

They whooped again.

Owen lunged past Duncan, shoved the skiff off the beach and clambered inside. Duncan caught the stern and flung himself aboard. Owen swung a paddle at him, but Duncan grabbed it. The boat turned and bumped the birch canoe.

One of the Indians shouted, "No good. Every gully staked."

Duncan hauled on the oar and toppled Owen into the bottom of the skiff. "Damn your hide. I should let you go out there and walk your feet raw in useless prospecting."

Owen had never been a fighter. Seeing that argument was useless, he hunkered down in the skiff and covered his face with his hands. In disgust, Duncan grasped the second oar and put his shoulders into turning the boat back to the clearing.

Indians were running toward the river, drawn by the prospectors' whoops. As Owen stumbled ashore, Duncan called, "Hang onto him. He has some explanations to make inside." To his stepbrother, he said tightly, "It's lucky for Joe you remember where he staked that claim."

# Chapter Twenty-Eight

Julia had never felt more set on a purpose than she did when Owen tried to block her from entering the skin house. She heard his protest and Duncan's hard, angry answer, but only one thought mattered. She lifted the dried caribou hide and stepped into the hut.

Her first impression was of a crowd of shadowy figures ringing a dimly lit interior. The second was of smells that nearly made her retreat. Redolent odors from a pot suspended over coals in the center of a grease-slickened dirt floor competed with the oily scent of drying fish, the stench of putrefying meat kept as bait for traps and the enclosing mustiness of tanned skins. There were other muskier odors she couldn't identify.

Disgust made her hesitate. Then she realized that once again Ruth and Aaron were ruling her. If she had stepped directly from their home in Seattle into this dusky hut, she would have pressed a perfumed handkerchief to her nose and fled into fresher air.

She had come a long way from Seattle and endured far worse than unfamiliar smells. Once she identified Ruth and Aaron's influence, a thrill of anticipation returned. Only a few seconds had passed since she pushed past Owen into the hut. In those seconds, while she recognized and accepted strange scents, her eyes adjusted to the darkened interior.

The shadowy figures resolved into men and women and a few children, who might have been tumbling like puppies before her sudden entrance but now clung to their parents in frightened shyness. Lumps along the walls became recognizable as skins, traps and clothing. In the silence, Julia became aware of a pallet at the far side of the hut. A plump woman in a cotton dress bent over a reclining figure.

With an effort, Julia found her voice. "Father? I'm Julia. Your daughter."

Her words echoed her fantasies. In the fantasies, the announcement was the prelude to an outpouring of love and wonder and a golden future with a man like Aaron Ames, but far grander.

Several people started to their feet, leaving a clear path across the hut. From the pallet, a querulous voice rose. "Hell's fire, girl. I ain't able to lay my eyes on you from way over here. Pack yourself closer."

The plump woman moved to one side, defiantly fingering the nugget necklace worn boldly at the collar of her dress. Squaring her shoulders, Julia walked between ranks of silent onlookers to her father.

Her heart pounded rapidly, and she felt light-headed. Every eye judged her, from the tight moccasins on her feet to the hastily rearranged hair beneath her rose-trimmed straw hat.

She felt resentment from the woman who stood protectively beside the pallet—her stepmother, the woman Joe had married. Feeling dazed, she looked at the gnarled sourdough. He hunched his shoulders and regarded her with bright curiosity. Beneath the pallor of illness, his lined skin looked weathered and dark. Stubble grew randomly from his chin and jaw.

With petulant motions, he ordered the woman to raise him on a nest of folded blankets. The same birdlike gestures urged Julia to her knees. She tried to rid her mind of distaste, to ignore the strange odors and the unfamiliar surroundings. After all, she had not expected to find him in a feather bed.

But she had expected to feel a swelling of pride. She had expected to find a man her heart would embrace. She had wanted to put her future in his hands. As every muscle tightened with belated caution, she leaned closer.

Her own gray eyes peered back at her. She remembered that Martha commented on the resemblance. It was more than the color. There was a curiosity and candor in Sodie Joe's eyes that she knew from looking in the mirror. Emotion surged through her.

"Speak up, girl," Joe snapped. "Reckon Ruth and Aaron ain't quite whupped the spark outta you."

She swallowed. "Owen said you were ill." Why had Owen come to mind, she asked herself with impatience, then knew that all her rehearsals had prepared her for the wrong scene. She was stumbling for new lines. When she reached for shared experience she found Owen.

Her father spat past her into the fire. She managed not to jump. "That damned fool. He's bad luck. Don't have nothin' to do with him, girl." With sudden suspicion, Joe demanded, "You ain't sweet on him?"

"Certainly not." Remembering Owen's proposal of marriage, she wondered what he might have said to Joe. "Father, there are so many questions I want to ask I don't know where to begin."

"Ain't had much practice at fatherin'," he said. "Guess you better begin by callin' me Joe."

She nodded, wanting to touch his hand but unsure that he would welcome the intimacy. "I'm sorry you've been ill. Are you feeling stronger?"

"Been off my head most of a month." He reached out and pinched the plump woman's ankle. She giggled and he grinned before returning his attention to Julia. "Guess I musta slipped somehow. The Indians found me layin' halfway down a creek bank. Recognized me as bein' married to this good woman. They took care o' me. Few days ago, I started rememberin'."

Julia listened helplessly, unable to find the emotional reunion she had longed for. Even the momentary recognition of herself in his eyes began to fade.

How naively she had set out from Dawson City, declaring that she would bring her father back with her. She forced herself to concentrate on his words.

"Weren't until the good woman here came home yellin' about some dolled-up city gal wearin' my nugget that I knowed how time had slipped by."

"I—I'm twenty-two," Julia offered.

He spat into the fire again, then cocked his head to study her. "I'll be damned if I ain't lookin' at a growed-up ghost of my purty little Amy." The gray eyes grew wistful. "Suppose you're wonderin' why a lady like your mother ever would've looked my way. But I ain't always been a dried-up sourdough. There was a time I gave the Seattle dandies a run for the money."

Julia tried to look as if doubts had never crossed her mind. Joe's sudden grin brought a momentary flash of youth to his face. "Little Amy was a dreamer and that ain't always a good thing, but I can see you're made of sterner stuff."

She felt a flush of embarrassment. How many times had Duncan called her a dreamer? "I'm here," she said simply. To her surprise, Joe reached out and clasped her hand. His grasp felt dry and warm and unexpectedly strong.

"There weren't nothin' to do but leave you to Aaron back then. I figured you'd find spirit enough to turn on the old boy. Happened, didn't it?"

"Something like that." Her smile answered him.

Grinning, Joe leaned back on the blankets. "Paid the old devil his due, eh, girl? Good for you."

They didn't need to discuss the pain Aaron had caused over the years or their mutual satisfaction in his defeat. Impulsively, she bent and kissed the weathered cheek. Joe wrapped one wiry arm around her in a tight, welcoming hug.

A glow of warmth spread inside her. There was strength in her father and a fierce independence. Never mind his failings. Joe was a survivor. When she looked into his sparkling gray eyes, she sensed a zest for living that nothing could extinguish. Duncan had that same inner strength. She knew she loved them both.

* * *

Duncan stepped into the hut and motioned for Owen and some other men to follow. Once inside, he looked for Julia. When he saw her kneeling beside a pallet, he crossed the hut to stand beside her.

She looked up with radiance, then turned to a figure on the pallet. "Here is Duncan Adair, who brought me over the Chilkoot Trail."

Duncan saw a grizzled miner who appeared tough enough to tackle the Yukon single-handed. There was no welcome in the man. Nor was there gratitude, although he held Julia's hand with a look of greedy possession.

His voice rasped. "A fellow don't make a hard trip like that without expectin' a reward. What are you after, Adair?"

Julia's apologetic glance flew from her father to Duncan. He placed one hand on her shoulder, claiming her in a gesture her father was sure to recognize. "You're right, sir. I do want a reward. Your daughter as my wife. She won't agree to marry until she has her father's blessing."

The old man became belligerent. He heaved himself upward on the matted blankets. "I ain't but just met her. You expectin' me to give her away?"

Duncan was about to say that whether Joe gave permission or not, he meant to marry Julia. Then the man's sharp gray eyes appraised him again. His canny look reminded Duncan of Julia at her most obstinate. "Hell's fire, son, if you ain't man enough to get 'er, you ain't man enough to marry 'er."

Duncan looked from Joe to Julia. In his rough way, the old miner had painted the truth over Julia's dreams of a godlike being who would solve all her problems. "Sweetheart," Duncan said quietly, "I believe your father has placed the decision in your hands—exactly where it belongs."

Julia looked from one to the other. She had always wished for a father who would love her. By placing the decision about her future in her hands, Joe had answered her quest.

In Seattle, the far north had gleamed with promise. And she *had* found treasures. The least was a gold nugget. The search for her father had changed and strengthened her. She would never be Ruth Ames, trembling in fear of her mate. But then, Ruth would never have made love in a sunlit glade. Perhaps her mother would have.

Slowly, Julia came to her feet. She realized that Duncan had always known her better than she knew herself. Like Sodie Joe, she was a free spirit, one that might occasionally surprise Duncan but would rarely disappoint him.

Linking her arms around his neck, she answered him with loving conviction. "He is man enough to marry me, Joe. And I am woman enough to marry him. There is nothing I want more than to share in Duncan Adair's future."

Their kiss was interrupted as the young Indian men talked excitedly in their own language. When they pushed Owen forward, he looked braced to defend himself against leaving Joe to die. Duncan moved to stand beside him. "My brother has some good news for you, Joe."

He saw Owen's startled relief. Duncan knew his stepbrother's failings were less important than the fact that a rich claim was within the old miner's reach. Through Julia, Duncan had discovered a willingness to look through another's eyes. Clearly, she had found the best in Joe. He made a silent promise to try harder to understand the young man who, like it or not, was his brother.

Sodie Joe's gleeful cackle interrupted Owen's halting explanation. "You sayin' I'm rich?" Turning to Julia, he added, "You hear that, honey? Looks like your pa's goin' to be able to give you anything your little heart desires."

He paused, then grinned even more widely. "Reckon what I'll be givin' is a hitchin' present, and after that, unless I miss my guess, there'll be a need for silver spoons and such for my grandbabies."

As Duncan reached out to embrace Julia, her father grinned at the silent Indian woman. "Hear that, old wife? How are you gonna like bein' a grandmother?"

Julia wasn't sure the woman understood, but she giggled and nodded, if only to please Joe. The crowded hut began to feel stifling. She was glad to agree when Duncan urged her outside.

The persistent late-afternoon sun cast a golden glow over distant dome-shaped hills. Julia imagined miners laboring over sluice boxes in nearly every canyon. That brought an image of Martha and a sobering memory of pain on a weathered face. That was one problem Joe was going to have to sort out. A rich claim might make it easier, but Julia knew one of the women would have to be hurt.

A sigh lifted her shoulders, and Duncan put one arm around her. "He wasn't what you expected."

"No." She leaned into the warm comfort of his embrace. Joe was far from the mythic figure of her dreams, yet in many ways he represented the untamed heart of this harsh country. "I wanted him to solve my problems. Now I find myself worrying over his."

"We'll stay in close touch with him, sweetheart." Duncan tilted her face upward. "You haven't heard . . . fishing and Seattle will wait. That pup off Caribou Creek is testing out rich."

"Rich!" She had been gratified to hear that her father had discovered a wealthy claim, after all, but she had never given her own claim a thought. "Rich? And we have two claims!"

Duncan smiled at her delight. "I'll be spending the next winter digging to bedrock instead of testing the sea. I hope you're willing to stay in Dawson and occasionally visit the mine."

She wrapped her arms tightly around his waist. "You won't so easily rid yourself of me, Duncan Adair. I mean to work at your side."

"I'll not have you turning into a hard, weathered old woman."

Laughter burst from her, then she gazed at him tenderly. "I don't think there's much chance of that as long as we're together."

As he held her, they gazed out across the wide, cold flow of the Yukon River to the rolling, sun-gilded hills, where wealth lay hidden in ancient riverbeds. This immense country resisted most cheechakos, but had offered a golden welcome to them. As her heart stirred with happiness, Julia knew that however hard the winter might be, the year they were to spend in the Klondike would be the most memorable of her life.

Duncan might be picturing sluices and gravel dumps, or the trawlers he meant to return to once the gold was won. Julia pictured their log cabin, made snug against the snow. There, they would explore the great treasure of their love.

Fantasy had carried her here from Seattle. Now, in her mind, she furnished their cabin with a deal table, a Yukon stove, a wide plank bed holding fragrant boughs. Near the stove, but within reach of her hand, was a magnificent, hand-carved cradle.

Delicate fingers waved within. Whether they belonged to boy or girl didn't matter. The cradle represented the center of their lives. Wherever they lived in the years to come, that heirloom would go with them, cradling other children, and their children after them.

Her eyes misting with happiness, Julia nestled into Duncan's embrace. His stepbrother had said one truthful thing. This great, wild country was growing. For awhile, she and Duncan would be a part of it.

"What are you thinking, sweetheart?" he asked.

So many answers swirled in her head that she laughed. The promise she made now held the rich vein of their future within it. "What am I thinking? Why, that one of the first tasks of our marriage must be to coax Martha into revealing the secret of those flapjacks."

\* \* \* \* \*

# PENNY JORDAN

Sins and infidelities...
Dreams and obsessions...
Shattering secrets
unfold in...

# THE HIDDEN YEARS

SAGE — stunning, sensual and
vibrant, she spent a lifetime
distancing herself from a past too
painful to confront... the mother
who seemed to hold her at bay,
the father who resented her and
the heartache of unfulfilled love.
To the world, Sage was
independent and invulnerable—
but it was a mask she cultivated to
hide a desperation she herself
couldn't quite understand...
until an unforeseen turn of events
drew her into the discovery of the
hidden years, finally allowing
Sage to open her heart to a
passion denied for so long.

**The Hidden Years**—a compelling novel of truth and passion
that will unlock the heart and soul of every woman.

**AVAILABLE IN OCTOBER!**
Watch for your opportunity to complete your Penny Jordan set.
POWER PLAY and SILVER will also be available in October.

---

# HARLEQUIN

## *Romance*®

**This September, travel to England
with Harlequin Romance
FIRST CLASS title #3149,
ROSES HAVE THORNS
by Betty Neels**

It was Radolf Nauta's fault that Sarah lost her job at the hospital and was forced to look elsewhere for a living. So she wasn't particulary pleased to meet him again in a totally different environment. Not that he seemed disposed to be gracious to her: arrogant, opinionated and entirely too sure of himself, Radolf was just the sort of man Sarah disliked most. And yet, the more she saw of him, the more she found herself wondering what he really thought about her—which was stupid, because he was the last man on earth she could ever love....

---

This August, don't miss an exclusive
two-in-one collection of earlier love stories

# M A N
# W I T H   A   P A S T

---

# T R U E   C O L O R S

by one of today's hottest
romance authors,

Jayne Ann Krentz

Now, two of Jayne Ann Krentz's most loved books are
available together in this special edition that new and
longtime fans will want to add to their bookshelves.

Let Jayne Ann Krentz capture your hearts with the love
stories, MAN WITH A PAST and TRUE COLORS.

And in October, watch for the second two-in-one
collection by Barbara Delinsky!

Available wherever Harlequin books are sold.

# MILLION DOLLAR JACKPOT
## SWEEPSTAKES RULES & REGULATIONS
NO PURCHASE NECESSARY TO ENTER OR RECEIVE A PRIZE

1. Alternate means of entry: Print your name and address on a 3″×5″ piece of plain paper and send to the appropriate address below.

| **In the U.S.** | **In Canada** |
|---|---|
| MILLION DOLLAR JACKPOT | MILLION DOLLAR JACKPOT |
| P.O. Box 1867 | P.O. Box 609 |
| 3010 Walden Avenue | Fort Erie, Ontario |
| Buffalo, NY 14269-1867 | L2A 5X3 |

2. To enter the Sweepstakes and join the Reader Service, check off the "YES" box on your Sweepstakes Entry Form and return. If you do not wish to join the Reader Service but wish to enter the Sweepstakes only, check off the "NO" box on your Sweepstakes Entry Form. To qualify for the Extra Bonus prize, scratch off the silver on your Lucky Keys. If the registration numbers match, you are eligible for the Extra Bonus Prize offering. Incomplete entries are ineligible. Torstar Corp. and its affiliates are not responsible for mutilated or unreadable entries or inadvertent printing errors. Mechanically reproduced entries are null and void.

3. Whether you take advantage of this offer or not, on or about April 30, 1992, at the offices of D.L. Blair, Inc., Blair, NE, your sweepstakes numbers will be compared against the list of winning numbers generated at random by the computer. However, prizes will only be awarded to individuals who have entered the Sweepstakes. In the event that all prizes are not claimed, a random drawing will be held from all qualified entries received from March 30, 1990 to March 31, 1992, to award all unclaimed prizes. All cash prizes (Grand to Sixth) will be mailed to winners and are payable by check in U.S. funds. Seventh Prize will be shipped to winners via third-class mail. These prizes are in addition to any free, surprise or mystery gifts that might be offered. Versions of this Sweepstakes with different prizes of approximate equal value may appear at retail outlets or in other mailings by Torstar Corp. and its affiliates.

4. PRIZES: (1) *Grand Prize $1,000,000.00 Annuity; (1) First Prize $25,000.00; (1) Second Prize $10,000.00; (5) Third Prize $5,000.00; (10) Fourth Prize $1,000.00; (100) Fifth Prize $250.00; (2,500) Sixth Prize $10.00; (6,000) **Seventh Prize $12.95 ARV.

   *This presentation offers a Grand Prize of a $1,000,000.00 annuity. Winner will receive $33,333.33 a year for 30 years without interest totalling $1,000,000.00.

   **Seventh Prize: A fully illustrated hardcover book, published by Torstar Corp. Approximate Retail Value of the book is $12.95.

   Entrants may cancel the Reader Service at any time without cost or obligation (see details in Center Insert Card).

5. Extra Bonus! This presentation offers an Extra Bonus Prize valued at $33,000.00 to be awarded in a random drawing from all qualified entries received by March 31, 1992. No purchase necessary to enter or receive a prize. To qualify, see instructions in Center Insert Card. Winner will have the choice of any of the merchandise offered or a $33,000.00 check payable in U.S. funds. All other published rules and regulations apply.

6. This Sweepstakes is being conducted under the supervision of D.L. Blair, Inc. By entering the Sweepstakes, each entrant accepts and agrees to be bound by these rules and the decisions of the judges, which shall be final and binding. Odds of winning the random drawing are dependent upon the number of entries received. Taxes, if any, are the sole responsibility of the winners. Prizes are nontransferable. All entries must be received at the address on the detachable Business Reply Card and must be postmarked no later than 12:00 MIDNIGHT on March 31, 1992. The drawing for all unclaimed Sweepstakes prizes and for the Extra Bonus Prize will take place on May 30, 1992, at 12:00 NOON at the offices of D.L. Blair, Inc., Blair, NE.

7. This offer is open to residents of the U.S., United Kingdom, France and Canada, 18 years or older, except employees and immediate family members of Torstar Corp., its affiliates, subsidiaries and all other agencies, entities and persons connected with the use, marketing or conduct of this Sweepstakes. All Federal, State, Provincial, Municipal and local laws apply. Void wherever prohibited or restricted by law. Any litigation within the Province of Quebec respecting the conduct and awarding of a prize in this publicity contest must be submitted to the Régie des Loteries et Courses du Québec.

8. Winners will be notified by mail and may be required to execute an affidavit of eligibility and release, which must be returned within 14 days after notification or an alternate winner may be selected. Canadian winners will be required to correctly answer an arithmetical, skill-testing question administered by mail, which must be returned within a limited time. Winners consent to the use of their name, photograph and/or likeness for advertising and publicity in conjunction with this and similar promotions without additional compensation.

9. For a list of our major prize winners, send a stamped, self-addressed envelope to: MILLION DOLLAR WINNERS LIST, P.O. Box 4510, Blair, NE 68009. Winners Lists will be supplied after the May 30, 1992 drawing date.

Offer limited to one per household.

LTY-H891

# Coming Soon

Fashion A Whole New You
in classic romantic style
with a trip for two to Paris,
a brand-new Mercury
Sable LS and a $2,000
Fashion Allowance.

Plus, romantic free gifts* are yours to
Fashion A Whole New You.

From September through November, you can take part in
this exciting opportunity from Harlequin.

Watch for details in September.

* with proofs-of-purchase, plus postage and handling

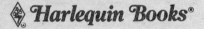